THE SECRET INGREDIENT

SUE HEATH

One More Chapter
a division of HarperCollins*Publishers* Ltd
1 London Bridge Street
London SE1 9GF
www.harpercollins.co.uk
HarperCollins*Publishers*
Macken House, 39/40 Mayor Street Upper,
Dublin 1, D01 C9W8, Ireland

This paperback edition 2024
1
First published in Great Britain in ebook format
by HarperCollins*Publishers* 2024
Copyright © Sue Heath 2024
Sue Heath asserts the moral right to
be identified as the author of this work

A catalogue record of this book is available from the British Library

ISBN: 978-0-00-853568-1

Printed and bound in the UK using 100% Renewable Electricity
by CPI Group (UK) Ltd

In loving memory of my great aunt Edith, and great uncle Norman — who truly were two halves of a whole.

Chapter One

Before

Sooner or later, most people will come across their 'day that will change everything'. For Kate it was April 22nd. Not this particular one – though the aroma drifting through from the kitchen as she opened the front door held quite a promise – but the one four years ago when she met Eddie.

She had just turned twenty-six and he was joking about his own thirtieth birthday looming over him. But the age difference was irrelevant; that first shared smile unlocked some deep desire inside her that she didn't know she had. She had never wanted anything, or anybody, as much as she wanted Eddie.

When she was little, and told her mother that she *needed* something, her mum would say she *wanted* not *needed*. But by her third date with Eddie, Kate knew with a certainty that this was the guy she *needed* to spend the rest of her life with.

She didn't tell anybody how she felt because just knowing herself was enough.

'Wow, that smells amazing!' Kate pushed the front door

shut and took a deep breath, letting the luscious smell of chicken fill her senses. Coming home was definitely her favourite part of the day; parts of her she didn't know were tense seemed to relax as the smell of Eddie's food wrapped around her.

She slipped her shoes off, and slid them neatly into the rack, giving herself time to savour this moment.

'It's going to taste amazing as well!' His deep voice made her glance up from the shoes. He was framed in the kitchen doorway. His chuckle brought her out in goosebumps, just as it had on that first date.

There was a broad smile on his broad face – everything about Eddie was broad. Strong. Dependable.

His long, curly hair was tied back, the chef's apron she'd bought him smeared with spices and tomato.

Eddie was a hands-in, rather than a hands-on, type of cook. He used every knife, every chopping board, every spoon, and then he used his fingers. He sprinkled and tasted as he went. He'd always wiped his hands on any tea towel that was handy, or the front of his T-shirt, which was why she'd bought him the apron. Well, two. One to wear, one in the wash.

He closed the space between them, his hands reaching for her waist. 'Happy anniversary, Mrs Shaw!' His touch made her pulse skitter; his steady gaze made her happy-dance inside. Those words were still the best ones in the world.

Kate couldn't ever remember feeling like she belonged, that she was with somebody who accepted her as she was and didn't expect more from her or want her to change.

And then Eddie had asked her to marry him, twelve months to the day after their first date, and Kate knew she'd been right about him. Them. He had no expectations, he loved her just the way she was. In a world full of uncertainty and rubbish, Eddie was the constant, the good.

Of course, they'd got married on April 22nd, and on this particular day it was their wedding anniversary, their second.

'Happy anniversary to you too, Mr Shaw.' She grinned back at him, her hands reaching up to his neck as his lips skimmed lightly over hers. A promise of something more later.

He pulled her closer, the warmth of his palms over her back, the gentle rub of his thumbs sending a tingle to the base of her stomach – in the same way it had the first time he'd touched her.

She called it the Eddie-effect.

'I'm starving.'

'For me or my food?' His eyes were dark, but his tone was teasing.

'Well…' She drew the syllables out and he laughed. Tightening his grip until her body was snug against his. 'When you put it like that!' Her stomach rumbled and he loosened his grip, laughing.

'You're always starving!' He kissed the tip of her nose, then was still for a moment, long enough for her to appreciate the gorgeous smile, the deep chocolate-brown eyes, the smell of him. Her man. The man she was so lucky to have.

Eddie wore life like a comfortable blanket. Where Kate fought her way through every step, he moved easily with it. They were the perfect combination; he was good for her.

'You can't blame me! It's the smell that does it. I didn't realise I was this hungry until I opened the door. What are we having?'

'Surprise.' He tapped the side of his nose with his forefinger, then took both her hands in his. 'Come on – I need you to taste something. Close your eyes!'

Eddie might leave the toilet seat up, his guitars (yes, plural) in the living room and his shoes in exactly the right spot for her to trip over – but she could forgive all the things he did wrong, because of all the things he did right. And that included knowing that one way to her heart was through her stomach. She ate like a goddess, and he even sometimes washed the pots and pans up as well. The kitchen was his domain, and she was more than happy to have it that way.

She closed her eyes, let him lead her into the kitchen. 'No peeping!' She stood still as he let go of her hands. Listened to the sound of the oven door opening and closing, of pan lids being lifted. Stirring.

The familiar aromas hit her senses, making her stomach rumble. Roast chicken, tarragon, mushrooms, garlic. It was roast dinner at her grandparents, mingling with the smell of the glorious buttery-garlic potatoes that Eddie had served the first time he cooked for her. The comfort food of her childhood mixed with the tantalising flavours that her husband knew she loved.

Her mouth watered; her stomach rumbled louder. 'Arghh, you're torturing me, feed me!'

'Shh!' His rumble of laughter rolled over her. 'Open up!'

The taste was even better than the smell. A spoonful of creamy sauce, soft chicken, the sweetness of leeks.

'Mmm, oh my God, how can food do this to me?'

This was different from that first meal he'd cooked for her, but the flavours were the same. She was right back there, in his tiny flat, gazing into his eyes – watching his face break into an enormous smile as she nodded her approval.

Their first proper dinner together. The first time she'd stayed over. The first time they'd made love.

'Nice?'

'Nice? Soooo good. Better than an orgasm.'

'Really? Are you sure about that?' The spoon clattered onto the board, and he was there – his arms wrapped tight around her.

She opened her eyes. 'It's awesome,' Kate said, her voice turning throaty at his intense stare as their gazes locked.

'I'm going to get you cooking one day.' His tone matched hers, as his eyes searched her face.

'But you're so good at it!' she joshed gently, but he didn't smile. 'Maybe, one day when I've got some spare time.' She'd not grown up with home cooking; her mum never had the time. Oh hell, she was beginning to sound more like her. *Be* more like her. She was not going to let that happen. 'How about tomorrow?' The words tripped out before she had time to think, but his lazy smile made her want to repeat them, say the words again. Make him happy.

'Tomorrow sounds good.' The light touch of his fingertips on her neck sent a shiver through her.

'How long until dinner's ready?'

'It needs a bit longer, but nearly there.'

'How much longer?' She knew she was teasing, asking him another question, but this familiar pang of hunger was nothing to do with chicken.

'Long enough,' he paused, 'to test out that statement of yours. I know my cooking is good, but I think you've forgotten just how amazing I am in other rooms of the house!' He swept her into his arms. Ignored her laughed shouts of protest.

'What about my dinner!'

'It's fine. It's simmering nicely.' He gazed into her eyes, raised an eyebrow. 'Just like me!'

'But I need a shower, to get changed.'

'I might join you. Everything,' his voice had turned throatier, in a way that made her pulse race, 'is bubbling away just how I like it.'

They lay naked on the bed, on their sides facing each other. His hand resting in the dip of her waist.

'That was good.' His voice was soft, post-sex languid. His fingers traced a line over her rib cage, his caress light as he reached up to tuck a tendril of hair behind her ear.

Kate smiled lazily back, wanting to snuggle in, but knowing they had to get up and dressed.

'We should do it more often.' His gaze was steady, and she knew what he was going to say before he said it. She half-reached out, to put a finger on his lips. Stop him. But he caught her hand and spoke again before the words could come out. 'As often as we can, before—'

The sigh broke free before she could stop it. She pulled away slightly, rolled onto her back. It was a reflex action; she couldn't help it, even though she hated herself for doing it. She stared up at the ceiling, tried to swallow the frustration away. 'Aren't you happy the way we are? Just the two of us?' She risked a glance towards him. 'What's the rush?'

'No rush.' His hand rested easily on her stomach. A light steady pressure. 'It's just…'

'If it happens, it happens. If it doesn't it isn't meant to.' She couldn't keep her tone light; a defensive note had drifted in. Kate hated it when that happened. It wasn't Eddie's fault.

'We can afford to give—'

'It's not about money,' she snapped, then instantly regretted it. She closed her eyes for a moment. 'IVF just seems so,' she hesitated, 'clinical.'

His smile was gentle. 'Yeah, guess it is clinical.'

'If we're going to have a baby, I'd rather give it time, let it happen naturally,' she said softly, resisting the urge to wriggle away. But her whole body had tensed. It was a defence reflex that she hated.

'We've given it time, Kate. I don't want to be an old dad.' His tone was soft, but she could hear the disappointment. The quiet determination. This was important to him.

'You've got years left in you!' She tried to keep her tone light, teasing.

'I want to be young enough to kick a ball around, to be in touch when my kids are teens. Don't you?' She shrugged. 'Wouldn't it be great to have kids and really enjoy it, not be knackered all the time, then still have years of fun left after they've grown up and gone?'

'Wow, that's some fast-forward. There they were, gone!' This conversation got worse every time they had it, or should she say Eddie tried to have it. Didn't he realise that life wasn't always how you wanted it? That kids didn't fit into every life. That parents could wish they'd never had them?

'We've got options, Kate. We should take them.'

Kate wasn't sure she wanted options. But was that fair? They'd never discussed having a family before they got married. It hadn't come up, because everything else had slotted into place so perfectly. They wanted the same things. She'd never questioned it, never dreamed that there would be something major that they didn't agree on.

But now she knew that what her grandad had said was true – two of the most important things that you need to discuss are money and children.

Kate and Eddie hadn't talked about either, because as long as they had each other everything would be fine.

And they'd got enough money; she'd always worked hard, earned enough to support herself. Earned enough to support both of them, if he followed his heart – ditched his job and retrained as a chef.

She swung her legs off the bed, her back to him. 'Maybe it's not the right time…'

'Lots of people say it's not the right time, but you just have to make it be.'

She moved away just far enough so that his fingers skated her body and his arm fell to the bed.

'I don't have to make it be.' She could hear the tightness in her voice as she struggled to do up the clasp on her bra.

He reached over again, his hand over hers. Stilling her. 'We, Kate. We, it's not just you.'

'And it's not just you. You can't make the decision.' She bit back the 'It's my body'. She was being unfair, she knew she was, but it always made her feel defensive. It always made her pull away from him, withdraw. It was too hard to explain. That was what it wasn't the right time for. Explaining.

'I'm not trying to make any decisions, I just want you to open up, talk to me, like we do about everything else. What's different about this? I don't get it.'

Everything is different, she wanted to shout. We don't need to pay out a ton of money so that some doctor can *make* me pregnant. I know why I'm not pregnant.

She didn't shout. Instead, she said, 'Please, can we not? Let's not spoil tonight. We can talk about it tomorrow.'

'Sure.' His finger traced a line down her spine, and she shivered in response. 'It's no big deal.'

But it was. There was a note of defeat in his voice that she hardly ever heard, and she hated. She'd done that.

Kate felt the bed bounce as he rolled off, came round and squatted in front of her.

She couldn't help but smile. He always knew how to make her smile.

She laughed with him, loved him, shared her secrets, her body, her hopes and dreams. Her life. So why was it so hard to talk to him about this?

He bounced on his haunches slightly, and she shook her head – unable to stop the smile broadening. 'You look like a giant frog!'

'Ribbit!'

This time she laughed.

He stood up, kissed the top of her head.

He had made her laugh, tried to lighten the atmosphere again, but she knew she'd spoiled things.

'I'm sorry I…'

'I'm sorry I keep pushing it.' He ruffled her hair. 'You're right, there's no rush. I don't know what it is.' He laughed as he pulled his jeans on, but he had his back to her now. She couldn't see his face, and she knew there would be disappointment on it. 'Maybe it's a mid-life crisis looming?' He shrugged. That boyish, cute shrug that she had fallen in love with.

'You're not mid-life!' She stood up, wrapped her arms around him. Buried her face in his back.

'Getting there.' He untangled himself, took a step away, but kept hold of one of her hands. To show he forgave her.

'I'm sorry, Eddie. I just can't—'

He interrupted her; maybe he didn't want to hear her say 'do this', or maybe he agreed that it was a conversation for another day. Not today.

'Hey, I've cocked up.' His voice had changed to more matter

of fact, but with a thread of hurt running through it, a slight tremor in his normal steady tone. 'There's some stuff, a couple of ingredients I forgot. I'll pop and get them, won't be long, dinner will be ready in,' he glanced at the clock, 'twenty minutes, so I've just got time. Have a chill for a bit! Anything you need me to get?'

Kate shook her head. She knew he probably didn't need to go out. He was giving her some space; he was giving them both time.

Pressing the reset button.

She tried to swallow the lump in her throat at his happy-sad wink. Eddie never could hide his feelings; it was one of the things she loved about him.

Kate listened as he went down the stairs. 'Hey, I love you!' she shouted out, just as the front door clicked behind him. Pretty sure he'd not heard, or he'd have shouted back. He always shouted back.

She slowly pulled the rest of her clothes on and sat at her dressing table.

She took her time putting her make-up on, styling her hair, and then decided to make more effort – picking out a dress he liked, to try and make amends for being such a wet blanket.

She put on some music, their favourite playlist. Pottered around the kitchen, his kitchen. She loved sitting at the island, watching him cook. She loved him; she loved their home. She loved their life.

It was as perfect as it could be, as good as she'd ever hoped. She just wished he'd hurry up back though. Then they could kiss, open the wine. Then she'd know it was okay between them.

Kate's mobile bleeped. The image brought a grin to her face instantly. A selfie Eddie had taken this time last year of them both grinning, holding up champagne glasses.

There were bumps in the road with any relationship; it would be plain weird if they never argued. They were good.

And tomorrow she'd help him cook dinner. She'd share that particular passion in his life, and maybe stop feeling so bloody guilty about this.

Still smiling she tapped out a reply.

'Love you, hurry back home! I'm ready and waiting [winking emoji] Xxx'

Her gaze stayed on the screen, wanting to know he'd seen the message, he knew how she felt. One tick, sent. Two ticks, delivered. She waited for them to change colour – for the status to change to 'read'.

It didn't.

Chapter Two

KATE

Three years, two weeks and one day later

Kate had always loved her job, which was partly why she was currently packing her belongings into a box. While she was still at university she'd opened a fortune cookie, which told her that her job would be 'a vocation not a vacation', and teaching was definitely that.

She might not want any children of her own but being in a school had always felt right. Maybe it was growing up feeling unwanted, not good enough, unnoticed, that had made her determined to make sure that even the lowest achievers academically were still valued – could find something to do with their lives that was good.

Kate hadn't been a low achiever – she'd been good at everything at school. But she didn't kid herself that it was because she was particularly intelligent, or things came naturally. It was because she worked hard. She was desperate to succeed because that way her mother might notice her. Her mother might be proud; she might actually have time to come to parents' evening or attend the 'Art Display' afternoon.

It was during the Christmas break in her final year at university, studying biology, that Kate had realised that when her mother said she wanted her to be independent, she meant this not just for Kate's benefit, but her own as well. She had performed her motherly duties and wanted to be released.

Kate had spent most of the holidays with her grandparents – which was nothing new. This year though, the new development had been that her mother didn't even appear for Christmas lunch. She sent a Skype invite instead.

She was in the States, sealing a deal on Christmas Eve, and there wasn't much point in paying the ridiculous air fare demanded to come back just for a turkey dinner, was there?

It was as her grandad carved wonky slices of Boxing Day honey-glazed ham that Kate realised she didn't need to do what she *thought* her mum would approve of any longer. It wouldn't make any difference if she was some Nobel prize-winning scientist or worked in an office. As long as she was standing on her own two feet.

As long as her mother had been freed of responsibility for the daughter she didn't want.

Whenever Kate thought back to that moment, whenever she was questioning herself and her choices, she remembered the taste of that ham – the sweet honey, the spicy-warm smell of cloves that turned bitter in her mouth.

She'd known in that moment, though, that it was time to move on. To do what *she* wanted.

Which was why she trained as a teacher, and why she was now moving on again – packing away that life for the last time.

How could she solve the kids' problems if she couldn't fix herself?

'Aww, how are you coping, love?'

Kate looked up from her box-packing. Rachel the cleaner had a sympathetic smile on her face. There was a clunk as she dragged her Henry vacuum around the desk with a force that sent him cannoning into the filing cabinet.

Kate tried not to flinch. She still found pity hard to deal with. If everybody carried on as normal, treated her as though nothing had happened, then she was fine. Totally fine. She could cope.

'It's not easy being a widow, is it?' Rachel prattled on, spurred on by Kate's reaction.

Kate had found there were two types of people – the ones who avoided risk of upset at any cost, and others who seemed to feed off another person's discomfort. Rachel seemed to be relishing this, and would no doubt be over-the-top sympathetic if she got a result and Kate broke down. Which she was not going to give her the satisfaction of seeing.

'I'm not surprised you need a break from work. When my sister lost her Dan, she was ill for weeks, withdrew right into herself she did. Pale like a zombie, not herself at all for weeks. Weeks it was. Said she didn't feel whole. She wasn't as young as you, mind.'

Kate's mind had stopped registering anything after the word 'widow'. She hated that word.

Rachel had not given Kate a chance to answer, just carried on talking about her sister as her Henry vacuum, smiling manically, bounced off walls and crashed into chair legs, the nozzle sucking the life out of the unfortunate spiders who'd sought refuge under the skirting boards. But the word had hung in the air almost accusingly.

'And it wasn't sudden like it was for you, she knew he only had months left, had time to get used to the idea. But for you, well, here one day, gone the next, now that's got to be a shock to the system, hasn't it, pet?'

'I'm fine, thanks,' Kate stuttered. Her face felt stiff as she picked up her bag.

'How long is it now?'

Widow. It felt an ugly word. A lost word. Sad and empty. She'd not thought of herself as one, it was a word she couldn't relate to.

At the funeral she'd been 'left'. Eddie had left behind his wife, not a widow. As though it had been some careless mistake and he'd be back. Or, she supposed, she'd be expected to join him.

It wasn't Rachel's fault she felt like this though. It wasn't Rachel's fault that today was her last day in work.

She'd loved working in this place. It had been her first real job (her only job); the kids were challenging and entertaining. Cheeky some days, on edge and nervous others. Needing reassurance on results days, needing a boost and a shoulder to cry on at other times. And the staff were great – supportive. You needed to be, in a high school. All for one and one for all.

They'd been there for her when she lost her grandparents – her gran following her grandad one month to the day after he died, because without him what was the point in hanging on, when you were ninety-three?

At the time she'd have said there was plenty of point. But now she understood.

She'd clung to her routine after Eddie had died. It was all she had left. But after that first year of anniversary dates that he wasn't there for, a year of getting home after work at her normal time but finding the house empty, a year of waiting for the weekend then realising she hated it, she'd learned that hanging on to the familiar wasn't helping at all.

It sharpened the loss. Magnified the gap in her life, the space that he was supposed to fill.

She didn't want to build a new life without Eddie, but she couldn't repair the holes in the one he'd left. She didn't know what she was supposed to do. She just knew that she had to do something.

'Two years, is it?' Rachel kept prodding.

'Three.' Corrected Kate. Three years, two weeks and one day.

'Well, doesn't time fly?'

Time had not flown by. Each second had ticked painfully, but it was still a shock that all those seconds had added up to more than three years.

She'd had support in the first few weeks; everybody had rallied round, until after the funeral. Why did they all think that once they'd laid a few flowers, it was all over?

Her really good friends had still been there to help her through the first anniversary, but then even they had moved on. Got on with their lives. But she hadn't been able to.

Their relentless optimism, their need for her to forget and 'live' had felt wrong. They didn't understand. It had been easier to say no when they invited her out, to go home and shut the world out, than to explain. But quite often these days she felt very alone.

Even Eddie was harder to hold on to in her head, even if he was still lodged in her heart.

'It's no wonder you're angry, love.' Oh God, was Rachel still prattling on? Kate would be angry enough to wrap Henry's hose round her neck and add to the death quota if she didn't go and vacuum somewhere else. 'No wonder at all. You off now?'

Kate nodded. 'I certainly am.' She knew her voice had an

edge. Rachel was actually right when she called her angry. She was. With Eddie, with herself. With life.

'Well, you look after yourself, love. There's groups you know, like AA, but not for drinking, you know support for stuff. My sister…'

Kate marched down the long empty corridor and took a deep calming breath as she stepped into the open air and the door swung shut behind her.

What did they call those groups then? Widows United, WU? Woohoo, fan-bloody-tastic.

Swallowing the yell of frustration, she dropped down into her car seat, slung her tote bag onto the passenger seat and rested her head back.

What was wrong with people? She didn't need anybody to remind her, it was with her every day.

Just like Eddie was.

Oh God, he would have found this funny. A woo club. He'd have told her that Rachel was just miffed she couldn't be part of it.

She put the car in gear, slowly reversed out of the parking spot.

Eddie would have been proud of her doing this. Breaking free, being daring.

He'd always liked a challenge. When he was the age that she was now, he'd been ready to move on.

She was doing the right thing. And he'd made it possible. He'd always said he'd look after her; whatever happened he'd make sure she was okay. And he had done. He'd saved regularly (his breaking free to start again fund), he'd taken out the kind of life insurance policy that only somebody who worked in finance would have thought a good idea.

She was doing what he'd have wanted her to do. What he would have done.

She gripped the steering wheel more firmly. She wasn't alone.

Rachel didn't understand because she hadn't had Eddie. She wanted to needle Kate, to live through her emotions, because she had never lived them herself.

The roads were busy, with the stop-start of rush hour traffic, but as Kate inched her way further from the school, from Rachel, her anger started to fade. She'd got this. What Rachel thought didn't matter. She had done it. For the first time in just over three years, she had made a decision. A life-changing decision that was her business, that she was doing for herself.

She had to believe that it was the right thing – and she did. Staying would have been about doubts, fear. Staying would have been about hanging on to a past that had gone, that she could never have back. Staying would have been about living with the judgement of people like Rachel.

Eddie had cruised along. She needed to do that. Sail, not fight the currents, the tides.

Just thinking about him, what he'd be saying now, made her feel better.

The bitterness inside her started to ebb away, the fury at Rachel lifted. It was replaced with a strange feeling. She was slightly shaky, her stomach fluttery – but she didn't feel panic, she felt…she felt… It took a while for her to work out what she was feeling, and then it hit her. It was relief that was surging through her – that was what she felt. Relief. Not fear or anger or despair.

'I made a decision,' she whispered, as a smile started to form on her face. 'I did it.' In a world where lately she'd not felt she had any control, any power to do anything, she'd actually stepped outside her comfort zone. Stepped off the conveyor belt. Made a move.

The traffic started to flow more easily, and she felt her features relax. She turned up the radio slightly, her fingers tapping in time to the music. This was good. This was day one.

'A new dawn,' she said softly. If anything ever went wrong, Eddie would always say, 'Hey, no worries, tomorrow's a new dawn, a new day.' Eddie had never been afraid of starting again.

She glanced in the rear-view mirror, indicating and slowing to turn off the main road, into the street where she lived.

The smile left Kate's face as she jammed on the brakes to avoid running slap bang up the rear of somebody bent double at the bottom of the open ramp of a removal van.

An involuntary squeak escaped from her, as she braced her arms and legs, her stomach lurching. The car stalled, her fingers clutching the steering wheel so tightly her nails dug into her palms.

For a moment she froze; all she could do was stare. Adrenalin and shock coursed through her body. Then she became aware of her heart pounding. Of the strange scene in front of her.

She forced herself back in the seat, willed her hands to relax.

What the hell was a van doing parked so close to the corner? Wasn't that illegal? And more to the point, why was some dork doing a very bad downward-dog pose in the road? It would be a dead dog pose if he carried on doing that for much longer.

The dark-haired, vaguely familiar man slowly stood up and looked at her in what, she had to say, was quite an intimidating way. His blue-grey eyes met hers in an unflinching stare. Never show fear, she'd been told during her teacher training, and it was a lesson she'd taken to heart. She clenched her teeth. If she could deal with a class full of mid-puberty, testosterone-driven teenagers, then she could cope with an idiot dancing in the road as though he owned it.

Except this was no teenager, this was an imposing adult whom she'd just unconsciously clocked as being well-toned, more man-in-a-magazine than the type you saw in the street. In this street.

He was scowling at her, and Kate scowled back, the heat rushing to her cheeks (there were some things she didn't have any control over), then he did that 'Pfft, who do you think you are?' dismissive gesture that really was guaranteed to make her blood boil. Kids had this down pat, and Kate never stood for it. She wound her window down, resisting the urge to get out and march over to him – he was rather tall, and broad, and well, you didn't know how people would react these days, did you?

'What the hell do you think you're doing, crawling around in the middle of the road? I could have run you over!' she spat out, her finger ready to whizz the window back up if necessary.

'So I gather,' he drawled back, in what sounded far too passive-aggressive for Kate to ignore in her stressed state. Which he was responsible for.

She narrowed her eyes. 'Did it not occur to you that you should check for traffic first?' Okay, she was joining in. Her grandad always said, 'Sarcasm is the lowest form of wit,' and her tone was dripping with it – though not in a funny way at all.

This was not the way she'd deal with a stroppy student, but then very few of them sent her blood pressure soaring by throwing themselves in front of her car.

'I did.' He said in an annoying reasonable tone. 'It was safe until you came whizzing round the corner. I heard you coming and thought I needed to grab this before you smashed it to smithereens!' He held something up. It looked like a photo frame – but with some kind of document in it.

It was Kate's turn to 'pfft'. If he was so careless that he dropped things in the road, then he deserved to be squished.

'The removal men dropped a box full of my kit and this fell off the top.' he added as though reading her mind. But Kate didn't want to talk to him, to even look at him for a second longer. She was already winding her window up and struggling to get the car into first gear. Which it was refusing to do – it was grating into reverse, then third, then finally into first. Right now, she wasn't in the mood to cope with this; narrowly missing him had really shaken her up, inside and outside. Her hands were shaking. She needed to get home and take a few deep breaths.

Kate stared ahead and pulled the car out and around the van. If it had been her box of valuable stuff, she'd have had the top taped up. But then not everybody was practical, she guessed. The sigh escaped before she could stop it. She'd probably been unfair, over-reacted. But it had been an instinctive reaction; he'd scared her. Shaken her up.

Great though. A new neighbour with attitude, that was all she needed. Not that she had really got to know any of her neighbours, so she could easily avoid him as well.

She pulled up in her own driveway, turned the engine off and waited for the tremble in her hands to fade away. For her heart to stop pounding.

What an idiot! Who in their right mind parked a van that size right on a road junction? She knew she was disproportionately angry, but she'd so desperately wanted to hang on to the good feeling she'd had as she left school. To arrive home calm and happy. Not shaken up and cross. She'd needed that good feeling, and some random idiot had ruined it.

Eddie would have cooked her his best hug-in-a-dish food, with a side of red wine. He'd have wrapped his arms round her and threatened to go and read out the riot act to their new neighbour. Except they'd have both known he wouldn't have done it because he was far too nice. They'd have just ended up laughing about it.

He would have made her feel better, he'd have made her smile again, and now that was her job. And she could do it. She *did* feel better. She'd have a shower, put some music on, recapture that positive feeling.

She was ready to go in. Start over. 'Come on, Eddie, let's cook!' she said softly as she slammed her car door shut, determined to leave her old life and *that* man behind.

Chapter Three

JACK

Moving on

Jack stared at the bright red front door and for the first time since he'd signed the rental contract, he wondered if he'd done the right thing. He did that a lot these days – doubted himself.

That had never happened to the old Jack. Doubts. He'd always steamed on with utter confidence in himself, and how things would work out. So, everything had worked out okay. Until he'd fallen ill, and suddenly the order of life had been rearranged. It was like some switch had been flipped, and chaos and failure had replaced his single-mindedness and success.

He'd been floored by the nasty virus for nearly two weeks. Really knocked sideways. Jack never threw a sickie, he was one of the healthiest people he knew, and being laid up unable to even *think* about cooking, let alone do it, had been a bit of a shock to his system. But as soon as he was back on his feet, he'd thrown himself back into work, forced himself to keep going until the end of the day even though the fatigue gave him brain-fog and left his arms trembling after a day of chopping produce and lifting heavy pans. After a few days, though, he was back into the rhythm and had dismissed the illness as an inconvenience. Until his head really was back into work, and he was able to concentrate on what he was doing properly. Then he realised his whole life had changed.

Jack had accepted that the virus has affected his sense of taste and smell when he was sweating it out in bed. His appetite had deserted him, but that's what being sick did, wasn't it?

But after a couple of weeks back in the kitchen, as he dipped into the sauces and stocks, it hit him. He couldn't smell the food he was preparing, and his taste buds had been obliterated. Wiped.

At first, he'd just been confused. He'd let people reassure him, tell him to give it time. He'd listened to the doctors who said that most people got over it, that their senses came back after a few weeks, or months.

But he hadn't got time, he needed to send out dishes, he needed to get as close to perfection as he could. He couldn't do half a job. And it seemed that he wasn't 'most people'.

Time went on and the strong cup of coffee that he started his day with still tasted metallic, the delicate sweetness of his desserts sidestepped his senses completely, and he had to rely on his staff to tell him that the flavours were spot on. And he couldn't work that way. It was doing his head in.

What kind of chef can't tell if the seasoning is too heavy? What kind of chef can't reject the fish that isn't quite as fresh as it should be?

Life seemed to have thrown him a curveball. He'd never thought about bad luck, he'd made his own good luck – with hard work. But he couldn't fix this. And nobody could give him an answer, tell him why he was different. Why he was one of the people who hadn't recovered fully.

Jack hadn't started to drink more to drown his sorrows, he'd not consciously reached for the bottle. He'd just found that a glass or two helped him sleep. That the bitterness cut through his senses – he could smell whisky, he could taste shiraz. He couldn't enjoy his food because it hurt to eat things that didn't carry the flavours that he knew they should.

And the *on* bit with his on-off girlfriend had disappeared.

His fault, he knew. He'd pushed her away. He'd distanced himself in the same way as he had with his parents. He preferred to spend his evenings alone, with a drink and mindless TV programmes that washed over him.

He didn't want them to hear the anger in his voice, or the despair. He didn't want them to hear the slight slur from tiredness and a whisky too many, which these days kept him awake rather than knocking him out.

He didn't want somebody 'never-minding', telling him to let his team do it. He did mind. This was his dream, his life, this was everything he'd ever worked for. One hundred per cent – not just a physical act, it was his heart, his soul. Food was his greatest love affair.

She'd never got that. Clara. She was with him because she liked what he did, his success, not who he was. Food was just fuel to her, so how could she ever understand him? The casual relationship had been fine, it suited him, he was too busy, too wrapped up in his career to be committed to another person. He'd always been clear on that, never wanted to mislead anybody.

But it had still been a bit of a blow just how completely she'd wiped him out of her life once she realised that he was serious about quitting. Up until that point she'd assumed he'd carry on, that they'd carry on. She seemed fairly oblivious to, or not bothered by, his withdrawal, his lack of communication. She'd drifted in and out of his daily existence in much the same way she always had. But the moment that she'd seen the contract he'd signed – letting out the restaurant, his home, to somebody else – the moment she realised he meant what he'd said, that he was quitting, that he hadn't got some other restaurant or job lined up, that it was over, then so were they.

'That's so fucking selfish,' she'd said as she swept her toiletries into a bag. 'Who's going to invite me out when they find out you're just a guy who *used* to be famous? You're just, just…' she'd stumbled '…normal, nobody now.'

It hadn't been just a casual relationship, she hadn't been with him because she liked his sense of humour or his dodgy taste in music, enjoyed his company or just liked hanging out with him – she had been with him because of his social status. He'd been a meal-ticket, and now he was a nobody. He'd outlived his usefulness.

But it meant he was now *completely* alone. Without his magic touch, without the love of his life, the food that had filled his waking and sleeping hours, he was lost.

It was the day his parents came round for lunch, and he didn't have any food in the house because he'd forgotten, that Jack decided enough was enough.

His father had insisted they drive to the local pub, and he'd shovelled in mouthfuls of something that he was sure tasted as bland to everybody else as it did to him.

His new level.

The look in his mother's eye had been sympathy. Jack had never needed sympathy, he'd been too driven, too motivated. That look made him feel more ashamed than admitting he couldn't cook any longer. He was a loser.

He knew he had a choice – go full-out pity-party or go full-out in another direction. Because there were no options for Jack that didn't involve one hundred per cent.

He had to get away. He had to start again, not hope that things would gradually get better (as everybody said they would) and he could pick up where he left off in the restaurant. He had to bury himself somewhere people didn't know him. To rebuild his life, then re-emerge when he was doing something he was proud of. When he could hold his head up.

Ben had been his mother's idea. Ben the therapist. If he wouldn't talk to them, he needed to talk to somebody else, she'd said, an outsider. The idea was completely alien to him, and from the look on his dad's face it wouldn't have been his first call either, but what else could he do but agree? He'd felt guilty, he'd felt ashamed for the version of himself he'd become, the son they could now see. So he'd said yes. It was the least he could do.

He'd had absolutely no faith that offloading on some stranger would help but booking that first appointment had given him the kick up the bum he needed. Upped his resolve to sort this out himself.

Ben had made it quite clear (well, as clear as a therapist ever makes anything) that he didn't think Jack was doing the right thing either. The platitudes had flowed out of him, like the trickle of water from a garden water feature. Splish-splash, with an annoying repetitiveness. A measured drip, drip. He'd thought therapists were supposed to listen, facilitate, not tell you what to do (or he definitely wouldn't have signed up), but Ben mustn't have got the memo. 'It might be good to face up, not back off. Not that I'm saying you're doing that.' Ben probably wasn't even his real name. He'd probably adopted it as it was nice, approachable. Easy-going and non-confrontational.

Like everything else about him. Jack had looked at him and imagined that before his birth his parents had probably given him a dynamic name – like Zak, or Finn – hoping he'd be a pilot or something big in the city. But it was totally at odds with his role as therapist.

Unless he'd been calm since birth and had genuinely been a gentle Ben.

Anyway, this hadn't been Ben's call.

When Jack had signed the six-month rental contract on the house it had seemed a good length of time. Long enough to eliminate routine, make a clean break. But now it seemed like a life sentence, and he'd not even moved in. It felt like a backwards stutter rather than a forward step.

Jack had done his cooking apprenticeship in Barcelona. There was an energy in the city, a feeling that anything could happen, a fluidity as the visitors changed as rapidly as the tides. It was a place to learn, create. A place of inspiration. A place of demands and rules set down by somebody else. Jack had looked around the modern, minimalistic restaurant one day and known he had done what he needed to. He was ready; it was time to go home. It was time to use what he'd learned and do it his way.

He'd loved his old place from the moment he saw it. It had felt right, it felt like home. The city had been fun, a good place to grow, but this was a place that captured his heart, the very essence of him.

The front door was oak – solid, understated. Most of the rooms might have been small, and the old beams might have been a hazard for a lot of his visitors (though let's face it, nobody had actually knocked themselves out or even had concussion), but the kitchen had been amazing. It had totally been the centre of his home, the hub, where it all happened –

where everybody wanted to be. He'd kept the old Aga that was there when he bought the place but added a state-of-the-art range as well. Pans hung from the overhead hooks that had been there for years, the traditional mingled with the new perfectly. He could have stayed in that kitchen all day and all night – and sometimes he got lost in what he was doing, and the sun was rising before he knew it.

That kitchen was a place where magic happened, where he used the skills that he'd been taught, but found his own style.

The old walled garden was his second favourite place, with its tangle of rambling roses, herbs that released their scent as he brushed past them down the narrow paths, sweet peas and runner beans that drew in the humming insects with their bright flowers. Quiet and calm. Inspirational. It was the only escape he needed.

And then there was The Orangery that had been a café, but effortlessly transformed into a light, bright but traditional-feeling restaurant. The perfect setting to serve his food. A place that reflected his thoughts, his aims.

He'd only been running his restaurant for three months when a local celeb posted a picture of one of his dishes on Instagram. The following weekend a food critic stopped by and wrote a glowing review about the 'inventive food that was still rooted in the countryside' and before he knew it, he was featured in a Sunday supplement and his tables were booking up a month in advance. Clara had appeared shortly after, happy (or should that be keen?) to be at his side whenever a photo opportunity arose.

He'd never sought fame. He wasn't a big talker, but he was proud. His parents were proud. And knowing people were loving what he created made him feel complete. He was doing what he was supposed to.

But that was then. And this was now.

Now the magic had drained out of his veins, and he was in no-man's land. The middle ground. No city buzz, no sleepy village – just the suburban middle.

Now he'd got a bright red front door and bedding plants in uniform rows. Neighbours across the road who could watch his every move. Neighbours who liked to speed up the road.

Bloody neighbours everywhere.

Jack had never really been into neighbours. He worked. Sure, he'd got some close friends, and he'd always made an effort to talk to customers. He didn't have anything against people in general, but he didn't have time to spend on idle chit-chat with somebody he hardly knew.

Actually, thinking about it, those close friends hadn't been so close for a long time. Before he was ill, he'd cut down on the socialising because work was pretty much 365/24/7 and he'd told himself that there would be plenty of time to go out drinking when he'd got to where he needed to. Done the legwork. And he hadn't needed some artificial high from booze or a buzzy atmosphere – he got it from the kitchen. His mates got it, but they didn't get the new him. They knew the original Jack and didn't know how to cope with the new moody one who didn't just feel like he was drifting down the stream without a paddle; he felt like he was caught up in a frigging whirlpool of nothingness.

So he'd done this. Moved. New start, new him – armed with a camera instead of a whisk. Hiding behind the lens.

It had been his idea. His choice.

To press the reset button somewhere new, where he wasn't being watched and judged. He needed space, to be able to breathe. To clean up his act and find a new direction so that he could go back to his parents and say, 'Look, I'm not a drunken pathetic failure.'

He felt now like his plan was about to totally fail – backfire. He didn't feel like he'd got away, he felt stifled. Suffocated. Packing a backpack and heading away from civilisation would have probably been a better idea.

At least then he wouldn't have had removal men moaning about the narrow road, spilling his gear all over the road, and some idiot driver nearly taking his left leg off.

Did it matter though? He probably should have just let her smash it all into little bits – his pathetic attempt at scraping his life back together. She certainly looked like she would have been happy to comply.

She'd also stared before driving off. That look of recognition that he had got used to identifying. He could do without that. He'd hoped that in his civvies, with slightly longer hair, he'd just be another guy. After all it wasn't like he was some 'A' list celeb, he'd only had a minor spotlight on him for a brief time. The guy next door who had a way with food.

He looked down the road at the driveway where she'd parked the car. She was clambering out, clutching a bag that was almost as big as she was. Tiny but fierce, like the terrier he'd had as a kid. That dog had not backed down from anything or anybody, even though you could pick her up with one hand. He'd not thought about that dog for years. He'd not thought about anything but food.

She'd been his best mate – he'd told her all his secrets, kicked a football round with her – until she destroyed it. The thought almost brought a smile to his face. Then he remembered the anger on the woman's face as she'd driven off.

Looks like he'd already fucked it up with his neighbours.

The story of his life right now. Isn't that what they said – the higher you go, the further you've got to fall?

Not that he'd ever been in it for glory, it had just been totally all-consuming. He'd wanted to be the best he could be. He'd wanted perfection.

'Where do you want this one, mate? There's no label.'

The shout snapped him out of his self-pitying thoughts. He really needed to get a grip. It wasn't his bloody surroundings; it was something in his screwed-up head that needed to change. This featureless house, this nosy neighbourhood were just a façade. Well, actually, more a farce.

He stared at the large box, then glared down at the framed menu he'd forgotten was in his hand. His first menu, signed by a handful of chefs he hero-worshipped. 'Garage,' he said flatly. 'Any that haven't got a label can be dumped in there.' It wasn't stuff he was likely to use again, but it had just seemed a waste to chuck it all. 'Hey, and this.' He tossed the menu on top of the box, then brushed the palms of his hands against each other and spun on his heel.

He'd have a garage sale or list it on one of those apps. He simply hadn't had the energy to do things, just the urge to get away. Start again. And here he was, already annoying the neighbours and making himself stand out.

He probably should apologise to her. Drop a note through the door or something. Try and make this work. They didn't have to like each other. Just co-exist, not annoy each other. At heart he'd always wanted to get along with everybody; he hated arguments. Unnecessary friction. Yeah, he'd write a note, or stick a bottle of wine on the doorstep. At one time he'd have cooked – it was his go-to way of making up. Well, his go-to for everything. He liked to feed people. He didn't cook for the sake of creating something that looked amazing, he cooked for people to enjoy. But that wasn't an option open these days.

He wiped his palms down the front of his jeans again — trying to erase the feel of that frame in his hand, the words from his head — then marched into the house, hoping that the men would hurry up and finish unloading so that he could shut his front door and put the kettle on.

Chapter Four

KATE

Pancakes with lemon & sugar. Bittersweet

The familiar feel of her fluffy keyring, a present from Eddie, nestled against Kate's palm as she put her key into the front door, and her determination wavered as Rachel's words came flooding back.

Well, one word. Widow.

She pushed the door shut behind her with slow, firm deliberation and then kicked her shoes off with a violence that stopped her in her tracks.

This was not her. This was not the person she wanted to be.

She did not want to be angry at the world, to be bitter. To be scared. But every time she took a step forward, something knocked her back. Was life without Eddie always going to be like this?

If she'd been the yelling and screaming type, the wailing type, she'd have done that. Instead, she stared at her reflection in the hall mirror.

Frowning brow, angry eyes, sad and lost.

She'd been right to leave her job – she hadn't been doing the kids, or herself, any favours. Not that their grades had slipped (she always hit or exceeded targets), or she'd not been there to listen if they needed it – she'd never have let that happen. But it had got harder. And she had a horrible feeling that listening to their problems had been a way of avoiding her own. It had been three years, and she knew she hadn't moved on at all. She'd been avoiding her emotions, her problems. She'd been avoiding herself.

She forced herself to look at her face. Her skin was drawn and tired, not fresh and tanned like it used to be. She had new wrinkles, frown lines across her brow. Her gran had always told her to stop frowning, that she'd regret the lines later. A small smile lifted the corners of her mouth. Her gran had been bossy, pretty blunt at times, but normally right. She'd be wagging a finger if she was here now, saying 'I told you so!'

A lump formed in her chest. She missed her grandparents. She'd not even given herself time out to cry when they'd gone. She'd ploughed on. Just like her bloody mother always did. Shit, she was turning into her. Becoming everything that she didn't want to be. Her mum was the queen when it came to avoiding emotion. It was as though she just hadn't been able to relax when she was with Kate. As though she was on edge.

Just like Kate felt now. Like she'd felt as she'd struggled with life since Eddie had gone. And now that word 'widow' had made her want to run away.

Her smile dropped, and she could see the pinch lines round her mouth. The look of exhaustion and resignation.

She was not going to turn into her mother. It was her mum's fault she was here now, in this state. She wasn't going to take all the blame. If her mum hadn't been the woman she was, then things might have been so different. *She* would have been different. *She* would have wanted different things. Eddie might still be here.

'Widow,' she said softly. Trying out the word on her tongue. It came out on a whisper. She repeated it, speaking louder, and the soft 'w' came out in an angry whoosh.

It echoed in the empty hallway. Because there was nobody there to hear it but her now, was there?

Eddie was gone.

He'd been gone for three years, but that word was the straw that broke the camel's back, the thought that tipped the balance.

Maybe this is what her therapist had meant when they'd talked about confronting things, owning the emotions.

It wasn't about closure; it was about being open to what had happened. Who she was now.

She hated the fact that Eddie had left her. That he wasn't there for their third, their fourth anniversaries. That he hadn't been here to celebrate their fifth anniversary, that they would never celebrate any more or have the child he'd wanted so much. She hated that today was her birthday, and she was now the same age he'd been when he died.

She hated even more the feeling that she was losing him all over again. For a long time – weeks, months – he had still been with her. She could smell him on the sheets, on his clothes that she'd refused to wash or throw away.

She could see him standing at the oven, as she sat with her glass of wine. She'd talk to him, ask his opinion. She could hear him playing the guitar as she sat in the lounge.

But lately it had been harder to see him. She felt like she was staring into a void. And it hurt. Oh my God, it hurt. She had cried herself to sleep too many times to remember, clutching the tea towels that no longer held his touch in their fabric.

She sank down onto her haunches, resting her back against the cold wall.

Shit, she could not let a stupid word do this to her. What had she let herself become over the last few years? An angry, bitter, sad woman. Eddie would never have let her do this to herself; it would have upset him.

She rubbed the heels of her hands over her eyes. Forced herself back to her feet.

Her job had been her last link with the past life they'd had. But their life would have changed, wouldn't it, over the past few years? It wouldn't have sat stagnant.

Eddie had been all set to start a new job, to finally turn his love of cooking into a full-time career. He'd said thirty-three was the perfect age to make a move, before it was too late.

She had to get her act together, start again.

Today had to be the first day of the rest of her life – or she might as well just give up altogether.

Her mother's voice rang in her ears. 'You're better than this, you're not letting me down, you're letting yourself down.' Right now, she hated her mother, for being right. For forcing her into the mess in the first place.

But she knew she was letting Eddie down – and she cared more about that than she cared about herself.

She strode into the kitchen before she had a chance to change her mind. Confront the past. Confront your fears.

Eddie's sparkling kitchen mocked her. His kitchen; it had always been his.

He'd fallen in love with this room the first time he'd set foot in it. Enthusiasm had shone in his eyes as he'd tapped on the plasterboard behind the cooker, convinced that it was hiding an old brick oven. That it would be the perfect spot for the range cooker he'd set his heart on. Eddie had plans to rip out the new, create a room that really would be the heart of their home.

But he'd never had time. They'd been too busy. They'd thought that tomorrow would be soon enough.

Kate hadn't had the same passion. She loved their home, but the main reason was because it was theirs. She had him.

Eddie had been the real homemaker, especially when it came to the kitchen, and she'd been happy to follow his lead, follow his inspiration. Chip in with little additions and ideas of her own. She'd shaped the bedroom, added colour to the living room. But this kitchen had been his.

She'd sneaked in like a thief over the past three years, to boil the kettle for coffee. Use the toaster. Scramble an egg. Grab a plate to load with takeaway food – when she was fed up with eating scrambled eggs on toast, or soup.

Or she'd just marched through, not looking around, when she headed upstairs – Eddie had loved that the staircase was in the kitchen, so they'd constantly pass each other, be a part of each other's lives. Since he'd gone the quirky feature of the house hurt her heart; it would have been easier to have side-stepped his domain. Rarely set foot in here.

But today she knew she shouldn't. Today she needed to be in here.

What would Eddie do, if she came home angry? He'd make pancakes. He'd toss pancakes in slow motion. He'd make funny fruit faces on them. He'd make her smile. He'd make her laugh.

She'd told him, that night, that tomorrow she would cook with him. Well, tomorrow had finally come.

She would make pancakes.

Soft, fluffy pancakes that melted in her mouth.

Hell, how did you make pancakes?

She'd never had pancakes as a kid; her mother was far too busy working. She'd never paid any attention to what Eddie had actually been doing, she'd been too busy just watching him, over the rim of her wine glass.

He had a recipe book. She knew he had a notepad where he jotted down ideas and tips. She glanced around, opened a drawer. A drawer full of food bags. She opened another. Receipts, scraps of paper. She rifled through: bills, paper, more paper, no book. Panic started to claw at her.

She forced herself to still. Take a deep breath. This was silly. She wasn't silly.

It didn't matter. She could do this without Eddie. She'd find his book tomorrow but right now she would do this herself.

She pushed the drawer slowly closed and picked up her mobile phone. Google, she'd google. She would find a recipe and do this before she changed her mind.

Pancakes with sugar and lemon

> 100g plain flour
> Pinch of salt
> 2 eggs
> 300ml milk
> Sunflower, vegetable oil or butter

- *Sift the flour and salt. Make a well in the centre and break the eggs into it. Using an electric or balloon whisk, whisk together until it starts to thicken. Gradually add the milk. Whisk until smooth, and the consistency is similar to single cream.*
- *Leave to stand for 15 minutes.*

- *Rub a frying pan with the oil or butter. Heat the pan on high until hot, then turn the heat down to medium and spoon in the batter. Tip the pan to evenly coat. When golden, flip over. Serve with caster sugar and freshly squeezed lemon.*

Fine. This would be fine. She had eggs, she had milk and butter. And flour didn't go off, did it? Well, if it did, it was tough. She'd die with a pancake in her stomach.

Why didn't she know these things though? She'd lived with an aspiring chef, a guy who loved to cook, who would have spent all day in the kitchen if you'd let him. She had never paid any attention. Never noticed what he was using, just watched the way his fingers moved, the strength of his arms as he carved, the look of concentration on his face.

She'd watched him cook. She'd just never *seen* what he was doing.

She'd been right – she was turning into her mother. Kate didn't grow up baking cakes or tossing pancakes. She grew up on fast food and shop-bought, because her mum never had time to cook, and didn't want to have to nurture a family. She'd always made comments like 'Your gran is better at making it how you like'. Why say something like that, when she was the woman who could do *everything* that she set her mind to, and told Kate she could do the same?

And it couldn't be that difficult, could it? Even kids did it.

'I won't let you down, Eddie,' Kate whispered, as she carefully measured out the flour and milk and lined everything up. 'If I can handle a classroom full of thirty teenagers, I can cook bloody pancakes.'

She could almost see him laughing, feel his warm breath on the back of her neck, his warm hands on her waist. It sent a shiver through her.

They could do this together.

She checked the recipe again.

'What the fuck is a balloon whisk?' Did it look like a balloon, or a whisk?

There was no answer from Eddie.

Google told her. But she was pretty sure she'd never seen Eddie with one of those in his hand. And then it came to her.

She remembered! He'd once told her that the best batter maker in the world was the blender. He had; he'd told her. She could almost hear him saying it, and it made her laugh – well, laugh-cry. It came out more like a sob, but before it took over she grabbed the step-stool and reached for one of Eddie's favourite gadgets.

Right, it said 'sift'; did she have to 'sift'? Oh, to hell with it, she was doing this properly. She balanced the sieve over the top of the blender, and held the bowl of flour up high, in the best chef fashion, then peered over as she tapped the side firmly with the heel of her hand.

The fine plume of flour shot straight up, dusting her face, getting into her eyes and choking her. Spluttering, she sneezed, dropped the bowl of flour and the sieve went flying.

Who knew that 100g of flour could cover so much, and that NONE would end up in the blender? Her best *black* fine-wool jumper was now a dusty grey, and she was pretty sure her hair was a matching shade.

She sneezed again, and the coating on the worksurface shot in all directions. 'You're kidding me!' She stepped back and yelped as something dug into her instep. She glanced down at the sieve. Which was now not very sieve-shaped, more foot-shaped.

'Oh, bugger that.' Kate threw the mangled sieve in the direction of the bin, then grabbed the nearly empty bag of plain flour and refilled the bowl to roughly the same level it had been before and tipped the contents into the blender. 'If you're lumpy it's your own bloody fault!'

Right, make a well and put the eggs in. They didn't need a well, whatever that was, they were going to be well and truly mashed up soon.

'And *voila*!' She poured the milk in from a height, with a flourish, then pressed the *on* button triumphantly.

The blender sprang into life. So did the ingredients.

Luckily, she had not been leaning over to watch her progress this time, she was standing back, hands on hips. So when the far from smooth mixture was launched into the air it was the ceiling that got splattered, not her face. And everything else within range. The worksurface, the once sparkling hob, the lovely clean frying pan that was ready to go. The floor.

She yelped, then tried to slam the switch to off but gave up as another splodge of batter narrowly missed her eye, and pulled the plug.

Kate stared; the blender was close to empty. Then she looked round open-mouthed. How could a couple of eggs and a bit of flour make so much mess?

She picked her mobile phone up, and slowly wiped the splattered screen. It lit up.

Tip the pan to evenly coat.

'Shit.' She took a step back, nearly slipping over. The floor had a fine misting of batter. In fact, most of the kitchen was pretty evenly coated. The frying pan seemed to have half an egg yolk and a few lumps of flour in it – so no hope there then.

She caught sight of her out-of-shape reflection in the kettle. There was a lump of something in her hair and a smear down her cheek.

Streaks down her jumper.

'Well –' she choked back the hysterical laughter that had started to bubble up in her throat '– I guess it's a good job I'm not going to be needing these for work.' She debated whether she should strip off her once smart work clothes in the kitchen and put them straight in the washing machine or get in the shower as she was.

She might as well bin the jumper, she was pretty sure it would never be the same again. It was halfway over her head when there was a loud knock on the front door.

She froze.

She would ignore it. Nobody ever knocked on the door at this time. She inched the jumper a bit higher.

The doorbell rang. She slowly pulled the jumper back down.

It rang a second time, and this time it was how Eddie used to do it. Persistent. And she would have flung the door open, frustration on her face, to see him standing there. Grinning.

And he would have helped her clean up the kitchen, and they could have had a food fight that took them all the way upstairs – to a shared shower.

She swallowed the gulp.

The doorbell rang again – and this time it didn't stop.

Chapter Five

CHARLES

The tearoom

Charles didn't like old age. It was cumbersome, mocking. Was it fair that the hardest things came when you were old, when you'd lived a lifetime and would like a bit of a break? A few quiet years to appreciate some home comforts.

He knew that his mind wasn't as sharp as it used to be, but it was his body that was the biggest burden. It was a race to see which would happen first – he'd forget where he was walking to, or he'd find he was physically incapable of getting there.

In some ways, the deterioration of his mind was getting easier to live with. Mary knew what he meant, even if he couldn't quite find the right word a lot of the time. It was only frustrating when he was with new people. That was when he missed his sharpness, realised his sparkling wit had gone for ever. It niggled him, brought regrets to the fore. Regrets that he hadn't made more of the last few years, pushed himself harder.

He remembered his old man telling him that there were people who trod the path of least resistance, who conservatively did what they knew they could do – and there were the risk-takers who either made it big or crashed. Charles had stayed in the safe zone, made sure he could provide for his Mary, buy a nice house, made sure they'd always be comfortable. But sometimes he wondered if he should have dared to take a chance more often.

Before it was too late.

Right now, though, his main concern was that it had taken him a lot longer than he'd anticipated to walk down to number 43. A few years ago – well, two hip replacements ago – he'd have marched from their home at the top of the street in five minutes flat and not broken a sweat. He'd have been straight-backed and determined. Now he wasn't quite sure whether he was doing the right thing, he was exasperated at his slow shuffle and dratted walking stick, and his shortness of breath had forced him to pause and lean on a fence or wall more than once.

He would also have enjoyed a walk in the bright afternoon sunshine (if you could ever call the soft April sun of England that), but now he was like some night-time creature – only daring out in the early morning or late afternoon. Even this gentle heat was just so exhausting, draining.

But at least he was alive, he supposed, having a lucid moment, and feeling a nostalgic lump in his throat as he glanced up at the building he'd stopped in front of.

The once familiar, white painted front door had been replaced with a solid-looking sage-green one, with a shiny brass knocker. Modern slatted blinds now shuttered the large bay window so that it was impossible to see in, or – he presumed – out.

He'd always loved sitting in that big bay window; it was the prime spot in the tearoom. He could show off his Mary, and they could watch the world go by.

The red brick still glowed in the soft sunshine though, as it always had done, and something about the building was welcoming in the same way that it had been all those years ago.

It had been a place of good times. It had been the start of something wonderful, so maybe it was fitting that his thoughts had brought him back here. Mary would call him a romantic old fool if she knew. And he quite liked hearing her say things like that to him.

He'd never thought there would come a day when she wasn't here to say it, but now he knew it was inevitable. That unless he took the coward's way out and stepped in front of a car or some such nonsense, then the day would come when he'd have to say a final goodbye, when he'd be left behind. And he would never try and leave her; he'd made his wedding vows and had no intention of breaking them. He would love and cherish her with all his heart until she drew her last breath.

He dabbed at his eyes with his handkerchief, stupid watery old eyes, then pushed the cotton square back into his trouser pocket.

Charles took a deep breath to straighten his thoughts out. He might have lost some of his shine, but he'd gained some things in old age. As a young man he would never have deliberately emphasised his weaknesses, showed himself in a poor light (as he was about to now). He hoped he'd had some humility all those years ago, but this was more. This was for somebody else; this was for his Mary.

Maybe he'd finally matured. He gave a wry smile, knowing that was a thought that would make Mary laugh.

'Oh, Mary,' he said softly. Then he straightened his back as much as it would these days. 'Well, what are you waiting for, you old fool?' he asked himself and set his walking stick towards the front door.

He really should have used his walking frame, but it made him feel old. Even the stick was a nod to his weakness, but one that he decided he could embrace. People of all ages used them these days, didn't they? Very Fred Astaire – or weekend rambler. He wasn't sure which.

But Zimmer frame? Just thinking the words sent a shudder through him. He shook it away impatiently and made his way up the path, tapping the stick decisively, leaning his weight on it as he squared his shoulders and reached out and pressed the doorbell.

There was no answer immediately. But he knew she was in. Her car was there, and she was always home by this time. So he pressed again. One long ring.

And then he leant on the bell and didn't let go, because he was beginning to feel a little bit light-headed standing for so long, and it gave him some support, if nothing else.

The door suddenly swung open with such force that he lurched back in surprise and nearly lost balance. But then remembered the importance of his mission and swayed back into position.

'Good morning my dear!' He raised his free hand to his forehead in a salute. She looked older than he'd imagined from a distance. Older than when he'd last spoken to her, on her wedding day. When Mary had insisted that they see her off as she left for the church. She loved a wedding, did Mary.

They had looked out on the day the hearse came as well. Mary had taken a card, offered their condolences and popped it through the door, but she hadn't wanted to knock. To intrude. Grief, she'd said, was personal. Everybody should be allowed to do it in their own way.

Now, Kate's skin was drawn and her gaze slightly blank, in the way of the sad or lonely. He'd seen that look on the faces of friends who had lost their nearest and dearest. He'd seen it more often than he cared to these days, but that was another downside of old age.

It was funny how each season of adult life was mapped out so clearly. The signposts of weddings, christenings and then funerals.

But right now, he wasn't here to think about death, he was here to remember life. To make sure Mary's last days were the best they could be.

She was staring at him blankly. She also seemed to have a blob of something rather strange in the middle of her forehead.

He dragged his gaze away from it. He must not let it deter him, he had to crack on as planned. He was doing this for Mary – for home baking and pork crackling – he must not be distracted! 'Are you open for business?'

She frowned and he remembered that she actually was quite pretty, when the pain was chased away from her green eyes. When she had something else to worry about.

And she hadn't just got a blob on her forehead, there was another on her chin, and a smear of something on her chest that he was trying his hardest not to stare at.

He set his cane centrally and rested both hands on it, willing himself to stay as upright as possible and look straight ahead – into her eyes.

'I –' Charles tilted his head slightly, let the hint of a smile lift the corners of his mouth (didn't Mary once call him debonair?) and glanced at her in what he hoped was a winning way '– would absolutely love one of your wonderful pots of tea, and –' he paused, waving a finger in the air, wondering if he was over-egging it '– a toasted teacake would be sublime!'

She took a step back, her eyes opening wider. 'Teacake,' she said weakly. The first word she'd said. 'I'm sorry, I…'

'This always was the best tearoom in town!' he added, to make absolutely sure that the message was clear, because these days people didn't always listen properly. It was at this point, now that she had stepped away slightly and he could focus more accurately on her, that he realised the smears on her face looked remarkably like cake mixture, and the black sweater she was wearing had a fine coating of what he could swear was flour! Which was amazingly opportune. His luck was definitely in. 'I don't suppose you have baked fresh scones today? You've obviously been cooking!' It might be rude to mention it, but he had been subtle.

She looked down at her front, then back up at him. 'Well, yes, I—'

Then all of a sudden, his darned knees decided they'd had enough, and quivered with an intensity that left his head spinning.

'Oh goodness.' He reached out blindly, meaning to grab the door frame, but somehow her hand shot out at precisely the same second and he found himself grasping it gratefully.

His gaze focused on hers and he realised she really was the prettiest thing he'd seen in a long time. She reminded him of Mary, his Mary all those years ago when they'd stood on this very spot, and he'd fallen in love.

Chapter Six

KATE

Egg and soldiers

'What the—' Kate reached for him without thinking, alarmed at the sudden wobble and the way the colour seemed to drain from his face. 'Oh my God, are you okay?' He was staring at her with a blank intensity that sent her into a panic. And swaying.

She got a better grip on him. He had to stay on his feet because if he didn't right now the only thing that she could remember about the recovery position was the name!

He took in a deep breath, shuddered and blinked, and the air came out of Kate in a rush.

With a sigh of relief, she loosened her grip on his elbow and tried not to wince as his own fingers tightened more firmly around hers.

Okay, he might not be feeling one hundred per cent, but she was now pretty sure he wasn't about to die on her doorstep. She smiled reassuringly, then glanced up and down the street. There was nobody else around – had he really come here expecting it to be a tearoom? Whatever the reason, she couldn't close the door in his face, could she?

'Do you want to come in, have a sit down for a moment?' She could cope with making a cup of tea, she wasn't sure about CPR – or scones.

He mustered up a smile, and an image of her gran jumped into her head. 'Nothing that a cup of tea won't put right' was one of her little sayings. Kate hadn't thought about her funny little sayings for a while; well, if she was honest, she hadn't thought about much at all. She'd wallowed. Her gran wouldn't have put up with wallowing. Oh wow, she wished she was still here.

'Are you okay, my dear?' He squeezed her hand gently.

'Oh yes, yes, sorry. Can you manage?' The second the words left her mouth she knew it was a mistake. Asking her grandparents if they could manage had always gone down badly. Independence and self-reliance had been everything. Admitting weakness was for wimps. But she was surprised to realise that the old man wasn't giving her 'the look', in fact, his features had softened.

'Old age is a bugger, if you'll pardon my language.'

She grinned. 'A pain in the posterior, as my gran used to say.'

'Now there's a woman after my own heart!' He smiled broadly, a smile that faded as he studied the step up over the threshold of the house. 'Now, if I can just…' He still looked exceedingly wobbly as he carefully took the step up – from the way his arm trembled she imagined most of his weight was probably on his stick and only the smallest amount on her arm. But at least she was in the right place to reach out and grab him if it looked like he was going to keel over. 'Phew.' He straightened slightly, though she was sure it had required a lot of effort.

They stood side by side and looked down the narrow hallway while he caught his breath.

'Well now.' He was frowning again. 'Have you redecorated? It looks different from last time I popped in! I could have sworn there was a door there!' He waved his stick. 'Though my memory does rather play tricks these days.'

'We decorated a while ago.' They'd given the place a lick of paint when they'd first moved in, but not made any big changes. They'd not had a chance; change had been something planned for the future. The one that never happened. 'But we, I, haven't moved any doors.' What did you do with confused people? Play along, or be honest? She didn't know, but she couldn't help it – being direct was her nature. 'Look, I'm sorry, it's not a tearoom. It never had been as far as I know.'

It didn't look like a café, did it? Why should he think that? Maybe his funny turn had meant he'd had a shortage of oxygen to his brain, and once he'd had a sit-down and caught his breath, he'd feel better. And know where he was.

Or maybe he'd taken a wrong turning and ended up in the wrong street?

She did recognise him though; she'd seen him walking up and down the street, with a woman of similar age, who, she presumed, was his wife. They must live fairly locally. Now she thought about it they must live *very* locally because they'd passed her house on a regular basis and it wasn't exactly a thoroughfare to the shops. Unless you lived here.

For a moment she felt a pang of guilt that she didn't even know her neighbours. They were just passing shadows, people she nodded hello to, people she'd hardly noticed.

But so much had happened since she'd moved in. They'd barely had time to unpack their boxes before…

She must not think about that right now. Definitely not. She gave herself a silent talking to and smiled as brightly as she could – hoping that she didn't look like Harry Potter's 'Professor McGonagall on a bad day' as Mark in Year 12 had kindly told her, as she'd tidied up her storeroom for the final time.

She might not be yearning for children of her own, but she had enjoyed the banter at the school. Dealing with teenagers had kept her on her toes, though they really could be little gits at times.

A shoulder nudged hers, and she realised he was wobbling again. 'Sorry, sorry, you need to sit down. I'm Kate, by the way.' She'd deal with the tearoom business when she took him home or found somebody to come and collect him. 'Please, go through.'

After a moment's hesitation, she indicated the kitchen. The living room looked, well, lived in. Very lived in. It was the place where she wrapped herself up in a fleecy throw and watched romances that made her cry, thrillers that she had to turn off, and reality TV that could just drift over her.

The kitchen was tidy, because it was a place she just passed through.

Then she remembered. It had been relatively unused – until about ten minutes ago. It now looked like there had been a food fight.

Oh hell, but it was too late to stop him – he was already heading determinedly through the open doorway.

'Charles,' he said, seemingly oblivious to the chaos, and the fact she was wiping a dusting of flour off the chair with her sleeve. He offered a formal handshake, which seemed to take the last of his resolve, as the moment she let go he sank down onto the chair.

He'd go home with a white powder coating on the seat of his trousers. But he didn't look like he was up to standing again, so she'd have to brush him down before he left.

She resisted the urge to shift him forward so she could check the back of the chair. She couldn't take him back to his nursing home, or house, or wherever it was he had come from, with a white imprint of a ladderback chair on his jacket, could she?

He gazed around, and she gave him a moment to catch his breath. 'Oh my goodness, this place has changed a bit. What on earth have you done to the bricks? You've covered them up!' He looked puzzled for a moment, then waved his stick in the direction of the oven. 'Flo had her magnificent oven there, you could see it from the seats at the front, magnificent it was. Black and polished to within an inch of its life, the old-fashioned way.' He leaned forward conspiratorially, even though nobody else was there, and lowered his voice. 'Mind, I remember when there was a proper brick oven there, baked the best bread in the street.' He suddenly tapped the side of his nose and laughed. 'Not that there was any competition! But I do have to tell you, you are most definitely mistaken, my dear.'

She raised an eyebrow.

'There was a tearoom here. *This* was a tearoom. Auntie Flo's Tearoom, the best for miles around if you ask me.'

Ah, he'd said it *was*, so he wasn't as completely confused as she'd first thought. And it seemed Eddie had been right; somebody had modernised this kitchen in a way that really would be better reversed. Not that she had the time, or inclination. Why even attempt to turn this into Eddie's dream kitchen when she'd just demonstrated that she wasn't even capable of making pancakes?

'And you do seem to have,' he paused, and waved a finger vaguely in the direction of her nose, 'a touch of flour…'

She put her hand up, and it came down covered in batter. Not quite cream consistency, more like the soggy bottom of a cake.

'A touch?' She couldn't help herself. She laughed. 'More like half a packet!'

He smiled back at her, then guffawed as he saw her gaze drift down to take in the rest of herself again.

'Tea.' Kate flicked the kettle on and decided that it was better to be blunt. He seemed very nice, but what if, after this cup of tea, he decided to pop in every day? 'I'm sorry, Charles, this –' she waved a hand to indicate the mess down her front '– is a bit of a one-off. I'm not much of a cook –' now that was an understatement '– and it's not a tearoom any longer. It wasn't when we bought it.'

'I can see that, my dear.' He was looking round, taking it all in. 'Unless it's gone all modern, with, what do you call them? Breakfast bars?' He watched in silence as she made the drink. 'There used to be round tables, with the loveliest lace tablecloths. Mary loved the tablecloths. And a view of the street.' His voice held a wistful edge.

'It's not been a café for a while, I don't think.' She was pretty sure the estate agent had never mentioned it had been a café when they looked round. Oh my, Eddie would have been over the moon if he'd known. The familiar pang caught at her throat. She couldn't tell him, he'd never know.

He'd known this was the house for them though, the moment they'd stepped over the threshold. Maybe he'd instinctively known that there was something special about it, that people had come here for food and drink. Eddie loved to cook for people, to feed people, and he would have been in his element. He would have been planning a reopening.

'Oh dear, oh dear. You're going to think I'm a right silly old fool.' Charles shook his head and sighed. 'I do get confused, lose track of time. But this place holds such wonderful memories.'

She sat down opposite him. 'You're not silly,' she said softly. What was silly about trying to remember the past? She of all people could appreciate the need to do that. The need to sometimes wish you could take back words, alter your actions. Change the past. 'I'm sure it was a lovely tearoom.'

'It was, it was indeed. That wall wasn't there.' He gestured towards the wall that divided the kitchen from the lounge. 'You could see right through from front to back. Now there was a counter of course, laden with cakes, but that was further back here. Just about where you are, I'd say. Made the tearoom bigger, if you follow? A grand room it was, grand.'

Kate nodded. Thinking about it, it did explain some of the quirks of the house. The fireplace in the front room wasn't quite central, which she'd always thought was a bit strange. It was also enormous, not in proportion to the size of the room at all. When somebody had converted the property, they must have decided the kitchen needed to be bigger.

Eddie had also been sure that the dividing wall between the hallway and lounge was a recent addition, but it hadn't seemed important until now. Though it would explain why the staircase was in the corner of the kitchen, if there hadn't been a hallway. And their bedroom with its central fireplace could so easily have been a cosy sitting room. The owners' living accommodation on the first floor.

'This was where I brought Mary on our first date. It was splendid.'

Kate wasn't sure if he was talking about the date, or the café.

'The first time I brought her in here was for a pot of tea and a slice of Victoria sandwich, back then we used to come in most weeks if I could afford it. It was what you did in those days, dated where there were plenty of people about. No sneaking off! We went dancing too, of course, but I like tea and cake.' His voice had softened at the edges, soft and light, like a slice of best sponge cake. 'You don't need to be touching to feel close, do you?' She shook her head. 'We had our first date here and I knew I wanted to spend the rest of my life with her. You just know in here, don't you?' He held his hand over his heart and there was a wistful edge to his voice that made Kate hold her breath. She nodded her head slowly. Yes, she knew what it was like to fall totally in love with somebody. 'Lovely Flo, who used to run the tearoom, made a special cake for us the day I asked Mary to be my wife. She had all those cakes we could choose from, but she made a special one just for us. I'd asked Mary's father of course the day before, not that I would have let him stand in my way!' He chuckled. 'She made the most glorious pineapple upside-down cake that left my Mary speechless!' His smile lifted his features, his voice, in a way that brought a lump to Kate's throat. 'We had pineapple upside-down cake every year on our wedding anniversary until Flo retired.' He paused for a moment, then his voice was softer when he spoke again. 'I'd like to bring Mary here again, share a slice of that cake.'

Oh my, what was she supposed to say to that?

'She was strong back then, my Mary. She knew her mind, had opinions, which my mother was never allowed to.' There was a note of awe mingled with the affection in his tone which caused a flutter in Kate's stomach.

'She's not...' She didn't like to use the 'd' word, it was devastating. She imagined that even when (if she ever made it) she was the same age as Charles, it would still hurt thinking about Eddie being gone.

Kate suddenly realised that Charles had snapped out of his musings, and his gaze, surprisingly direct even though his eyes were clouded over with age, was on her. He rested his hand over hers. The skin was mottled, thin as paper, but his grasp surprisingly firm and reassuring. 'Oh no, I'm sorry, dear, I didn't mean to upset you.' There was a pause, a shared look that brought a lump to her throat. He understood. He definitely wasn't as muddled or confused as he seemed. There was nothing wrong with Charles, apart from the type of forgetful that came with the years, whatever impression he'd tried to give her. He patted her hand, then pulled slightly away. 'No, my Mary is still with me, not as young as she used to be, but still with me.' The softness of his tone, the way his words lingered, worried her, made her want to swap roles — reach out and comfort him.

'No scones then?' The touch of hope in his voice as he gazed round for evidence of her baking broke the feeling of sadness that seemed to be hanging in the air.

She laughed and shook her head. 'I'm afraid I never got that far!' Then she fetched the pack of biscuits from beside the kettle, feeling vaguely disappointed that it was all she could offer.

Charles studied the proffered packet for a moment, before taking one with what seemed to be polite resignation.

'I'm sorry,' she said. 'I've never been much of a cook.'

'You should make some,' he said firmly.

'I don't really know—'

'When Mary used to bake them, it filled the house with the smell. Nothing like the smell of good food to get the taste buds going. Delicious!' He had that faraway look back in his eyes.

Her throat tightened. She missed so many things about having Eddie around, but Charles had just hit the nail on the head. Oh wow, did she miss the smell of his delicious food. Not just the taste. She had always come home to a house full of warmth, and smells. It was a promise of what was to come, it was love, it was – well, if she really had to define it, it was comforting.

These days her home smelled of air freshener and cleaning products, not life and love.

'They're very easy to make, according to Mary.' Charles glanced at his watch and then started struggling to his feet. 'I really should get off; she'll wonder where I am and it's fish and chips night!'

Kate followed him to the front door, glad that there was some colour back in his cheeks.

'I could run you back, in the car?'

'Nonsense.' He waved his stick in the air, narrowly missing the vase on the hall table. 'It's only up the road – number 89, you know?' She should know; she didn't, she'd never stopped to watch where he went. Never wondered about Charles and Mary. 'And I'm sure you need me out of your hair. I'll let you get on, get those cakes baked for tomorrow!'

She couldn't help the smile. He reminded her of her old headmaster.

'But I don't need to…' He'd obviously forgotten again that it wasn't a tearoom – or decided to ignore the fact! But what did it matter? 'Wonderful!'

'Goodbye, my dear, thank you so much for the tea! I'll get

Mary to pop in and let you have the recipe for the scones. She doesn't bake these days.' He tapped his wrist. 'Arthritis in the joints, she's got. Right bugger it is. She used to bake every Tuesday and she'd make the most delicious dinner on a Sunday. Roast beef and Yorkshire pud was our favourite, and apple crumble. Nothing like an apple crumble with warm custard, none of your cream nonsense. She misses being able to do it, we both do.' His voice had softened, but then he straightened, and the words came out more briskly. 'Oh well, life and all that!' His stick swung in the air, and she ducked instinctively. 'Toodle pip!'

Charles took a step out of the door, then hesitated and looked back over his shoulder. 'If you've never made them before I'm sure Mary can help. Scones, that is, not the Yorkshires. She'd be happy to boss you around. She's good at that!' He grinned. 'Right-oh. How about Monday? Or are you busy?' His look was hopeful and challenging at the same time. There was something about people once they passed a certain age, thought Kate, when they really did think you'd fit in with their plans.

She hesitated.

He gave the lightest of sighs, and when he spoke his tone was soft. 'She's not been well, you know. She thinks I don't understand, but I do.' He shook his head and hesitated as though he wanted to say more but was undecided. Then he straightened up, his voice stronger, as though determined to put a positive spin on his request. 'It would mean the world to her, my dear, being back here. In the tearoom, but at the business end, if you know what I mean!' He winked.

She could say no, she could say she was busy. But did she really have any reason not to spend her Monday baking? She wasn't going into school, and she hadn't made any plans yet.

She could spend the day moping on her own, or she could make scones with Mary. She could help an old man who wanted to please the love of his life. She could help Mary bake again. After all, how bad would Eddie have felt if he'd been deprived of the thing that he enjoyed most?

'Lovely! Is ten o'clock okay?'

'Splendid! And don't forget – they must be served the Cornish way!'

'Definitely!' Kate closed the door behind him and made a mental note to find out what he meant, before 'his Mary' came by on Monday. The only things that stuck in her mind about Cornwall were early morning sea mist, sand and King Arthur's sword – and she wasn't sure that any of those were involved when you served scones.

'Oh my God, what a state.' She looked round the kitchen. She'd been too focused on Charles and his physical and mental state to really worry about the carnage in the once-clean kitchen. What the hell had he thought of her? It was no wonder he was offering to send his octogenarian wife round to help her out.

Her feet practically squelched as she walked around to where the blender was.

But strangely enough, the room didn't feel quite as empty as it did before. 'Oh God, I'm sorry, Eddie! What have I done to your beautiful kitchen?' she said out loud, about to rest her hands on the worktop, then hastily changed her mind.

Her place had always been perched on a stool on the opposite side, a glass of wine in her hand as she watched him cook. Tidying up as he went. He might have had half his dinner smeared down his apron, but the worktops were pristine.

She could almost see him sitting opposite her now, roles

reversed. He was laughing, his head thrown back as she grinned at him bashfully.

'Guess I better tidy up then.' And she could feel his nod. She gathered up the cups and saucers, ran water into the sink. Then stopped, her hands covered in suds, staring out at the garden but not seeing it.

She felt closer to Eddie than she had in ages, and suddenly she thought she knew why. It had taken an old man to point out the obvious. He missed the smell of his wife's baking, he said she missed doing it.

And she missed the smell of Eddie's cooking.

She'd cook. Not just pancakes.

She'd bring Eddie back that way. She'd felt she was losing him, but maybe the way to feel close to him was through his food? She'd find his recipe book, she'd cook the food he used to cook for her, or at least she'd have a good go – there were enough YouTube videos to help her out. It was time to stop being angry.

The floor was still sticky beneath her feet as she moved across the kitchen, opening cupboards for inspiration.

The pancakes hadn't exactly been a success. She had a feeling she'd be finding splatters of congealed batter in unexpected places for weeks.

Runny, sticky... and then it hit her. What she really, really wanted right now wasn't some complicated Eddie recipe. It was the thing that her gran used to make for her, when she felt down, when she was poorly, something simple and wholesome. And she was more than capable of making that.

Dippy egg and soldiers.

She didn't need a recipe. She'd watched her gran do this enough times to know that she popped the eggs in a pan of boiling water and left them for four minutes. It had been Kate's job to turn the old-fashioned egg timer. To watch the sand trickle through. To shout out when it had all gone – not a second too early, not a second too late.

Gran didn't care whether any chef said that was the right or the wrong way to boil an egg. It was 'how we do it in our family'.

And Gran always pushed the mess to one side and said the kitchen was the heart of the home, and who wanted a disinfected heart?

Kate grabbed the smallest pan and pushed the blender to the back of the kitchen counter. She'd clean up later. There were two eggs left in the box, and right now she was going to make perfect runny-yolk eggs and hot toast dripping with butter.

Chapter Seven

DELLA

Bacon butties

Della stared at what had once been a neat bed of spring flowers and didn't know whether to laugh or cry. Instead, she shook her head and frowned. She loved her garden; she loved the act of gardening. She liked the warmth of the sun on her back as she snipped and trimmed, the damp soil on her fingers as she planted, the peace and quiet. Nobody asking questions or giving pitying looks. It was her therapy, giving her some control of her surroundings, of her life. If she planted carnations, that was what they were, carnations – they didn't grow and turn into something else.

After the Justin affair she'd very nearly thought about selling up, running away from the memories and the shame – but then she realised that she couldn't let herself give up so easily. Why should she? She'd lived in this house, on this street, for years and she liked it here – she had the biggest garden, quiet neighbours and a cottage with character.

At this second, though, as she surveyed the mess, she did

feel like she could give up on this puppy. There was a muffled bark, and she glanced down to her right. He was at her feet, a little bundle of fluff, wagging his tail so hard his whole body was wriggling.

'What have you got now, you little tinker?' Her previous dog, Skip, had never been this naughty. She was sure, positive.

She stooped down and held out her hand, and he dropped something into it, then looked up at her, his mouth hanging open as though he was laughing.

It was a potato. It was hard to be upset or angry when your pup brought you a potato.

She shook her head, smiling reluctantly. 'Oh, you little horror, that's your idea of an apology, is it?' She pointed at what had been a beautiful flowerbed. 'You do know you've just desecrated Skip's grave?' The puppy wagged his tail harder and barked. 'You're shameless!'

'Very cute though.' The softly spoken words held a smile in them, and Della turned round. The young woman standing on the other side of her gate was paler and slimmer than the last time she'd stopped for a chat (goodness, how long ago was that? Two years, three?). She knew, of course, that Kate had lost her lovely husband a few years ago. Since then, Kate had always rushed past, barely acknowledging the world, as though she was afraid of what would happen if she did. But then Della supposed she'd done much the same herself – avoided talking to people. She'd kept her own head down. But today her neighbour looked stronger, more – what was the word? – optimistic than Della had seen her in a long while.

She opened her mouth, about to say, 'Long time no see', then realised that it was probably better to leave the obvious unsaid.

Kate was bending now, stroking the puppy. 'What's his name?'

'That is Clint, because he was very nearly the dog with no name. I just couldn't decide what to call him! You know, Clint Eastwood, Man with No Name? Oh, what am I saying? You've probably never heard of him, long before your time.'

Kate chuckled. 'Everybody has heard of Clint Eastwood. My gran loved him!'

'But he's more often called devil dog, or little git for short! Goodness, he wears me out.' She shook her head. 'Look at the mess!'

'Ahh, but he brought you a potato!'

'Exactly. He knows exactly what to do to stop me being cross with him!' She paused. 'He loves to raid the vegetable rack, little horror.'

'What does Skip think of him?'

Della shook her head sadly and pointed to the newly dug earth. 'I lost him a few months ago.'

'Oh no, I'm so sorry, I didn't—'

Della waved the words away. 'I wouldn't for one moment have expected you to know, you've got more than enough on your plate with work and your own place to look after. I swore I wouldn't get another dog, because they do break your heart, but then the house seemed kind of empty, and a friend of mine told me about this little horror. Although,' she smiled wryly, 'her description was *adorable bundle of fluff who'd be no trouble at all*. Not evil devil dog grave digger! Poor Skip was resting in peace until this one decided to dig up all the plants that I'd put in.' Clint barked with delight and started to chase his tail. 'Skip used to lie there sunning himself. It was his favourite spot.'

'I remember, he was gorgeous. Eddie pointed him out to me once when we were walking past!' Kate smiled, then half frowned as though trying to remember something. 'He'd always stop and say hello to him; he was quite fond of Skip. Didn't he make him some kind of smelly treat?'

'Liver!' Della laughed. 'Very smelly, I bet your house stank. I did tell him it was very kind, but he shouldn't feel he had to. He offered after I'd said I wished there was an alternative to all these expensive dog treats that have all kinds of rubbish in them.'

'I remember. He'd got some cheap liver from the butcher and couldn't wait to experiment, but the smell of them baking was…' She screwed her face up.

'That bad?'

Kate nodded, still grinning. 'Afraid so.'

'Well, it was very kind of him, they were appreciated. Skip loved them, you know. He adored Eddie! He knew when he was on the way long before I did.'

'Probably the smell of liver cake.'

Della smiled back at Kate. She didn't really know her, she'd never actually been friends with Kate – there was quite an age gap between them, for a start – but she had instantly warmed to her when the couple had first moved in. There was something about her. A gentleness, a warmth.

Eddie had been a different story though; she'd got to know him quite well. He'd often wandered past at the weekends saying he was 'keeping out of Kate's way while she was marking books and preparing lesson plans', or in the late afternoon, after he'd finished work, he'd often pass on his way to the local greengrocers. He'd stop if she was out in the garden and make a fuss of Skip, and it had soon become a bit of a routine. One thing had led to another, like it did when people had time for each other – Eddie had given her cooking tips, in return for fresh veg and cut flowers. They'd had a love of gardening and growing food in common, the type of things that had no age barrier, and she'd enjoyed chatting to a man who was young enough to be her son, instead of just Justin and his fuddy-duddy friends.

But she'd never really seen much of his wife. Kate had always been friendly if they did see each other, though more often than not she'd been in a rush. Teaching was a full-time occupation, and, after all, what did a young girl like Kate have in common with a menopausal woman like her?

The couple were wrapped up in their own lives, and each other. And Della tended to see Eddie more during the week, as at weekends Justin liked them to go away. Oh, he loved nothing more than a 'city break'. Her whole life, now she came to think of it, had been a bit of a compromise. She would have been more than happy to spend their spare time at home, in the garden, with the dog. Art galleries, posh cafés and highbrow shops were nice now and again, but she'd found the lifestyle tiring, and, frankly, a little bit tedious. She'd felt like she always had to be on her best behaviour, dressed up and presentable – rather than dressed down with a dog on her knee and soil under her fingernails. 'Chill' was not a word in Justin's vocabulary.

She'd not often crossed paths with Kate, but she had watched from a distance. She'd been a tiny bit envious of her – young, carefree, too busy to worry about the tiny niggles in life. And she had always thought how nice it must be to have some-body who complemented you like that, two halves of a whole. Kate and Eddie had made such a wonderful couple. Unlike her and Justin, who'd been two pieces of the jigsaw that didn't quite fit but had been jammed together.

She could understand Kate's devastation – now more than ever – when she'd lost her husband, and she'd known that empty platitudes didn't help at all. She'd dropped a note through the door, offering help, then kept her distance.

And then, of course, Justin had gone, and she'd retreated from the world even more.

But there was something different about Kate today, perhaps a readiness to tackle the world again, and Della felt an almost maternal urge to encourage her. She also felt a motherly instinct to feed her up. But that was none of her business really, was it? Asking her in would be silly.

'I suppose I should get those plants back in before they dry out. It was lovely to say hello though.'

'It was,' Kate said softly, running her fingertips through Clint's fur, so that he stretched up for more, and made her laugh. 'I could play with him for a bit if you want, keep him out of your way – if it would help, that is?'

Oh, she wished she was younger, and had that easy way of offering help, of making friends. Of being able to talk to people. But she was out of practice. 'Oh, that would be wonderful! He'll be straight back in helping me dig otherwise. If you're sure you've got time. You're not too busy?'

'Not busy at all,' Kate said firmly. 'To be honest, I've left my job and it's so nice to be out of the house and not worrying about lesson plans on a Saturday morning.'

'Wonderful! Not about your job, about being able to get out, that is.' She grabbed Clint with one hand and opened the gate with the other before she talked Kate out of helping. Clint immediately dashed off, delighted to have a new friend, and came back with a tatty old tug toy that he loved to bury and then dig up again.

'Come on then, Dirty Harry, let's see what you're made of!' said Kate, grabbing the other end and laughing as he play-growled in response.

With a smile Della picked up her trowel and started to dig, hoping that at least some of the plants would survive their ordeal. Ten minutes later, the bed looked almost as nice as it had before Clint's digging frenzy and she straightened up, rubbing the small of her back.

Kate was sitting on the lawn, tossing an old tennis ball from hand to hand and laughing as Clint ran around her in circles, barking excitedly. She watched for a moment, smiling, until Kate glanced up.

'All done? That looks lovely!'

'All done! It's not too bad, is it? Whether they'll all survive is another matter.' She rubbed the soil off her hands and paused, then acted on impulse, asking before she had time to overthink things. 'You wouldn't fancy a cuppa with me, would you? If you've got time, that is?' The words came out in a rush. 'And you drink coffee? I've only got plain old cow's milk, I'm not very vegan-friendly, if…'

Her voice drifted off as she saw the hesitation in Kate, the inner battle. She was wondering why she had asked – what on earth were they going to talk about? What did they have in common?

'Say no if you're busy! I know how much you've got on your plate, I'm sure you've got places to be.' Clint pawed at her foot, and she hesitated. She should do this; it could do them both good even if they were very different. 'But it would really help me out – this one is such a terror I end up having to put him in his crate even when I'm doing things like boiling the kettle, or he's into everything! I feel a bit guilty, actually. I'm sure he doesn't mind, but it feels cruel to constantly…'

'Of course, I bet you need a break, he's got so much energy!' At Kate's words, Della felt her breath come out in a rush of relief. 'And like I say, I've got a pretty much free day!' She gave Clint another stroke. 'I bet it's a bit like having a toddler, constantly needing to be on your toes.'

'Worse in some ways, but at least with dogs you're allowed to lock them up in a playpen or crate and rush out of the house to calm down when you're on the verge of strangling the little darlings!'

'I sometimes would have loved to be able to do that with my students. Lock them up, that is, not strangle them!' Kate laughed again as she followed Della into the house. Della found herself smiling as she filled the kettle. 'And don't worry, I do drink coffee, but I'm not vegan!'

'You don't fancy a bacon butty with your coffee then, do you? I'm famished. I was just about to make some breakfast when I spotted what Clint had been up to and got distracted.'

'Well…'

'You'd be keeping me company.' She hesitated, not wanting to overstep the mark. 'I must confess I hate eating on my own. It's weird, isn't it, the things that are hard?' As the words came out, she suddenly realised that she hadn't shared any personal details, like how she *felt*, with anybody since she'd admitted to her parents that Justin had gone. But there was a certainty growing inside her that it would be okay, that Kate wouldn't judge. And she also really did feel like she wanted to look after the young woman – if she didn't mind.

Kate nodded. 'It *is* weird. I've turned into a bit of a grazer. Eddie would be horrified – he loved sitting around a table and eating properly.'

'I bet that was nice,' Della said softly. Justin had liked a *proper* meal, on a properly laid table, but she was sure that for Eddie and Kate it was more about sharing, relaxing. Enjoying the food and company, rather than worrying that the cutlery hadn't been polished. But she couldn't share that, could she?

'It was nice, he looked after me. But even sharing a coffee and cake with him was different to doing it on my own. I can't seem to sit still.'

Whatever their differences, they had things in common, thought Della. She paused for a moment, but Kate understood. And she wasn't exactly baring her soul, was she? 'I suppose that's why I got Clint. I couldn't bear the empty house, I felt like I was just existing in a vacuum rather than having a purpose in life.' The words died on Della's tongue as she clattered around, feeling slightly embarrassed but determined, getting bacon and bread out before Kate could say no. She was talking to fill the silence. Why was she telling a complete stranger things like this? The poor girl would wish she'd never said yes. 'Dogs are such good company; I've always had one.'

Sometimes, she knew, you just had to give people a bit of a push in the right direction. If it hadn't been for her friend Jane, she would never have got another dog, because losing Skip had broken her heart. But without a dog, she wouldn't go out walking and talk to anybody, and it was so easy to become practically a recluse these days when everybody was so busy. It had been easier when she'd been part of a couple. Couples got invited out. You always had company, and you felt as though you had a kind of shield; it wasn't as awkward if you stopped to speak to somebody you hardly knew. It didn't feel as though they might think you were desperate for company.

Looking back, she'd gone from being at home with her parents to marrying Justin. She'd always had somebody to hide behind. But now she was alone. She'd lost her husband, her shield, nearly a year ago. Skip had been the gentle soul to help her through her anger, shock and shame, but Clint (as her friend had said) was about new starts and an appetite for life.

He certainly was a happy soul, and made friends a lot more easily than she did, so she had to at least try, didn't she?

She'd always been reserved, happy with her own company and being part of a couple with Justin – but becoming a hermit, shutting herself away from everybody, wasn't really her. She'd realised recently, as more and more often she saw the same faces on her daily dog walks, and share 'hellos', that the isolation wasn't good for her. She needed contact, she needed people. Heat stung her eyelids as she moved the slices of bacon around to try and keep her mind off feeling sorry for herself.

She buttered the bread carefully, right up to the edges. She sighed as she turned the bacon over, and bent to pat Clint's head as he pressed himself against her leg. Her age hadn't helped either. The hot sweats and brain fog of the menopause had drained her, but it had been nothing compared to being left by Justin. It had scared her, the thought that she was alone. Unwanted. That everybody would see her as a fool. She knew she'd never be a self-confident, life-and-soul-of-the-party type of person – she wasn't going to have a personality change now. And she'd been quite content having one person in her life. But in the past year one had become none. If she carried on alone much longer there would be no way back; she'd never have the courage to talk to anybody properly again.

'Skip was so good for hugs, he was warm, and loving, and I could chat to him in the evening about the rubbish on TV.'

'Sometimes the hardest bit is not having somebody to talk to about the silly things, isn't it? I wish I'd had a dog or something.' Kate's wistful tone brought Della's frantic buttering to a halt. 'Do you still miss him? Justin?' The question was so unexpected that for a moment Della froze.

'Yes.' She very slowly and deliberately made up the bacon sandwiches, giving herself time to think, then went to sit down opposite Kate. 'I do miss him. I felt a bit like an abandoned dog, but I suppose at least I know it wasn't the menopausal moods and my old age that sent him running off!'

'You're not old!'

She laughed then. 'I'm definitely well into middle age!' Reaching her fiftieth birthday hadn't felt like a milestone, even fifty-five hadn't left her feeling old, but when she celebrated her fifty-ninth birthday, alone, it suddenly hit her just how many years had sped – no, sauntered – by without her really noticing. She was nearly sixty. Sixty! She had a strange urge to tell this young girl all about the problems, but she was old enough to be her mother. What would she think?

'Well, you don't look it! And you're nothing like an abandoned dog, I'm sure…'

'It's okay, I know he didn't mean me to feel like that, but it's how I felt.' She half-smiled. 'He does love dogs though; he'd never abandon one! He said Skip would help me, and he was right, but now Skip has gone as well. You know what I miss most? I don't miss his fastidiousness, or his funny taste in bowties, or his snoring, but I do miss the hugs, the human contact.' There, she'd said it, admitted it to herself. She looked Kate in the eye and Kate matched her gaze, a sad smile on her face. 'Men are like dogs really, aren't they? The sods bog off and leave you before you're ready.'

'They do.'

'Oh goodness, what am I saying? I'm going on about my silly problems and you could never have been prepared for…' She'd reached out and touched Kate's elbow lightly before she'd had time to think about it. 'I'm sorry, I didn't mean… I'll be upsetting you.'

'It's okay. It's quite nice to actually talk about him –' she paused '– Eddie, instead of piles of sympathy or people just avoiding mentioning him.'

'He was a lovely man,' Della said softly. 'So nice, everybody liked him, but I'm sure you know that. I don't need to ask if you miss him,' she added tentatively, searching Kate's face for signs that she'd upset her.

'I miss him so much. I've not really got out or chatted to anybody since…'

Della could see the door being closed, but that was fine. She didn't want to pry. 'People understand. Well, actually, a lot of people don't really chat anyway these days. I mean, it's hard, isn't it? Though I do talk to people when I go out with Clint because he makes friends quite easily. People always like to talk about dogs!'

'And scones, some people like to talk about scones.' Kate grinned at her, moving the conversation on neatly in a way that Della had to admire. 'I had a visitor yesterday, somebody thinking my house was a tearoom!'

Della frowned. 'I think it was, but that was years ago. I think it had shut before I moved here, but I've seen photos. I'll have to see if I can dig any out – if you're interested.'

Kate nodded. 'It would be nice to see it. The place seemed so important to him, and I felt really bad that it wasn't the place he remembered. I think he was a bit muddled.'

'Who on earth was it that thought it was still a café? I mean, it doesn't exactly look like one these days, does it!' Della felt a sense of relief that they were on safer ground, talking about other people. It was silly to try and unburden herself on the lovely young Kate, who'd suffered far more than she had. The last thing she wanted to do was bring back upsetting memories.

'I think he said his name was Charles?'

Della smiled. 'Ah, oh yes, I know who you mean! He's married to Mary? That makes sense. I think they've lived round here for years. They're lovely. They used to wander up and down hand in hand, chatting over fences, but he's not as mobile as he was. Well, neither of them is – I think she's got arthritis – and you're right, he can't always remember things. It must be hard, they're so independent. I used to let her have some of the apples, and she'd bring me an apple pie.'

'He said she missed cooking.'

'I bet he does too! She was amazing – you know how they say pastry is melt-in-the-mouth? Well, hers was, and the apples were just right – she knew exactly how much sugar to put in so that you still had a hint of the tartness.' She couldn't help but smile at the memory. It was making her long for a slice, still warm from the oven. Della loved Nature's seasons, and autumn had always been linked with apples. Gathering windfalls, climbing onto a rickety stepladder to pick them from the tree, enjoying a warming slice of one of Mary's pies.

'He seemed lovely, and –' Kate paused, mischief in her eyes '– he's sending Mary down to teach me how to make scones tomorrow!'

'Really? Wow, that's a bit, well, forward, even for him.' She laughed.

'He probably felt sorry for me, seeing as I'd let the tearoom fall into such a state.'

'State?'

'I'd been cooking, well, trying to make pancakes, and the kitchen was covered in lumpy batter mix.' She held up her hand. 'Don't say anything. I had to ask him in because he looked like he was about to keel over. It was a bloody good job he didn't need CPR because the floor was disgusting, he'd have gone to hospital lightly battered.'

Kate grinned and Della started to laugh, and soon neither of them could stop. Della thought that she could rather like Kate; they seemed to share the same sense of humour. She was also very pretty when she laughed.

'So now I'm not quite sure whether he thinks it is still a tearoom and he'll be back again, or whether he just thinks I need help.'

'Or maybe he does?' said Della softly, as it hit her that she hadn't seen the lovely elderly couple for a long time. 'Need help? Maybe they're lonely, struggling. I haven't seen them out and about for ages, now I come to think about it. I've been so bloody wrapped up in feeling sorry for myself, I'd not really thought about it.'

'He did say Mary was struggling with her arthritis, and he *was* very wobbly.' Kate screwed up her mouth. 'Oh God, I feel so guilty now! I didn't exactly welcome him in, and the tearoom obviously means a lot to him – it was where he fell in love and where they courted.'

'Maybe I should make them a pie or something, take it down.' Della felt a pang of guilt. 'They're probably far too proud to ask for help.'

Kate frowned. 'I don't know them at all. You're the only neighbour I've ever really chatted to, I vaguely remember them waving me off on my wedding day, but…' Her voice drifted off. 'I was always too busy, isn't that terrible.'

'It's not terrible at all,' Della said firmly. 'Don't beat yourself up. Teaching is pretty intense, I'd imagine, and you'd just moved here and got married and…' She stopped abruptly. That was a sentence she really shouldn't have started.

Kate filled in the awkward gap. 'Well, now I've packed in teaching, I have got time. I feel like I should do something.'

'Well, you are doing something, you're cooking with Mary. Let me know how the scone-making goes! Bring me a sample!'

'Maybe…' Kate drew the word out slowly, her gaze unfocused for a moment as though she was thinking something over, then she seemed to come to a decision. 'I can do better than samples. Maybe I should re-open for the day and you can have afternoon tea with Charles and Mary? What do you think?'

'I think that sounds lovely,' Della answered softly. 'I'm sure they'd love it.'

'Well, I might regret it, but I'm willing to give it a go. Any idea what he meant by "Cornish style"?'

'Jam first.'

'Jam?'

'Jam first, then clotted cream on top. They do it the other way round in Devon.'

'That's it then? No pixie dances, or pulling swords out of stones?'

Della laughed. 'Nope, that's it!'

'And there was I thinking they must have some magic spell or be crimped like pasties! You learn something new every day.'

Della grinned, then pointed at Kate's plate. 'Eat up, it will go cold!' Then she took a bite of her bacon sandwich, the crispy bacon crunching very satisfyingly, the saltiness mingling with the sweetness, and the rich melted butter carrying the flavours and urging her to take another bite.

'Oh wow,' breathed Kate, closing her eyes, 'that is the best bacon butty I've ever eaten!'

Della nodded. She'd eaten a lot of bacon sandwiches in her time, alone, but having Kate here seemed to make this one taste different, better.

They both sat in comfortable silence for a moment, eating, and

Della thought how nice it was to have human company – especially at mealtimes. Sitting alone in a café just wasn't the same. True, you could people-watch, but you were an outsider. You weren't *with* anybody. 'I think re-opening is a fantastic idea. Maybe you need to re-open for more than one day, just for a selected few!' She winked.

Kate laughed. 'You wouldn't say that if you'd tasted any of my food! Hopefully, Mary will be able to help. Oh well, I guess I better get out of your way. That was great, not had a bacon sandwich for ages. It's one of those things, isn't it? Just the smell.'

'Oh yes.' Della smiled. 'Skip loved sharing a bacon sandwich with me.' For a moment, emotion blocked her throat, but she swallowed it down. 'When Justin first went, I practically lived on bacon butties.'

'Do they make you sad?'

Della paused, trying to work out exactly *what* she felt. 'Thinking about Skip makes me sad; he was such a gentle soul and such good company. He just knew how I felt, do you know what I mean? He'd come and rest his chin on my knee and stare up at me with his kind eyes. It was as though he was asking me to tell him all about it.'

Kate nodded, and her eyes said that she did know what Della meant. Totally.

'And,' she sighed, 'thinking about Justin going still churns me up inside … but I've always loved the smell of bacon.'

'Eddie did.' Kate nodded again, her gaze faraway. 'He used to say bacon reminded him of being on holiday, of camping. It makes me think about being cold, going on one of my grandad's hearty walks and Gran warming us up with bacon butties and hot chocolate when we got back.'

'Oh my God, yes, hot chocolate *is* winter!' Clint gave a sharp bark, and Della suddenly realised that she'd been so busy talking, she'd completely forgotten that she always saved him a bit. 'Oh no, sorry, Clint.'

'Here.' Kate held out her last bite of sandwich, and before Della could object, Clint had jumped up and grabbed it, then dived off into the corner of the kitchen. They looked at each other and laughed as he put it down, carefully sniffed it, then swallowed it whole.

'I guess I better get going. Thanks though, that was just what I needed. It might sound totally over the top, but I can't remember enjoying anything that much since…'

Della squeezed her hand. Oh, if she'd had a daughter, she'd have loved her to be like Kate. 'Same here,' she said softly. 'Thank you. You do realise you will be Clint's friend for life now? He'll be hunting you out!'

'I don't have a problem with that. I'll let you know how the scone-making goes, and if they're edible we'll have a pop-up tearoom for the day!' Kate said as she stood up.

Clint wound his way round their legs, like a cat, as they walked to the front door.

Kate paused in the open doorway. 'You've got such a beautiful garden. Mine's a bit wild. This is amazing, it all kind of flows together and all the colours blend, it's like one of those perfect country gardens you see in the Sunday magazines!'

Della's cheeks warmed up. 'Thank you! It was something me and Justin did together, but when he left, I realised just how much I enjoyed it.' It had actually been quite liberating, being free of his judgemental opinions when it came to garish annuals, and his desire to snip everything into oblivion. Her poor garden had been topiary-ed to death.

'Right, I better go and leave you in peace, and buy some food. My cupboards are pretty much bare, and I need the stuff for baking scones as well, plus clotted cream. Do they sell that in the village?'

'Go to the farm shop. You know, the one past the petrol station.'

Della watched as Kate walked down the road and it suddenly didn't feel such a big deal that Clint dug holes in the garden, his chewing the chair legs, the stress of him disappearing after squirrels and barking at the neighbours. Somehow a bacon sandwich with Kate had left her feeling not quite so alone as she had for the past few months. Less useless. Less invisible.

Who knew that a bacon sandwich shared tasted one hundred times better than one she ate on her own?

Chapter Eight

KATE

Second impressions

Kate picked up one of the wicker baskets from the stack just inside the farm shop doorway and glanced around, trying to decide which direction to head in first, unable to stop herself from smiling.

She had only been in here once, just after moving into the house with Eddie. She knew that he'd been back, but Eddie had always done more of the food shopping than she had. He'd tell her not to worry, to finish off her marking while he 'popped out' for a crusty loaf, or some delicious pâté and cheese, so they could enjoy lunch in the garden while the sun was out.

But she didn't have Eddie now, and she didn't have marking to do. And this was like an Aladdin's cave!

If afternoon teas were going to feature in her future, then she had a distinct feeling she'd be back here again.

Making a decision, Kate headed towards the first chiller cabinet. She needed to find what she came for, clotted cream, before she got distracted by all the other goodies – including the amazing smell of freshly baked bread.

Then she stopped dead in her tracks as she spotted the deli meats that Eddie had loved so much. He would always buy more than the two of them could possibly eat, then spread them out on a massive platter with slices of tomato, salted and drizzled with balsamic vinegar. Just the thought made her mouth water. She needed to get some of those fresh tomatoes, still smelling of the vine, of summer, she thought as she reached out and picked up a pack of the meats – and then a small pot of herby olives. Those olives had been incredible, juicy but with a slightly nutty edge as she bit into them, leaving behind a tang that called out for a sip of crisp white wine. Nothing like the tart ones she'd first tasted in a bar as a teenager and hated. And, oh my God, those sweet cherry peppers stuffed with cream cheese. Sharp, creamy, sweet and spicy in one mouthful. She had to have some of those!

She didn't need to cook, she just needed to put some of these on a plate, with a rocket salad and some of that amazing olive bread that Eddie had brought home. Or the walnut bread, that had been out of this world! She looked at the things already in her basket – the perfect balance of texture and taste, without her even trying. Kate suddenly felt like she needed to celebrate, to mark this moment. It would have been a thousand times better if Eddie had been here to share it with, but the growing feeling inside her, that she actually did want to live, that she did want to be the person he'd have wanted her to be, this new positivity was making her feel – well, actually it was making her feel *alive*. Leaving her job had not been a solution to the wasteland that had been her life, but it had been a – she frowned as she searched for the right word – a facilitator.

Not having the shield of work to hide behind, removing the

comfort blanket of a career that she could easily bury herself in – work 24/7 – was forcing her to face up to real life. Her job had served a purpose, she had always loved it, and over the last few years she had needed it, but she had to move on. Find out who she was going to be for the rest of her life.

Because there had to be a 'rest'.

If she'd still been going into school, she wouldn't have felt she had time to chat to Della, she wouldn't have ventured into the kitchen to attempt pancakes, or even to make her egg and soldiers. She would never have agreed to make scones. Oh heck, the scones! She had to stop eyeing up the tantalising selection of local cheeses and find some clotted cream.

As she scanned the shelves in the chiller cabinet, she spotted a familiar blue and white carton almost immediately, and, grinning, she strode up towards her target, reaching out before she got there.

And cannoned into somebody who was reaching for something else.

'Oh, sorry.' She glanced up, the smile on her face dying as she saw who it was. The tall figure was instantly recognisable. The man from the bottom of the street. The guy she'd nearly run over. He'd burst her bubble then; he was the last person she wanted to see right now.

'This is getting to be a bad habit,' he drawled. 'Bumping into each other like this!'

There was the slightest lift of the corner of his generous mouth.

'Shit, sorry, that was my fault.' It was, she had to admit that. She didn't add 'this time', but the slight glint in her eye let him know it was on the tip of her tongue.

'After you.' He took a step back and waved her through, just as she did the same.

And then he did smile. Properly. Kate had to admit that without a scowl on his face he was quite approachable. Good-looking, in fact. Well, very good-looking.

She'd clocked the blue-grey eyes, the well-toned arms and broad shoulders last time she'd seen him. But what had really hit her then was his attitude, the way he'd got her back up when she'd already been feeling vulnerable, when she'd been desperate to hang on to the good feeling she'd had. So she'd not really noticed just how attractive he actually was – not suited-and-booted smart but casual boy-next-door good-looking. The type who did it without even trying.

And maybe the way she'd prickled at his attitude had been more about her than him. Maybe it had been a bad moment for both of them. And she did like to give people the benefit of the doubt.

'You first. I insist, I'd feel safer.'

Or maybe she'd read his attitude right, and he was cocky.

'Sorry, that was uncalled for,' he added, his tone softer.

She didn't quite know how to read this man. There was humour in his eyes, but a kind of edge, as though he didn't really want to engage – but didn't want to offend her either. But he was a neighbour, and wasn't her new life all about doing new things, having time to at least chat to the people who lived around her?

'Thanks. Sorry, I spotted that clotted cream and felt I had to go for it!'

'Good choice.' The corner of his mouth lifted again, just a little. Maybe he wasn't the type of guy who belly-laughed like Eddie used to. 'Looks like you're feeding the hordes!'

She looked down at her rapidly filling basket, and blushed. How on earth, why on earth, had she picked up so many of the goodies?

'Bit personal.' Jack had read her discomfort and held a hand up, taking another step back. 'Sorry again, none of my business.'

'No, no, no problem. It's just for me though, I got a bit carried away. I'm not used to shopping.' The words faded.

'I'm not used to just getting stuff for myself either, I'm used to cooking in bigger quantities.' He glanced down at his own, very empty, basket. She didn't like to say that it wasn't that she wasn't used to shopping for one – she just wasn't used to food shopping at all, except for ready meals, food on the go, day-to-day survival. But he was being nice. 'I think I'd better shut up now, leave you to it! I'm being presumptuous. You, er, shop!'

She met his gaze. His own cheekbones carried the slightest hint of pink now.

Maybe they did have things in common. Maybe, like her, the last thing he'd needed the other day was aggravation. Maybe he too was making a new start. On his own.

Her first impression could have been totally inaccurate: he was stressed with moving, she was stressed with leaving work. You never knew what burdens people carried, did you?

'Thanks.' She smiled. 'The deli stuff here is really nice, if you're into that kind of thing, and the local cheese tastes amazing!' she added on impulse.

'Great. Enjoy!' Then he turned away before she had a chance to say anything else.

What was it with this man? He was making her bristle again, just as she was trying to give him the benefit of the doubt!

Was she being over-sensitive, or had he sounded a tiny bit flat, uninterested, dismissive? And if he was, why was he even in a place like this? The food here was wonderful, but not exactly cheap. It was a place to come for special treats, to find ingredients that were out of the ordinary, or ideal if you were a foodie like Eddie had been and really appreciated the freshness, the tastes and smells that only came from locally grown fruit and vegetables, and chicken and meat that had been reared with care.

With a small sigh, Kate drew her gaze away from the retreating man. He obviously had worries of his own, and maybe he just didn't like to cook. But at least they'd spoken again, and now it wouldn't be quite so awkward next time she passed him in the street. Which she was bound to do at some point.

She glanced at the bakery counter. She'd get some nice freshly baked bread, and maybe a croissant for breakfast tomorrow. And she could treat herself to a bottle of pinot grigio or, better still, push the boat out and open that Chablis she'd spotted in the wine rack.

It was just as she dropped the still-warm baguette into her basket that the shrill shout of alarm rang out. She spun round, just as her near-neighbour dived past her and behind the large baskets of bread, to where a toddler was wobbling purposefully towards a pile of what looked like fresh-out-of-the-oven hot trays. He'd scooped the little boy up and swung him in the air before the child had a chance to realise the danger he'd been in, so that what could have been screams and tears turned to chuckles.

'Thank God.' The breath she didn't know she'd been holding rushed out in relief, and his gaze locked with hers. For a moment it was as though she was seeing the real man. Not the dismissive man, not the embarrassed one or the one who got her back up. There was an honesty, something so real about the relief and concern on his face. About the warmth in the blue-grey eyes that had seemed assessing before.

And then the woman dashed between them, reached for her child, and the three of them moved away together.

Kate added a cinnamon bun to her basket with a slightly shaky hand. It was so lucky he'd been there, so lucky that he'd had fast reflexes. The child could have had nasty burns, and the shop facing health and safety enquiries, if it hadn't been for him – by the time she'd got her senses together it would have been far too late.

She turned round, watching as he accepted the woman's thanks and offered to carry her shopping out for her while she clutched the child to her body as though she'd never let go.

And for a moment, Kate forgot about whether he had worries of his own or not, whether they'd talk next time they saw each other; she just stared at the woman. The way she had her arms wrapped around her son, the way he clung to her.

Is that what motherhood, life, could have been like for her, if she'd not pushed Eddie away? If she'd not said no?

Chapter Nine

KATE

Love is ... liver treats

K ate felt slightly sick as she stared down at the dark blood-red slab of liver. She could not touch it, definitely not. She'd have to handle it with a knife and fork. She must be going crazy. This was not how she'd ever pictured herself spending a Sunday morning.

Sunday mornings were for lie-ins, for fresh coffee and croissants, for long walks or catching up on paperwork.

But she hadn't been able to get Della's comment about Eddie's kindness out of her head as she'd done her shopping, and on impulse she'd picked up a bargain piece of offal that she would have normally steered clear of.

But Eddie wouldn't have avoided it. Eddie had, in typical chef fashion, been keen not to waste and she could imagine his delight at being able to cook offal treats for Skip.

After unpacking her shopping, she had still been on the verge of binning the liver, until she had sat down at the kitchen table with a cup of coffee, and something (she had no idea what) had made her open the small drawer underneath. And there it was.

Eddie's notebook.

At first glance, it was nothing out of the ordinary. An A5 lined pad, with a plain cover. But to her it was like Eddie, extraordinary on the inside. It didn't hold just his recipes, just words, it held his hopes and dreams, his inspiration, his enthusiasm. Eddie had been quiet and unruffled on the outside, not standing out, not wasting his energy fighting life. But inside, his passion, his positive energy, bubbled. He was the underground spring that never stopped trying to fulfil its destiny.

Eddie had not been an over-the-top optimist, he'd been a realist who believed the right things would happen.

As she'd stroked a finger over the cover of the notepad, Kate felt glad that she hadn't found it earlier. Now was exactly the right time. The time she needed it, the time she'd already made her own decision to cook, to bake, to try and help the people around her.

It was almost like Eddie had put it here for her to find at just the right moment. As though he'd know that she'd be stronger, less angry, less sad now. It didn't make her want to cry. It did make her sad, sad that here in these pages was so clearly his dream – a dream that he didn't have time to make happen (and she knew he would) – but it also made her smile with recognition.

She'd flipped over the pages slowly. Eddie's book was *him*, not just recipes. It was a monologue, a – what was the word – homage to the ingredients he worshipped.

It hadn't been difficult to find the recipe for Skip's liver treats.

So what choice did she have but to make them?

. . .

She fetched the blender, plugging it in next to the chopping board, her mind on what Della had said.

Everybody, it seemed, had known Eddie. Charles had mentioned that he'd made them jam sponge. Della had shared gardening tips with him.

How many more of their neighbours had he made friends with? She frowned as she thought about all the cards of commiseration she'd received. She'd hardly looked at them, she'd been too raw. She'd been too sure that if she refused to acknowledge that he'd gone, then it wouldn't be true.

The cards had gone with the bag at the bottom of the wardrobe. Eddie's bag. The bag of his belongings that the police had brought round. She'd not wanted to look at them any more than she'd wanted to tip out the contents of the bag and admit that he'd gone.

But they'd sent those cards because they cared. They knew him. While she'd been marking books and nurturing the minds of children, he'd been nurturing the people who lived on the same street.

He hadn't kept it a secret, of course. He'd told her. But it hadn't seemed significant when he'd mentioned that the apples in the crumble had come from Della's tree, or the pungent smells were dog treats in the making. She'd never really thought about the friendships he was forming, or the things they talked about. It was just Eddie. Eddie liked to cook for people. Eddie liked to look after them. And Eddie loved animals of all kinds.

Maybe if he hadn't died, they could have had a dog, instead of a baby.

She pulled a face and leant back slightly as she picked up a sharp knife, and a fork, to tackle the liver with. The smell rose up as she cut into it. Eurgh, it really was yucky.

It had been bad enough when she'd taken it out of her

shopping bag, and even though it was already wrapped, she'd shoved it in another plastic bag before putting it in the fridge, because she was sure she could smell it.

She glanced down at Eddie's notepad, and couldn't help but smile, even though what she needed to do was gag.

Skip's Liver Cake

(Liver, the once-a-week superfood, this dog is going to live forever!)

- *Oven at 160°C, mask at the ready, windows open, extractor fan on — you're in for a rough ride!*
- *Slice up 500g liver and chuck it in a bowl with a couple of eggs and if he's a dog that loves a bit of flavour add half a clove of garlic. Whizz it up with a hand blender, or stick it in the blender with the lid very firmly on (and your spare hand over your nose!) until you've got a disgusting slimy smooth mess! (It's worth it for man's best friend.) Fold in 200g plain flour with a fork until it's a gooey, sponge-mix consistency, yum!*
- *Add a splash of milk if too stiff.*
- *Pour the gloop into a lined or greased baking tin.*
- *Slam it in the oven for 35–45 mins. Just enough time to clear the airways with a brisk walk in the fresh air, and a fortifying glass of beer. Leave to cool (more beer!) and then slice up into bite-sized treats. Deliver to the gracious pooch who will love you unconditionally for the rest of his life.*

Taking a deep breath, and keeping it at arms' length, she chopped the liver into (very) rough pieces before dropping it into the blender and very carefully putting the lid on.

She'd thought that doing this would bring a part of Eddie back, and it did. She felt like he was there every step of the way. Joking, teasing, laughing at the look of disgust on her face and her wrinkled nose.

The smell, if anything, was worse when the tray was in the hot oven. Even though she'd shut the door through to the hallway, and opened the window and back door, it permeated the whole house. Eddie had been right: she really did need a drink and some fresh air. But when she opened the oven door and took the tray of golden-brown sponge out, she had to admit it looked good. Practically edible. Even if you had to be a dog to appreciate the taste or smell.

In fact, it looked the best thing she'd cooked so far, she thought, grinning. She put the tray by the open window to cool, then carefully cut it into small cubes.

It looked pretty professional when she piled it into a brightly coloured bowl – so professional she took a photo of it.

She took her mug of coffee into the lounge, to get away from the smell, and stared at the photo on her phone.

Why had she done this? For Eddie, or because she'd wanted to. To say thank you to Della for the bacon sandwich, for asking her in, for asking questions without any pressure, for saying the things that were hard to actually voice.

What she'd said to Della was true – people either offered the kind of sympathy she still found hard to cope with, or they avoided mentioning Eddie altogether.

She didn't want either.

And Della seemed to understand. Was it odd though to go round today, after only seeing her yesterday? She didn't want her to feel pestered, because she struck her as the type of person who was quite happy with her own company – even if from time to time it was nice to chat to somebody else.

The knock on the door made her jump, and when she

opened it she was surprised to see Della's smiling face. Well, that solved that problem!

'I'm not bothering you, am I?'

'Of course not, that's what I call perfect timing. I've got something for you.' She felt her cheeks start to glow. 'Well not for you, for Clint, to say thank you for the bacon butty yesterday.'

'I didn't expect…' Della paused, sniffed the air, then started to chuckle. 'You've been baking!'

'I certainly have. I need the practice, and I thought a puppy might be less discerning than Charles and Mary!'

'Oh, you lovely girl, Clint is going to love you.' She shook her head. 'But liver? That's worth way more than a couple of rashers of bacon.'

Kate smiled, leading the way through to the kitchen. 'It was nice to have a chat, I enjoyed it.'

Della nodded and smiled back. 'It was.'

Why hadn't she had a mother like Della – a gentle, generous, nice person who didn't mind a dog digging up the lawn and took people as they were.

'Wow, those are impressive!' Della spotted the treats and her eyes opened wide. 'Very professional looking!'

'They are, aren't they? Even if I say so myself!' Kate grinned back at her. 'I'm not sure I'll be doing them regularly though.' She pulled the door to the garden shut, and partially closed the window.

'I don't blame you. You do know Skip loved the tuna treats as well?'

'Tuna?'

'Oh yes, it wasn't always liver!' Della nodded, looking almost mischievous. 'And sardine and cheese, oh, and he did some with sweet potato.'

Kate stared at her. 'You have to be kidding me? You mean I could have done my good turn without making my chopping board look like there'd been a fatal accident?'

Della shook her head.

'You mean I could have used a tin of fish instead of that…' Kate could almost picture the look of dismay she was sure had settled on her face – but she could see that Della was fighting a battle not to laugh. Which she was losing.

'Your face!'

'My blender! Oh God, that was so disgusting to clean out!'

'Sorry, oh, I am sorry, but…' Della really was losing the battle and her shoulders started to tremble with suppressed laughter. Kate shook her head, which made Della's eyes water.

'At one stage I thought I'd have to resort to a mask and oxygen!'

The laughter burst out of Della, and Kate couldn't help herself. She joined in.

'It's no wonder Eddie suggested an alcohol break!'

'It's his recipe?'

'Yes, I found his notebook. I almost wish I hadn't!'

'Oh, Kate.' Della wiped the tears from her eyes, which made Kate laugh even more. It took several minutes before they could both control themselves. 'Oh, love.' She shook her head, then reached out and hugged her. 'I appreciate it though, I really do, it was a lovely thought, Kate. And Clint will think he's in heaven!'

Kate felt a rush of warmth, and suddenly understood that feeling of being wanted, of being admired by a virtual stranger. Eddie had known this, he'd loved this feeling – and now she was starting to understand things about him that she hadn't realised she didn't know. Even liver cake had the power to make somebody happy, life wasn't all about sweet treats or fancy meals.

'I'll put them in a box for you. You don't fancy a quick cup of coffee?' She wanted to hang on to this feeling a tiny bit longer. She wanted Della to be here.

'That would be lovely. Oh, I nearly forgot why I popped round – I've found some photos for you, of the tearoom. They were in the loft when we bought the cottage, and although I tried to find out who they belonged to, I didn't have any luck. They're a bit fuzzy, pre digital cameras and fancy phones I suppose, but it looked such a pretty little place.'

She took an envelope out of her pocket and passed it to Kate, who spread the contents across the table.

There were half a dozen photographs, some sepia, some with faded colours, but all – without a doubt – of her house.

'Oh wow. Look at that cakestand! And that bit there is where there's a door now.' A lump blocked Kate's throat. 'And that lovely cast-iron spiral staircase in the corner! The new wooden version might be safer but it's nowhere near as nice. Eddie would have loved these photos,' she said softly, touching one with her fingertip. 'Quite often, still, I'm about to shout to him, to show him something, then I remember he's not there. Is that ridiculous?'

'Of course, it's not ridiculous.' Della reached across the table and rested her hand over Kate's for a moment. 'You had something special, and you're bound to miss him.'

Kate blinked away the threatening tears. Della would never understand that it was more than just Eddie she missed. Not being able to share, tell him stuff, had an added hurt – because there were things she wanted to have, should have, said to him the day he died. Things she'd always regret not saying, so much that it brought a pain to her chest. Things that might have made the difference between him staying and going out… She'd missed her chance.

'I don't want this to sound spooky, but I used to watch you walk up the street and I was slightly jealous. Pleased for you, but jealous.'

Kate blinked and looked back up at Della's softly spoken words. She frowned. 'But…'

'Oh, I know I had Justin, but it was never like the relationship you had. I guess,' she smiled, 'the nearest I got to that was with my dog. His kisses were a bit sloppy, but his listening ability was out of this world!'

Kate couldn't help herself, the corners of her mouth lifted. It seemed to encourage Della, who obviously wanted to cheer her up.

'When Justin went, Skip became even more important to me. Justin was more of a companion than a big love affair, but with him gone I didn't have anybody else to talk to, I'd shut myself away and it was such a mess, and I knew Skip wouldn't judge me.'

'Oh, Della, I'm sure nobody would judge.'

'Oh, they do,' she sighed and Kate, sensing she might be hesitating about saying more, raised a questioning eyebrow. It was far, far easier listening to Della than trying to explain her own feelings. 'My parents were appalled. I mean, what kind of woman is left by her husband for another *man*?'

'It wasn't your fault! But —' she hesitated herself '— people do say hurtful things, they don't mean to, it just sometimes comes out wrong.' Didn't she know that herself? All the well-meaning people who with a few careless words could make things seem even worse.

'I know they weren't really having a go at me, they didn't know how to deal with it, but… Well, I'm old enough to be your mother, and it was a different generation. It was easier for me not to try and explain. Skip was the only contact I could bear with another breathing being. I know he was only a dog...'

Kate squeaked an objection, 'I'm sure dogs are far more sensitive to the way we feel than most people are.'

'You're right. They are. You asked me yesterday if I missed Justin. Well, he left me for his best friend, and it wasn't the shock of it being Mick, it was the shock of being left that turned my world upside down, and I couldn't even start to explain that to another person. But Skip just waited, he was just there. I mean, after over thirty years of marriage, you just don't expect a bombshell like that, do you? I felt so bloody stupid, as well as, well, like some abandoned dog that he'd got bored with. Although, to be honest —' she paused '— if he'd left me for another, younger, woman I suppose that would have felt like I'd been thrown out because —' a small smile tugged at the corner of her mouth '— my breeding days were over.'

'Over thirty years?' Kate stared at Della. She was motherly in some ways, and obviously older than Kate herself, but she didn't seem *that* old. 'You must have been a child bride! I had no idea, it's no wonder it came as a shock. I'm sorry.' She'd thought she'd spend the rest of her life with Eddie, but she'd never even started to think about what that really meant, about what losing him after thirty years would feel like. Thirty years was a lifetime!

'It caused a bit of a rift with my parents. We'd never had children because our once-a-week sex sessions weren't enough to make it happen! You'd have thought I'd have guessed there was something wrong when he rationed our rumpy-pumpy, wouldn't you?' Della gave a gentle laugh. 'It's all so ridiculous, isn't it?'

Kate smiled back. 'No, I don't think you should have guessed. Not everybody is sex-mad!'

'At least it means I don't miss it! I just thought it was normal. I was a silly naïve twenty-year-old with no experience of men when we met. Oh well, you live and learn. I'm learning to manage.'

Kate found herself nodding. She'd not thought about it that way. 'So am I, I'm getting used to the idea, I guess. It just takes time, but he's been gone over three years and I know it's time to stop hiding and move on.' She tried to suppress a sigh. 'I decided it was time to pack in work so that I could do that properly and work out where I'm heading. I was worried that I'd be at a loss, but I'm now beginning to think that even baking with Mary is too much – there's so much I've let slip, so much to do, like decorating the front room, and the garden. I mean, have you seen the state of that? I haven't had the time or the motivation.' She'd spent too much time feeling sad, wondering how they'd have done things together.

'Well, I could help with that, if you want?' Della's words came out in a rush, as though it was on impulse.

'Oh, I wouldn't like… I'm sure you're very busy.'

'I don't want to interfere, so just say no and I won't be offended. But I do like gardening.'

'Really? Say no? You must be kidding.' Wow, if Della could help her with the garden, it really would help her feel more positive, she was sure of that. She knew that she needed tidiness, she needed order, and part of her struggle was that it had all got a bit too much.

'I do mean it, if you'd ever like a bit of a hand. I know what it feels like suddenly having to cope with everything.'

'That would be amazing!' Kate hesitated. 'It is a total mess though; it would take you ages.'

'Let me look, then I can tell you what I can do?' She got up and walked over to the window.

Kate held her breath as the silence lengthened.

'Oh, it doesn't look bad at all. We could have a go at those weeds –' she pointed to the overgrown herb garden '– together. You could soon have fresh thyme and rosemary again!'

Relief rushed through Kate, and on impulse she reached out and hugged Della. For a second she stiffened with surprise, then relaxed and laughed, squeezing Kate's hand.

'We'll soon have it sorted!'

'Tell you what, if you could help me in the garden, I could make Sunday lunch for us next week. Nothing posh, I'm a bit of a novice.' She couldn't accept help unless she felt she could pay Della back – food had always been Eddie's way and suddenly it felt like it could be hers as well.

'Oh, now don't be modest, I'm sure you picked up loads of tips from Eddie!'

Kate shook her head. 'My pancakes were a disaster.' She sighed. 'He was the chef, I drank the wine and chatted. But I do miss his food, I miss him.'

'I bet you do. Sunday lunch would be lovely, even cheese on toast would be fantastic.'

'Cheese it is then! Next Sunday at 1pm? Bring Clint if you like, he can have a good run in the garden and dig as many holes as he likes!'

Della laughed. 'You're going to regret saying that!'

'Believe me, anything he does is probably an improvement! Hey, let's swap numbers, then if I have a disaster on the cheese front, I can let you know!'

'Here you go.' Della held her phone out. 'You put yours in, you'll do it much quicker than I can, I'm all fingers and thumbs! And then I suppose I better get going and take the little horror out for a walk. Try and work off some of his energy.'

As they walked to the door, Kate was surprised at just how comfortable she felt with Della. She was so nice, unassuming and gentle – why on earth hadn't she stopped and talked to her earlier?

'Thanks so much for the dog treats, they were a lovely surprise.'

'No trouble. Well, okay, if I'm honest they did make me gag – I'll be doing tuna ones next time!' Della smiled. 'And thank you for the photographs!'

Della hesitated at the front door. 'Look, I don't want you to think I'm a nosy old bat, but you can manage now you're not working? Everything is so expensive and…'

'I'm fine.' Kate smiled, feeling better than she had for a long time. 'I'll be okay for a while, and I can always consider re-opening the café! That's a joke by the way!! Let me know what Clint thinks of the treats. And Della? Thanks for asking.'

She closed the door gently behind Della's back, smiling to herself. Teaching had, she supposed, given her satisfaction, made her feel at least useful – but this was different. This had lifted her inside. She felt lighter than she had for ages.

She went back into the kitchen and paused as the photographs caught her eye. She picked one up and carried it into the lounge, looking round, trying to work out what had changed.

You couldn't turn back the clock. She knew that. But maybe, maybe when she'd joked to Della about re-opening the café, maybe she could do something like that. Not knock down the walls, but maybe rearrange things a bit. Maybe give Charles a proper reminder of how the place used to be.

Well, whether she did or not, she was sure he'd love to see the photographs.

Which reminded her, she needed to check she'd got everything she needed for her scone-making session.

But first of all she was going to have another look in Eddie's notebook – how on earth had she missed his fishy dog treats?

Chapter Ten

MARY

Monday scones, Cornish style

Mary knocked tentatively on the door and took a step back. She had not been convinced that her husband hadn't imagined his conversation with 'lovely Kate at number 43'. But he'd been quite insistent that she'd be letting the lady down if she didn't come here today, and it had been easier to agree than refuse. He could be quite cantankerous these days. She worried about him. She knew he was frustrated that his memory wasn't what it used to be, that everyday words were often elusive, that some days it was hard to know if he was living in the past or the present, but she still wanted him to know that she loved him. That she respected him. That she looked up to the strong man she'd adored for so many years. So, she'd said, 'Of course,' and dug out her tattered old notebook of recipes.

It was a long time since she'd opened it, but it felt familiar, like an old friend. Just holding it had put a spring in her step that seemed to have been missing these last few months.

Now that she was standing on the doorstep, though, she was feeling a bit like a silly old woman. She knew, of course, that Eddie had died, but she also knew he had been a keen cook. Quite often he had been out in the front garden on a Thursday when she'd walked past on her way to withdraw her weekly housekeeping from the bank, and he'd ask if she'd be kind enough to give her opinion on his latest traybakes, or hand her a little pack of sauce because 'he'd cooked far too much and she'd be doing him a favour'. He was a wonderful young man and she had to admit to missing him, so she was sure his wife missed him a thousand times more.

She was also fairly sure that Kate would know how to cook, and was used to fancy TV recipes, not scones. How could she not?

But now, however silly she felt, she had come because she had to. For Charles.

Mary had always assumed that Charles would die before she did, and that she'd miss him terribly and not know what to do with herself, but now she dreaded the thought that he would be the one left behind. It had been just the two of them for years now, and he relied more and more on their habits, their routine. He was quite often befuddled (goodness knows what he'd said to young Kate), and she worried about him even when she popped down to the shops. With Saul, their son, far away in Canada, they had nobody to turn to if things went wrong. She sighed. If only things were like they'd been years ago, when this village had a real community feel, when people knew each other, helped each other. She would have known there was somebody to keep an eye on him.

There were many things about the past that weren't good, but as long as you had good people around you, what else did you need?

'Hi, you must be Mary!'

The door had swung open while she was still musing about the past, and Kate was smiling at her.

'I am!' Relief flooded through her, that at least she was expected. 'I'm not sure if he's got this right, but Charles told me you needed to learn how to make scones?' She really did feel silly, but Kate's warm welcoming smile gave her confidence.

'I certainly do. I hope Charles hasn't told you I'm totally hopeless in the kitchen?'

'Certainly not, and I'm sure you're not, my dear.' She decided it was better not to mention Kate's late husband. She looked frail, brittle at the edges, and definitely in need of some feeding up.

'I'd been making pancakes when he came round,' Kate said, as though that explained it. 'Well, trying to – most of the batter ended up on the kitchen floor.'

Ahh, well, that explained why Charles was covered in flour. 'Well, kitchens are for food and for living, and bathrooms are for keeping clean! A bit of a mess is a good sign.'

Kate grinned, and her whole face was transformed. Charles had been right; she really was a beautiful girl. Mary remembered watching her leave the house on her wedding day; she'd made a lovely bride. It was so sad that within such a short time she'd lost her husband and her joy in life. It was different, Mary thought, when you got to her age. When these things were to be expected, when you'd lived your life – good or bad. But when you were so young, so hopeful, had so much ahead of you. Together. So many dreams and plans. It was heart-breaking.

'Come in, come in. Is he okay? He was a bit shaky when he came, but he wouldn't let me give him a lift home.'

'He wouldn't.' Mary smiled. 'That's my Charles, stubborn as a mule, but his heart is in the right place.'

'It certainly is. He's lovely.'

Mary followed Kate into the large kitchen, gazing around her as she went, and placed her basket on the table. It really had changed enormously since the last time she had been in here, although goodness, how long ago had that been? She really should stop gawping though, it was somebody's home now, not a place to gather and natter.

'I've got to warn you, I'm a complete beginner when it comes to scones, but I think I've got all the ingredients.'

'I'm sure you have. There's not much to them really, easy as pie! My mother had me baking when I was eight years old. Half the recipes in here were hers.' She took her tattered recipe book out and placed it on the table, then pulled her pinafore over her head. 'Well now, how much baking have you done?'

'Probably best if you assume none.'

She raised an eyebrow. She wasn't one to judge, but she would have loved to have a husband who liked to cook – they would have been joined at the hip! Although actually, come to think of it, it had always been quite nice to have time to herself in the kitchen. Time to think and relax – she'd always been a firm believer in a couple working apart as well as together.

'I'm a complete novice, but good at following instructions!'

'Well, that's perfect. I can't lift with my wrists being like they are. We seem to put everything in the micro these days. So frustrating.' She washed her hands, and for the first time in ages felt a feeling of contentment drift over her.

Life had seemed a bit tricky recently, so much to worry about – but baking always used to be her go-to if life got her down. She missed it. When she was baking, nothing else mattered. She lost herself in whisking and stirring, she knew what she was doing, she was in control. When she baked, she stopped worrying about yesterday, and all the maybes that tomorrow might bring. She filled the kitchen with wonderful smells, and the look on Charles's face as he tucked into her cake was like a warm hug. Old age, and arthritis, had robbed her of the one thing that could have helped right now. But maybe being here with Kate would be a good second best.

With a smile she opened her worn notebook at the right page.

'Here we are. This was one of the recipes Mother started me on. My oven is newer than hers was, so I've altered the recipe from Fahrenheit to Celsius, and, of course, she used pounds, ounces and inches, so I thought I'd better update that, but everything else is the same. If it isn't broken don't mend it, as Charles says. Oh, and she often used granulated sugar, but these taste just the same as the ones I used to make with her, I'm sure they do.'

Mother's recipe for scones - one day these might be as good as hers

350g self-raising flour

1tsp baking powder

50g caster sugar

100g butter (unsalted)

175ml full-fat milk

1 beaten egg for glazing

- *Preheat the oven – it's 200°C with my new fan oven.*
- *Mix the flour and baking powder in a large bowl. Rub in the butter with your fingertips until it resembles fine breadcrumbs. Stir in the sugar. Make a well in the centre and add the milk. Stir with a knife to bind the ingredients into a thick dough.*

> *Dust a work surface, and your hands, with flour and then work lightly until smooth. Form into a round about 4cm deep. Use a smooth-edged cutter to cut out the scones. Brush the tops lightly with the egg, then place on a heated tray. Bake for 10-12 minutes until golden.*

- *Delicious served when still warm, with the best homemade strawberry jam topped off with Cornish clotted cream (or just lashings of butter if we're in a rush!)*

'Oh now, isn't that wonderful, you've got a lovely big bowl just like mine!' She touched the rim of the brown-glazed earthenware bowl, and the familiar, solid feel made her feel at home. 'I think Mason Cash bowls have been around longer than me!'

It was after they'd popped the scones into the oven, when they were drinking a welcome cup of tea, that Mary decided to tell Kate. The baking had given her a feeling of optimism – not for her own future, but about the time she had left.

'Thank you for letting me come round today, it's made me feel happier than I have for weeks. It's taken my mind off things, and I've felt useful.'

'That's brilliant.' Kate smiled. 'But it's me that should be thanking you. I've really enjoyed it, you're so good at explaining. It's quite nice, isn't it? Stirring and mixing and rolling.'

'It is.' Mary smiled. 'Soothing.'

'Will you come back again? We could try something else from your book?' Kate hesitated. 'One of the last things I did was promise Eddie that I'd cook with him, and I never had a chance, and to be honest, I've not really wanted to. But today it felt different.'

'I'd love to.' Mary dunked her biscuit into her cup of tea. It didn't instantly melt, like biscuits used to. Today they were made of sterner stuff. Maybe she could come round another time, and they could bake shortbread. 'I'm dying,' she added, matter-of-factly, before she had time to change her mind. She was sure from Kate's tone that she must be wondering what on earth an old lady needed to take her mind off.

Kate glanced up, her direct gaze meeting her own.

'Oh, Mary, I'm—'

'I'm not expecting sympathy,' she said firmly, 'but I wanted you to know. I've probably only got a few months left, but it would be lovely to end my days feeling needed, not some useless doddery old thing.'

'Nobody could ever call you doddery!'

'And I am sorry, because I'm sure you've had enough bad news and death in your life, but if you really have enjoyed baking then maybe we can be a help to each other? It takes my mind off things. If you're not too busy, that is. I know how much you youngsters have to do these days.'

Charles had sent her here, she'd come to keep him happy, but as they'd baked, a plan had started to form in her mind – a plan that involved bringing Charles here, coming back and baking again.

Kate stirred her tea slowly. Mary was pretty sure she'd already done that, and she found herself holding her breath, until Kate glanced up, her bright eyes shining with what Mary hoped weren't tears. She wasn't that good with tears; she'd been brought up to get on with things, and not feel sorry for herself – which was what she was trying to do now.

'I think I'd like that,' Kate said quietly, and Mary felt like a huge weight had been lifted. She didn't know why, but that feeling she'd had as they cooked together had come back. She couldn't beat the cancer, but she could give it a bloody good run for its money. 'And I think Eddie would have liked it too. I'm sorry this isn't a tearoom any longer, but maybe you could come round now and then, and we could bake and *pretend* it's still a tearoom? We could invite Charles round, and I can get my gran's best china out.'

Mary felt a sheen over her own eyes, and a lump in her throat that didn't seem to be leaving enough room for words to come out. So she nodded. But after a sip of tea, she managed, 'That would be wonderful. I only came today to keep Charles happy. He gets so confused sometimes and I don't like to leave him on his own too long, but he really would love that. We had so many happy times here.' She gazed around the kitchen. 'Wonderful times.' She wouldn't say it, even though it was on the tip of her tongue – that she didn't know just how many more good times they had left to share. 'He remembers what we were doing years ago far better than what's happened today. I really don't know how much of what we talk about really sinks in.' It worried her, the way Charles prioritised her arthritis as the biggest problem she had, rather than the more significant diagnosis that would soon do far more than stop her baking. He'd been with her when she went to the doctor, the hospital, but she wasn't sure if he had forgotten or was in denial. But Kate wouldn't want to know about their silly problems. She did her best to smile, and then peered down at her watch while she gathered herself together again. She was shocked to see how much time had passed. But it had always been like that when she'd baked. She lost track. 'Oh goodness, look at the time! I should get back and see what mischief he's been up to!'

'And you'll come back around 3pm so that we can all sample them together? I'll ask Della if she'd like to join us!'

'Della? Oh, the apple lady with the naughty puppy!' Mary

chuckled. 'It's a right little monkey. It will be lovely to see her, it's been a while. I think she's been busy; everybody is so busy these days. And of course, that lovely boy left her. It was a real surprise, he did seem kind, the type that would have stayed whatever happened.' The oven timer beeped, interrupting her, as they reached the front door. It was probably a good job; her tongue did tend to run away with her sometimes. Some things were private, and she was sure Della would be upset if she thought people were discussing her. It was so sad when relationships ended. 'You'd better go and check if they're ready. Don't forget to use the oven gloves.'

'I won't.' Kate smiled.

'Oh, what kind of a fool am I! I nearly forgot to give you this.' She had just been about to go when she remembered. She reached into her handbag. 'Strawberry jam! Homemade is much tastier than shop-bought. It was lovely Della who gave me the fruit last summer when I could still lift a pan. Oh, this old age is such a nuisance.'

'I bet!' Kate's smile was soft and brought a sheen to Mary's eyes.

'I'd better get back, the old fool will wonder where I am.'

'See you both later!'

'Maybe we could make a trifle one week? I know it isn't baking, but Charles always did love a trifle. I'm a bit of an apple crumble girl myself, but he's still a big kid, a trifle is party time!' She grinned at Kate, who chuckled.

Kate studied her for a second, her head slightly tilted as though she was thinking. 'My gran used to make an amazing trifle; I'll see if I can find the recipe! I've invited Della for lunch next Sunday. Would you like to come? Maybe you could help, well, tell me what to do? I was going to just do cheese on toast, but maybe we could do something a bit better? I'm not sure I'm ready for making Sunday lunch, but maybe a pie?'

Mary chuckled and squeezed her hand. 'Oh Kate, that is the loveliest idea! You find your trifle recipe and I'll have a think. I'm sure we can rustle something up between us.' She paused, feeling like an excited child at Christmas. 'With your brawn and my brain.'

Kate giggled. The sound stayed with Mary all the way down the road, and it was still making her smile as she put the key in her own front door.

Chapter Eleven

KATE

Afternoon tea

Kate pushed the door shut and wondered what on earth had come over her. Since leaving her desk at school for the last time on Friday, she seemed to have turned her life upside down.

The persistent beeping of the oven timer broke through her thoughts, and she dashed down to the kitchen – she was pretty sure that if the scones burned to a frazzle, Mary and Charles would know if she'd replaced them with a shop-bought offering. They'd never forgive her. She'd be 'a disappointment'.

She grabbed the oven gloves, and carefully pulled the baking tray out.

They were a wonderful golden brown and perfectly risen, and for a moment all she could do was stare at them – until the heat from the tray started to burn through the oven gloves, and with a yelp she put the tray down with a clunk on the top of the hob.

They really did look fantastic though, like *proper* scones, and the smell they filled the air with wasn't just sweetness and cakes, it was warmth. It was the hug she'd been missing since Eddie had gone.

She opened her mouth, to shout to him and tell him how clever she was, then remembered.

The familiar sense of loss hit her, but it wasn't quite as bad as it had been recently, she realised. Mary and Charles would be round later, and possibly Della, and they'd share her happiness. They'd share her food.

'Oh, Eddie,' she said softly. 'I think I get it.' She reached out and touched the top of one of the scones lightly, breathing in the mouth-watering aroma that shouted out *home*. Why the hell hadn't she woken up to this earlier, why hadn't she shared Eddie's obsession with him?

The sigh escaped. She must not turn everything into a regret.

Kate picked up her mobile phone and sent a photo of the scones to Della.

Success! Have you got time to come for a tasting @3??? Kate x

The reply was almost instant.

Wow, they look amazing! You bet! Can't wait. Della xx
p.s. liver treats were a huge success!

Kate was surprised that it was only just gone noon. Mary was probably making salmon sandwiches for Charles, and a pot of tea. The house felt suddenly empty without her and her gentle manner, and Kate felt a pang of loneliness.

She untied her apron and threw it on the table decisively. She was not going to wallow. Mary was dying, and Mary wasn't wallowing – she wanted to feel useful. To do things.

And the least Kate could do was help her, give her a reason to feel good.

She wondered what she was dying of, probably cancer, at a guess. Cancer often came with a death sentence and a good estimation of the time you had to serve.

Eddie used to say there was a recipe for every ailment, from a broken heart to a broken leg. She wondered if there were recipes to make you feel better if you had cancer. She was sure she'd read something somewhere. Or maybe that was just if there was a hope of remission, or if you had chemotherapy? She wasn't sure. Eddie would have known.

She'd google later. She'd see if there was a way to sneak healthy ingredients into their baking sessions. But in the meantime, today, she had fine china and a clean tablecloth to find, and she might as well see if she could locate her gran's trifle recipe.

When she'd cleared her grandparents' house there had been a box full of photos, and mementoes, and she was sure there was a notebook full of recipes – just like the one that Mary had brought with her.

Kate checked the time again and ran through what she needed to do before everybody arrived at 3pm. She loved a plan; her days at school had been driven by her lesson plans, and so it came naturally to order what she needed to do, rather than run around flapping. The time she really did flap was when she had nothing to do, and then the time spread ahead endlessly, and she got into a panic. That was what she'd been most afraid of when she'd handed in her notice at school: the fear that she wouldn't find anything to fill her time. But so far that didn't seem a problem at all – even if it was only Monday.

The first thing she needed to do was find the nice tea set and give it a quick rinse. Antique shops and fairs were full of old-fashioned tea sets that no doubt had been part of house clearances, but Kate had hung on to the one her grandparents had left behind. It was so pretty and delicate, it spelled out 'special' – it was their 'Sunday best', only appearing when there were guests, or on special occasions like Christmas day.

She was sure Charles would love it. She hadn't got a lace tablecloth, but she could at least serve their tea in the type of cups they probably drank from when this was a tearoom.

She laid out the plates, cups and saucers, filled the milk jug and popped it in the fridge and put some sugar in the sugar bowl. There was even a cake stand and small bowls that were perfect for the clotted cream and jam.

Kate had no idea where the pretty gingham tablecloth they'd bought when they first moved into the house had gone. But she decided that napkins and placemats would have to do today, and she'd invest in a new tablecloth before next weekend. She really hadn't got time to faff around searching for something that wasn't that important – as Eddie always said, it's the company not posh plates that people come for. Although she wasn't one hundred per cent sure that applied where old people were concerned. Her gran had always been very conscious about what people would think, but right now Kate hadn't got time to wonder about that. And, after all, Charles had already seen the kitchen at its worst.

Finding her grandmother's book, and the trifle recipe, was a bit trickier. She knew she'd unpacked it because she remembered seeing Eddie grab it. He homed in on anything food related – and then he spent a whole evening flicking through the pages, chuckling to himself. At the time she'd wondered in passing what could possibly be funny, but then she'd gone back to marking mock exam papers and never asked him.

Eddie had gone up to bed, taking the book with him, long before she'd finished work – shouting down that he was picking out old favourites that he promised he'd make for her.

He'd not had time. The six months between her gran's death and his had been filled with other stuff. Life.

Live in the moment, they said, but maybe she'd got it wrong. Maybe the important thing is to do the things you'll regret not doing, rather than doing the things that drift your way.

The book wasn't on the kitchen dresser, or in any of the drawers. She went through each one systematically, keeping an eye on the time. There was only one other place it could be.

Eddie had kept going back to it, so maybe Eddie had the answer.

Kate hadn't kept to her side of the bed after he had died. She'd spread out across the king-size mattress, migrated to his side so that she could smell him, imagine his warmth. Rest her head in the indent his head had made on his pillow.

She'd forced herself, as time went by, to sort through his clothes – his cupboards, his wardrobe – but she hadn't gone through all of his personal stuff. She hadn't sorted through the books and bits and pieces on his bedside table – for much the same reasons that she couldn't sort through the bag at the bottom of the wardrobe. She couldn't. If she sorted through the stuff, she'd be throwing things away, packing things. Admitting he'd gone. She wasn't ready to sweep him out of her life. Not yet.

The book was there.

Not food-splattered, as it would have been if it had been Eddie's. It was unstained, no page corners turned down – just worn at the edges from constant thumbing, her gran's small, neat handwriting faded in places.

Kate sat on the floor, her back against the bed, and turned the first page over.

Apple & Blackberry Crumble (Kate's favourite with custard!)

She smiled. She had loved it, and hadn't Mary said it was one of her favourites as well?

Baked Stuffed Apples (Norman prefers these to apple sauce if we've got too many)

She flipped over a few more pages. Mary's recipes had notes of the changes she'd made, and lots of little tips and asides about how to serve them, but Gran's recipes were as precise as the ones in a book – apart from all the little notes about who loved them most. All of her gran's recipes were in her special book for a reason – for a person. About a person.

And Eddie's? Well, from what she'd seen, Eddie's were just like him. A story, a conversation, ideas straight from his head onto the page that told you how he felt. Generous, natural. Emotional. She paused for a moment.

Eddie had worn his heart on his sleeve; it was the way he was. Gran had been quieter, more reserved, brought up in a different time – but her recipe book held the words she hadn't always said.

Yorkshire puds with sugar (Guaranteed to mend Kate's scrapes and bruises!)

She smiled. She didn't know anybody else who made giant Yorkshire puddings and served them with a good sprinkling of sugar – they were like massive, bouncy pancakes.

A coloured card slipped onto the floor, and she instantly recognised Eddie's handwriting. It was a list of recipes, and as she flicked through her gran's book, she realised it was all the ones that had been marked as her favourites – including Gran's notes from '*mend a 15-year-old Kate's broken heart?*' to '*picnic favourite*' and '*always makes her smile*'.

Kate wasn't sure that her thirty-three-year-old heart was mendable; maybe hearts as well as bones took longer to knit back together as you got older. Maybe the bits never quite fitted together again the same. Maybe the fault lines remained weak points. Reminders of what could have been. Her heart ached right now.

She'd never given herself a chance to think about her gran when she'd died – she'd rushed about being busy, burying herself in work. She'd run away from her emotions – just like her mother had run away from her. It seemed to be a family trait.

She let the book fall onto the carpet and closed her eyes.

How had she never realised just how much her gran loved her? How every meal she made was picked with care – not some random dish on the table?

And Eddie had been doing the same.

Kate had always recognised that she had spent the first part of her life consciously trying to do things to please her mum, to get her attention. But she had thought that when she left university and became a teacher she had moved on, was following her own path. She now realised she wasn't.

She had been doing the things her mother had done, running away from her feelings, from people who loved her, who might want more than she was confident of giving. Being a workaholic was a lot easier than being emotionally available.

Kate wasn't being her own person at all, because that huge shadow was still hanging over her. A shadow that was filled with emptiness. An illogical and impossible concept, she knew, but that was the best way of describing it.

She'd not appreciated the people who did love her, who tried so hard to make her happy. She'd not realised until now, when they were gone. She'd not faced up to the loss of her grandparents, she'd pushed Eddie away when they should have talked. Not explained why she was making the decisions she was, and not letting him in. Maybe she'd been frightened that she was wrong, that he'd talk her round? If they *had* sat down, he'd still be alive. They might have the child he so desperately wanted.

Kate rubbed her eyes with the palms of her hands and felt weary. She wanted to curl up and sleep.

The doorbell chime echoed in the empty hallway, and Kate jumped.

How on earth could it be 3pm already? And she hadn't even found the trifle recipe, let alone brushed her hair or put any make-up on. Scraping her hair back into a band she scurried down the stairs as the doorbell rang again – more persistently.

And this time she knew it wasn't Eddie, it was Charles.

Kate flung open the front door and then took a step back, her hand flying to her mouth to cover up her shock and the big smile on her face.

Her tiny doorstep was crowded, Mary was at the front, in a very *Darling Buds of May* frock that shouted out 'British summer' in the best way possible. Behind her was Charles, doffing his hat, a broad grin on his face. He had one hand on Mary's shoulder, and Kate very much hoped it was protective and not because he might otherwise fall over.

'We're here!' announced Della, who was standing at Mary's other shoulder and waving the most beautiful bunch of colourful spring flowers, which Kate was sure she must have just picked from her garden.

'Wow, come in! You'll be very pleased to know that the scones turned out fine.'

'Fine?' questioned Charles, winking at her. 'They will be more than fine if Mary had any say in them.' He waggled a finger, before hastily putting his hand back on Mary's shoulder.

'They are,' said Kate with a smile.

'Wait!' He waved his stick (Kate really did need to clear the hall of ornaments if he was going to be a regular visitor), stopping Mary and Della in mid-step. He took a deep breath. 'Isn't that the most delicious smell?'

Mary gave a little shake of her head, a smile lifting the corners of her mouth as she gave Kate a conspiratorial look. 'It is, darling, but we'll all have died of hunger if you keep us hanging about any longer!'

'Oh heck, I haven't put the jam and cream out yet! Come in and sit down, give me a minute – just one minute!'

'I'll spoon it out, while you waitress?' offered Della with a cheeky smile that made her look much younger.

Kate laughed, shaking her head, then settled Mary and Charles in their seats and took the teapot over.

'Oh, my goodness, Mary!' Della had opened the jar of jam and was wafting her hand over the top. 'Smell those strawbs, Kate! Were these the ones you had from the garden?'

Mary nodded.

'Nobody makes jam like you do. How do you keep so many whole strawberries? Mine turn to pulp. And that smell – it's summer all over again. That's exactly how they smelled when I picked them!'

'I'll give you the recipe.' The smile on Mary's face was so full and happy, Kate forgot what she was doing and overfilled the cup with tea.

'Eek! Sorry, sorry, let me just get a cloth.'

'This tearoom has really gone downhill!' admonished Della, and they all laughed.

'Ahh but these scones are the bee's knees!' declared Charles, who had already taken a big bite out of one.

'I take it back,' said Della, 'they're delicious – this is the best tearoom I've been to for a long time.'

'It's all down to Mary.' Kate glanced over at the older lady, who had cut her own scone into delicate quarters, but was looking thrilled at how well their baking was being received.

'Nonsense, you've either got it or you haven't, and I have to say, my dear, you definitely have got the knack.' She smiled. 'Eddie would be so proud.'

'Hear, hear,' boomed Charles, and everybody laughed.

Kate felt colour flood her cheeks, but it was a nice embarrassment. If Eddie was here, he'd be laughing, and hugging her, and planting a big smacker on her lips.

'It was a lovely tearoom,' Mary said quietly.

'Oh, I nearly forgot! I've got photos to show you. Della found them.' She fetched them and spread them out on the table so that everybody could look. 'It's really got me wondering about how this place used to be.'

It had. She hadn't been able to stop glancing around, trying to work out what had changed and how.

Of course, it was silly to imagine turning the place back into a café. But it did feel nice to have people here, to bake for them.

'It was a happy place.' Charles's voice was firm.

'Oh yes, lots of laughter. Flo was lovely, she used to send us home with full tummies and full hearts.' Mary glanced up at Charles, and Kate felt a pang as she watched them.

'She was a gem, just like you.' Charles squeezed Mary's hand, and then pointed at one of the photographs. 'That was our favourite table, wasn't it? There, just by the window, you could see everybody walking up and down the street and wonder what they were up to!'

'You did, you cheeky monkey!' Mary smiled at Kate and Della. 'He used to make things up about them to make me laugh!'

Kate brewed another pot of tea. Maybe it would be nice to open out the kitchen into the front room again. Get rid of the dividing wall. Open-plan was very popular, and she could see why. It let in the light. Eddie would have loved the idea. He would have enjoyed cooking and being able to chat to his guests at the same time. If the house went back to its original layout, it would make little get-togethers like this so much nicer. They wouldn't be cramped around the kitchen table. And she could quite easily turn the study into a cosy sitting room.

It didn't have to be a tearoom again, just a nicer place to live.

She glanced around the table. A nicer place, with people. There were three generations of them sitting together, three generations from different families. But maybe sometimes that was better – a made-up family, of people who wanted to be together. Of people who were there because they wanted to be.

Kate popped the last bit of her scone into her mouth. They really were as delicious as Charles had promised. The smell as she'd taken them out of the oven had left her practically drooling, but they were even better than she'd imagined they'd be. There was the smallest of crunches as her teeth bit into the crispy top, followed by a surprising softness. A light and fluffy inside that practically *melted* on her tongue – all buttery and gorgeous. She closed her eyes for a moment, and she could almost feel the touch of her gran's hand on her arm, see the pleasure in her eyes as she watched Kate devour her baking. She'd not tasted scones like this for years, not since she'd been in her grandparents' small, cramped but cosy kitchen. She swallowed the small lump in her throat. She missed them, she missed all the little things, all the things that she'd never really appreciated at the time – the things that made her feel safe, cared for. Loved.

Kate opened her eyes as she felt the lightest of touches on the back of her hand. It wasn't Gran, as she'd half expected; it was, of course, Mary, who was studying her, a question in her eyes. Kate smiled back reassuringly.

'I'm fine, your gorgeous scones reminded me of Gran,' she whispered.

'Food is like that,' Mary said softly. 'It's more than just a recipe, isn't it?'

It was. Kate nodded. Warm scones weren't just scones, they were her gran's baking, they were holidays in Cornwall when her grandad would compare the expensive cream teas to Gran's (Gran's were always better). Scones were childhood memories, something that she'd almost forgotten about until now.

'And this is more than just a kitchen!' Charles pronounced, before launching into a story about the building's history, and how it had been a bakery, and always a place of warmth and people.

Kate sat back, surprised how much fun it was just being there, in their company, and listening to them all.

Della regaled them with tales of her naughty puppy, and Mary told them how to make the perfect loaf.

Kate felt more relaxed, more her old self, than she had since Eddie had gone. Charles was right, this building did seem to be a place of warmth. Even Della had come out of her shell. She'd struck Kate as being quite a reserved, self-contained person, but as she knew from the kids at school, even the quietest ones wanted to share and be with people. And hadn't Kate cut herself off from people as well? Maybe it was the right time for both of them to let friendship back in.

It was funny really, Della was probably of a similar age to her mum, but they were as different as two people could be. Della would have made a good mother, if the way she loved and cared for Clint was any indication. But she'd said yesterday that they'd never had children because she didn't have that kind of relationship with Justin. Did she regret it? Would Kate herself regret it in the future? Oh yes, she regretted not talking to Eddie on that night about having a baby, but she'd been so sure that to have one would be a mistake.

'Oh, I do hope we can do this again,' Charles said, cutting into Kate's thoughts, as he made a neat pile of his crumbs in the middle of his plate. He took Mary's hand in his. 'It's been top-notch, just like the old days! I was so lucky to meet my lovely Mary and be able to bring her here.' He planted a kiss on her cheek.

'No pressure then,' Della said with a cheeky wink.

'Well, Mary and I —' Kate glanced at Mary for confirmation '– were wondering if everybody would like to get together again next Sunday for lunch?'

'How splendid!'

Kate had always thought that the phrase 'his face lit up' was a bit improbable (and dangerous, as it probably would have involved flames and an accelerant), but that was the only way she could have described Charles. It was as though he was glowing from the inside. His already wrinkled skin formed deeper creases as he smiled with delight, and his hand shook as he put his teacup down hastily.

'Oh my goodness, homemade roast dinner! How splendid.'

Her stomach did a flip. 'Well, I didn't mean Sunday lunch, as in Sunday *lunch*.' Charles raised an eyebrow and Della laughed. 'I was going to make a trifle,' she added hastily, trying to temper expectations, 'if I can find my gran's recipe, and Mary can help.' Mary nodded, once, in a gentle way, in complete contrast to her husband's excitement – but her hands weren't quite steady, and her eyes gleamed. 'But –' Kate hesitated, not wanting to dampen the mood '– I've never made a roast dinner. That was Eddie's thing. I was going to make something simple.'

She shared a look with the grinning Della, and knew they were thinking the same thing. Cheese on toast!

'Oh, nonsense, my dear, his expertise will have rubbed off on you!'

She didn't have Charles's confidence. It had not rubbed off on her.

'And there's always that new chef fellow if you need a hand, what's his name, you know the one. Though Mary will have it all under control, I'm sure.'

Kate glanced at Della, raising her shoulders in a question. Chef fellow?

'New neighbour,' mouthed Della.

'Splendid chap, young, good-looking!' said Charles, with a thumbs-up.

'He's that lovely young man that moved in at the bottom of the road, on the corner?' Mary said softly.

The corner? The only new arrival at the end of the road was… Kate frowned, then her stomach did a tiny lurch as the truth of the matter dawned on her. That obnoxious idiot who liked to wander around in the middle of the road was a chef? Well, no, she was being unfair. He might have been obnoxious then, but when she had bumped into him in the farm shop, it had been a bit strained, but he'd seemed nice enough. Well, very nice, kind to some people. Okay, he'd averted a disaster. He was a hero.

But a chef? Oh my God, that explained his throwaway comment about being used to buying food for lots of people – and there was she assuming he wasn't interested in food. What an idiot. No wonder he'd not been interested when she was recommending the cheese, telling him what was nice – what on earth must he have thought? She tried not to wriggle in her seat, but she suddenly felt so uncomfortable. No way was she asking him for help now.

Mary seemed to sense her mood; she squeezed her hand gently. 'We'll manage, won't we, Kate? We don't need some fancy chef telling us we're doing it wrong!'

Fancy? Fancy chef? That made it even worse.

'I don't think he is a fancy chef any longer actually,' said Della. 'I'm sure I read somewhere that he'd shut the restaurant and gone into hiding. He was the local wonder boy,' she explained, 'well, not very local really, about fifteen miles up the road, but we claimed him! He's been in the newspapers, and

I'm sure that was the most recent mention – rising star goes into hiding – or something like that.'

This made absolutely no sense at all, and Kate, Charles and Mary shared a look. 'Well, he's not done a very good job of hiding, has he, if you all know he's here?' Kate, it seemed, was the only person who didn't know he was – or had been – some kind of super chef. But she hadn't lived here for as long as everybody else, so it made sense if he was a local hero.

'Shall we get together later in the week, dear? And you can tell me what you've got in mind?' Mary diplomatically ignored the comments as Kate was trying to work out just why a mention of the man was making her bristle like a cat. He really had got under her skin, but she should follow Mary's lead and just ignore it. She wasn't interested in some talented Adonis who was trying to hide – in fact, given the way he looked, he was going to find that a challenge anyway. If he really wanted to hide, he'd shave his head, grow a beard and stop posing in the middle of the bloody road.

'Lamb!' announced Charles, suitably distracted. 'Roast lamb was always Mary's favourite, wasn't it, dear?'

Kate's stomach did another flip. Lamb? She'd been planning on a simple pie, topped with ready-made puff pastry. Or maybe a cottage pie because mince and mash had to be achievable even for her.

Mary nodded. 'But I don't do it now.'

'She can't lift the trays. Her wrists.' Charles's tone was soft as he briefly touched her arm, and they shared a look of understanding. 'A right old pair, aren't we, love? You with your aches and pains, and me all doddery and forgetting what I've gone upstairs for.'

'But you can remember right back to the day we met in the tearoom.' Mary smiled and squeezed his hand.

'That's embedded deep in here. I'll never forget.' He tapped his heart. 'But the stuff in here —' he tapped his temple '— everyday stuff…' He sighed. 'It's a right bugger when it's taken me so long to get up the stairs and I stand there wondering what I'm doing, and Mary isn't able to do the things she loves.'

'I did love cooking, and the garden,' Mary said wistfully. 'But what we can't do we can't. We manage, don't we?'

'I'm always happy to help with the garden,' Della offered softly.

Kate could see the hesitation. Charles and Mary had always been independent and they didn't want to accept help, even though it clearly would make life much easier. 'We can't afford to pay—'

'You're not paying me anything! I'm going to help Kate out with her garden, so I'll spend an hour or so here, then pop over to yours. You'll be helping me, actually, because I intend to be hitting sixty as fit as a fiddle. It would be no trouble at all, I'll have my tools with me, and coming here to share lunch with you all is more than enough.'

Kate tried not to let her feelings show on her face. The idea of sharing one lunch had sounded doable, but it seemed to be escalating into a regular thing. She wasn't even a one-dish wonder, she didn't have *any* dishes she knew how to make!

'Well, that sounds lovely, thank you.' Mary smiled. 'It's good to share, isn't it, dear?'

'Lovely,' said Kate weakly.

'Spot on.' Charles beamed. 'Sorry, what were we talking about, sharing a minibus to Brighton?'

Kate forgot about the challenge of a weekly dinner as they all looked at him, open-mouthed. Is this what happened when you got muddled, you time-hopped?

Charles suddenly chuckled. 'Haha, gotcha!'

'You old fool,' tutted Mary, 'always like to be centre of attention.'

It brought a lump to Kate's throat; she wondered just how many times Charles actually did forget. There were recipes that brought back memories of the past, but she wasn't sure there was any type of food that helped in the moment. She was sure she'd read somewhere that music often helped people – could food do the same?

'And that's why you love me!'

Charles and Mary, she thought, were muddling along, making the most of the time they had, so surely she shouldn't be feeling sad for them? She needed a dose of whatever gave them their joie-de-vivre attitude.

Oh well, in for a penny, in for a pound. How could she let them down? 'Well, that's settled, Della is head gardener, I'm head chef, and Mary is second in command! And we'll do lamb on Sunday.' She was mad, totally mad. 'Though you will have to help me, Mary.'

Mary smiled.

'Lots, I will need lots of help!'

'And I'll make some mint sauce from my herb garden,' Della added.

It was nearly 5pm by the time Charles and Mary got up from the table.

'We've had a wonderful time, my dear. Thank you.' He squeezed both her shoulders. 'I'm so glad I popped in the other day.'

'So am I.' And Kate meant it.

'It has been lovely.' Mary gave her a proper hug, her dry lips brushing Kate's cheek. 'Oh, silly me, I nearly forgot! I've got you a present.' She reached into her large handbag and drew out a notepad. 'Your own book for recipes. Everybody needs one to write down their favourites!'

Kate smiled, wondering just how many goodies Mary had in that large handbag.

'Thank you.' She kissed her on her cheek, taking in the delicate flowery perfume. 'And you'll have to give me that strawberry jam recipe to start me off.'

Kate didn't glance at the notepad again until she'd cleared all the dishes away. She sat down and picked it up.

There was a picture on the front of the most beautiful cottage, complete with colourful garden. Inside there were tabs, splitting it into sections.

For a moment she sat quietly thinking. She thought about her gran's book, about the notes in it. She thought about the card that Eddie had written out, and she thought about her new friends.

She didn't want to split the recipes in her book by courses, or ingredients. She was going to divide it into themes. She would have a section on feel-good comfort food, she would have a section on winter warmers, of sunny summer memories and – she traced her finger over the cover – she would have a section on Mary's favourites, and of food that might help her illness.

Della had confirmed that Mary had cancer, and Kate was going to find out how to cook the best food for her. Mary was going to eat ingredients that were good for her, but ones that were good for her soul as well as her body. Kate couldn't save her, but she could make sure she felt wanted, needed and loved. And she had a feeling that was why Charles had come here – why he'd brought his Mary back to the tearoom where he'd met her all those years ago. He was trying to recreate more than an afternoon tea.

Kate sat quietly and thought about the way they looked at each other, about the way they referred so much to her arthritis, but never her cancer, and it was then that the tears sprang into her eyes.

Chapter Twelve

JACK

Roses

It was Tuesday. Tuesday had always been Jack's day off. The day he was supposed to do whatever he wanted – which usually involved experimenting with new recipe ideas. Today he found himself inside the local supermarket, staring at buckets filled with garish flowers.

'Can't go wrong with a bunch of carnations,' a voice said at his shoulder.

Jack half turned, to find an elderly gentleman inches away from his shoulder.

The man gestured at the buckets with his walking stick, as though he thought Jack was either deaf or stupid.

'Carnations! Not much scent, but they last for weeks. Can't go wrong. Bit like roast chicken and two veg, eh?'

Jack stared back at him blankly.

'Can't go wrong, can you? All that fancy stuff you cook is fine at the right time and place, but roast chicken wins every time.'

Jack felt the words chip away at his resolve. He didn't want to get into a discussion about roast chicken, or any kind of 'fancy stuff'. He had got up this morning determined to make the most of the day. Recently it seemed that he had been getting out of bed the wrong side every morning, but although he had not slept much last night – due to the creaks and groans of a house he wasn't used to yet, and the absence of his normal (now banned) nightcap – he had woken up with a new determination.

He had worked out what Ben, his laid-back overpaid therapist, had not been able to. The answer to his current predicament was to stop mulling over the past and getting 'to the root of why it had affected him as it had' (as suggested by Ben) and to find a new obsession.

Jack needed a passion, he needed a goal, something to strive for.

Before cooking had completely taken over his life, Jack had been a keen amateur photographer. He loved still-life (which came in very handy when he was putting together a portfolio of recipes) – and it didn't matter if it was a basket of wild mushrooms or a person who was as yet unaware that they had his focus. In fact, people fascinated him, and quite often when he'd looked around the corner of the kitchen door, he would have loved to be able to capture the expressions on the faces of his customers.

He hadn't, of course, had the time – but now he had. It was time to move on from food; he'd tried to be patient and wait, but his senses hadn't sharpened as he'd been told they might. He couldn't tell cumin from coriander; the tantalising smells no longer tickled the back of his throat and told him he'd got the seasoning just right.

He'd lost it, and it felt like a bereavement. But his mourning period had gone on for too long. His kitchen was the past, and he needed to immerse himself in some new experience.

Jack had never done things by halves, whether it was working, sleeping, partying or sulking. Well, nothing that mattered to him; buying flowers seemed to be another thing altogether.

'I would have thought flowers with a scent were better than ones without?' he said mildly, deciding that just ignoring the chicken comment was the best tactic. The old man was still staring at him so intently he looked like he might topple forward at any moment, straight into his arms.

'Modern flowers don't seem to smell of anything these days, not like the old-fashioned home-grown ones we used to have.'

Jack had to agree with that statement. His best ingredients had always been the ones he'd foraged, grown himself or bought from a local producer, and he guessed the same must be true of flowers.

He wasn't a big buyer of bouquets. He'd only ever bought flowers for his mum and for women he was dating. It felt too personal to give them to a complete stranger by way of an apology.

Flowers said, 'I love you,' didn't they? Not 'I guess I'm a jerk'.

But he had been a jerk. Not once, but twice. He'd hurt her the second time, he'd seen it in her eyes, and she didn't deserve it. She was being friendly, nice, and he'd just turned away because it had been the easy way out.

And the easy way had never been his way.

'Now Della at the end of the road has some old favourites in her garden, but you can't exactly go and help yourself, can you?' The old man nudged Jack, who found that he had no sensible response to that. 'My Mary always liked freesias. She'd fill the kitchen with her baking, and the front room with the smell of freesias. A right smelly house we had!' He chuckled, and Jack felt himself drawn to the stranger, despite himself.

'What's happened to you then? My son treated us to a meal at your place before he moved to Canada. You – now what's the term you youngsters use? – smashed it! That's it, you smashed it with that pork crackling stuff, lad. I wasn't sure about those flower petals on everything and those smears of sauce on the plate, nowhere near enough to dip in, but the pork was bang on. Mary would have loved the recipe, but she can't do it now.' He paused. 'Can't carry the heavy oven trays, like, she's got arthritis in her wrists. I bet if you gave it to me, though, that little Kate could make it with my Mary's help.' He shifted his weight from foot to foot and moved his stick slightly, and for a moment Jack thought he was going to have to dive in and catch him. Actually, the old man was standing so close, there wouldn't be much diving involved. What was it about old people and personal space? Was it because they couldn't see or hear as well as they used to? 'She's doing us lamb next Sunday. We're having mint sauce.'

Jack nodded, and half-smiled, wondering how he was going to get away.

'Any hints or tips? On the sauce, that is. I bet you put that balsamic vinegar in it, don't you?' He smiled and winked, and Jack couldn't help himself – he smiled back.

'Well,' he leaned in conspiratorially, 'don't tell anybody, but I reckon the best mint sauce is made the way my mum used to make it, with white wine vinegar and the freshest mint leaves she could pick. Simple, it's all about clean flavours, then let the lamb do the talking.'

The old man nodded. 'My Mary would agree there.' He waved his stick back in the direction of the flowers again. 'I'd go for the carnations, lad. Forget the smell, none of them smell like they used to.'

Jack nodded. Nothing smelled like it used to. And trying to jolt his senses back to life with alcohol had definitely lost its appeal. He didn't even enjoy it that much. It had just filled the gap in his evenings when he'd normally have been devising recipes. Drinking was a bad habit, and he knew he needed to change his habits if he wanted to change his life.

But he wasn't convinced that pouring all his booze down the drain, the day before he moved into this new place, had been one of his best ideas. He wouldn't have noticed the unfamiliar noises if he'd had a drink or two.

But hey, this was supposed to be a new place, new start, so all the old habits had to be dumped. Clean break. He wasn't even forty; he had years ahead of him, years to form a new career. A new life.

'You shouldn't have stopped your cookery, lad.'

Jack had almost forgotten about the old man. But he was still there, his eagle-eyed stare fixed on Jack. 'I might not have liked everything you cooked, but it's a gift when you can do something like that. God's gift, I'd say, not that I'm religious.'

'God gives and God takes away,' Jack retorted, his tone dry.

'And the devil finds work for idle hands,' the man shot back, but his eyes were twinkling.

Jack laughed. He'd never been one to stop and chat, and to be honest, his initial reaction when this guy had started to talk had been to get away as quickly as he could, but the old man was actually quite entertaining. Maybe it was time he was less of a hermit. One downside of his previous occupation had been that it left little or no time for family and friends.

He didn't regret it, but maybe there was a life out there that could satisfy him in different ways.

He winked, then fished the camera out of his rucksack. 'Well, if this is the work of the devil then you're spot on!'

'Depends what you're taking photos of, I suppose.' He chuckled again, but this time it turned to a cough, and his whole body wobbled alarmingly.

Jack instinctively put a hand on his elbow to steady him. 'Do you need to sit down? There's a chair by the till – I could get it.'

'No, no, no.' He waved him away, then clutched the walking stick so firmly his knuckles turned white. 'But I reckon if you're a photographer now, then that thing should be hung round your neck, shouldn't it? Ready for action.' He held his hand in front of his face and made a click noise as he pressed an imaginary shutter.

'You could be right.' Jack slung the strap round his neck.

'When you get to my age you usually are, lad. One of the few benefits of old age. A bit of nous, insight.' He tapped the side of his nose. 'And my head still says you've done the wrong thing packing up that restaurant, but that's just me. If you're not sure about the carnations go for one of those mixed bunches, spread the bet! Better be off.'

Before Jack could say anything else, the old man headed slowly up the vegetable aisle. He was sure he could hear him muttering, 'Fresh mint', or it could have been 'Silly twit'.

His hand hesitated over the carnations, then he reached past them and picked up a bunch of roses. The old man had seemed bright and on the ball – he'd definitely been right about idle hands: Jack needed something to occupy his, and his mind – but he'd been wrong about the flowers.

They were mixed, soft colours – old-fashioned. They reminded him of his cottage, of his mum, and as he held them up to his face, he was sure he could detect just the faintest hint of scent.

Or it could have just been a memory.

The camera bumped gently against his chest. If taste and smell were going to be just memories, then building a new life based on sight had to be a good idea, didn't it? Sight and touch – he could create images that made you want to reach out and feel them beneath your fingertips.

Chapter Thirteen

DELLA

Digging

Della tightened the green string around the peg and wondered if she'd made a mistake. Nobody had ever accused her of being impulsive, in fact, her nickname at school had been 'dithering Della', so she didn't quite know what had got into her. In the space of a few days, she'd told Kate she'd help tidy her garden, and promised Charles and Mary that she'd give them a hand as well. To cap it all, after a couple of glasses of wine last night she had come up with the bright idea of a vegetable garden. Kate was keen to help support Mary and Charles, and although neither of them really had a clue about what constituted the perfect diet for Mary, they agreed that fresh had to be best.

Della might have had a few herbs and some strawberries in pots recently, but she hadn't grown as much as a single runner bean for years (Justin hadn't been a fan of 'wonky' veg), but the idea had actually quite excited her – which was what two glasses of merlot and an enthusiastic Kate had done for her.

Now, when she eyed up the plot she'd marked out and realised that the next step was to dig it, she wasn't getting quite the same feel-good vibe. She could do with somebody half her age, or at least with twice her stamina, to help out. This was really going to do her back in – she wouldn't be able to move tomorrow. Well, she'd said she'd do it, so she supposed she'd better make a start. She wasn't about to let everybody down. She rolled her sleeves up.

'Probably a better idea to do that round the back, out of sight!'

The deep voice broke into her thoughts, and she spun round to see a man grinning at her from the other side of the fence. The first thought that popped into her head was that he looked a bit weathered (in quite a nice, solid way rather than a battered-old-building kind of way), the second was that he had smiley eyes, and the third (and most important thought) was that he looked rather strong. He was no spring chicken, and her impression was that he was lean and wiry rather than a body-builder, but he had muscles, definitely digging biceps, on full show.

Could she ask him? No, no, she definitely couldn't. What on earth was she thinking? She wasn't the type of person who accosted innocent strangers who were passing by.

'Sorry?' she said, her mind still weighing up his spade-wielding potential. Oh, it was so tempting. But what did he mean, round the back?

She was determined to ignore the big six-oh and treat it as just another birthday. She'd always been capable of digging her garden, but she had to admit that it took it out of her more these days. Sometimes she wished she was more like the young-sters, readier to ask for help, but it didn't come naturally to her. She'd always been more the 'soldier on and manage' type. Her father had always been stubborn, not admitting his failings, never saying he couldn't do something – and she was more like him than she sometimes liked. Was it really weak to ask for help?

She glanced down. Through the picket fence she could see very workmanlike shorts, strong calves and the type of boots that said 'mud-proof'.

He might look a few years older than she was (possibly even older than Justin), but he definitely didn't look like a man who liked to spend his days on his backside.

'Burying the body! I think it's normal to do it under the patio so nobody will suspect.'

'Ah.' She'd spoken to him before – well, said 'hello' in passing as you do with people that are vaguely familiar– but never actually *seen* him. He wasn't a total stranger; they were nodding acquaintances. Neighbours. 'What about potatoes?' She supposed, looking at it, the plot she'd marked out *was* like a large grave. She could fit two bodies in it, Justin and his new partner. Not that she wished them dead; it wasn't really Justin's fault that he was born the wrong sex, was it? Although she *could* blame him for pretending. She could never forgive him for *using* her like that – as though she was some lab mouse to experiment his sexual preferences on. The female that he could marry and see if he could live with. He'd probably picked her because she dithered, knowing that she'd never throw him out even if she suspected he hadn't married for love. She'd play along, making the most of it. Which she had. For bloody years.

'Would it be easier to put them in a barrel?'

Della frowned at the man. Who on earth put dead bodies in a barrel? Unless they'd been minced or put through a wood shredder. She was sure she'd seen something like that on some Netflix series. But if you chucked a barrel in the canal, wouldn't it float back up? This was the strangest conversation she'd ever had.

'Potatoes, not bodies!' He laughed, as though he could read her mind.

She grinned back at him. 'Ah, right. I get you! It probably would be easier, but I've promised to supply half the flaming street with fresh salad and veg.'

'That's a lot of barrels,' he agreed. He kept a straight face, but she was sure he was laughing inside. 'Am I in the wrong half of the street then?'

'Sorry?'

'To benefit?'

'Ah, I get you. Well, that depends where you live.'

'Up there.' He pointed up towards the top of the street. 'Number 3. Oh, it's David, by the way.' He held his hand out. 'I don't think we've really met properly?'

'Della.' She smiled back, thinking how easy that had been. Then she took his large, slightly calloused hand and was surprised at how reassuring the rough skin was against hers. His touch lingered for slightly longer than it needed to, but she didn't feel the need to pull away. Instead, she smiled at him, and a small tremor of pleasure at the human contact warmed her inside and out. He took a step back, their hands parting in a way that felt quite natural. 'And no, I don't think we have, though I don't know why.'

'Sorry for butting in. I didn't mean to interrupt. It's just nice to see somebody using their garden.'

'Oh, you're not interrupting.'

'And you looked like you mean business!' He nodded towards her rolled-up sleeves.

'I was mentally gearing up to start digging.'

'Big patch,' he said, and Della nodded.

'I think I got a bit carried away, to be honest. It *is* a big patch.'

'Well, if you find you need a hand – you know, many hands make light work and all that – I know a man with a spade who'll do anything for a cuppa.'

'You do?' She raised an eyebrow, and as the corner of his mouth lifted, heat rushed to her cheeks. 'Ah, you mean you!'

''Fraid so. Not that I want to be pushy or anything, and you look like you've got it all in hand.'

'Oh, I haven't.' She paused. Oh, for heaven's sake, she could do this, she had to. She could be impulsive and brave. 'Well, to be honest, I suppose you could, erm, benefit...' Her cheeks felt hotter than ever now, and it was far too late in life to blame the menopause. 'From the veg and salad, that is, when it grows. It could be like an exchange.' She looked him straight in the eye. He had quite nice eyes, brown, with wrinkles around them that looked a little deeper than her own. 'If you really don't mind helping me out with the digging, then you really will have earned some, won't you?'

'Sounds like a good deal.' She got a blast of his full smile, and a glimpse of his chipped front tooth. 'Give me five minutes and I'll put my scruffs on and bring a decent spade.' He gave her a thumbs-up, then hesitated. 'If you were planning on carrying on right now, and you're sure I'm not interfering? I know some people have their own way of doing things.'

'Not at all,' she said firmly and smiled as she realised that she really meant it. It would be quite nice to have a helping hand.

'I'll be back as soon as.'

'Wonderful, and you can let me know when you're ready for that brew.' As she watched him stride out back down the street, she thought it was probably the fact that he was so totally different to Justin that had made her brave.

He also had quite attractive legs, which surprised her. She'd never thought of a man's legs as attractive before.

It was as Della was making the second cup of tea for them both that she realised this was the first time she had spent any time alone with a man (unless you counted the octogenarian Charles, or the teenage paperboy who liked to play with Clint) since Justin had left.

She didn't like to ask David how old he was, but he'd told her he had one cat and two grown-up children.

She paused at the door, a tray laden with cups and a plate of scones in her hands, and watched him. He was sinewy rather than heavy, which was nice. She didn't want some big brute of a man throwing her soil in all directions, but David just looked healthy and strong in an active way. He dug steadily, not wasting any effort. Efficient.

She liked aesthetically pleasing things, beautiful things, which she supposed – she thought with a sigh – was why she'd made the mistake of marrying Justin. If anything, though, he'd been rather *too* perfect. He would never have picked up a spade or wanted to get dirt under his fingernails. Whereas she liked the feel of the earth, and she didn't mind a bit of hard work, so long as her back and her knees could stand it. She loved the idea of transforming the rough into a diamond. When it came to a garden, of course, not a man.

'You're very fit.' She blushed, the tray in her hands wobbling, as she realised what she'd said. 'For your…' She'd nearly said 'age'. What on earth had got into her? She might not make impulsive decisions, she might spend too long mulling over decisions, but she'd always known how to speak to people. Well, obviously not today. David had left her tongue in a knot. 'I mean you've done that far more quickly than I could.'

'I like to be out in the fresh air,' he said, ignoring her confusion, and carrying on digging. 'Do a lot of rambling in my spare time. Nothing like a good walk to clear your head. If you're ever at a loose end, you're welcome to join me.'

He left it open, as a half question – but when he glanced up and reached out for the mug his gaze met hers head-on and she felt like he wanted an answer.

'That sounds nice. I'm quite often at a loose end, actually, but I'm not much of a walker – I'm sure you'd leave me behind. I wouldn't want to hold you up…'

'We could start off with something easy, a nice stroll. I like some time on my own, but it's good to have company, share the sights.'

She smiled back at him and nodded. It *was* nice to have company, to share.

'The number of times I've spotted a lesser mottled toad and not had anybody to point it out to!'

She frowned. 'I'm not sure I'd know what … ah, you're having me on!'

He chuckled then, showing the chipped front tooth, and Della felt something inside of her lift. 'You're a quick one! But you know what I mean.'

'I do. The number of times I'm about to comment on something stupid on the TV to Justin, then I remember he's not there.'

'We've got something in common, I guess.' He sat down next to her on the garden bench.

'Oh?'

'My other half ran off with another man.'

Della laughed. 'Well, yes, mine did that. But at least your other half was a woman!'

'True.'

He grinned at her, and she found herself grinning back. Good heavens, she didn't feel in the least embarrassed. They were discussing her husband leaving her for another man, and it was funny, not terrible. She could make a joke of it, rather than feeling like the most stupid, deluded person on the planet.

'And I bet your new dog hasn't tried to dig up the remains of your other one!'

'Okay, okay!' He held up a hand. 'You win. Though my daughter did threaten to put a picture of the cremated pizza I made her on Instagram.'

'You've got two daughters, haven't you?'

'Yes, Sally got married five years ago, but little Harry, Harriet that is, only left last year. Just me and the cat now! Right, better get back to it.' He stood up, brushing crumbs off his knee. 'I was ready for that cup of tea, and you can't beat a homemade scone!'

'Kate made it, Kate and Mary.' Della didn't want to mislead David into thinking she could bake. She could cook a mean shepherd's pie, but she'd never been into baking really.

'Well, it was grand, whoever made it. Come on then, you grab that rake and start at the other end, and I'll finish digging over at the top end. We'll soon be done.'

Della wasn't sure she wanted to be done soon. She was quite enjoying working next to David, and she was surprised, when she glanced at her watch, to find that it was late afternoon. They'd worked in companionable silence, with just the odd comment passing between them. She felt quite sad when he straightened up and took a step back.

'Not a bad job, if I say so myself.'

'Not bad at all.' She smiled. 'Thank you, this would have taken me days.'

'Just being neighbourly.'

'Thank you,' she said again, wanting to talk but not sure what to say, now that the job was complete. 'I hope I didn't mess up your day, you didn't have anything else on?'

'Oh, I like to take each day as it comes. Not much of a plotter and planner. The best things come when you least expect them to, I always find. Don't you?'

Della, who *was* a planner, and liked to know what to expect, wasn't sure how to respond. She thought for a moment and realised that David probably had a good point. She never acted on impulse, and yet his offer of help today, though unexpected, had been rather a success. And she hadn't planned to invite Kate in for bacon butties the other day either.

'You could have a point!' she conceded.

'Well, do you fancy that ramble?' His words had a slight brusque edge as though he was embarrassed. 'I told myself when I hit sixty last year that I'd keep going, every day. But it's always better with a bit of company.'

'How can I say no?' She smiled. Della loved her dog walks and often stopped to have a brief chat with people she bumped into regularly, but a proper walk with a human companion would be wonderful. And maybe David was right, maybe the best things could happen when you weren't expecting them – when you're brave and willing to step outside your comfort zone. 'I'll be sixty soon, but although it looked like a bit of a milestone when I was fifty, now it feels important for a different reason – like it's marking the start of my new life.' She felt flustered as she realised just how much she was telling David. It was very unlike her.

'Well now –' he paused '– that sounds like a good way of

seeing it. And a bit of company can't do any harm in this new life.'

'A bit of company sounds a good way to start.' Much as she loved her new friend, Kate, David was actually her own age. It would be nice to spend some time with somebody of her own generation.

'Only if you want to, of course. I know walking isn't for everybody.'

'Are you trying to talk me out of it?' She was surprised to hear the teasing edge in her tone. Since when did she joke?

'I'd be over the moon if you want to come, I just didn't want you to feel —' he shrugged '— pressured.' His gaze met hers, and he didn't look away but just kept looking at her.

'I'd love to come.' There, she'd said it! She'd spent the afternoon alone with a man — well, in the side garden where every passer-by could see them; she'd joked about Justin, and now she was agreeing to go walking with him. Not a date, just a bit of company. 'Do you mind if Clint comes?'

'Of course not — as long as you don't tell my cat!' He pulled her gate shut behind him, then turned back, as though he couldn't help himself. 'It's nice to see you back out in the garden.'

'It's nice to be back out,' Della said, smiling as she watched him walk down the street. He side-stepped as a younger man marched past, a determined look on his face and a bunch of roses dangling carelessly by his side. David glanced over his shoulder and waved one hand briefly over his head, then turned back before she could wave goodbye.

The younger man drew level with her, and nodded briefly, not breaking stride and she realised it was the guy who had moved into the house on the corner recently. Jack, the chef.

She was glad she was older now, that she wasn't so caught

up in life that she didn't have time to slow down and notice things. People.

Why had she never spoken to David before though? He must have walked past because he'd noticed her in the garden. He'd noticed when she *wasn't* there.

She guessed she had been in a little 'married couple' cocoon for a long time (Justin had liked it to be just the two of them), and then she'd been in a self-imposed prison of embarrassment – though she was beginning to think she had nothing to be embarrassed about at all.

Chapter Fourteen

KATE

Pork crackling

'Oh, it's you.' Kate stared at the man standing on the doorstep, the last person she'd expected to knock on her door. 'Sorry, that sounds rude. I didn't mean...' She forgot what it was she didn't mean, as he abruptly swung a bunch of flowers up in front of her face.

Jack.

She had, of course, googled him after Charles, Mary and Della had all confirmed that the guy she'd narrowly missed flattening was something of a minor celebrity. It had been bad enough realising she'd been giving food advice to a chef, but worse to discover just how well-known he was (though obviously not to her).

It wasn't difficult: she had typed in the name of the town they lived in and then the words 'local chef', hit enter and there he was. He looked so young and carefree. Happy.

In the photograph, he was leaning against the timbered frame of what looked to be a picture-postcard-perfect country cottage, one hand in the pocket of faded jeans, the other cradling a hen. He was slim, with a fashionably well-worn T-shirt hanging slightly loose, his mid-brown tousled hair framing his face, his smile broad, his chin not quite clean-shaven.

Wholesome country boy, but with the kind of sex appeal that made something at the base of her stomach tighten. A physical reaction that caught her by surprise, that made her hate herself – and him – because nobody should make her feel like that. Him especially.

There was something about the way he seemed to be looking directly at her. He had this magnetic quality. The dishy chef. Pfft.

She'd not known what to make of him before. She didn't know whether she liked him or not, but the more she'd found out about him the more churned up inside he'd made her.

He might have made friends in the farm shop, but was that all show? Play acting?

She hadn't been able to help herself – she'd carried on staring at the image. And it was then that she'd felt a distinct twinge, no, a surge of jealousy, build up inside her. Anger replaced the superficial attraction – because that's all it was, superficial. She was looking at a bloody photograph (and an old one at that), for God's sake.

This man had everything, everything that Eddie wanted. The future that he would have chased. The future he had been denied.

Now, a slightly older version of the media image was staring at her – minus the happy-go-lucky smile. This was the third time she'd seen him up close, and it was like she saw a different version every time. He might not be wearing the bad-tempered scowl he had on the first occasion, but he wasn't looking exactly happy, or friendly. Which was a bit rich, considering he was living the dream. Maybe he was actually one of those swearing chefs, and the online version was pure media image.

Except that even this version of Jack had a casual attractiveness about him. He was older, slightly weary, but if anything it made him more real. Even more bloody sexy.

He probably looked good whatever mood he was in.

Her fingers were itching to slam the door in his face. She'd been ready to overlook her first encounter with him, but she now knew she'd feel better if she never saw him again.

The easiest thing would be to hate him, for who he was, what he had.

She'd not been able to shake him out of her head after hearing Charles talk about him. She'd obsessively searched for information because she'd felt almost tricked by him. Unfair on him, but it was how she felt. And she'd spent far too much time staring at his photograph, thinking about how he'd looked at her in the shop, because it was almost like they had a connection. But the unsettling flutter in her stomach, the way his gaze locked with hers, was – well, it was wrong, so wrong. She didn't want a connection with him.

Only Eddie had shared looks like that with her.

Only Eddie was supposed to stir her up and send a shiver down her spine.

This wasn't fair. She knew life often wasn't, but having him here, standing in front of her, was making her angry at him, at herself, and she'd promised herself that she was going to try and move her life forward.

He waggled the flowers more obviously in front of her face, and although she would have liked to rescue them before he shook all the petals off, she folded her arms. If this was an invitation to take them, she wasn't sure she wanted to.

She didn't want to get any closer to him. She didn't want to even talk to him. Because it was wrong.

'Sorry about the other day. Well, both times we've met,' he said, and her arms, her whole body, loosened slightly. She couldn't help herself. It was an apology, a slightly grudging one, but an apology. She always tried to be open to people saying sorry (you really had to be if you worked with kids), because it could be hard for them. It was a reaction she had no control over – a forgivingness that she hated herself for granting so easily. 'Sorry about being rude in the shop, but mainly sorry for letting you nearly run me over.'

'Letting me?' Her arms tightened around her body again. It was easier to be defensive. 'You were in the middle of the road!'

'Well, by the side actually.'

'My side, when I came round the corner.'

'Rather fast.'

'It was not fast,' she retorted, warmth flooding her face. She really should have gone with her first thought and slammed the door on the stupid man and his stupid flowers. 'What is the matter with you? You come round to –' she glanced at the flowers '– apologise, then say it was my fault!'

'And what's wrong with you? Why are you so angry at me? What did I ever do to you?'

'You tried to dent my car with your, your body!' she stuttered, feeling even warmer. 'I'm not angry at you! I don't even know you!' They glared at each other, and then Kate couldn't help herself. She laughed. It wasn't because it was funny, it was the absurdity of it all. She wasn't being truthful though, because she *was* angry at him. Not for jumping in front of her car, but for being who he was. A hot man who didn't appreciate just how lucky he was.

The look of shock on his face made her laugh fade. It wasn't funny. He wasn't funny.

Then he raised one eyebrow, and the opposite corner of his mouth, and he had that kind of beguiling look that meant if she hit out, she'd feel like she was attacking a sweet puppy.

And he slowly raised the flowers again.

They were roses. Faded, old-fashioned roses that rather fitted his online image. Even if they were the only thing that did. 'I am sorry −' his tone was softer now, and he held up a hand to stop her interrupting '− for giving you a shock, and trying to dent your car, and being a jerk. And −' he paused '− still being a jerk. I know these are pretty crap, but it was the best I could do at short notice, and I reckoned if I left it any longer the moment would be gone.'

He looked about as contrite as a fifteen-year-old who had been caught smoking behind the cycle sheds. Which was not very contrite at all. He also looked cuter, and considerably more mature.

Kate took a deep breath. Sure, she had all this conflict in her heart, but that wasn't his fault, was it? He didn't know that right now she felt like a spitting cat and had no idea why.

He was trying to be nice, conciliatory, offering an olive branch.

'I take it you're not going to say, "and I promise not to do it again"?' She gave him the smallest of smiles. *Smile*, they always said, *it shows in your voice, it makes you feel better however bad you think things are.*

'Nope.' He shook his head, his blue-grey eyes looking directly into hers.

'Thank you.' The words came out shakily. His gaze was unnerving, but Kate couldn't look away as she reached out and clumsily took the flowers. Her fingertips brushed against his hand, and the warmth of his skin caught her by surprise. She snatched her hand away.

She was suddenly conscious of what a mess she looked. Not that she had particularly wanted to look nice for him; she just liked to be presentable. It made her feel more in control, instead of on the back foot like she did now. Unsettled. A bit of eyeliner and a smear of lip gloss, and she could face the world more confidently. They were armour, not battledress. Being smart made her feel businesslike, and she really could do with that right now.

After her chat with Della last night about recipes, Mary, and growing their own fresh ingredients, Kate had been feeling inspired. So inspired that this morning, after a quick shower, she'd left her hair pinned loosely up, not bothered to put any make-up on, and instead had grabbed hold of the new recipe book Mary had given her, and the old one that had belonged to her gran, and her laptop.

She was going to make a start with her own recipe book. She was going to find the trifle recipe. And then she was going to pop down and chat to Charles about his wife.

Much as she wanted to have the 'Mary' section in her book crammed full of healthy recipes, she knew that wasn't the right thing. She wanted to find out what Mary's favourites were — because if she'd learned anything over the last few days, it was that food could make people happy, and the *right* food could make the whole day feel better. She needed to get this right. She wanted Mary to feel loved, wanted, needed. She wanted to cocoon her in a foodie hug.

She'd just spotted the trifle recipe and was copying it out when Jack had knocked on her front door.

He'd caught her on the back foot. She wouldn't have reacted to him like this if he hadn't, she wouldn't be feeling all stirred up and, well… She searched for the word – a word she didn't want to apply to herself – vulnerable.

He'd stirred up her anger at the injustice of the world, the pangs of loneliness. That was why she'd reacted as she had to that potent mix of good looks and confidence. He'd caught her unawares.

It wasn't his fault.

She'd switched from thinking he might not be too bad after all, to wanting to hate him.

'Sorry about advising you on food. You're a chef, aren't you?' Trying to make conversation, she filled the silence with the first thought that came into her head. He'd made a nice gesture and she needed to show she appreciated it. Then they could both move on.

'Nope. A photographer.' He lifted a camera that she hadn't noticed hanging on a strap over his shoulder.

She frowned, confused. 'But you are Jack Shepley?' It was the same guy she'd been reading about; she was sure it was. And Della had said the same. Everybody said it was him.

He sighed. 'That's me. I was a chef, I'm not now.'

She vaguely remembered Della's comment about the papers saying he'd gone into hiding, and the one very brief article she'd read about how he had walked away from his restaurant, which was now empty.

'Oh.' For a moment she hesitated, but what harm would one little question do? She might not have known Charles long, but even though he might get muddled at times, he was remarkably persistent – and stubborn. He'd dropped by a short time ago, on his way back from buying his daily newspaper, telling her to make sure she made the mint sauce with white wine vinegar, and that she had to ask Jack for his pork crackling recipe. He said it had been one of Mary's favourites – so how could she not ask? She was supposed to be putting together some of Mary's favourite things. And here by coincidence was Jack on her doorstep.

'You couldn't tell me how to make pork crackling, could you?' There was a rush of heat to her cheeks. One minute she was yelling at the guy, the next she was asking him for help. It was ridiculous; she shouldn't have asked, she could look it up on the internet. Charles would never know. 'It's not for me, it's for this elderly guy, Charles, who lives up the road, and his wi—'

'Nope.' The flat word cut across her explanation, and the shutters came down over his features, catching her by surprise.

'Sorry?'

'I don't cook any longer.'

'You're a chef!'

'No, I'm not.' His lips had tightened. He hadn't folded his arms, but it didn't take an expert on body language to recognise his rigid stance as a no-entry sign.

She bit back the 'you are' before they entered pantomime territory.

Then, suddenly, he laughed. 'Oh my God, don't tell me you're little Kate?'

It was her turn to scowl. What did he mean, 'little'? And how did he know her name?

'I just got told off by some old guy for packing up the restaurant, and—'

Kate bristled and jumped in before he could say another word. 'You leave Charles alone, he's just a confused old man!' How dare he attack lovely Charles.

'Confused? He might be old, but there's nothing wrong with him at all. I hope I'm that on the ball if I get to his age.

And according to him I'm the devil, but you –' he paused '– lamb and mint sauce Kate, are a saint.'

'Huh, I don't know about me being angry. You're, you're –' she was stuck for polite words '– not nice at all.'

'You'd find it hard being nice if everybody you spoke to had a go at you!' he snapped, the angry tone making Kate draw back. 'What is wrong with people these days, sticking their nose into everybody else's lives? If a teacher gave up teaching and ran off to sit in a cave doing yoga, nobody would start asking why, would they?'

Kate's cheeks were really burning now. He couldn't know, he could not know she'd been a teacher, that she had just left. That she was not, definitely not, going to live in a cave and do yoga. She wasn't bendy enough for a start. Or chilled enough to breathe slowly and make funny noises. It might come in handy right now though, before she gave in to the urge to slap him round the face with his bloody flowers – and to hell with their poor delicate petals. There was a long silence, while she tried to get herself together enough to speak.

'Maybe if that teacher had had the perfect life, was living a dream, and then they just threw it away because they couldn't be bothered, then maybe they'd be glad if somebody asked why they were trying to tie their ankles round their bloody neck!' she spat out.

Jack stared back at her; his jaw dropped.

What on earth was she doing? Why had she said that? Any of it, especially the bit about ankles.

He had hit a nerve though, and she was so wound up it had just all come out – the feelings, if not the right words. She stared at the man standing in front of her, and the pain sparked her nerves – sharp, immediate.

Eddie would have killed to have the opportunities Jack had.

To have his own restaurant, cook his own food. Cuddle his own bloody egg-laying hen outside a dream cottage in the country with a big kitchen garden.

Eddie had been so close. If he'd still been alive, he would have been a chef now. He'd been about to take the plunge.

She suddenly realised that her eyes had brimmed over, and she brushed away the dampness with the back of her hand. She was not going to cry, and definitely not in front of this jerk (he'd called himself one, so she was fine doing the same). How could any part of her even *think* he was attractive?

'You're right, I am bloody angry with you, for having it all and not giving a fuck.' Her anger was seeping away though, and even as the bitter words came out, she wanted to take them back. She couldn't stay angry for long. Ranting and raving never helped anybody, it just fed negative feelings. It was exhausting. 'Eddie envied you,' she said quietly. 'He wanted to change career, cook, and he can't.'

'That's not my problem. If he wants it enough, let him work for it.' His tone was clipped now.

'He can't.' She blinked the fresh tears back. 'He's dead.' Oh God, why had she locked horns with him, why couldn't she have just taken the flowers and shut the door? Why even raise his being a chef? It didn't matter. Except that she had promised Charles she'd get the recipe and she liked to keep her word.

She was an idiot; she could have just googled. Or asked Della to talk to him.

There was a long pause, and he just stared at her.

'I'm sorry.' When he finally spoke his voice was soft, and the gentle tone made her feel far shakier than his anger had. 'I really am. Are you okay?'

She nodded, wiping away the tears with the heel of her hand. Relieved that he hadn't moved closer.

'Life can be shit,' he said softly, his gaze unwavering, 'I do know that, but I just want to be left alone. I've got stuff in my life that needs sorting and I want to do it my own way.'

They stared at each other. She got that. She'd wanted to be left alone. She didn't want people interfering, even if they meant well.

'You don't always get the ending you planned. I didn't. But I do know that I have the power to find a new one. That's what I'm doing.' His tone was flat, unemotional, but his gaze was so searching it stopped every thought in her head.

'I'm sorry too,' she finally squeaked out. She cleared her throat. He was trying to be nice; he deserved some kind of explanation. 'I shouldn't, I mean, oh, fuck it. You're right, I'm angry, angry at you and lots of things, but it's not your fault. You're just in the wrong place at the wrong time, with some crazy woman. I miss my husband, he was awesome, and it just seems so unfair that you basically were living his dream, and you don't care.' The fight drained out of her, and she finished on a whisper, the hurt welling up in her chest.

'I do care. I did really care, believe me. But like I say, sometimes you have to rewrite the ending, and I want people to leave me alone and let me do it.' His tone was measured, calm, but had an edge of finality that said the conversation was over. He didn't want to talk about it.

Kate nodded, not trusting herself to speak until the trembling that had replaced the anger stopped.

He was right. She was in the wrong. Wasn't that what she was trying to do herself? Kickstart her life again, find a new path to follow?

He half-smiled, took a step back, then hesitated at the bottom of the path. 'Give me your number and I'll send you a recipe for crackling, Kate.'

'Thank you, I appreciate it. I need all the help I can get,' she said softly, then recited her number. He obviously thought messaging was safer; he wouldn't risk ever knocking on her door again, and who could blame him.

'I doubt it. You'll manage fine, you're stronger than you think.'

'I'm sorry I…'

'It's fine.' He didn't look back, but his words carried.

Kate closed the door gently and felt like all the fight had been taken out of her. She wasn't strong at all. She was exhausted.

Poor Jack, why the hell had she taken it out on him? The cookery dream had been Eddie's, not hers, but she was taking it personally. Hitting out at a stranger who'd had what he couldn't.

She walked through to the kitchen, sat down and looked at the recipe books. Deep down inside, she knew what the problem was. She felt guilty that she was here and Eddie wasn't. Guilty that he'd gone out that night because of her.

Guilty that she'd looked at another man and felt something inside her react to him in a way she'd only ever reacted to Eddie.

But yelling at strangers wasn't going to alter anything.

Her phone pinged.

Charles's Crispy Crackling

- *Preheat oven to max. Ask the butcher for a nice skin – slice into 1cm strips. Lay fat-side down on a baking tray, add a few scraps of fat in the tray. Weigh down with a second tray and cook for 10 minutes. Remove top tray and cook uncovered*

for another 12-15 minutes. Keep an eye on it as it can crisp quicker than you expect (i.e. burn to a frazzle!)
- *Allow to slightly cool, place on serving platter, sprinkle with some flavoured salt (any herbs/spices you like).*

Enjoy. J

She couldn't help the half-smile; the flash of humour was unexpected. But so was Jack's comment about Charles.

Poor Charles. Except Jack hadn't thought he was muddled at all; he thought he was on the ball.

Was he really as forgetful and confused as he wanted her and Mary to think?

Chapter Fifteen

DELLA

Paella

'Nice flowers!' Della was drawn to the pretty roses on the kitchen windowsill. For some reason they seemed to suit Kate, even though most things about her and her home were quite modern. Maybe it was because of their delicate, almost fragile, edge, and the fact that roses were tough. Roses coped with whatever you threw at them.

Kate rolled her eyes. 'That chef guy brought them.'

It was Della's turn to raise an eyebrow.

'You know, the one that moved in at the bottom of the road? That you were all talking about when we had our scones?'

'Jack? Oh, I saw him walking down the road with some flowers, I didn't realise he was on his way to yours. How lovely, and such a handsome man. I didn't know you were friends; you kept that quiet. If I was a few years younger he'd tempt me as well!'

'Don't start!' Kate said in a firm voice. She had, Della

thought, probably been a great teacher. Nice, but firm. 'He doesn't tempt me. And we aren't friends.'

Della tried not to smile. Kate seemed quite flustered. But she hadn't been joking; if she'd been Kate's age, she'd have been very pleased to find Jack on her doorstep with a bunch of flowers. In real life he was even more swoon-worthy than he'd appeared in the newspaper reports. There was something very masculine about him – even when (well, probably even *more* when) he was being all mean and moody. He was positively smouldering.

How nice would it be if the two of them could get together? Not that she wanted to matchmake or interfere, and she did appreciate that Kate's heart had been broken. But a mild flirtation with a handsome guy like Jack could do her good.

'Don't look like that! The flowers were an apology. I nearly ran him over the other day.'

'And it's him that's apologising?' Della chuckled. 'That sounds interesting.'

'Because he was messing around in the road, right on the corner. He scared me to death!'

'Did you give him detention?'

'Della!' Kate topped up their glasses with wine. 'I didn't know who he was then, or I might have done. You were right though – he says he's not a chef, he's into photography now.'

'Really? Well, that is quite strange. I mean, it was in the local newspaper that he'd closed the restaurant down and nobody knew where he was, but he had rave reviews when he opened that restaurant, there were even articles by fancy food critics in the Sunday supplements. He was quite the superstar. People loved reading about his success because it was only a few miles away – like I said the other day, we could claim him as our own! I'm not sure now whether it all happened before you moved here, or after. I lose track of the years these days.'

'Hmm, I don't remember hearing anything when we moved here, and I'm sure Eddie would have known him, but I looked him up online after you mentioned him.'

Della raised an eyebrow.

'Just to check it was the same person!' Kate added swiftly, but it didn't escape Della's notice that she'd coloured up again. Whatever Kate said, Jack had definitely made some impression on her. 'But he flatly refused to even admit he'd been a chef.'

'Don't you think that's a bit odd? We didn't go and eat there, but even Charles thought he was brilliant, and he's not given to exaggeration.'

Kate rolled her eyes, and Della laughed.

'Oh, come on, aren't you just a tiny bit curious? I am! The man was brilliant, everybody said so, he could have been something big, and he just totally ditched it.' She leant forward and lowered her voice, even though there was nobody else there. 'Do you think he had his heart broken?'

'If he has one.' Kate's tone was dry, which made Della grin even more.

'Oh, come on, he brought you some lovely flowers. He didn't have to do that.'

'True. And —' Kate paused and reluctantly continued '— he sent me his recipe for pork crackling.'

'Ohhh!' Della couldn't help herself; this was getting more interesting by the second. 'The great chef handed a recipe out to a total stranger, after —' she could feel her smile spread over her face '— giving her flowers.'

'I knew I shouldn't have told you!' The tinge along Kate's cheekbones had spread to a full blush.

'He's either totally off food and happy to hand out his

secrets to any Tom, Dick, or Harry…' She laughed again at the affronted look on Kate's face. 'Or he fancies you!'

'He does not fancy me!' Kate said hotly. 'He did it because Charles told him to.'

'Wow, I feel really left out now. How come he's chatted to everybody but me?'

'We didn't chat.'

Della limited herself to raised eyebrows.

'And Charles met him in the supermarket and told him to come here and give me his recipe, so he probably told him to buy the roses as well!'

'I don't think anybody tells a man like Jack what to do. You don't get where he did by letting other people take over, do you?' Della asked, wondering if there was a way of roping Jack into their Sunday lunches. Kate would no doubt object, and, given the stormy look on Jack's face when he marched past her place when David was leaving the other day, he might not be feeling particularly neighbourly. But who knew? He might be open to the suggestion. Charles was probably the right person to broach it. She was beginning to think that Charles might not be quite as muddled as he liked to lead people to believe. He'd very neatly brought Kate out of her shell. If it hadn't been for him, they wouldn't have had their recipe project to think about, she wouldn't have been digging a new vegetable patch – and she would have never started chatting to David.

And he'd very craftily directed Jack to Kate's doorstep. He was either a genius or very, very lucky. Quite the master facilitator.

She was pretty sure Jack could contribute in a lot of ways. He had to know a lot more about food that would help Mary and Charles than they did, and he could probably advise her on the best varieties of herbs and veg to plant. She'd seen pictures of the amazing kitchen garden he'd had, which flourished without pesticides or other nasties. She could even adopt some hens! No, no, no she admonished herself. What was happening to her? She was turning from dithering Della into some kind of crazy try-anything woman. Justin would be appalled.

David wouldn't be. She was fairly sure he'd actually encourage her. She tried to suppress a smile. Something about the idea of shocking her ex but pleasing David was making her feel all sparkly inside.

'What are you plotting?' Kate's tone was laced with suspicion.

'Nothing.' She felt herself blush at the direct question.

'You've done an amazing job digging that patch in your garden. You're superwoman – that would have taken me weeks!'

It was Della's turn to feel a little bit hot and bothered. 'Well, I did have a hand. You're not the only one attracting the men!'

'I'm not attracting anybody!' Kate denied. They laughed together, but Della knew that Kate was waiting for more.

'It was David, from the top of the road. Do you know him?' Kate shook her head. 'Well, I don't really. I've only said hello to him before, but he stopped to see what I was doing and we got talking.' She shrugged. 'And I told him about the veg patch and he was really lovely. He's got two grown-up daughters, but they've both left home and he was at a bit of a loose end, so he offered to help in return for some of our veg!'

'I hope you've not invited him to dinner on Sunday as well!' Kate said, laughing, then her laughter dried up as she saw the look on Della's face. 'Oh no. You're kidding? I mean, I've not got anything against him, but I haven't got a clue what I'm doing. I've never cooked a proper dinner for one, let alone half the street!'

'Well, I haven't exactly invited him,' Della said, choosing her words carefully. 'But I thought it might be nice as a thank you some time? He's on his own, and he was a great help. I couldn't have done it without him. Well, I could, but it would have taken ages and I'd have been laid up with a bad back!'

'Hmm. So what else did you promise this David?'

'Nothing! Well, I am going for a ramble with him I mean, I'd have been taking Clint out anyway,' she added quickly, 'so it's just a bit of company. I hope he doesn't expect me to climb any mountains. I've got my limitations.'

'I'm sure he won't. It sounds lovely. Go for it!' Kate's voice had lost its teasing edge, and was soft, which embarrassed Della even more. She wasn't sure why she was feeling so excited about the prospect of going for a walk with David. After all, it was just a walk, and she did that every day. She lifted her wine glass, to give herself time to think.

She took a sip of the red wine and was slightly surprised to find it was lightly chilled – just how they always served it in Spain. It stopped her short. Justin loved Spain, and they'd spent a lot of holidays there – and now it was the place he called home.

'Is it okay?' Kate was frowning.

'Yes, great! Sorry.' She paused, but her tongue seemed to have been well and truly loosened tonight. It was as though she'd been given courage, a willingness to share, to be, well – *different*. 'It just reminds me of Justin and that makes me mad because I don't want to think about him.' One minute she'd been thinking about a nice walk with David (a step in the right direction, haha) and the next, Justin was back in her head.

'I'll open another bottle, a white?'

'No, don't be daft,' she said firmly, batting Kate's hand away. 'This is lovely, it just caught me on the hop a bit. But I'm not going to let him ruin this as well!' In fact, now she thought about it, it might have evoked memories of Justin, but they *had* just caught her by surprise. She didn't feel upset, or angry with him, as she had been since he left. 'I'm just annoyed with myself, I'm not upset.' And it was true. 'But it's perfectly normal to associate things with people, isn't it? It's always going to be like that. We did have happy times.' They did, they had some wonderful times together. 'I shouldn't let the fact that it was all based on a lie sour my memories, should I? It's my life, my past. And —' she glanced up at Kate, '— it's what happens to you, what you do, that makes you who you are, isn't it?' She had to stop running away from the past, the bad bits, because she'd been with Justin for years. She was denying half of her life if she tried to wipe that time away.

'I suppose,' Kate sighed, and Della was sure that she was thinking about Eddie. 'It's funny, isn't it, what triggers things, reminds you of people, things that have happened to you?'

Della nodded. 'Chilled red wine will always remind me of Spain, which reminds me of our good times, and —' she paused, tracing a line in the condensation on her glass '— he actually invited me over there for a week with him and Mick.'

'You're kidding? Wow, that must have been...'

'Mmm, it was a bit odd.' She took another gulp of wine, trying to find the right words. She knew Kate would understand, that she wouldn't judge. 'I suppose I always knew he wasn't exactly one of the lads; it was one of the things I liked about him. He was gentle and kind and good fun, and I liked the friendship and companionship, but he was always, well, tentative about sex. It didn't bother me at first, I kind of thought that as time went on things would warm up a bit, but honestly the nearest I got to hot sex and abandon was reading a romance in a steamy bath!'

Kate grinned, and Della felt herself smiling back. The girl was young enough to be her daughter, and she would never have dreamt she would find herself chatting so openly to somebody who wasn't of her own generation. But maybe it was *because* of the age gap that it felt easy to talk to her. Young people were so much more used to talking openly, to judging less. Sometimes she wondered how life would have been if she'd had a daughter. But it was a waste of time thinking about things that she couldn't change.

'He stayed in touch after he left and told me he was getting married so that I wouldn't hear it from somebody else. He was very loyal, a bit like Skip. He, they, seem very happy so he invited me over to stay. Justin doesn't like bad feelings; he wants everybody to think the best of him.' She sighed. 'Sometimes he doesn't make it easy. He didn't want to hurt me, I am sure of that, but I felt so stupid.'

'You're not stupid at all, Della.'

'I know, but I do miss the hugs and having somebody there. For a long time, I really hung on to the thought that he'd come back, and we could just carry on as we were. But that wouldn't be healthy, would it?'

'You don't still want it, do you?' Kate asked softly.

Della shook her head. 'You know what? I don't now! It was strange going over to Spain and seeing them, but it was good in a way, to see them together in his new life, you know? I always knew he wanted to move over there, but I like it here. I like the seasons. I know people these days go all over the place travelling and living, but when I was a teenager the idea of abroad was a big adventure. That's how I always saw it, I suppose, just an adventure.' Her voice drifted off. She'd never thought about just how different they were. How badly suited really. 'It did help, and Mick cooks a mean paella! He sent me the recipe, but I've never made it. It's not the same cooking and eating it on your own, is it? Oh my God, I miss that paella and all the tapas. Does that sound terrible? I probably should hate them now, and going over there to see Justin should have soured the place for me, but…'

'It's not the same cooking stuff just for one.' Kate stared into her wine glass. 'It hardly seems worth it.' Then she looked up, her gaze meeting Della's. 'But there's two of us now! Why don't we make one? We could do this again next Thursday, but eat as well as drink? Oh my God, did I just suggest we cook paella? I haven't got a clue how to do that! I blame you, and this Spanish wine!'

'It's a brilliant idea! Really? You'd do that for me?'

'We,' Kate said firmly, topping up the wine glasses. '*I* won't do it, *we* will! We'll make one. Together.'

'You know what? It's a really brilliant idea. Hang on, let me find the recipe. He messaged it to me.' She flicked through her messages from Justin, talking as she did. 'We need to put it in your book, it needs stuff in it that we like now, not just memories. New, good stuff.' She paused, realising what she'd said. 'Oh God, sorry, I didn't mean to take over your book, it's yours for your stuff.'

'It's fine.' Kate laughed. 'I don't think it is mine, I think Mary gave it to me for all of us. She was telling me all about Charles's favourites, and what her son likes. And you're right,' she said firmly, as she picked up the book Mary had given her and traced her finger over the picture on the front. 'It's not about memory food, it's about the future as well as the past. It's Eddie, and Gran, and Mary, and well … us.' Her clear gaze met Della's. 'I think it's about healing. Mary told me that she misses baking, because she could lose herself in it and forget her problems.' She tapped the cover. 'Spain needs to go in here!'

Della grinned and held up her phone. 'Tada, one recipe for black rice – arroz negro.'

'Hang on, let me grab a pen, it's going in!'

Arroz Negro (Black Paella), serves 4 – Della's Spain!

She paused, then added – perfect with chilled red wine because that was what had reminded Della of it, wasn't it?

6-8 large prawns (shells on)
1 large squid tube – sliced into rings, or cut into pieces
2 tbsp olive oil
1 onion – finely diced
1 red pepper – diced
2 cloves garlic – finely chopped or grated
2 tbsp tomato paste
2 tsp smoked paprika
1 tsp ground cumin
Saffron threads (optional)
300g paella rice
240ml dry white wine
1l seafood stock
2 sachets of squid ink
Lemon wedges to serve

- *Heat up the olive oil in a paella pan (or large frying pan), sauté the squid for 30 seconds then set aside.*
- *Sauté the onion and pepper until soft, then add the garlic and spices. Heat through for another minute or two. Stir in the*

tomato paste. Add the rice and stir until coated. Add the wine and simmer until it has almost evaporated.

- Add the stock and squid ink, stir. Season, bring to the boil and then turn the heat down to a simmer. Leave (do not stir!) for 15 minutes until the rice is almost cooked and the liquid reduced.

- Put the squid back in, lay the prawns on top (in a circle for maximum appeal!) and leave to cook for 4-5 minutes. Remove from the heat and allow to settle before serving with lemon wedges. Enjoy!

'That's next Thursday evening sorted then!' Kate put the pen down, smiling.

'I'll get Justin on Zoom if we get stuck and he can talk us through it!' Della could hardly believe she'd just said those words. She'd avoided communicating with Justin as much as possible (apart from the trip to Spain, which was supposed to give her closure, but hadn't) because it wound her up, but right now she didn't care. It might be the wine giving her a false confidence, but she didn't think it was (well, she hoped not). She was moving on. She wasn't sure they could be friends, but they'd always be there for each other. They'd shared too much to just write it all off.

Della glanced down at her watch. 'Oh wow, I didn't realise it was so late. We haven't even started to think about what we should cook for Mary!' They'd arranged to get together so that they could come up with some ideas to help Mary, and time had sped by. Della couldn't remember the last time an evening had passed by so quickly. 'I feel so guilty! We've not made any progress.'

Kate smiled. 'You know what? I think we have. It's been great.'

Della smiled back. Kate was right, they had made progress – well, she had. In fact, she'd really surprised herself, telling Kate so much. 'Is that your gran's book?'

Kate nodded, picked it up from the table and handed it over to Della. 'I found the trifle recipe, but then got a bit distracted trying to work out how to cook a leg of lamb with all the veg. It's all the timings – I'm going to need a spreadsheet to keep track of everything. I would duck out, but Mary seemed quite excited when I saw her on the way to draw her pension out of the bank this morning. She was talking about goose fat and rosemary. You've not got any of that in your garden, have you?'

'Rosemary I have plenty of, but goose fat is a no! Oh wow, look, there's cottage pie. I just love cottage pie! I've not had it for years. And lasagne. We're doing Spanish paella, we need to do Italian food as well. We could have a themed evening! My nana wouldn't have had a clue how to make lasagne.'

Kate frowned. 'It wasn't the type of thing mine normally made. Most of the food she cooked was pretty traditional. I don't know what got her into lasagne.'

'Debbie.' Della tapped the page. 'She cooked it for Debbie. *Debbie's treat when she's home for the hols from uni.* I didn't know you had a sister!'

'I don't.' Kate's voice had an edge that made Della look up from the recipe book.

'There's a little menu here with the recipes. Lasagne and garlic bread, and Millionaire's Shortbread.' Her voice tailed off at the look on Kate's face.

'Maybe that's what gave her the idea.' Kate's tone was flat.

If Debbie wasn't her sister, who was she? 'What idea?'

'To be a millionaire. All she was ever interested in was work and making money.'

'Who, Kate? If she's not your sister…'

Kate topped up their glasses with a hand that shook. The wine splashed, drops landing on Della's hand, but she hardly noticed. 'She's my mum. Debbie is my mother.'

Della waited. Kate was such a private person, the type that kept things to herself, tried to solve her problems on her own. But Della knew that sometimes saying things out loud to another person – even a dog – could make all the difference.

'We're not close. I've not seen her for years. She moved to the States as soon as I went to uni and I didn't need looking after. Not that she did much of that. What kind of mother does that, leaves the country? That was a bit extreme even for her!'

Della blinked. Kate's voice had a hard edge to it that she hadn't heard before.

'What do they say about being able to pick your friends, but not your family? I had my grandparents though.' The soft smile on her face reached her eyes. There was love there even if there was sadness as well. 'And they were the best, both of them,' she added firmly. 'I'd have picked them any time. They were always there for me, and she wasn't.'

'Oh, Kate.' Della reached out and put her hand over Kate's. 'Children need their mothers. Mine is hard work at times, but I can't imagine not having her. Maybe she worried about not being able to provide for you? It's not always easy to get the balance right. I think children can be a worry sometimes. They're a huge responsibility, aren't they?'

'Do you regret not having children, Della?'

Della smiled. 'It wasn't a choice for me, but –' she sighed '– sometimes I do wonder what it would have been like to have a daughter, like you. A friend.'

'It doesn't always work out though, does it? Mum was never a friend to me. She kind of held me at arm's length.'

'Lots of mothers and daughters aren't really friends, just like brothers and sisters aren't. I suppose the answer to your question is: no, I don't regret it. Even if I'd married somebody else, I don't know if I would have wanted a family. My main regret is that I didn't come out of my shell earlier and make more friends. But it wouldn't have been me – I was very shy when I was younger, and it's only recently that I've felt more comfortable in my skin and happy to talk to people. Would you and Eddie have had children?'

'Oh no,' Kate said vehemently, surprising Della with the force of her words. She was surprised; she was sure Kate would make a lovely mother. 'Eddie would have liked to have kids, but it didn't happen, and to be honest I don't think it would have been a good thing.'

'Oh?'

'I might have made a terrible mum!'

'Like your own mother?' Della said softly. 'I'm sure you wouldn't, Kate. But sometimes things aren't black and white, are they? Like me and Justin, sometimes there's more going on than you realise, and things aren't what they seem. She always made sure you were safe and looked after, even if she wasn't doing it herself, didn't she?'

Kate nodded reluctantly. 'I suppose so. Anyway…' Her voice now held a decisive note that shouted out loud and clear that she wasn't going to say any more, and Della respected that. 'I think we need a plan of action for Mary, don't we? She's coming round on Saturday to help me with a shopping list and plan for Sunday so I can try and find out what she likes.'

'And if either of us sees Charles, we can see if he can help out with ideas? He might seem a bit muddled at times, but he can remember the important things about Mary. He's so devoted, isn't he?'

Kate nodded. 'I'm beginning to wonder if some of his forgetfulness is put on, you know, exaggerated. Jack was saying how on the ball he is, and he's right. I mean, at his age he does forget, but so do I!'

'You wait until you get to my age, Kate. Honestly, I'm already starting to do that thing when you go into a room, then can't remember why! You are right though.' She'd not really thought about it, just accepted Charles's ways, and Mary's concerns about the onset of dementia, but most of the time he was as 'with it' as a man half his age. 'I was thinking the same. I wonder why he'd do that though?'

Kate frowned. 'I wonder if he understands full well about Mary's illness, but he's putting a brave face on it. He doesn't want her to worry about him, and I think he's just doing his best to make her life as good as it can be.'

'Which is why he came to yours?'

'I do wonder if pretending he thought it was still the tearoom was just a way of making sure I wouldn't turn him away. I mean, if he'd just knocked on the door and said, 'You don't know me but can I bring my wife round for tea and cakes?' I wouldn't have said yes, would I?'

Della laughed. 'I suppose not.'

'He really wanted to bring her back to the place they met and dated, and he really wants her to have somebody to bake with, doesn't he?'

'She certainly misses her baking.'

'She was so happy when we were making the scones. It seemed to give her energy.'

'So he might not be quite the daft old codger he wants us to think he is.'

'He might –' Kate's voice was soft, and Della thought again that she must have been an amazing teacher '– still be her knight in shining armour. I think he just wants her to be happy.'

'And I think Mary just wants Charles to have somebody there for him. When we were all sitting round the table, she looked so pleased that he was in his element and entertaining us all.'

'And I got the impression she was quite keen for us to get together again,' Kate said thoughtfully. 'I don't want her to think we're interfering, or feeling sorry for her, but I don't think she will. I think she worries about how he'll cope when she goes. She asked me if we could bake together because it took her mind off things, but I wonder if part of it is because we'll all get together and get to know Charles.'

Della nodded. 'They care about each other so much, don't they?'

'They do, and I really do want to help them if I can. But I'm not sure about the best recipes health wise. I've googled, but it's mainly about just healthy and fresh, and eating calorie-rich food little and often.' Kate sighed. 'I'm not sure where to find the best things. At the moment I just want to cook her favourite things, which will make her feel good and hopefully give her an appetite.'

'I know you're not going to like this, but you do know who we need to ask, don't you?'

Kate raised an eyebrow.

'Jack.' Della gave it a moment to sink in. 'You might not be keen on the guy, Kate. But you have to admit he knows loads more about food and nutrition than we do.' She paused. 'And it is about Mary, not how we feel.'

'Definitely.' Kate nodded, then repeated the word as though to persuade herself. 'I'll leave that to you then!'

Bugger, that wasn't quite what she'd had in mind. But she

was quite happy to make the first approach, and then hopefully back off if he agreed. Kate was the chef, she was the gardener. They both needed his help.

It was time to go though. 'I'd better get off. Clint will be crossing his legs!'

Kate smiled. 'It's been lovely.'

'It has.' She nodded as she put the recipe book down and picked up her jacket. 'Thank you for listening, Kate. It was good to talk about Justin to somebody. And if you ever want to talk about, you know, anything, I'm a good listener.'

'Thanks. Enjoy your walk with David!'

'Oh my God, don't remind me. If he has me climbing over stiles and wading through streams, I am so going to regret this! I'm really not as young as I used to be.'

'He won't have you climbing.' Kate laughed. 'Though I want photo evidence if he does! I'm sure you'll have a great time.'

Della joined in the laughter. Despite her fears about what the ramble was going to involve, she was looking forward to it. And she was pretty sure that even if she didn't, talking to him had already done her good. He'd made her feel more positive. A man had shown an interest in her, a man who might never mean more to her on a personal level (as in the hot sex she'd definitely missed out on in life) but had shown her that she could move on. That there was life beyond Justin. That she didn't need to feel stupid or naïve.

'That lasagne did look tasty. I do like the idea of an Italian evening.' What had come over her? David had made her more than brave, he'd made her reckless. She was pushing her luck now. Talking to Jack and sharing a dish her mother loved was probably several steps too far for Kate right now.

'It was tasty,' Kate said softly. 'Everything Gran made was good. She was like Eddie, she cooked to make people happy.'

'With love,' Della said, squeezing her hand as she kissed her on the cheek.

'With love,' Kate echoed. 'I didn't realise how much until I found her book. I've been so busy ploughing through my own life, I never appreciated her like I should have. I'm as bad as Mum.'

'Nobody is bad,' Della said. 'They just sometimes make bad decisions.' Like she had, like Justin had. 'We all have our reasons —' she paused, smiling at Kate '— but we don't always share them!'

'True.' And then Kate did something Della hadn't expected. She hugged her. 'Thanks, Della.' Her voice was muffled against her shoulder.

'Thank *you*.' Della hugged her back, and the smile that it gave her stayed all the way home.

Chapter Sixteen

DAVID

Runner beans

'David!'

David had wondered if he was doing the right thing when he'd decided to go and knock on Della's door.

Would it seem pushy going round again so soon after they'd spent a pleasant afternoon digging over her new veg patch together. After all he was seeing her tomorrow for a walk, so she might think that was soon enough.

He felt awkward. The problem was he really liked Della, and she'd stuck in his head. He couldn't think for the life of him why anybody would marry her then leave her – she was so nice and easy to talk to. He'd felt they gelled, were comfortable from the off. It was a feeling he wasn't used to and the fear of making the wrong impression was making him question his every move.

When Harriet had come over yesterday evening, she'd asked him why he'd cleaned his walking boots.

'I regularly clean them, you cheeky madam!'

'Not that clean,' she'd retorted, then her eyes had narrowed. 'Have you met somebody?' Surprise, or embarrassment, must have shown on his face, because her hand had flown to her mouth, then she'd sniggered. 'Oh my God, you have!'

'If you mean, am I going walking with somebody instead of on my lonesome, then the answer is yes.' He half held his breath, waiting for the fallout. Harry hadn't been happy about her parents' split, so she definitely wasn't going to be happy if she thought there might be another woman on the horizon.

'Good. Can I borrow your bike?'

'My bike?' That request had taken him by surprise, even as much as the 'good'. 'What do you want with my bike?'

'To ride it.' she said tartly.

'Last time you got on a bike, young lady, I was holding the back of it.'

'Well, maybe I've got somebody else to do that and won't be on my lonesome!'

There was a twinkle in her eye, and a cheekiness that hadn't been there for a while. It made him feel lighter. Maybe there was something in the air for all of them, positive new beginnings.

'Enjoy your ramble, Dad.' She'd kissed him on the cheek as she said it – emphasising the word 'ramble' which for some reason she always found funny.

He'd been glad she hadn't asked anything about Della. For once he was glad of a young person's lack of interest, but even if she didn't want to know anything about Della, he did. He wanted to know all kinds of things, and they'd barely started.

He couldn't remember feeling so keen to see somebody again. Tomorrow seemed such a long way off. It was like being an awkward teenager all over again. Except now he didn't know the dating rules. She wasn't a kid – would she think he was being weird? Would he scare her off?

He'd spent a morning agonising over it, before deciding he'd do what he always did: just get on with things. What was meant to be would be. So he'd gone down to the allotment and cadged some seedlings from a mate. He was just being neighbourly, helping her out.

Now, standing on her doorstep clutching an array of vegetables, he wondered if he was just being a stupid fool.

'Wow, you've got plants!' Della pointed at the trays full of potting compost and the first shoots of life.

'Well, I don't know whether I've done the right thing, but I've got a friend at the allotment who's got a bit of surplus, and I told him I knew just who could make use of them. Runner beans, carrots and sprouts. Not to worry if you've already got some or got different plans.'

'I haven't got any proper plans at all. They look amazing!' She paused, and they stared at each other, smiling for a moment. 'You haven't got time for a cuppa, have you?'

'Certainly have, but I can pop these in for you first if you like?'

'Really? You'd do that, now?'

'No time like the present. You just show me where and I'll get cracking, unless you want to do it in your own time. You might have your own way.'

'Not at all. Come on.' Della did better than show him, she picked up string and pegs to mark out rows, and a trowel, and between them they soon had them all planted out, with neat labels at the end of each row.

'It looks quite professional, if I say so myself.'

'It does, doesn't it?' Della brushed the soil from her hands.

'It looks great. Now all we've got to do is make sure Clint knows it is out of bounds!'

They shared a smile, as they stood shoulder to shoulder admiring their handiwork. He liked that they'd done it together. He liked the fact that she'd just said 'all *we've* got to do', rather than 'I'.

An hour later they were sitting in a sunny corner of the patio, with Clint at their feet, and a nice piece of lemon drizzle cake in their hands.

'Kate's inspired me to do a spot of baking. Is it okay?'

'Perfect.' David nodded his approval. 'This nice weather must be giving everybody some get up and go. My Harriet asked if she could borrow my bike! Never been the biking type, she hasn't.'

'Maybe there's a boy involved?' Della grinned, and he found himself grinning back.

'You could be right, you could be right. Full of the joys, she was!'

'I've not been on a bike for years.' Della gave Clint the last bite of her cake and sat back. 'I'm not that keen really, I prefer walking on my own two feet.'

'Nothing wrong with that.' He hesitated, not quite sure he should ask the question in case he got the wrong answer. 'Still up for our walk tomorrow?'

'Of course I am!' Her response and big smile sent a wave of relief through him. He'd always considered himself to be on a fairly even keel, he didn't do emotional highs and lows – but Della seemed to be having a strange effect on him. She was making him feel like he was on an emotional wave. 'I'm looking forward to it, and so is Clint. He's had a brush, so he'll look his best.'

'Champion, I even cleaned my boots in your honour!' She

laughed, and he was glad he'd made her laugh. 'Well, I'd better be off, get out of your way.'

'You're welcome to stay for another cup of tea if you like, I've not got anything I need to rush off and do. Unless you have? It's nice to have a bit of company.'

'It is nice.' He nodded. 'That sounds spot on.' So he stayed, and they sat in companionable silence, listening to the birdsong and letting the sun warm their faces. And then they planned out the vegetable plot, and talked about pruning and weeding, and he felt useful and comfortable all at the same time.

Chapter Seventeen

KATE

Lasagne

Kate poured herself a second cup of coffee and curled up in the armchair, then opened her gran's book at the trifle recipe. Her Thursday evening with Della had stirred up all kinds of emotions in her. She'd almost forgotten how to care about others, which was a shocking self-revelation, but it was true. She listened to her students' issues, encouraged them to talk, offered a shoulder to cry on, and advice, but she'd been detached since Eddie's death. It wasn't just that she'd turned inwards out of grief, more that she'd had an emotional overload with her own feelings. She couldn't cope with caring about anybody else as well. She'd been brought up to be determined, to drive onwards and not give herself time to think. She'd never been very good at self-care. But when Della talked about Justin so openly something stirred inside her. Della's pain was real, and she'd felt a pang, a sadness that had made her want to reach out and comfort her. To genuinely care.

She'd never had time to feel like that about anybody but Eddie.

And then there was the book. The recipes that Della had noticed. Her mother.

Della had been right; her mother had always made sure she was safe and looked after. But that wasn't enough, was it? She'd wanted love, hugs, approval. She'd been desperate. But it had always been as though her mum had been scared to get too close, had not known how to give what her daughter needed.

It was no wonder she had decided that having a child of her own would be a mistake. Because she could end up like her mother, unable to love a child – and no child deserved that.

The familiar lump of regret, or guilt, hardened in her chest. She should have told Eddie what she'd done. He didn't deserve the way she'd treated him.

She'd been sure she wouldn't sleep, but she had. She'd fallen into the deepest sleep she could remember, since the medically induced ones in the early days. The moment her head hit the pillow and she'd closed her eyes she must have fallen asleep, because she couldn't remember anything else. Apart from flashbacks of her grandparents, of Eddie cooking, of her mother sitting next to her helping her read. Of her gran's hugs, telling her she was loved. Eddie holding her, telling her she was amazing. Of them all writing in the small notebook.

Fleeting images that could have been dreams or memories. But they hadn't upset her, hadn't disturbed her rest.

Friday, fully refreshed, she'd felt more enthusiastic about her shopping trip into Manchester, and her meet-up with a schoolteacher friend, than she had about anything for a long time.

She'd cut herself off from her friends after Eddie's death,

pushed them away because they couldn't understand, but she hadn't realised just how much she'd isolated herself until Charles, Mary and Della had come into her life. But fond as she was of them, a day out shopping with somebody her own age had given her a spark, a feeling of enthusiasm that she couldn't remember having for a long time.

She also knew now that she'd been right to move on from her career, to give herself some time, some space to think, and a small space for the things she needed to come into her life.

Della had come. Charles had come. She didn't feel useless – without work, and a purpose – like she'd expected; she didn't feel like she was wasting her life. She felt strangely more power-ful. More in control.

She'd returned from the shops with a new determination to move on but take Eddie with her. She also came home with a new, *very* bright and colourful top (which seemed a good idea at the time but might never get worn – the jury was out on that) and enough groceries to feed a small village for a fortnight. If her Sunday lunch was a one-off and Mary and Charles didn't need her after all, then she'd be filling the freezer. And buying a second one. Eddie would have laughed at her – the girl who had only ever bought strictly what she'd gone out for. He'd been the impulse buyer, and she'd laughed at his lack of self-control.

But something in her heart told her that Sunday wouldn't be a one-off. Della had been right; Mary did want to know that somebody would be there to look out for Charles. She'd looked almost relieved when they were all sitting around the kitchen table, and he was entertaining them with his outrageous tales. If getting together for lunch would help ease Mary's worries, then Kate was more than willing to do it.

Friday had been good, but today she was looking forward to

a day at home, cooking. Who on earth could have known she'd ever be thinking that!

She stared down at the trifle recipe, then, still thinking about Eddie finding it, reading it, she started to copy it into her own book.

It was strangely calming, and therapeutic, writing out the familiar ingredients. She could almost smell the fruity jelly, see her gran's smile as she handed a cube over to Kate, a finger on her lips. Their secret. Her mum would never have approved of eating jelly cubes.

Or would she?

Was saying no her way of showing she cared, doing what she thought was right? The *easiest* way.

Halfway through the task, Kate stopped. She couldn't help herself; she flipped the pages over to the recipe that Della had found. Lasagne. She loved the pasta dish herself, but how had she never known that it was one of her mother's favourites as well? They'd never been close, however hard she had tried to please, but now she felt more than ever that the only parent she'd known was a complete stranger.

Her father, Mum had told her, had been a foreign language student. Passing through, with no intention of stopping or picking up any responsibilities. He'd created a child that he never knew about – because when her mother had finally tracked him down, she found him on social media in the arms of the girl he'd promised his heart to before he'd headed to England. She'd told Kate that much. But no more. He was not to be spoken about. He was not a part of their lives – because to bring him into theirs would destroy his.

Who had her mother been, what was she like, when she'd fallen for that guy – or at least fallen into his bed? If she'd been brave and selfless in refusing to ruin his life, why couldn't she have shown the same love to her daughter?

Had she ever been a carefree student. Had she been pleased to be home for the holidays when each university term finished – cooking lasagne and garlic bread. Had she ever loved her baby daughter.

Kate had a faint memory of hugs and kisses, of the smell of her mum's perfume, but she was never sure it wasn't false – that her memory was playing tricks, and instead she was remembering her gran. She wasn't sure which was worse – her mother never loving her and holding her tight, or the knowledge that once she had and then Kate had done something to drive her away.

Was Della right, that things were sometimes more complicated than they seemed. Her mother had been guilty, in her eyes, of many things. But maybe Kate had been guilty too – of not questioning things as she'd got older, of not finding her mother and asking her why. Why she'd found life easier to cope with, without a child. Had she not wanted Kate, or had she not known how to love her.

She stared at the recipe for garlic bread. At the side there was a heart drawn in a heavier pen, and 'love you, Mum' written in a different hand. She knew she hadn't written that as a child; it had to be her mother. A note to Gran.

Her mother had held this book, just as she was doing now. Reading the recipes, helping Gran make them. Her mum had had a *mother* to cook with, something she'd deprived Kate of. She felt the familiar knot form inside her chest. For a moment she closed her eyes, forced her clenched hands to relax, tried to push the image of her mother frowning at her out of her head. She opened her eyes, stared at the book, tried to replace the image of her mother with one of her grandmother. Gran cooking, Gran writing these recipes down.

Lasagne. And then she noticed it, in the adult hand of her mother, tucked in tiny letters in the margin as though she didn't want the words to be seen: '*Kate loves this as well*'.

For a second her vision blurred, then she angrily flipped the pages over. She'd mourned the absence of a mother–daughter relationship for too long. She'd let it wreck her life and it was time to stop. It meant nothing, nothing at all, that her mum knew she liked lasagne.

What had Della said? She missed Skip because he had been like her shadow, which was why she'd had to get Clint. Well, Kate missed Eddie's actual shadow beside hers, because it had been big, bold. She used to jump as they walked to try and make her shadow taller. She'd swung their joined hands, loving the fact that they were linked in a way she never remembered as a child.

In the early months after his death, she'd walked (when she had to go out) in the shade, as she felt even more lonely when she could see her shadow ahead, on its own.

But it was time to move out of the shade. Della was being daring. She'd talked about Justin, she'd dug a vegetable patch, she'd agreed to go for a hill ramble with David – even though she had never been out with any man other than her husband, even though she said she was the least adventurous person ever. Dithering Della, she'd called herself. But she wasn't dithering at all, she was taking action, deliberately stepping out of her comfort zone, and she looked happy.

Kate wanted to be happy again. Not just in passing, she wanted to feel the kind of happy that stays with you when everybody has gone, the kind of happy that lingers on.

She flipped through the book again. Searching for some kind of answer in the pages. Could cooking really help her.

The book fell back open again at the page Della had stopped on. That's why it was open on this page, because Della had recently bent the pages back right here. Not because it was important, not because Gran had opened it there many times, not because Eddie had. Not because this dish – lasagne – had any importance at all.

The card with Eddie's notes slipped from the pages. Seeing the familiar loop of his handwriting tugged at Kate's heart, and for a moment she just held it, then forced herself to read the words.

Lasagne was there on his list. Of course it was, he'd written down every recipe that Gran had noted as one of her favourites.

He'd written his own note at the side – a dish to unite 3 generations of broken hearts?

Three generations? What did he mean by that? Her gran hadn't been broken-hearted, she'd been loving, giving, always there for Kate. Always telling her that her mother loved her. Always telling her that sometimes it was hard to be as brave as you needed to be, that one day she'd understand.

Maybe Gran felt like piggy in the middle, trying to support her daughter and her granddaughter. Who knew.

But Eddie seemed to. Eddie, who always said that food brought people together, food didn't care about the past or the future. Food was about enjoying the moment.

'Oh Eddie,' she said softly, swallowing the lump in her throat.

Eddie and her mum had never met. Two of the people who had shaped her into the person she was had never been in the same room because they'd been the good and the bad. Opposites, with Gran in the middle. But is that the way Eddie saw it? She'd never know now.

But her mother had actually loved her, or at least cared enough once upon a time to notice that she loved lasagne. That they had something in common. They might never share the dish again, but maybe cooking it for herself would help her freeze that moment before it had all gone wrong?

Was this one of those moments in her life that she had to take notice of if she was really going to be able to move on?

She picked up her pen again slowly. Eddie had wanted to cook this for her, but he wasn't here now. Maybe she needed to do it for herself.

Lasagne.

She hesitated, looking at her gran's comment... Debbie's treat when she's home for the hols from uni.

Gran's recipe book was about people, about love, about doing things for other people. What was her own recipe book about? Why was she doing this?

If she was ever going to find a way to move on, maybe the first step was forgiving. Acknowledging why she was copying this recipe into her own book – her own life. That maybe it was okay if they were similar in some ways.

Her hand trembling slightly she wrote, ***Gran's recipe for Mum*** – before taking a steadying breath and adding – ***and I love it too*** – before copying out the rest of the ingredients.

Olive oil
> *2 streaky bacon rashers*
> *450g mince*
> *2 celery stalks - chopped*

1 clove garlic – finely chopped/minced
¼ teaspoon mixed herbs
400g can tomatoes
1 tbsp tomato puree
¼ tsp sugar
9-10 sheets of lasagne (dried)
75g gruyere cheese
75g ricotta cheese
75g/one ball of mozzarella
Parmesan – grated (a couple of generous handfuls)
Milk

- *Fry the meat in the oil until brown, add the celery and seasoning, add the tomatoes and puree – adding extra water if necessary. Simmer for 30-40 minutes.*
- *Cook lasagne sheets if necessary (most don't need pre-cooking).*
- *In a large dish add 1/3 of the mince mix, lay 1/3 of the lasagne sheets, top with 1/3 of the cheeses. Add enough milk so that you can just see it through the layer. Repeat twice more.*
- *Cook in the oven for 45 minutes at 190°C.*

She couldn't personalise the recipe Mary-style, because she'd not made it yet, but maybe she would. Maybe she'd come back and add notes once she'd had a go at cooking lasagne, because there was something really lovely about Mary's recipe book. Kate was so wrapped up in her thoughts as she copied the recipe into her own book that the ring of the doorbell made her jump.

When she opened the front door, Mary was there holding a basket.

'I'm not too early, am I? I can go to the park and come

back in half an hour.' She smiled tentatively. 'This might sound silly, but I was so excited about coming round to cook again that I had my basket packed and ready an hour ago.'

'It's not silly at all! I'm looking forward to another lesson. Come in, come in. I've just been writing some recipes down in the book you gave me, and completely lost track of the time.'

'I hope you don't mind, but I brought some sprinkles for the top of your trifle. I know it's silly, and your trifle is probably much more sophisticated than mine ever were, but Charles did like his sprinkles. Oh, I am being silly, I'm sure—'

'Of course we need sprinkles! And it's Gran's recipe not mine, it's not sophisticated at all. You can't have a trifle without sprinkles! You haven't got any of those little silver balls, have you?'

Mary smiled as she set her basket down on the table and pulled her apron out. 'The ones you're scared of breaking your teeth on. I thought you'd never ask!' She smiled. 'I've also taken another liberty. Tell me if I'm being an interfering old woman though, I don't want to take over.'

'I want you to take over! Honestly, there is no way I could do this without you, Mary.'

'I thought maybe we could be a tiny bit sophisticated, and do some of those fancy pork crackling bits that Charles enjoyed so much when we went to that posh restaurant? He said Jack had given you the recipe. Is that true?' Her eyes had opened wider in what could have been disbelief, and it made Kate laugh.

'It certainly is. They're very simple, but Charles must have liked them a lot – he told Jack to tell me how to make them.'

'Oh, isn't he a one? He did like them. He liked them so much he went down to the butchers first thing this morning and came back with this.' Mary fished into her basket and drew out a package. 'Pork skin. I asked him what on earth I was supposed to do with that, and he said give it to you. You'd know what to do with it! He also told me that Jack had told him how to make mint sauce.'

Kate took the packet. Charles really was a one. Who else could have somehow talked her into cooking a Sunday lunch and challenged the 'not-a-chef' Jack into parting with his secrets.

'The funniest part is,' said Mary, taking out the other ingredients she'd brought, 'he has never before shown any interest in cooking – only eating!'

'Wow, really?' Kate unwrapped the pork skin. And the thought came to her again - was Charles as muddled and forgetful as he seemed. Or was he doing what she and Della were trying to do – encourage Mary to eat, to enjoy food. To enjoy her time. Except Mary had said he seemed in denial; he wasn't acknowledging her illness. It could be true, or, Kate was beginning to think, he just didn't want to talk about it. He preferred to try and make his wife feel as loved and happy as he could and not let sadness take over the remaining time they had together.

'From what I remember, the best thing with that is to pop it uncovered in the fridge until tomorrow and then it's nice and dry.'

Kate did as she was told. 'Trifle next?' She reached for the packet of jelly, flicking the kettle on.

Mary nodded. 'And then we can chop up the veg and write out the timings for tomorrow.'

As Kate tore the jelly cubes apart, dropping them into the jug and pouring hot water over, she couldn't help but smile. 'Eddie used to do that at Christmas. He'd prepare all the veg on Christmas Eve, then put them in the fridge, then we'd have mulled wine and sausage rolls.' She stopped stirring the jelly cubes, which had slowly started to dissolve, for a moment. Eddie had been flamboyant at times with his cooking, but certain things followed a ritual. Christmas was done in a certain way. It was nice, comforting, to sometimes know exactly how things would happen.

'He brought us some of that mulled wine one year,' Mary said, surprising Kate. She knew he was generous, that he loved to share his food, but more often than not she'd still be at school on Christmas Eve – and just come home to the delicious smells.

'Are you cross with him for dying, dear?' Mary sighed. 'That's one thing that worries me, that Charles will find it hard to forgive me for going before him.'

'I'm sure he won't.' Kate put her spoon down and squeezed Mary's hand, then sighed. 'But I was cross with Eddie. I might have been able to forgive him if he'd had—' She paused and met Mary's direct gaze. Mary finished for her. 'Some terminal illness?'

Kate nodded. 'We didn't have time to put things right, to talk things over, because it was so sudden. He was there one minute, then gone and he never came back.' She bit her bottom lip. 'I hated him for it, isn't that terrible?'

'You can't have love without hate, Kate. They're bedfellows. You're not a terrible person at all, you're just human.'

'And then I hated myself for hating him. I really hated myself and felt so guilty. There were things I had to tell him.' She bit her lip again to stop the tears welling up. 'Things I had to explain. I'd done something and I'd never told him, but I was going to. I was just waiting for the right time, Mary, and there wasn't one, it was too late.' With a shaky hand, she poured the jelly into the bowl to set, and then took the pile of carrots that Mary had peeled and started to chop them. She'd never told anybody how she had really felt, never admitted it. But somehow it was easy to talk to Mary, as they cooked. It could have been the repetitive, soothing chopping, or the gentle acceptance on Mary's face. 'He walked out of that door, and the next time I saw him he wasn't my Eddie at all. He was like some caricature with no smile or warmth, and Eddie was all about warmth.' She rubbed the dampness away from her cheek and reached for another carrot. 'Eddie wasn't the most handsome man on the planet.' She carried on chopping.

Mary smiled, the pace she was shelling the peas never changing. 'The good ones never are. Make sure they're all the same size dear, or they'll cook differently.'

Kate took a deep breath, and forced herself to slow down, take care. Cooking, it seemed, was all about a steady rhythm, she thought, an evenness, a routine, which might be why she was finding it possible to talk about this. She smiled; she could practically see Eddie watching them.

'His hair was all over the place —' she'd loved his untamed hair '— and he had slightly too thick eyebrows, and the best chocolate brown eyes, they were meltingly soft.'

'And a beautiful smile, a generous smile,' added Mary. 'That was one of the things that drew me to Charles, you know, his smile and naughty twinkling eyes. Full of mischief, they were. He was so dashing in his own way.'

'When Eddie smiled it made me feel all warm and scrunchy inside, and his voice always made everything better.' Kate scraped the carrot pieces off the board into a pan. 'But he wasn't any of those things when I went to see him. I couldn't say that broken, empty man was my Eddie, because he wasn't, Mary. He wasn't.'

Mary squeezed her hand again gently.

'I was so angry. I hated him for not taking more care. I hated myself for not caring enough. I hated his family for not being there to help, I hated strangers for saying it would get easier, and I hated all my friends for telling me that keeping busy at work would make me feel better, so I stopped talking to them. Nothing made any of it better.'

'There are many silly platitudes spoken by well-meaning people, Kate. They want to offer comfort but aren't quite sure how. They say things like "some things are better left unopened", and "some things are better left unsaid", but that is because they don't know. How can they?' She dropped the last of the peas into the colander and placed her hands over Kate's. 'Things are only best kept to yourself if you are certain that one day, a day of your choosing, you'll be able to share them.'

'Will you share how worried you are with Charles?'

The lightest of smiles danced over Mary's face. It was, Kate thought, not happiness, but memories. Fondness. A lifetime of sharing. 'I think he knows really,' she said softly. 'He did come to the hospital with me, and he sat there and listened, but we don't talk about it. He remembers my bad wrists, but sometimes it's as though the past is crystal clear but there's no room in his head for what's happening now, today. It's in, then it's out. I do worry how he'll cope without me.'

She'd said a similar thing only a few minutes ago, so it was obviously on her mind, bothering her and Kate felt a sudden need to reassure her – but she wasn't quite sure how.

'I don't want him to feel alone when I've gone, I want him to know that somebody is there for him.' There was the slightest quaver in her voice, and all Kate wanted to do was reassure her. Persuade her that she didn't need to worry, that Charles would be okay. 'You'll put his favourite recipes in your book?'

'Of course I will, and I'll look after him, Mary,' Kate said softly. This was why Mary was baking with her, not just to take her mind off her illness but so that she'd know what Charles needed when she was gone. Had Charles known this would happen when he'd knocked on Kate's door, when he'd sent Mary over? 'Della will be here as well; we won't let him feel he's got to deal with his grief on his own.' She paused. 'He worries about you too.' He did, she was sure he did – but like her he didn't know quite how to show Mary.

'You could be right, dear.'

'And I think he knows how ill you are. He does understand, he just doesn't want to dwell on it, he wants to do things for you, with you. Make you happy.'

'He has made me happy, bringing me back here, to your home. We used to sit in here by the big window at the front and watch the world go by. Such a wonderful time.' Her soft tone brought a lump to Kate's throat, and her whole body stilled, her full attention on Mary. 'There was no need to talk, he wasn't a chatterer. We'd watch everybody else and were happy with the silence. It was comfortable. Charles never was a big talker, but he's deep, a thinker. He's always been a kind man, which my father never was. I don't think my mother ever knew what it was to have the love of a man. I've been lucky.'

'You have.' It was on the tip of Kate's tongue to ask about Mary's family, when Mary moved back and straightened up.

'But I will talk to him again, when I'm ready, when it's time. Tell him I'm worried about him.' Her tone was decisive. 'We seem to have stopped talking lately. I haven't wanted to tell him how worried I am about how he'll cope. I think you're right. He's been avoiding the big C word, because he always has been a glass-half-full person. He's always tried to look after me and make sure I'm happy.'

'You'll talk when you're ready.' Kate nodded. Mary was so sensible, it all seemed so logical, so easy. It was all about being ready. She hadn't been ready before to do this. To talk, to admit (even to herself) how she felt. 'I didn't even want to go to the funeral, you know,' Kate said. Chopping again. 'Because funerals are about mourning, and I wasn't ready for that. I wasn't ready to admit that he wasn't going to come breezing in through the door apologising for taking so long.' Funerals are about cold, dry bones and hot flames, and Eddie was about warmth and life.'

They kept his car for months. The car took time to process, to investigate before cause was established. But Eddie's body was different – it was obvious what had gone wrong. Clear what had caused the end. And Kate had that part of him back before she was ready to let go of the man she remembered. 'Oh God, I'm so sorry, Mary. I've been going on and on about myself, and there's nothing wrong with me. But you…'

'Broken hearts aren't "nothing",' Mary said briskly. 'But—' She stopped, and Kate felt a stirring inside her. A feeling that she needed to hear whatever Mary was hesitating over.

'But?' she said softly.

'I've realised that the trouble with cancer is, it doesn't care who you might have been. It only matters who you are. And that, my dear, is why I've decided to be positive, to do the best I can do in the time I've got.'

Kate felt the hot tears prickling her eyes again. Death hadn't cared either, about what Eddie might have been. How their life could have turned out. It only mattered now who *she* was, what she did with *her* life.

She had to do the best she could for Mary and Charles, and Eddie, as well as for herself. She had to bring back the magic moments that they'd shared here. She had to try and stop Mary worrying about Charles.

'And that is exactly what we are going to do, the best we can! Can we sort out the timings for tomorrow, please? How long will this lamb need, and does it matter if the plates don't match?'

Chapter Eighteen

DELLA

Parkin

Della looked at her waterproof jacket, hanging in the hallway, and wasn't sure whether to take it or not. It was probably too warm to wear, but if she didn't wear it what should she do with it? She didn't really want to carry it as she'd have Clint's lead in one hand and the other ready to dispense treats. But she didn't really want to tie it round her waist either – she really felt her waist had spread too far to do things like that these days.

She took it down off the hook. Then hung it back up again.

Della had an unfamiliar flutter in her stomach. An excited flutter that she was sure was about anticipation not dread. The same kind of anticipation she'd had on the day she picked Clint up from his breeder, but had never really felt before when going out for a walk with somebody.

She was, she had to admit, in a bit of a dither, because she didn't want to get this wrong. It seemed important to show herself in the best light she could. Which was a bit silly, it was just a walk with a friend after all.

'What do you think, Clint? I don't want to look like a silly old fusspot in front of David, do I?' Clint rolled over onto his back for a belly rub, which she obliged with – but he was no help at all.

Footwear had not been a problem, as she always wore quite sturdy, waterproof walking boots when she went out dog walking. The boisterous Clint was stronger than he looked, and after landing on her bottom in the mud a couple of times – and having to walk down the street soggy-bottomed and feeling a bit silly – she'd decided they were well worth the investment.

As was the lovely lightweight jacket.

She took the jacket off the hook again and was still trying to work out what to do with it, when the doorbell rang.

David, she was relieved to see, was kitted out in a very similar fashion to herself. Except he had shorts on and was showing off his muscled calves. He seemed to be the type of man who wore shorts whatever the weather.

'You can pop that in the rucksack!'

She suddenly realised that she was actually staring at his legs, which left her a bit flustered. 'I never thought about taking a bag. Do I need one, should I…?'

'Not unless you're bringing anything else? I've got plenty of space in this, I thought we should be prepared in case of a shower.' He grinned. 'Or do you think I need to bring the crampons or climbing ropes this time?'

Della shook her head. 'Very funny!' She snapped Clint's lead on, and then had a sudden thought. 'I couldn't pop a bottle of water in there for the dog, could I? I completely forgot!'

'Sure.'

After getting the bottle, and shoving a few more dog treats in her pocket, she pulled the door shut behind her. She was dithering, fussing. She really had to stop. 'Sorry, I'm ready, honest.'

'No problem, you take your time. Don't want to forget anything, and there's no rush, is there? We've got all day.'

Della smiled. 'No, there's no rush.' Justin had hated it when she'd had to mess around, remembering things she might need just as she was ready to go out. David's relaxed attitude was wonderful and left her thinking that she really didn't need to worry about covering every eventuality. If she forgot something, she was sure David would come up with a solution, without making a big deal at all. That had been the trouble, she realised. Justin made such a fuss if she forgot anything important, he made it feel like it was her fault. Why the hell hadn't *he* made sure they had what they needed, instead of leaving everything to her?

'All ready?'

'All ready!' she said decisively, furtively checking she had her front door key. 'Where are we heading?'

'I thought we'd go to The Cloud, if that's okay with you?'

'Fine, though I have no idea where it is!' she said, laughing, feeling a buzz of excitement. She was being adventurous, trusting David, and it felt wonderful. 'Although "cloud" makes it sound like it might be a bit of a steep climb!'

David laughed. A hearty laugh, not at all like Justin's. Oh, why did she have to go and do that –compare them. She kept doing it. She had to stop. David was David, he was different. This was her new life; she was trying to move on.

'It's near Congleton, I used to live there. There are some wonderful walks, it's one of my favourites.' He paused. 'It's not too steep. I wouldn't want it to be too tough to talk, not when

I've got you to talk to and share it with.' His gaze met hers. She could have sworn there was a pinkness along his cheekbones that wasn't there before, and she was fairly sure she was blushing as well. And there was a warmth inside her that was really quite nice.

She busied herself with Clint, as David opened the back door of the car for him. The moment could have been awkward, but it wasn't. They were brushing shoulders as Della leant in to put the seatbelt attachment in for the dog's travel harness and it was a *nice* kind of embarrassment, if there was such a thing.

Clint jumped into David's car without hesitation, and David waited for Della to settle herself in the passenger seat.

'There is parking very close, so it's only about an hour's walk to the top, but if you're up for it I thought it would be nice to park near the canal and do a roundabout route, if that's okay. If you've got time.'

'I've got all day!' They shared a look again.

'I think you'll like it.' David smiled as he pulled away from the kerb, and she found herself studying his profile – the unremarkable nose and chin, the laughter lines around his eyes and mouth – and thinking that sometimes it's the unremarkable that's the most remarkable.

Two hours later, Della found that David had been right. She did like it. They'd had a lovely walk along the canal, and then across a meadow that sent Clint dashing round in circles, chasing the scent of rabbits, and even his own tail. His tongue was lolling out, his ears pricked and he wasn't pulling at all when she snapped his lead on for a short walk along the road. He meandered at the side of them happily but was ready to be off again when they moved off the lane and onto a track. He bounded off, as they tackled the path and steps that progressively got steeper.

The ground levelled out, and David led the way towards a white concrete post. 'The trig point.' He pointed. 'It's got a toposcope.'

She blinked at him, slightly short of breath from the steep climb. 'A what?'

He grinned, and her gaze was drawn to the chipped tooth again. The best things in life, she decided, were the imperfect things. A face was far more interesting if it was slightly rugged. If it showed it had had a good life. 'Here.' He put an arm round her shoulders to draw her closer. 'It tells you what you can see in each direction.'

Clint put his front paws up on the rock at the base of the trig point and she stroked the silky fur. She felt exhilarated as she gazed across the Cheshire plain from the top of The Cloud.

'Wow, I didn't know there was a place like this so close to home. What a view!' It really was amazing, it was causing a flutter in her stomach – although that could have been the touch of David's hand on her shoulder, the warmth of his body so close to hers.

David grinned. 'Congleton is that way, Staffordshire that way, and if you look –' he pulled her in even closer, so that she was sure she could feel the beat of his heart as he lifted a hand to point '– Jodrell Bank. It can get a bit busy up here in the summer, but it's great on a lovely clear day like today.'

They settled down on a rock, a happy Clint at David's feet.

'He likes you,' Della said, watching as David stroked his head. She liked him as well, Clint was a good judge of character.

'He's a good boy, aren't you?' He stretched his legs out, and Clint rested his chin on one of his knees. 'Ah, I nearly forgot! Refreshments!' David pulled his rucksack off his shoulders, set it down between them and reached in.

'You've brought a flask?' Della, who after sitting down had realised that she was a bit tired after the walk, and very thirsty, resisted the urge to grab the rucksack herself.

'Better! I brought a flask, and, tada.' He held up a foil-wrapped parcel, then carefully started to unwrap it. 'Parkin.'

'Oh wow, I've not had parkin for years.'

'It was a special treat for the girls when they were little. We had it on Bonfire Night, and Harry loved it.' He held out the pack towards Della, and she took a piece of the rich, dark, sticky cake. Her mouth was already watering from the spicy smell before she'd taken a bite. 'She won't touch it, or anything much at all now.'

Della raised a questioning eyebrow, her mouth too full for her to risk speaking.

David sighed and looked more despondent than she'd ever seen him. He'd always been so upbeat and positive in the few encounters they'd had. 'Anorexia. She picks, and she used to be such a big eater.'

'Until?'

'Until her mother ran off.' He sighed. 'I've tried to do my best, but I guess it's not the same, is it? She wants both her parents, together.'

'How long ago did she go, your wife?' Della asked softly, suddenly realising that she had never asked when they chatted in the garden. It had all been one-way; he'd listened to her more than she'd listened to him. She'd offloaded and never thought about the fact that although his comment about his wife leaving him for another man might have sounded a bit throwaway, it must have hurt. It must have had consequences, for the whole family. She'd been lucky, she supposed; not having children had made it easier for Justin to go.

'Nearly five years ago, just after Sally's wedding. She said —' he gave a short, harsh laugh '— that she would have hung on until Harriet left home, but there weren't any signs of that, and she couldn't carry on as we were.' He took a flask out of his rucksack and slowly poured them each a coffee, his fingertips touching Della's as he handed over her drink. His touch lingered, his steady gaze meeting hers. 'Poor Harry, she seems a bit of a hippy on the outside, a bit of a tomboy, couldn't care less — takes after me that way. But inside she's soft, she's a homebird. She might love to wander, but she wants everything to be the same when she comes back.'

'She still sees her mum?'

'Oh yes, Vicky makes sure of that, but she wants more than that. She wants her family back.'

'So she stopped eating?'

He nodded. 'Can't stomach my terrible cooking!' David laughed, then it died. 'I don't know what to do with her, I really don't. She's a grown woman, I can't make her go to the doctor.'

'Maybe,' Della said softly, resting one of her hands over his, 'it's her way of gaining some control. She can't control her parents, but she can control her body.'

David nodded again, but this time she could see his thoughts dancing across his features. 'Maybe you've got something there.'

'I don't want to interfere, but…'

'You interfere away, any help is good as far as I'm concerned. She was such a bonny baby, you know.' He sighed. 'I've pretty much given up trying to tempt her with food when she comes. It takes all the pleasure of food away, knowing she's not enjoying it.'

'Maybe she needs to feel she has some say in you and, er, Vicky. Who she sees, when, how it all works. You could even get her to cook a meal. I don't know anything about kids, but I do know how it feels to have what you believed would be there for ever taken away. To have no say, no control over the situation at all. Your whole world is kind of thrown up in the air and all the pieces come down in the wrong place.'

David slowly turned his hand over and squeezed hers. 'It must have been tough.'

'It was, but I'm not saying this for sympathy, I'm just trying to understand how Harry might be taking it.'

'I know. Thank you. I'll talk to Vicky. I think you're right. Little Harry has had the rug pulled from under her feet. It's different for Sally, she's older and she's got her new life to think about. Yep, I think you're right. I'd never thought about it that way before.' He nodded again, more decisively this time. 'But I didn't bring you here to solve my problems, I brought you to have a nice time.'

'And I am.' Della smiled. 'I could manage a bit more of that parkin if it's on offer though!'

He laughed. 'It certainly is!'

'It's amazing, I'd forgotten how much I loved it. This is one for Kate's book if you can give me the recipe.'

David blushed, then held his hands up. 'You've got me there – shop bought! You've no idea how long it took me to peel that sticky paper off so you'd think it was homemade!'

Della laughed. 'Well, I'll have to dig out a recipe. I need more, and I'm sure Mary and Charles would love it.'

'So, what's Kate's book, if you don't mind me asking?'

'Ah, well, it's her recipe book. Well, she said it's for all of us.

Mary gave it to her, but she's putting her favourite recipes in there that her gran used to make, and ones that we think will help Mary.' She paused. 'She's dying. Mary, that is, not Charles.'

'Oh.' They sat in silence for a moment, until Clint rolled over for a belly rub and made them both laugh.

'I said I'd help out with their garden if they needed anything doing, and Kate is cooking with her, because she misses that. And the café, they both miss the café – that's Kate's place, or it was. Sorry, I'm rambling!'

'No, you're not! And even if you were –' David winked '– I'd still listen. I like listening to you.'

Della batted on, not giving herself a chance to wonder why David might like listening to her. 'And she's even got some tips from Jack – you know, that chef guy that moved in at the end of the road? He's famous!'

'The grumpy guy with the battered roses?'

'That's the one, they were for Kate!'

'Well, I never.'

'I suggested she ask him for some hints on recipes for Mary.'

'Now you wouldn't be trying to matchmake, would you, dear Della?' His eyes were twinkling as he said, it, and Clint started to bark and wag his tail so hard he nearly rolled down the hill.

'Oh, stop ganging up on me, you two!' Della had been feeling slightly guilty about insisting they talk to Jack – but she just had a feeling that sparking off him might do Kate good. Sometimes people treading warily round you was no help at all.

'We wouldn't dare, would we, Clint?' Clint jumped up and kissed David, then sat down and started to inspect his own bottom.

'Good job he got those two activities in the right order!' David said drily. 'What else is in this book then?'

'Well, we're going to make a paella. I love paella, it reminds me of Spain.'

'I've only been to Spain once.'

'Really, I thought you loved travelling?'

'Oh I do, but I somehow missed Spain out. South Africa was my go-to place for a while, and the Canadian Rockies, where I could pretend I was in the Wild West.'

'Very exotic!' Oh God, thought Della, I must seem so boring.

'Some parts of it were, but I always like coming back and being boring and normal for a bit. It's nice to have some home comforts. That's the side of me that Harry's inherited.'

'I've never been very adventurous, I'm afraid.' But maybe she could be.

'Adventurous isn't about where you go. Sometimes the bravest thing is to stay where you are. Sometimes people are just running away, hoping a new buzz can replace the things they're scared of.'

'I suppose so,' she said reluctantly.

'But maybe if you're feeling in need of a change, we could go further afield some time?'

'I think I'd like that.' Della stared out into the distant landscape. 'Yep, I think I would really like that.' She could see for miles; she had no idea what was out there. Maybe she could broaden her horizons, learn new things, go to new places.

'Start off with the Lake District?'

'I've always wanted to go to North Cornwall actually. You know Tintagel?'

'I know it well. Now there's a place that's worth exploring. Ah well, I think young Clint is getting restless.'

'He is.' He was chewing his lead, looking for mischief. 'Thanks for the parkin, it was nice. Maybe —' she hesitated; she really was getting pushy '— we could try that pub at the bottom of the hill if we do this again.'

'Sounds like a good idea to me.' He was on his feet and holding out a hand to help her. He had a firm grasp, an honesty about him that gave her courage.

'And maybe you could look into a little trip to Cornwall? Would Clint be able to come?'

'I'm sure I can sort that. And if you need a hand with all this extra gardening you've taken on, then you know where to find me. Can't have it cutting into your trip time, can we?'

'We certainly can't.' Della smiled, and she was still smiling when they got to the bottom of The Cloud, and started to head up the road.

She'd definitely look up a recipe for parkin when she got home, and she'd make some to take on their next walk. She'd make it for David.

Oatmeal Parkin

> 225g plain flour
> 2 level tsp baking powder
> 4 level tsp ground ginger
> 100g butter or margarine
> 225g medium oatmeal
> 100g soft brown sugar
> 175g golden syrup
> 175g black treacle
> 1 egg, beaten
> 4 tbsp/60ml milk

- *Preheat the oven to 160°C. Grease and line a 20cm cake tin. Sift together the flour, baking powder and ginger. Rub in the fat, and then stir in the sugar and oatmeal.*
- *Gently heat the syrup and treacle, then make a well in the centre of the dry ingredients and pour it in. Stir, then add the milk and egg.*
- *Pour into the tin and bake for 45–60 minutes. Cool slightly in the tin before turning out onto a rack. Once cool, cut into squares.*

Chapter Nineteen

JACK

Sunday snaps

Jack turned out of his driveway and looked down the long road stretching ahead. It was deserted, apart from a single black cat that was sitting in the middle of the road, with its back leg stretched over its head.

He couldn't help it, he smiled. It wasn't far from Kate's, and he was sure she would have some health and safety advice to dole out if she saw it.

It was strange, he'd been determined to keep himself to himself in his new home, but in the few days he'd been here he'd learned the names of more of his neighbours than he ever had at his old place. It had taken years to be accepted in that village, whereas here he seemed to be being pulled in despite his reluctance. There was the old guy, Charles, who didn't seem to miss a trick, even if sometimes he didn't seem to remember his own name or what he'd gone to the shops for. There was his wife, Mary, who'd thanked him for being kind to Charles, and the middle-aged woman who was always out in her garden, digging. Delia, or something like that, she was called. He'd been very tempted to tell her she needed to mix more compost into the soil before she planted. But what was it to do with him?

He'd watched her puppy launch into the newly dug soil with delight, and dig a big hole, and wondered who was going to win that particular battle.

And then there was Kate. Kate, the widow who spat at him like an angry cat, but everybody else seemed to think was a saint. He didn't know what to make of Kate. But strangely, she stuck in his head. He felt drawn to her. Probably because she had a spark, she was passionate – even if at the moment all that passion was directed into disliking him.

He didn't need her help with that; he was perfectly capable of doing it himself.

The weight of his camera reminded him of his resolve to stop beating himself up – though taking photographs seemed a bit, well, indulgent. He'd prepared food knowing that somebody would eat it, enjoy it, but what was he going to do with his carefully shot pictures? Jack couldn't remember doing anything without a definite goal in mind, a purpose.

He slowed a few metres from the cat, not wanting to startle it. It stopped licking its nether regions, pausing with its pink tongue still out, and stared at him. Assessing. Then, deciding he didn't pose a threat, it lay down, its front paws tucked neatly under its body.

Jack squatted down and edged closer. 'Hey kitty cat, mind if I take a photo?' The cat didn't move. It didn't even blink.

There was something about a cat, he thought, beautiful but contained. A total confidence in its ability to tackle the world full on and win. 'Maybe I need to be more cat, eh?'

He lifted his camera. The glossy sheen of its black coat was like the shine on a perfect sauce. The indignant but serene expression on its face was so like…

'Just the man!'

Jack jumped, his train of thought broken by the voice. The cat swished the very tip of its tail, as though annoyed that it was no longer the centre of attention.

It was her. Angry cat lady.

Although *her* eyes were green, and the cat's were golden, with startlingly black pupils that made its gaze more piercing.

'Sorry?'

'I saw you out here, and, well… Can you do me a favour?' Kate's tone now had a hint of hesitation in it that her first words hadn't. An uncertainty that made him want to look up, look at her. See the expression in her eyes.

Instead, he paused. Reached forward, stroked the cat. It tilted its head, pushed it against his hand. Then he slowly stood up, took his time. If he attempted to touch cat lady, he wasn't sure he'd come away unscathed.

Why did he want to meet her gaze? Why did the tone of her voice hit some nerve deep down inside of him, create a physical response that he couldn't control? Why had he stopped to take photographs here, when he knew that her house was only across the road? It was almost like he was *asking* for trouble. Looking for a battle.

When his gaze met hers, though, she looked far different than at their last two encounters. Her features were gentler, and her shoulder-length mid-brown hair framed her face with a softness. He studied her in silence for a moment, even though something inside of him told him not to. Told him he should walk away.

He couldn't quite pin down the colour of her hair. It was broken up with lighter sun-streaked sections, and it didn't have the severe straightness that it had the first time he'd seen her, but it wasn't waves or curls. It was, like the rest of her, a bit of a mystery. Fluid.

He wanted to capture it. Analyse it. Look at her.

She was frowning slightly.

'Sorry, I was thinking.' He was gawping. 'What kind of favour?' he asked warily.

'Nothing big.' She looked like she wished she'd never asked.

'A favour for a favour?' Why was he saying this when he didn't even know what she wanted? 'You let me take your photo and I'll answer your question if I can? I need the practice.' He held up the digital camera. He'd asked on impulse, but he really wanted to take her photograph. He wanted to test out his eye, that was all. He wanted to see if he could capture that elusive quality about her. The conflicting emotions that he could feel under his skin, as though he was touching her.

Oh hell. He should stop right now. He didn't want to touch her. That's where trouble started. After Clara, he'd sworn to himself that he wouldn't go within a million miles of a woman, let alone *touch* one who knew who he was – *had been*. He'd been burned, and it wasn't happening again. It still hurt that he'd never realised who she was, what she wanted. If he'd been that blind, then how would he be able to stop it happening again?

'Well, I don't… I'm not very photogenic.'

That was the worst thing she could have said. The moment the words left her full lips, he knew he was doomed. He couldn't help himself; it made him want to take the photo even more. 'I don't want posed. I need to experiment with natural light and form.' That was all. He wanted to see what he could capture. And he didn't want her to think he was some weirdo stalker or anything. 'That's –' he pointed at the cat '– why I was…'

'In the middle of the road?' Her frown had melted away, and her eyes danced with laughter. It lifted the tension between them, and he couldn't help but respond with a small smile of his own.

He held up his hands in surrender. 'Guilty as charged! Seems to be a new hobby of mine.'

'Dancing with death?'

'I always have liked to push the boundaries.'

'I gathered that!' Her retort was half-teasing, not at all like the confrontational Kate he'd met before, and even though she hadn't said yes, he had to do it. He wanted to capture this moment. When he'd asked, it had felt like just a whim, but now it felt important.

This was a glimpse into what he was sure was the real Kate, too important to pass on.

He held up his camera. The sunlight filtered through her hair, halo-like, surrounding her in a warm glow that reflected in her face. The old-fashioned blue and white patterned bowl that she cradled in her hands was almost like an offering. Reverential.

Oh hell, what on earth was he thinking? Reverential?

She glanced down, and his gaze followed hers. Drawn back to the bowl. It wasn't what he'd expected, though. What was that? Something modern, clinical? Something aesthetically engineered.

He wasn't sure. But this chipped, colourful bowl was the type of item he'd always liked in his own kitchen. Used, work-manlike.

There was a shyness in her face now, and he wanted to capture that as well. Kate was constantly shifting, ambiguous. Intriguing.

'Can you just taste this, please, if you've finished with the snaps?'

'Snaps? This is art!' He pretended to sound affronted. It made her grin.

'And this is pork! Can you tell me if I've got the seasoning right? I really want it to be good for Charles. I mean, I know it won't be as good as when he had it last time, at your place, but…' The words tailed off, no doubt at the look on his face.

The familiar clenching in his stomach had started up as soon as he'd realised what she was about to ask, and even though it was completely irrational, his heart started to race.

'Please?'

He reached out reluctantly and took a piece of the crispy crackling, because for some reason he didn't want to disappoint her. He wanted to try.

The texture was just right, the roughness under his fingertips promising a crunch.

'It feels good.' His voice was scratchy. Maybe. Just maybe though… He lifted it to his mouth, a satisfying snap as his teeth bit into it.

Then… nothing. Disappointment hit him in the guts. Why had he done it, tried to please her? He turned the scrap over on his tongue, willing something to happen.

'And it tastes?' She was waiting, expectation and hope in her face.

Oh yeah, he knew those emotions well.

'Like cardboard,' he said tautly, then watched the light fade from her face. He hadn't wanted to do that to her, it wasn't her fault. 'It's not you, not a fault with your cooking.' He put a hand out on impulse, covered hers, then rapidly pulled back as he realised what he'd done. He'd just wanted to reassure her, make her feel better. Wow, that was a new one. When had he last done that? Stepped out of his own pity party to worry about how he was affecting another person? 'Look, I'm sorry, this is absolutely nothing to do with your food. Everything tastes like cardboard, I'd kind of hoped…' He studied the pork crackling strips for a moment, then glanced up. Met her gaze. Wanting to be honest. 'It could be worse, some stuff tastes of sawdust, soap or metal.' He tried a smile; it was probably a pretty twisted attempt.

She was staring at him as though she didn't quite believe him, as though he'd grown another head.

'I had a virus, and when I recovered enough to get back in the kitchen I realised after a few days that I couldn't smell or taste things properly.' He'd not really admitted that to anybody, apart from Ben, and his immediate family. It had been admitting failure, and he wasn't used to failing. 'After a while my sense of smell started to come back, so it took me a while to realise that I was using that, not actually tasting stuff.'

She was frowning now. Turning the bowl with long slim fingers.

'The doctor said it would come back, but –' he paused, watching her movements '– it hasn't. I'm one of the unlucky ones, I guess.' Massive understatement.

'So that's why you stopped cooking?' she said slowly.

'I can't cook if I don't know everything is as good as it can be. I relied on my chefs, asking them to taste and tell me, making them think I was testing them out.'

'When actually they were doing the job for you.'

He nodded. 'That was when I thought I'd be back to normal after one week, two. When it didn't happen.' He shrugged. 'Sorry, they do look good. Incredible in fact.' He nodded towards her bowl. 'I'm sure they taste good.'

'Has your taste not come back at all?'

'Not that I've noticed. It's kind of there, but wrong.' So, so wrong.

'It might, don't give up.'

'I can't just keep hanging on.' He shook his head. 'I've realised I'm wasting my life; I need to just get on and do something. I can't let the maybe tomorrows steal my todays.'

'True.' She stared directly at him, unmoving, like the cat had. There was a long silence, but he let it lie. She was thinking, he could tell. 'I like that,' she said slowly, '*maybe tomorrows*. I've been letting the *could have been tomorrows* take my todays.'

Their gazes locked.

There was so much more to Kate than angry Kate, bereaved Kate. He wanted to know how many other Kates were in there. Which one was future Kate. Except she was nothing to do with him. He couldn't let her be.

'So the photography is your new tomorrow?' She finally broke the silence.

'You got it! Tell you what, I'll tweak the photos and pop over in the week with them, then you can say they're shit in return for me saying what I did about your food!'

She laughed. It lifted something inside him, brought a smile to his lips that he couldn't prevent. Her happiness seemed to have that effect on him.

'Deal. Though I warn you, I don't pull my punches.'

'I know.' He met her gaze, and this time there was none of the intensity. This was okay, they shared a smile. 'I wouldn't expect anything less.'

'I'd better get back in the kitchen, I guess. I'm supposed to be cooking lunch for Mary and Charles.'

'I guess you had then. Good luck.'

'Good luck to you too!' Her words were soft as he stepped away from her. But he heard them perfectly, and for some reason the buoyancy inside him seemed to spread through his whole body and as he walked up the street, he felt like his stride was lighter. That he might actually believe the words he'd been saying over and over to himself: he was going to move on.

'Jack?' The shout stopped him in his tracks. He half turned. She was running after him, still clutching the bowl. 'Can you, well, describe how they should taste?'

He half closed his eyes, memories of the restaurant and the food he loved flooding back. 'You've got the crispness spot on, that snap and fizz in your mouth, but you don't want any fatty taste, which I don't think you have. You can just lift it with some salt sprinkled over.' He paused. 'The ones Charles had at my place probably had some salt flavoured with fennel on them. Or just dish up some apple sauce. Whatever flavour you fancy, but not too strong.'

She smiled. 'I think Charles would approve of fennel.'

'I think he might.' He smiled back, then raised his hand in a brief wave. 'Enjoy.'

And this time as he walked away, he could almost taste the crackling laced with fennel and lemon. Okay, it might only be a memory, a phantom taste, but for the first time since he'd been ill, he didn't mind.

Chapter Twenty

MARY

Sunday best

'I don't half fancy you!' Charles grinned at Mary and her heart gave the little flip it always had done when he looked at her in that way. Well, it probably didn't flip quite as violently as it had all those decades ago when they'd first been dating, but that was a good job at her age. She'd be worrying she was having a heart attack.

'And I fancy you the other half back,' she answered, smiling, before picking a piece of fluff off his lapel.

It had been Charles's idea for them to dress up in their Sunday best to go for dinner at Kate's. For a brief moment she'd been worried that they'd look silly, but then Charles had squeezed her hand, his gaze meeting hers. 'It's too long since I took you on a date,' he'd said and she'd squeezed his hand back. She knew what he was saying, they'd not got many dates left and they needed to make each moment count.

'You're not as daft as you pretend, are you?' she'd said, and he'd wrapped his arms round her and told her he loved her more today than he had in all the yesterdays added together.

She knew then that on her next baking day with Kate she had to be more direct; she had to ask her to look after Charles when she'd gone. Yes, she'd mentioned it the other day, but it needed mentioning again. She'd never asked for much her whole life, but sometimes she knew she had to forget about being independent, about being strong. Sometimes she had to ask for help – and it wasn't for her. It was for Charles. He was a good man, he'd always looked after her, and now she wanted to make sure that there would be somebody looking out for him. It wasn't worrying about dying that was keeping her awake at night, it was worrying about Charles living. If only Saul had been closer. But it had never been their job to tie him down, it had been their job to bring him up with wings. Show him that he could be anything, go anywhere. She was proud of him, proud of them. They'd done a good job. There should be no regrets.

'Ready for the fray?' Charles said softly, bringing her back to the present.

She nodded. She felt so tired these days, it was frustrating. She had so much left that she needed to do, but sometimes even getting out of bed was a struggle. Only knowing that Charles was there kept her going, made her do it. 'I am.'

'We've no need to go if you're tired?'

'Nonsense.' She slipped her hand into the crook of his arm. 'Kate has put quite an effort into our Sunday lunch, and I've got the most handsome man in the world to take me, why would I miss it?'

'Mary!' he said warningly.

'I'm fine.' Her tone was soft as she looked into his eyes. 'I'll be perkier when we get there, it will do me good.'

'That's my girl!' He kissed her cheek then, and it brought a rush of emotion to the surface. She'd underestimated her Charles, like she had so many times. However befuddled he was about where he'd left his glasses, or why he'd gone out of the room, or how to make a cup of tea, he understood. He knew.

She picked up the small box that she'd left on the sideboard in the hallway so she wouldn't forget it. After she'd helped Kate with her timings yesterday, the young woman had been adamant that she'd cope okay, and she'd shout out if she had a problem, but Mary had felt that she wanted to do something. So she'd made a batch of chocolate truffles, which didn't put any unnecessary strain on her wrists. 'Do you think these will go down okay?'

Charles hugged her. 'My absolute favourite, my dear, they'll go down a storm!' He took the box from her. Then winked. 'I hope some of them have got rum in!'

Mary smiled back. 'Of course!' When Charles had whisked her off to Gretna Green, they'd stayed overnight in a boarding house, and the very lovely landlady had given her a box of the truffles, the recipe and some advice, 'My great aunt gave me this recipe and told me that there's one type for the ladies, and one for the gents, but I've always ignored that. Gretna isn't about rules, is it? It's about following your heart and knowing that a bit of what you fancy does you good!'

Whenever Mary made the truffles, it took her back to that day. Charles had been what she'd fancied and she'd never for a single second regretted running away with him.

Gretna Green Chocolate truffles

200g good quality dark chocolate
2tbsp (25g) butter

200ml double cream

For the gents — rum to flavour and desiccated coconut to roll them in

For the ladies — sea salt/orange liqueur to flavour and cocoa powder to roll them in

- *Chop the chocolate into small bits so that it will melt easily. Gently heat the cream and butter in a pan until the butter is melted (Saul says I can place it in a microwave and use 30 second bursts until melted). Pour the mix over the chocolate and stir until smooth. Stir in 1tsp of flavouring if required. Leave to cool in a fridge for a few hours, preferably overnight — if I can keep Charles away for that long.*
- *Divide into small balls, then roll in the cocoa powder or coconut.*

Chapter Twenty-One

KATE

Sunday lunch

K ate spooned the mint sauce that Della had brought into a small jug, listening to the murmur of voices behind her.

Cooking the dinner had filled the house with delicious smells, but it had still felt empty – until her visitors had arrived. Eddie would have loved this; he'd have been in his element serving dinner to a crowd. She was hot and flustered. Even with the careful plan of timings that Mary had written out for her, she seemed to be juggling far more tasks than she was comfortable with, but apart from a bit of over-caramelisation on the carrots, and the odd lump in the gravy, it was going remarkably smoothly. And now everything was keeping warm as she took through the dishes of pork crackling.

Jack's response to the impromptu tasting session had not been what she had expected at all. She'd had a whole list of expected reactions in her head – contempt, derision and mockery had been top of the list. 'Cardboard' had been the last word she'd expected, and she might well have tipped the lot over his head if it hadn't been for the look of dismay on his face, and the explanation he'd given her.

He'd tried to hide his feelings, studying the cat and then glancing up through those incredible thick eyelashes that should have looked effeminate but didn't, and instead gave her eyelash envy. Then he'd looked her straight in the eye, his tone expressionless, as he'd described how his delicious food tasted of soap, metal or worse.

She'd wanted to reach out and hug him. But she hadn't. Sympathy was the last thing he wanted, she was pretty sure of that. Now that she could see beyond the cocky, abrasive act that had been all she was aware of on their first encounter, there was something about Jack that drew her to him. When he smiled it was warm and genuine – it reached his eyes. When he looked at her in that intent way it was as though he could see inside of her. In her grief, she'd closed herself off from the world, and she was sure Jack had done the same. And now, as she'd started to push those doors open and let life back in again, it was as though he was stepping into that gap, making her feel the type of connection with another person that she'd thought she would never be able to feel again.

She closed her eyes. He did make her *feel*, but she couldn't let herself. She'd only ever wanted Eddie. She would only ever want Eddie. Falling in love wasn't on the menu – definitely not with somebody like Jack.

And even though he'd had that spark of recognition in his eye, even though that syrupy soft voice had made her want to step in closer to him, he wouldn't want her anyway. There was a wariness about him. They had so much in common, things that weren't the basis for even a friendship. They'd both suffered a loss, both retreated from the world. Isolated themselves. That connection was mutual sympathy, knowing what hurt felt like. Being drawn to somebody who was on the same wavelength.

She took a deep breath. Opened her eyes. Looked at the pork crackling.

It must have been so terrible for him, losing his ability to do what was quite clearly his passion in life. The more she thought about it the worse she felt. She'd laid into the man, shouted at him for packing up what would have been Eddie's, and was obviously his, dream job.

'Oh, my goodness!' Charles's face was one big smile as she put the dish on the table, thankfully driving the image of Jack out of her head. 'Oh my, those look just like the ones I had in that chap's fancy restaurant. May I?'

She nodded, unable to stop smiling at his reaction.

'You don't have apple sauce, do you? A meal is not complete without apple sauce.'

'Ignore him, Kate. He doesn't need apple sauce; you sit down and join us.' Mary patted the seat next to her. 'I don't think this is the whole meal, darling.' Mary's own eyes were shining at her husband's delight as she told him off.

'Really? There's more! Splendid, splendid, I didn't like to assume, you know.' Charles was already dipping into the bowl of pork crackling, closing his eyes briefly as he bit into one. 'Exactly the same, you're a genius!'

Kate grinned, warming up inside with a feeling of satisfaction and happiness that she couldn't remember experiencing for a long time.

'In fact, I think it's better. Don't you, Mary?'

'They're lovely.' Mary took a small bite. 'I'm afraid my appetite isn't what it was, Kate, but these are wonderful. I might have another one.'

'Did he help you? That Jack fellow? I told him to, but he's a strange one. Can't fathom him, he cooks lovely stuff. I told him off for closing that place of his. It's not right, you know.'

Kate took a breath. Should she tell them? She wanted to defend him but was it up to him to explain why – not her choice to gossip about him? 'I think he has his reasons. He, er, didn't help, but I did show them to him and he said they had just the right crunch in them.'

'And they taste wonderful!' Charles wasn't going to give up. 'Did he tell you that? Or was he afraid of the competition?' He winked and smiled.

'He didn't say that, but I don't think I'm any threat to him at all.' Oh, she had to tell them. She was sure he wouldn't mind, or else why would he have told her, a total stranger? 'He didn't say they tasted good, he said they tasted of cardboard.' There was an intake of breath, and all of them stopped eating and stared at her. Della's mouth was opening, no doubt with an indignant comment on the way. 'Everything tastes of cardboard to him,' Kate said quickly. 'Or worse. He lost his sense of smell, and it affected his taste after he'd been ill.'

'Oh, how awful.' Della grimaced. 'I can't imagine not being able to taste bacon, or coffee, can you?'

Kate shook her head.

'Poor man,' Mary said softly. 'Oh, that explains so much. And his food was so pretty, it wasn't just the taste, it was everything about the dishes.'

'I think he's quite artistic,' Kate said. 'Right, if we're all done, I'll go and dish up our dinner!' She didn't want to talk about Jack or think about Jack. He kept popping back into her head – his look of dismay, his gorgeous smile, his gentle voice – and it wasn't right.

She uncovered the leg of lamb, which she'd left to rest

while they ate the crackling, and as she started to slice it she forgot all about Jack and found herself humming. It wasn't exactly the neatest carving in the world, but the way the meat fell away was very gratifying. The butcher had assured her that this was the absolute best time of the year to eat lamb and that she had to include his secret ingredient – a small tin of anchovies – alongside the garlic and rosemary (which Della had brought from her garden).

Mary's Favourite Roast Leg of Lamb – a collaboration!

> *2kg leg of lamb*
> *A small tin of anchovies, drained (Adam, the butcher)*
> *4 cloves of garlic & rosemary sprigs (from Della's garden)*
> *Sea salt*
> *Olive oil or butter*
> *Red onion, lemon*

- *Total cooking time guide – allow 20 mins per 450g, plus 20 mins, adjust if you prefer the meat well done (Mary says that Charles likes it with the slightest hint of pink). Check the internal temperature (Eddie had a note about this in his book).*
- *Preheat the oven to 200°C (fan oven). Slice the garlic thinly, then cut into 'fingers'. Halve the anchovy fillets. Using a sharp knife, make slits evenly over the surface of the leg of lamb. Push some rosemary, anchovy and garlic into each slit so that the flavours will be evenly distributed. Rub the surface of the meat with butter or olive oil, and season with sea salt.*
- *Place the lamb into a lightly oiled roasting tin, on a bed of garlic, a quartered red onion and a halved lemon.*

- *Cook for 20 minutes, then lower the heat to 180°C for the remainder of the cooking time.*

She didn't want to over-face Mary and had no idea how much of an appetite Charles would have (though he'd devoured the crackling), so she spooned the vegetables into colourful serving dishes that would brighten up the centre of the table.

'Here we go. I'm sorry the plates aren't Jack-style pretty, but I hope it tastes okay.'

'Oh my goodness, doesn't that smell wonderful, and it tastes –' Charles was already taking a mouthful of lamb '– delicious! And as for the mint sauce, a triumph, Della! Just what the doctor ordered.'

'It's lovely, dear. Melt in the mouth.' Mary squeezed her hand and took another small mouthful of meat.

Kate felt herself glowing on the inside as well as the outside. Everybody was tucking into the food and chatting. 'I'm so pleased you could all come and do this. Thanks, Charles. It's all down to you, if you hadn't stopped by…'

'Silly old fool that I am!' He chuckled, waving his fork in the air, before stabbing another roast potato with it.

'I'd love to add a photo to my recipe book, but…' Kate looked down at her own plate with slight dismay. She'd completely forgotten about taking pictures, and her lunch was half eaten. 'It didn't look exactly pretty, and I think I've left it a bit late!'

They all laughed.

'It's not how it looks, it's how it tastes that's important,' said Della.

'Well, next time, you could ask young Jack how he does it.

Even if he can't taste it there's no harm in him putting it on plates, is there? He can, what do you call it?'

'Style it?' Della chipped in.

'That's the word they use! And you can do the tasting! Not that there's anything wrong with the way this looks,' he added hastily, making them all laugh again. 'It's champion! You cook, and he can make it look fancy. How about that? Job done.'

Kate nodded. Charles might have a point. For some reason she hadn't been able to get the look on Jack's face, when he'd sampled her food, out of her mind.

He'd had a loss, just as she had. He'd lost his passion. Bereavement came in many forms, and each of them around this table was doing their best to handle their own loss. Della had lost her faith in love, and belief in the truth – and then her dog as well. Mary had lost the chance to bake, the one thing that might have given her some comfort as she tried to make the most of each day she had left. Charles was losing his sharpness, and she was sure he knew that soon he would lose the love of his life.

And she had lost Eddie – and the future she had mapped out.

But they were all coping in their own ways, and they were helping each other in a way that she couldn't have imagined just a short time ago. So why shouldn't she try and help Jack? Her attraction to him was just a passing thing, probably just a reaction to him being nice to her – because he definitely had a way with him. He probably had always had women falling at his feet. That was all it was. She could keep a polite distance, treat him like a normal friend and help him. They could all help him. She'd rope Della in, then it would definitely feel less personal.

She could ask him for tips on how to present the food.

Come to think of it, if photography was his new thing, surely he was the person to take the photos for her? They'd look much better than her attempts, then she would have pictures of the food she cooked, and she'd remember the dishes more clearly. He definitely had an artistic flair, which no doubt used to show in his food. She'd ask him. What had she got to lose? He'd said to her that sometimes you had to write a different ending, and he was trying to do that with his life – but did he really want to shut food out altogether? He could say no, but she would definitely ask him. It could do them both a favour.

And maybe one day she'd pass on her recipe book to somebody else, just like she'd inherited her gran's. Not that she'd ever have children, but maybe there would be someone who would want her little book, want to know about the dishes that meant something to her, care enough.

Actually, thinking about children, and the next generation, surely an online recipe book would be an idea. The thought made her pause. If she had decent photographs then she could put them on Instagram. They could be a professional team, her and Jack, which would be a far easier idea to sell to him. She might not have a tearoom any longer, but how about an online one? The perfect café at home? She could even call it 'Auntie Flo's' after the tearoom. She would of course keep her recipe book, but this could be a glossier version – one that anybody could find.

'That was amazing.' Della put her spoon down, distracting Kate from her thoughts. 'You'll have to give me the recipe for that trifle, I'd like to make it for David.'

Kate raised an eyebrow, and Della blushed. 'He doesn't bother much with cooking these days, now he's on his own.'

'Well, he should join us!' declared Charles and didn't look at all abashed when Kate stared at him with her mouth open, and Mary sighed.

'And what makes you think you're going to get invited again, darling.'

'Oh, we've got to do this again.' Della's unexpected enthusiasm caught her by surprise. 'Please, Kate. I'll help!'

'We'll all help.' Charles chuckled. 'Well, I'm about as much use in the kitchen as a chocolate teapot, but I'll be there in spirit.'

Kate looked from one to the other. How could she say no? It had been lovely, but hard work. 'Maybe once a month?' She glanced around the table, her gaze resting briefly on Mary. How much longer did she have? 'And maybe we could do afternoon teas in between. If you'll help me with the baking, Mary?'

'Definitely.' Della smiled. 'David gave me this wonderful parkin when we went on our walk, so I found a recipe when I got home. Could we try that?'

Kate grinned. Exactly how many times had Della mentioned David? She had been so bubbly today, and Kate wondered if this was the *real* Della that was emerging. She had a new confidence that made Kate want to hug her.

'Sounds great! Where did you go?'

'Up The Cloud!' Della grinned. 'I was in walking boots, scrambling up a hill, can you believe it?'

'Well, actually, I can.'

'And he's talking about us going away together. We thought we'd start off with Cornwall but then maybe go on a safari or something.'

'Wow, I'm impressed, and slightly jealous!'

'You should go to Canada, that place where the polar bears go into town!' Charles waved his spoon at her.

'I don't think I'm quite that adventurous yet.'

'You ignore him, dear, he's never been anywhere near a

polar bear. And stop sneaking extra trifle, I'm watching you. Don't think I didn't see you helping yourself to extra roast potatoes either!' Mary tutted, but Charles just grinned, his eyes shining with mischief.

Kate watched them, listened to the chatter and felt more at home, happier, than she had for years.

She was so pleased for Della, talking about adventures. Ready to take a risk, try something new. Reinvent herself. She felt proud of her in the same way she used to when her students achieved more for themselves than they'd believed they could. Except this time she'd had nothing to do with it at all.

'David's welcome to join us next time,' Kate said softly and was pleased she had when Della blushed.

'That would be lovely, I'm sure he'd appreciate it now his daughters have left home.'

'They are lovely girls, and he always looked so happy when he was out with them,' Mary said softly. 'A lovely family. Such a shame about their mother, but I suppose these things happen. He must miss them though.' She frowned. 'I think the younger one, what is her name – a man's?'

'Harriet, Harry.'

'Ah yes. I think she still visits quite a lot, doesn't she?'

'She does, but she isn't a big eater.' Della sighed. 'He says she hardly touches her food, and she won't go to the doctor.'

'It's hard to lose somebody you love. You feel so helpless,' Mary said, and for a moment they all fell silent.

'Well, you should invite them all here. One big family, the more the merrier, eh?' declared Charles, sneaking another spoon of pudding out of the bowl. 'I reckon this is a house that needs people in!'

He had a good point, Kate thought. Cooking, filling the

house with the smells of food, had helped her feel a little bit better – but actually having a group of people here, people that she was growing quite fond of, enjoying a meal together, was something else. Even Mary looked relaxed, her gaze constantly on Charles. It was nice, and it was bringing the life, the heart, back into her home.

'A family, children!' Charles's words snapped her out of her comfortable thoughts, crunching her heart. 'Nothing like children to make a house a home, eh?'

'Charles.' Mary's tone was warning, as she glanced from Kate to her husband. 'Shhh. Sorry, Kate. He sometimes doesn't think before he speaks.'

Charles looked from one to the other of them, and Kate could practically see the moment when he realised what he had said.

'Oh, my dear, I am sorry. I didn't mean to upset you. You and your young man must have had all kind of plans for a family in the future.'

Kate could feel the emotion welling up. He was making it worse, but how was he to know that children were the one thing she hadn't been planning on – but Eddie had.

'Will you shut up, Charles!'

Kate started, swallowing the hard lump of grief. She had never heard Mary sound so cross, had never imagined that she could.

'I'm a stupid old man, please—'

'It's fine,' Kate said as calmly as she could, but she could feel the tremor in her words, in her throat. The lovely lunch was disintegrating. The last thing she wanted was to upset Charles and Mary. To have them at odds. 'It's okay. You're right, it must have been lovely when it was a tearoom and there were children in here. Children do make a home.'

'And so do dogs,' added Della.

'Well, not everybody wants children anyway,' said Mary, looking at Kate assessingly. Her tone was brisker than normal but had lost its anger. 'I certainly didn't think I did!'

Kate frowned at her. 'But I thought you had a son.'

'We do,' Charles chuckled, 'and she loves him to bits. Made our lives even better, he did.'

'I do love him.' Mary smiled. 'Saul's always been a good boy, but we adopted him.'

'You could adopt, you know. Splendid idea, splendid,' Charles said to Kate, totally oblivious to the truth of the matter. That she could have had children with Eddie, he'd been more than willing. It had been her that didn't, couldn't. 'They don't mind if you're single these days, and you can get babies from other countries, what do they call those families? What was it?' He frowned. 'Blended! That's the one, blended. Or am I thinking of tea? Memory just isn't what it was.'

'Charles...' Mary sighed.

'Ah, I think that's my ten-second warning.' His eyes were twinkling. If Kate didn't know for a fact that she hadn't served wine with the dinner she would have suspected he was tipsy.

'He's a bit giddy,' Mary said under her breath to Kate, as though she'd read her thoughts. 'I think it's time I took him home.'

'Indeed I am. It's all been so splendid, but I think I'll just go and use your facilities before we go, if I may, my dear? Don't want to be caught out, do I?'

'You may,' Kate said, trying to suppress her laughter and match his serious tone. 'It's upstairs, I'm afraid. Can you manage?' The final words drifted out of her mouth, and she hoped she hadn't offended him. But he just chuckled.

'It's my mind that's the problem, my body is still willing!'

'Which reminds me.' Mary fished about in her handbag and drew out a piece of paper that she gave to him.

'Much obliged, my dear!'

Mary tutted, but she was smiling affectionately. They cared so deeply for each other, loved each other, that was clear.

'I think I'm a bit giddy too.' Della laughed as she got up from the table as well, then hugged Kate. 'It's been wonderful, but I'll get out of your hair. See you all soon?'

'You certainly will!' Charles did a little dance. 'We'll be down to investigate that vegetable patch, won't we, Mary?'

Mary nodded. 'One thing at a time, dear.' She pointed at the note she'd given him a moment before, that he was still holding in his hand, and he stared at it, a slight frown on his face. 'Bathroom,' she added softly.

Kate looked from Charles to Mary, and a surge of emotion filled her throat. She hadn't known them long, but she'd miss Mary when she went, and she'd be sad for Charles. Mary was right to worry; he would be lost.

How would he cope? She understood now the weight that Mary felt, the weight of a love that was about affection, years of togetherness, knowing somebody so well that they almost felt a part of you. That feeling of really, really wanting to be with somebody.

She looked back at Mary again. All of a sudden, she looked tired. Her face had paled. She'd willed herself to come here, have a good time, but it must have felt like a long day. Charles and Mary were so keen to carry on *living* that it was easy to forget how old they were. How ill Mary was.

Kate reached out, squeezed her hand. 'I'll give you both a lift home.'

'Oh no, no, you've made us a lovely dinner and we can manage. We don't want to be a bother.'

'But I haven't made you a lovely dinner, I've just sat back and had a lovely time,' Della suddenly cut in. 'I'm off to get my car, and by the time Charles comes back downstairs I'll be back. No arguing!' And she gave Kate a quick kiss on the cheek before rushing off before Mary had a chance to object.

Kate felt a rush of gratitude.

'Ah yes, bathroom!' Charles proclaimed out of the blue, as though the jigsaw pieces had suddenly fallen into place.

Mary turned to Kate, as he started to make his way up the stairs. 'The note is to remind him why he's there when he gets to the top. He forgets so quickly. He can remember which shirt he wore on our first date, but he'll get to the bathroom then forget why he's up there and start wandering around the bedrooms and then come back down.' She paused. 'I am sorry he upset you, my dear. After you've made such a lovely dinner for us.'

'It's fine. I'm fine, honestly.'

'No,' Mary said firmly, 'you're not. He didn't mean anything by it, but he's very good at putting his foot in it.' She put her hand over Kate's. 'If you ever want to talk, you know I'm here to listen, don't you?'

Kate nodded.

'Kate, there's nothing wrong with not wanting children, you know. I never was the over-the-top maternal type, and I was so naïve and positively shocked at the idea of a baby growing inside me.'

Kate couldn't help the small smile. 'It's not that.' She'd never even thought about a new life growing inside her. 'But I decided I didn't want a baby.'

'I didn't want to bear a child, and Charles's parents were so pushy it hardened my resolve even more. But after we'd been married a few years, we both realised that we did quite like the idea of a family, and we wanted to make our own decisions. It was Charles who pointed out that there were far too many unwanted children in the world, so to shut his parents up we adopted! They were furious.' Kate was amused to see the glee on Mary's face. For a brief moment the years dropped away. She could imagine the young girl that Charles had fallen head over heels in love with. 'And they couldn't do a thing about it!' Her features softened. 'It was the best thing we ever did. We loved him so much. He was perfect. We both wanted a child in our lives. Charles was a wonderful father when Saul was little.'

'I bet he was.' Kate's throat started to close up with emotion. 'He's so lovely.' The words almost came out on a sob, and Mary looked so worried she forced herself to calm down.

'I don't mean to be an interfering old woman, Kate. It's none of anybody else's business whatever you decided in your personal life.'

'It's fine.' She really must stop saying 'fine'.

'Not all men are cut out for fatherhood.' Mary patted her arm again. 'And it doesn't suit all couples.'

Kate suddenly couldn't help herself; the words wouldn't stay inside her any longer. Eddie would have been a wonderful father too. She'd deprived him of that opportunity. She was responsible for everything going wrong. And now Mary was starting to think that it was him that hadn't wanted a baby – not her. 'It *would* have suited Eddie. Eddie wanted a baby; he wanted a baby so much, but I didn't,' she blurted out.

'And there's nothing wrong with that, that doesn't make you bad.' Mary squeezed her arm.

'I couldn't. I just couldn't, it would have been wrong.'

'And I'm sure he understood. You don't have to see eye to eye on everything in a marriage.'

'But you don't understand, it was my fault he left the house, it was my fault he died, it was because we'd been arguing about it!' The hurt started to bubble up inside her.

'Ah, you said you didn't have time to put things right, is that what you meant?' Kate nodded; she couldn't trust herself to speak. She was trying to hold the anger, the anguish inside, but Mary's calm tone was helping. It was giving her something to hold on to, to anchor herself.

'It *was* my fault.' She wiped the dampness off her face angrily with the back of her hand.

'You weren't just angry, you felt guilty. Oh, Kate.'

Kate knew she was trembling, but it felt more like exhaustion than anger now. She wanted to hang on to Mary, listen to her words, accept her comfort. But she was old, frail, ill. Kate should be the strong one.

'Kate.' Mary waited until Kate was looking her in the eye. 'Guilt is a terrible thing, it gnaws away at you, it doesn't let go. It wasn't your fault. It was Eddie's choice to deal with it that way, and I'm sure he respected your choice to say how you felt. It was the driver of the car that ran into him that was at fault, and who knows if you should call the rest God's will, fate, predestination or something else altogether. It doesn't really matter, does it? All that matters is that he was good and kind and loved you, and that he respected your feelings, and that is why he left you to gather yourself, isn't it? That –' she patted her hand '– is why I've always felt lucky that I found Charles. He might be a daft bugger at times, and he might be losing his mind, but he's never held my decisions against me. And I don't think Eddie would.'

'I remembered!' shouted Charles from the top of the stairs, making them both laugh. 'Now, what were we talking about?'

'We,' Mary said firmly, 'were talking about getting back home so that you can calm down before it's your bedtime.'

'Oh, you're a bossy woman.' He landed heavily on the last step and lurched forward, planting a very heavy kiss on her cheek. 'And that's why I love you!'

'See?' Mary winked at Kate.

She watched them walk down the driveway and get into Della's car, then gently closed the door behind them.

She felt exhausted, but she also felt strangely relieved. Her recipe book caught her eye as she walked into the kitchen, and she opened the cover and glanced at the first recipe.

'What do you think, Eddie, should we help make everybody happy and put these on Insta?' There was no response to her soft question, but she could imagine him nodding. 'And –' her words were even softer now '– would you mind if Jack helped me?'

A gentle breeze from the window, which she hadn't been aware of, stirred the pages of the book. They fluttered and, as she reached out to stop them, they settled. She stared at the recipe. One she'd copied out of her gran's book.

Chocolate brownies. The recipe that Gran had written '*mend a 15-year-old Kate's broken heart.*' against.

Chapter Twenty-Two

CHARLES

Cherry Frangipane Tart

'Just off for my constitutional, dear!' Charles picked up his stick and waved it in the air, and Mary smiled. 'Will you be okay? Is there anything I can get you?' She looked tired. She had started to look tired a lot. It worried him – well, it more than worried him, it made his stomach churn, and it sent a flutter through his bloodstream that made him feel quite weak and helpless. He was trying to soldier on, put on a bright smile, but he was frightened.

Mary had always been a part of his life. He felt like in the days, years, before he met her, he'd simply been marking time. Waiting for that moment when she would be there. Life before Mary had simply been growing up. Life after Mary was unimaginable.

He'd wanted to show her that he would be okay, that the good people around here would support him. He'd wanted to make the time they had left together less of a worry for her, because he knew she worried about him. He'd wanted to bring as much enjoyment back into her life as he could, to bring her baking back, even if she couldn't actually lift the heavy trays herself.

It had been easy at first, but in the last week or so it was almost as if the disease had picked up speed and was about to take over their lives.

Charles had never been the fearful type, but now he was scared.

'I'm fine, darling.' She squeezed his hand. 'You have your walk, but don't go too far.'

'I won't! I might pop into the tearoom, grab a cup of tea maybe.'

'Charles.' She shook her head in admonishment. 'Now you know it's not a tearoom any longer, don't you?' She couldn't help the question.

He kissed her on the top of her head, as he often had through the years. He did forget lots of things, but this was not one of them. 'I do, but Kate is always happy to put the kettle on.'

'Well, don't bother her if she's busy.'

'I regale her with tales of when it was a tearoom, and of our dancing days, and the day I proposed.'

Mary chuckled softly. 'You old fool, a young girl like that doesn't want to be regaled!'

'I'm trying to get her to talk to that Jack fellow, slip him into the conversation.' He winked.

'Oh, you are naughty, she might not want to be bothered with men.'

'Nor did you, until I dived in and you realised what you were missing!' He smiled at her. Mary had been a challenge; she hadn't realised, in the same way that he had, that they were the perfect match. That they were supposed to be together. It had taken a lot of persuasion, smooth talking and cake before she'd come round and agreed to seeing more of him. But it had been worth it.

'I was being careful,' she said primly. 'Nobody likes a pushover, do they?'

It was his turn to chuckle. 'Oh, I do love you, my Mary.'

'And I love you too! Now, on your way and let me think about what I'm going to help Kate bake next week. Honestly, you don't give me a moment's peace!'

He knew she didn't mean it. That they had always been happy in each other's company. Mary wanted to sit quietly in her chair, close her eyes for a while.

'I just want to be with you,' he said softly, his hand resting upon hers, ignoring the teasing. There would be too many moments of peace in the future. Too many moments without her.

'I know.' She smiled up at him. 'I want to be with you as well, I always have. Don't you ever forget that.' Then she shuffled about in her seat and sat up a bit straighter. 'Now off you go and get some exercise. I'm not going anywhere for a while yet. I'll be here when you get back. Oh, and Charles, ask Kate if she'd like my sloe gin recipe. Gin is all the rage, isn't it, these days. I know it's a while until Christmas, but nothing like being prepared, is there.'

'There's not.' He shook his head gently. He didn't want to be prepared. He wanted life to carry on as it always had. 'I'll be off then. I won't be long.'

'That's nice, bring a bit of cake back, why don't you?'

'Will do.' He patted his pocket, to make sure he'd remembered his notepad, then stepped out and carefully pulled the front door shut behind him – giving it a gentle push to make sure it had closed properly.

Mary waved at him through the window, and he waved his stick and doffed an imaginary hat, pausing to see her smile, before setting off determinedly up the street. Trying to look like the man she'd married so many years ago.

When Kate had first asked if he could secretly bring her some of Mary's favourite recipes, so that Kate could surprise her, it had given him a purpose, made him feel useful. And the tiny subterfuge had been exciting. He'd rifled through Mary's recipe book when she'd been at Kate's, or if she'd insisted on going to the shop on her own, or had the hairdresser around, and he had carefully copied her favourite dishes out into a little note-book he'd bought specially for the purpose.

The last few days it had stopped giving him as much of a buzz, because he'd been too worried about Mary. She was getting tired – tired of battling. But, having promised to do it, he had, and it had at least proved a distraction. Fretting, as Mary said, never solved anything. You just have to get on with things. So he had. Today he had a recipe that Mary changed with the seasons. It had been her mother's recipe originally, made with love and passed down.

As puddings went it definitely came into the hug-in-a-dish category, with its luscious fruit and sticky warm inside.

In the spring she bought cherries, in the autumn she'd pick plums for it, in the summer the raspberries would find their way from the canes in the garden to the cake in the kitchen. They'd not had raspberry canes for a long time though. Maybe he should stop by Della's on the way back from Kate's. Raspberries would make a nice addition to her fruit and veg patch, though – and he felt the sigh well up in his chest, clogging his lungs – Mary might never get to taste the first crop. She always had loved raspberries fresh from the garden.

'Charles!' Kate's voice startled him. He'd not even noticed that he'd reached her house and knocked on the door. 'Are you okay?'

'Good morning, dear!' He recovered his composure, but she was still looking at him warily, as though worried he was about to keel over. 'I'm tickety-boo, dear! Tickety-boo. Miles away for a second, I was then!' He was tempted to try a little skip in the air to prove how full of energy he was, but that could result in a nasty slip – or worse. Sometimes bravado had to be left, with pride, in the past.

'But you are okay?' She was frowning slightly at him. 'Is Mary all right?'

'She's a little bit tired.' He wouldn't worry Kate with their problems, she had enough of her own. 'Glad to get me out of her hair for a bit she was!'

'Oh Charles.' Totally out of the blue, she wrapped her arms round him, and he could see he'd upset her. 'I should come round, maybe cook for her at your house, then she doesn't have to come out.'

'She'll be fine, dear.' He squeezed her arm. 'We'll be fine. She just has some days that aren't as good as others.'

'I am sorry,' Kate sighed. 'I wish I could do more.'

'You are doing more than enough, although this—' He whipped his notebook out of his pocket with a flourish, though rather messed up the gesture when a page got caught and flew off, fluttering like confetti. 'Oh dammit, old age!'

He bent down to retrieve it at exactly the same time as she did, and they nearly hit heads. She was grinning as she straightened up, and he immediately felt better.

'This,' he said with a wink, 'is one of her absolute favourites and she would be thrilled if you could make it!' He handed over the notebook and she read, her smile broadening.

Mother's Fruit Frangipane Tart

Ready-made shortcrust pastry — she made her own but why not move with the times?

Fruit compote (supermarket jam is just as wonderful!)

500g plums, stoned and sliced (or substitute with cherries or other in-season fruit — frozen cherries are the easiest these days, I find) — sprinkle with 2tbsp sugar, and 2tbsp brandy and leave for 2–3 hours minimum

150g caster sugar

150g butter

3 eggs

1tsp baking powder

150g ground almonds

Zest of a lemon

- Lightly grease and dust with flour a 25cm loose-bottomed flan tin. Line with pastry, prick with a fork and blind bake for 20 mins at 180°C (in the fan oven — mother did it at 360°F). If necessary, remove the baking beans and parchment paper and return to the oven for a further 5 minutes.
- Spread a thin layer of jam onto the cooled pastry case.
- Mix together the sugar and butter until pale and fluffy. Add the eggs one at a time, beating until smooth. Stir in the baking powder, almonds and lemon zest then pour into the pastry case.
- Arrange the fruit slices in circles on the top, pressing down lightly, then pour the syrup over the top.
- Bake for 45–50 mins at 180°C, then allow to cool for 10 minutes.

'Oh goodness, frangipane tart! My gran used to make this. It was so light but all sticky and gooey inside. That's wonderful, Charles. Thank you, you're doing an amazing job!'

'Splendid, splendid! She's converted all the temperatures and measurements, you know. My Mary has always moved with the times. And cherries –' he tapped the place in the recipe '– they're her absolute favourite. The tops! And isn't it a lovely day?'

'It is. Come in, if you've got time for a cuppa, that is.'

'I've always got time for a cup of your tea, and maybe something to go with it?' She grinned. 'And how is your own recipe book coming on?'

'Oh it's great, specially now you're giving me all these wonderful recipes from Mary. I can't wait to surprise her with some of them!' She bustled about the kitchen, making the tea and slicing a cake. It made Charles feel more relaxed. He'd always loved watching Mary in the kitchen. Kate had been hesitant when he'd first come here, but she looked so much more confident, so happy, and he was pleased. He was more than pleased, he was proud. His Mary had helped do this; Mary with all her caring and common-sense had helped young Kate. Who said old people were useless?

'It really would look better with some good photos though. I mean, I know Mary's book hasn't got them, but it would be great to put it all on Instagram, you know, the internet? It was just an idea I had after you came for lunch, I thought maybe the kids of today would be more interested then?'

He nodded wisely. Not really having a clue what she was talking about, but wanting to encourage her enthusiasm. She'd also given him an in, and he wasn't going to miss the opportunity.

'Well, I said it then, and I'll say it again. You should ask that young lad up the road, Jack. All about photography he is now. He's champion at making food look pretty.'

'Well, I did think about asking him, but I'm sure he's far too busy to waste time with me. I mean, my cooking is very basic, isn't it? Not at all what he's used to.'

'Food is food, and it tastes splendid! If you want it to look all fancy like his used to, then I'm sure he's the man to ask! And I'm sure he's into that Insta thing as well. Nothing ventured, nothing gained, eh? Talking of which, I couldn't have a tiny slice of that to take home to Mary, could I?'

'Of course you can! It's quite light, I'm sure she could manage a piece, I'll wrap one up. And maybe if I put in some of my soup. I mean, it's nothing special, but my gran always made it when I'd not got much of an appetite, she said just the smell would help, and she was right.'

'That's very kind, dear. I'm sure she'd love a bit for her supper.'

'She is okay?'

'Battling on! You know Mary. The doctor did warn us she might be tired, and he did say at our age —' he rolled his eyes dramatically, and Kate laughed, as he'd hoped '— that we couldn't expect to be running up the stairs. Anyway, it's a good thing she's moving slower, or I wouldn't be able to get away with copying her recipes out! I'm sure she doesn't suspect a thing, I'd make a good undercover cop. My talents have been wasted!'

'I think you could be right!' She chuckled, then pushed her plate to one side so that she had room for his notebook and hers, side by side. 'I'll copy this out before I forget. You're doing a brilliant job with these. I thought we could put on a nice spread of some of the ones she really loves. Maybe for her birthday?'

'Well, I don't know about her birthday, it's our wedding anniversary coming up in a few days.'

'Oh wow, I didn't realise!' She hesitated for a moment, and then the words rushed out of her mouth. 'Well, I've got to make pineapple upside-down cake, haven't I – would you like me to? I mean, I'm sure it won't be a patch on the ones you used to have in the tearoom, but I can certainly try.'

'Oh Kate!' He blinked, glad that he was sitting down. 'That would be splendid.' The final word stuck in his throat, came out in a croak, so he tried again. 'Really splendid. Thank you. It will be our last one, and I want to make all our lasts the best I can.'

'Oh Charles.' Tears had welled up in Kate's eyes, which was the last thing he wanted.

'Now, now, don't go daft on me. Facts are facts, aren't they?' He sighed. 'And we can't change the inevitable.'

'Oh Charles.' She shook her head. 'You do know she's worried that you don't know how ill she is? She thinks you've forgotten.'

'Oh dear, have I got it wrong?' He sighed. 'In my cack-handed way, I thought if I didn't go on about it then she wouldn't dwell on it, and I could just try and make sure these weeks were happy ones. That's why I came here, to you. I knew the baking would help her.'

'I know.' Kate's voice was soft, and her gaze was gentle. It made him feel tired, and he was trying so hard to be brave, to battle on like Mary needed him to. 'She's worried about leaving you.'

'I know she is, my dear, and I've been trying to stop her. I thought baking would take her mind off things, and when she saw how lovely and welcoming you were, she'd know that although I'll be only half of myself without her, I won't be on my own. I don't want her to worry about me, only herself,' he finished quietly. All he'd ever wanted was for Mary to be okay.

'Oh Charles, you're so amazing, but –' Kate paused '– I think the two of you need a chat. I don't want to interfere, but I think – though I don't know – that you've always told each other everything, and I think you'd both be happier if you did that now. I've never known two people who care about each other so much, but I think you've been trying to protect each other because you're frightened of the future.'

'I am frightened, my dear, and I'm sure she must be too.' Charles nodded. 'You're a wise child.'

'I'm not wise at all, I've messed up so much in my own life, but I love you both. You might not be quite as frightened if you do this together.'

'We might not.'

'If you tell her everything, if you tell her you understand what's going on.'

'Everything?' He raised an eyebrow. 'I'm not sure we should tell her about stealing her recipes, should we?'

Kate grinned, and he was glad he'd lightened the atmosphere.

'Or our anniversary plans?'

'Oh no, don't tell her about the pineapple cake, in case it doesn't work! We can just say it's afternoon tea.'

Charles nodded. 'Mum's the word!' He put a finger to his lips.

'Maybe I should invite Della as well.'

'I am so pleased I got confused and popped in to see you that day,' he said.

'So am I!' Kate smiled. 'Though if I'm totally honest, I'm beginning to wonder just how confused you actually were.'

'Oh dear.' Charles frowned and gazed around him. 'What

am I doing here? Did I come to buy something? Is this the new flower shop?'

'There's nothing wrong with you at all, is there?' Kate laughed and he knew then that she'd seen through his act. But it didn't matter. All that mattered was his Mary. He couldn't transport Saul back here to reassure her, but she'd definitely been happy since they'd got to know Kate.

He reached out to take her hand and kissed the back of it. There was nothing that wrong with him. Not yet.

Chapter Twenty-Three

KATE

Pineapple upside-down cake

K ate finished washing up the dishes and stared out at the garden.

When Charles had knocked on her door yesterday, he'd looked his normal dapper self, but there had been something strained. Something sad about him.

When she'd offered him a cup of tea, he'd jokingly suggested cake and raised an eyebrow expectantly in the way he always did, but she'd known him for a while now and something about him was waving a warning flag.

He popped in at least once a week, often more, bringing her copies of Mary's favourite recipes, and the forgetfulness and vagueness that had hung around him like a weight had lifted. Something seemed to have happened to Charles over the past few weeks – since he'd first knocked on her door looking for the tearoom.

He seemed to have more of a spring in his step, a twinkle in his eye. He seemed more – she struggled to find the perfect word – sprightly. But yesterday he was quieter, more distracted. She was sure that he was worried about Mary – and so was she.

The couple were so independent, so strong … but they were old. And Mary was ill.

It was nearly three weeks since they'd had their lamb dinner, and Mary had seemed frailer then. She had popped in to bake with Kate each Thursday, but she'd hardly bustled about to offer a helping hand. More and more she'd just watched and advised. Kate, in her ignorance, had put it down to the fact that she was getting more proficient and needed less help, but it was probably more to do with Mary's failing health.

She sighed. She was already so fond of the couple; she couldn't imagine one of them not being around. And Mary had helped her so much. Given her confidence, encouraging her.

It was almost like having her grandparents back. Two people she'd loved but probably never appreciated enough. And never given herself the time to mourn. She hadn't even noticed when her gran had decided to stop fighting to stay alive, but she could see the weariness creeping up on Mary. She couldn't stop that, but she did want to help her make the most of the time she had. To bake, if that was what gave her pleasure.

Kate realised she was getting hooked on cooking. Mary had been right; she could lose herself in the gentle and sometimes repetitive tasks, forget all the niggles of everyday life – and the pain of losing Eddie. While she was in the kitchen, she was in control, she was creating something that gave her pleasure. And she could actually remember Eddie in a good way; imagine him by her side, chiding her for the mess she left, cheering and high-fiving her when something came out how she wanted it.

Oh goodness, she really hoped that Charles was right, and

it was just a bad day. She didn't want to lose Mary, and she was sure Charles would be devastated, however much of a brave face he put on things.

She slowly dried her hands and sat back down at the table, picking up the recipe book that Mary had given her. She'd been updating it most days with the help of Mary, Della and Charles but she knew that it would be far more attractive if she had some good photographs of the dishes and cakes. She'd been reluctant to ask Jack, but then the other day she'd come downstairs to find an envelope on the doormat, with 'Kate' written on the front, underlined, and 'As promised. Rgds J'.

There were two photographs inside. One of a rather superior-looking black cat, and the other of herself. She was looking rather pensive, her hair a mess, a bowl in her hands (making her look a bit like Oliver Twist begging for more), and she had her slippers on.

Her first instinct was to laugh with despair at just how messy she looked, and she put the photo down on the hall table. But then it drew her back, and she picked it up for a second look.

It was clever, way different from the snaps that other people had taken, most of which she hated as they seemed to capture all the bits of her that she didn't like, rather than the bits that were okay. Jack had captured something about her. Her mussed-up hair looked almost artistic, the way the light filtered through it, and he'd somehow managed to make her wrinkles disappear. Either a clever trick of the light, or good editing.

She shook her head slowly. He was obviously one of those people who was good at things, naturally talented. Artistic. These weren't the casual snaps she thought he'd taken. These were good. He'd think her attempts at cooking were shocking.

Except… She paused. The hurt she'd seen in his eyes when

he'd tried to laugh off the effect of his illness had been genuine. It had made her pause, think about how much she took for granted. And Della was stepping out of her comfort zone with David, being brave, so why not just risk asking him? The worst she could suffer was mockery, and did that matter?

At one time getting things right and being good (well, perfect), had seemed important. Until the accident – when doing things her way had…

She shook the thoughts from her head. When Mary had said that guilt was terrible, she'd been right. Hers had been gnawing away at her. Whatever anybody said, it *had* been her fault Eddie had gone out at that moment. But fate, or something else, had meant he was precisely where he was when that car rammed his. It wasn't her fault that some guy they'd never met had had a massive heart attack that sent his car careering across the lanes out of control, his foot jammed on the accelerator. She could see that.

But Mary didn't know she'd lied to Eddie. Mary didn't know that their last moments together had been everything she hated about herself. She couldn't change that moment. She couldn't make amends with Eddie, but he'd have loved to see her helping Jack. He had been generous, positive. She could be a bit more like Eddie.

Before she could change her mind, she picked up her phone and sent Jack a message. She'd put it off for far too long, and she wasn't sure why.

Thanks for the photos – could I ask a favour, could you come and take some more for me? My food? Maybe tomorrow if you're free. It's a little project I'm doing and I'm the least artistic person in the world.

She pressed send. When, if, he came she'd ask him for hints on how to arrange the food.

She had set up her Instagram account for 'Auntie Flo's Tearoom', but so far she hadn't uploaded many photographs. The first picture hadn't even been food, it had been the roses that Jack had given her. They'd been old-fashioned, nostalgic, and looked perfect when she'd put them in the jug on the windowsill – as though they belonged here. Well, in the tearoom.

And they'd been a gesture of goodwill, an apology – accepting them had been part of her nature, but she'd stared at them for a long time after he'd gone. She'd forgiven Jack, she'd accepted his flowers, and they were a reminder that she had to do that in other parts of her life. Those delicately coloured, fragile petals held their heads high because they had strength and thorns. She wasn't sure she wanted the protection of thorns – it was time to *stop* being prickly – but she did want to be strong.

She'd liked the photograph she took. The simple jug, the old-fashioned paned window blurred in the background, the beautiful softness of the roses. So when she set up the account it felt right to upload it.

She jumped as her phone vibrated.

Sure. Mid-morning? J

She smiled. A man of few words, but the right ones.

p.s. the photos weren't shit, they were rather good! Surprisingly? J

The single-word reply made her laugh out loud. Jack had a dry humour. He interested her – maybe too much.

Charles had been very excited when she'd told him she was thinking about making their cake, he had promised to keep it a secret – and find Mary's recipe for her. He'd been as good as his word and dropped it off that morning, along with a beautiful bunch of heavily scented freesias. 'For you, my dear.' He'd leant forward and raised her hand, kissed the knuckles and made her blush. 'They've always been Mary's favourites. She says they're the scent of summer in a vase. I'll miss her.' He said the final words very quietly, before waving his stick in the air and setting off down the path.

Kate's heart sunk. Did this mean Mary was worse rather than better? She'd lifted the flowers to her nose and felt touched in a way she never had before when she'd been given flowers. Which admittedly wasn't often, but something about the flowers was so personal. So carefully selected, as though they weren't just a gesture, they were a genuine thank you. And something about Charles's final words brought hot tears to her eyes. However forgetful he was, however muddled he could seem, he did know how ill Mary was. He was just handling it the best way he knew. He was trying to stop her worrying about him. But she really hoped he'd talk to Mary. Be open. Because that's what their whole marriage had been about, until now, when they were both skirting around their fears for each other. Because they were so deeply in love.

'No pressure then, Eddie,' she'd said softly as she'd closed the front door behind Charles, but she so wanted this cake to be perfect. How Charles and Mary remembered it.

She popped the flowers into a vase, thinking they'd look perfect in the background of a foodie photo, then paused for moment – staring at the stairs.

Charles's words sent her upstairs to the bedroom. To the bag in the bottom of the wardrobe.

She didn't quite know why she'd decided it was time. Maybe it was to do with love, love and loss. Maybe it was to do with the way Charles was handling things, quietly accepting each layer of his life.

Kate sat cross-legged on the floor and stared at the bag. The bag that the police had brought round, Eddie's 'personal effects'.

The bag she'd been avoiding, because it was all she had left of him. His last goodbye. Once she'd opened it there was no turning back, it was admitting he was never coming back.

She laid the commiseration cards to one side. One day soon she'd read them. Just not yet.

Was it weird that she'd never sorted through his things, she wondered. To lose somebody you loved with all your heart and leave their things untouched. But she knew why she'd done it. She'd looked at his things and felt hate. She hated Eddie for leaving life, leaving her, so abruptly. And she'd been frightened of facing up to what he had gone out for, what he would have brought back. Because this represented the tomorrow he hadn't had. That she'd been partly responsible for.

But she knew it was time to stop. To face up to everything. She had to see this last little bit of her husband, or she had lost even more of his short life, of their marriage, than she needed to. She'd lost those last few seconds, the last thoughts he'd had. She'd been treading water since he went, and if she didn't want to sink, she needed to learn how to swim. Cooking, her new friends – and yes, they were friends in a way workmates never had been – had taken her on the first step, but she knew she had to start taking bigger steps on her own.

She tipped the contents of the bag onto the floor. A surprisingly sparse collection for the last day of a life. Car keys – she blinked the tears away and pushed those to one side – his wallet, mobile phone, scraps of paper and bits and pieces that he kept in the car. And an envelope.

She picked up the envelope, with her name on the front, and the big heart he always drew.

Is this what he'd forgotten? But he'd already given her a wedding anniversary card that day. She was sure he had. So, what was this?

For a moment she hesitated, and then she stood up and slowly went downstairs, and put it on the kitchen dresser.

She wasn't sure why, but she didn't feel that now was the right time to open it.

But she did feel ready to make a pineapple upside-down cake for Mary and Charles.

Kate sat down at the table and looked at the recipe. One she really had to put into her own book.

Auntie Flo's pineapple upside-down cake

The sweetest, lightest, loveliest cake – the perfect celebration of my darling husband and our wonderful life together. I always make it exactly to her recipe, because it is perfect just the way it is. (The only thing I've done is update to grams and alter the oven setting because in my old age I get very confused)

Sponge

100g softened butter, 100g caster sugar, 100g self-raising flour
1tsp baking powder
1tsp vanilla extract
2 eggs

Topping

50g butter, 50g light soft brown sugar
Pineapple rings in syrup
Glacé cherries
You will need a 20cm cake tin. Preheat fan over to 170°C

- *Topping - Melt the brown sugar and butter together in a pan, pour into the tin. Drain pineapple slices and arrange on the bottom, put the cherries in the centre of the pineapple.*
- *Sponge – cream the butter and sugar together until light, gradually add the eggs. Stir in the vanilla extract. Sift in the flour, baking powder and salt. Add 2tbsp milk, or 2tbsp of the pineapple syrup. Beat together until smooth. Pour into the tin.*
- *Cook for 30-35 minutes, testing until a skewer comes out clean. Leave to cool slightly in the tin, before turning out.*

The knock on the door was brief and decisive, very Jack-like. The man, though, when she opened the door, looked much more chilled than the last time she'd seen him. He also looked like a man on a mission.

Chapter Twenty-Four

JACK

The secret of change

J ack poured himself a cup of coffee, took a bite of the hot, freshly buttered toast and realised that today had a different feel about it. It took him a while to pin down exactly how he felt, then he realised that the only applicable word was 'happy'.

There was a lightness inside him, or rather an absence of the weight of failure and loss that he had become used to.

Jack had never exactly been carefree; he'd been focused, driven, determined. But he had been content with that, it had kept him on an even keel – which was why he'd been hit so hard when his life had lost its direction.

He took a sip of the coffee, and the corner of his mouth lifted; he was sure it tasted better. More like coffee – or that could have been the smell, combined with the memory. But did that matter? It tasted less metallic, and less could be more, couldn't it? Less metallic meant more of the true earthiness of coffee. Less metallic meant more hope.

The thought of drifting from a cup-half-empty to a cup-half-full type of person made him laugh out loud. But he got now why Ben had told him to celebrate the small wins. Enjoy them. Feeling less negative might not have been how he had felt in his old life, but in his new one maybe it was a good start.

His gaze drifted from the view of the garden to the photo on the table. Kate. He wiped his buttery fingers clean, then picked it up and sat down.

From an artistic point of view, it was good. The light was filtering through her hair, giving it light and dark shading, but it was her eyes that pulled him in.

He saw more of Kate in her eyes than he had face to face.

She didn't have cat's eyes; hers had a depth. A reflection of a past. There was a look in them that he couldn't quite pin down. A question, an uncertainty. She had a hint of little girl lost that her body language was at odds with. Is that what they meant when they said eyes were the window to the soul?

And she was holding the bowl out to him like a gift. Offering him an olive branch.

Kate was a giver, not a taker.

The corner of his mouth lifted again at the thought. He was being fanciful. But that wasn't just because of the photograph, it was the text she'd sent. The text that for some strange reason had meant he'd got out of bed today feeling like he was getting out on the *right side*. That today could be interesting. He had a purpose.

'Hey!' He lifted his camera in a greeting. Kate grinned. She looked more relaxed than she had in the photograph he'd taken a couple of weeks ago. More confident. His fingers itched. 'May I?' He held the camera up to eye level and she nodded. So Jack stepped back and snapped away, capturing her standing in the doorway – head tilted to one side, a half-smile lifting her generous mouth, her chin lifted. Pretty, confident, ready to face the world. 'Sorry.' He shrugged self-consciously, unable to shake the words from his head. 'Need all the practice I can get!'

'I know that feeling! I need you to practise on my pineapple upside-down cake though.'

'Your what? Cake has never really been my thing, I had a pastry chef to make the desserts, but that conjures up all kinds of strange images – none of them good.'

She laughed. 'It's not that bad! Come on in. I'm doing it for Charles and Mary, but I really could do with some help. I've got a picture from the recipe I found online but I want mine to look different. And I just need some general tips on making all my food look a bit better.'

An hour later, Jack had his sleeves rolled up and a knife in his hand. The only knife skills he'd used recently involved spreading butter or cutting his food up, but a chopping knife felt like a familiar friend. His knife had always felt like a part of him, an extension.

'Okay, so you can go for the sophisticated small-plate precision or the thrown-together casual look. But it's like most things in life – natural takes a lot of effort, if you know what I mean.'

'Yeah, I know exactly what you mean! My bedhead look isn't at all like the version you see on TikTok, I look a right state!'

She laughed, her eyes twinkling, and Jack couldn't imagine her looking a state. He wondered what she'd look like while she was asleep, her hair strewn over the pillow, her features soft. Why was he thinking like that? Kate in bed. Hiding behind a lens was turning him into a stalker.

'I look like I've been electrocuted, definitely bad hair day,' he said to hide his discomfort. 'And I dribble out of the corner of my mouth in my sleep apparently.' Wow, he was doing an ace job of making sure they'd never spend a night in the same room, let alone bed.

'Dribble as well? Definitely electrocution.'

Their gazes met. And Jack felt a sudden urge to kiss her, which was scary. Jack hadn't got anything to offer anybody else. What the hell could a jobless, directionless ex-chef do for anybody?

And he was pretty sure Kate wasn't a snog-and-move-on kind of girl. For God's sake, she'd lost the love of her life a few years ago. She was floundering nearly as much as he was.

He switched his attention to the potato instead. Repositioned it. 'So anyway, back to the food. Potatoes are easy to start on, plenty to go at and an even texture, and if you cut one in half you've got a steady base. Even thrown-on-the-plate needs to be done carefully. It's all in the chopping. Evenly done, even if you're going for rough cut.'

'Oh yeah, sure.'

He laughed at her dry tone, keeping his eyes on the chopping board to concentrate on root vegetables, not her long elegant fingers and slender wrists. 'Let's start with precision, it's easier. Okay, so you need even-sized pieces for cooking as well as presentation, yeah?'

'Mary said something like that.'

'Or they won't all cook properly. Then it's easier to make it look pretty as well.' Muscle memory kicked in as he took the potato and effortlessly cut it into perfect slices. Chopped them into identical cubes.

'Wow, how do you chop that fast?'

'Plenty of practice. I've been doing it most of my life.'

'Most?'

'I was helping Mum as soon as I was old enough to hold a knife. She was fairly relaxed about sharp blades and kids.' He couldn't help the smile. They had been good times, helping his mother. He'd not stopped to think about that for years. 'Hey, hold your knife like this.' He leant round, covered her hand with his. Adjusted her grip. 'Now, try again.' He wasn't sure if this made things worse or better. At least now he wasn't watching her lips, but he could feel the warmth of her skin beneath his.

Kate chopped, then glanced up at him, happiness shining in her face. 'Look at that!'

'See? It's easy.' He moved away reluctantly. 'We'll make a chef of you yet.' He picked up his camera, to give himself something to do with his hands. Stop him from cradling her face in his palms, kissing her. He captured the concentration as she adjusted her grip and sliced carefully.

She brushed the hair out of her face with the back of her hand. 'This is hard. I don't think I've concentrated this much for years!'

'It gets easier.' He smiled. It was nice to watch her.

'It's almost therapeutic, isn't it? Cooking, preparing food.'

'It certainly is. I've always spent hours on my own in the kitchen, working on techniques, recipes. I like my own space; I've always enjoyed my own company.' He'd had hours of his own company, until he'd started to hate himself and tried to run away. Tricky one.

Kate nodded, thoughts chasing across her face, a slight frown furrowing her brow. 'I never really gave myself space, I don't think, until Eddie went. I was scared of it, I think, it was easier to just keep going than stop and question anything. But when Mary was helping me she said much the same; she's always spent hours in the kitchen and I think it really helps her right now. It's like an escape.'

He nodded.

'But I guess it's different for you.'

'It was my whole life. My obsession. A very close friend, Ben, said I needed to reimagine change.' Why was he calling him a friend? Why couldn't he be honest with her? She didn't know him, wasn't judging him. It wasn't like admitting it to friends, or his parents.

She was waiting, her knife still.

'Not that close,' he added. 'Not a real friend.' He sighed. 'Well, to be honest he was my therapist.'

'Was?' She didn't sound surprised.

'We parted company when I insisted on working this out my way.'

Her smile was soft. 'Sounds like Bea, my therapist. Bossy.'

'Very bossy,' he said, smiling back, 'but in a non-confrontational way.'

'Of course. Your decision, you have to decide, but their look says, just listen to yourself!'

'Exactly. You've got it wrong!'

They both laughed, then he stopped feeling awkward.

'I don't think you've got it wrong,' she said softly, then sighed. 'I think I need to get to enjoy my own company more. But reimagine change, what does that mean?' She wrinkled her nose. Even her nose was cute. Kissable.

'He said I was using too much of my energy fighting the past, instead of focusing it on the new life I was trying to build. And that is the secret to change, letting go.'

'And are you? Fighting the past?'

He frowned. 'I think I've been thinking too much about what I've lost and assuming that defines me. Which I guess cocks up any chance of a different life. I guess I need to put the lid down on the dreams I had and replace them with new ones. Reinvent myself.'

'You can put the lid down on those dreams, but hold onto the special bits, the good memories.' Kate was looking out of the window as she spoke, and he was pretty sure she was talking about herself, not him. Convincing herself.

'Reinventing is about the future, not your past. Reinventing that image, redrawing it, not shutting off what happened. I guess I struggle with where to put that line, how much to hold onto without it stopping me moving forward. I needed to get away from Ben, from my old place, to try and work it out. He was driving me nuts, made me feel cornered. Well, actually —' he paused '— I suppose it was me that was putting the pressure on myself, a deadline on how quickly I should work it out. I finally understood that I couldn't do that.'

She blinked at him. 'Was that hen you were holding in that interview yours?'

'She was. That was Mary, Mary Berry to give her her full name. I also had —' he smiled '— Clarissa, Delia and Isabella.'

'Isabella?'

'Mrs Beeton! They were all formidable in their own right. You don't mess with chickens. I think you've chopped up enough potatoes to feed the whole street.'

'The way we're going, I might end up doing that!' She hesitated. 'You should come round some time. Maybe take photographs of us all enjoying the food.'

He raised an eyebrow.

'And join us eating it as well, of course!' she added hastily.

'I can tell you were a teacher, offering enticements.'

'I don't think teachers are allowed to do that.'

'You know what I mean.' He smiled. 'I might do, sometime.

Thanks for the invite.' He wouldn't, of course. He wasn't ready to be interrogated, talked about. He could imagine how it would go. Or was that his ego? Would nobody be interested, now he was old news. But that aside, was it really a good idea to spend even more time with Kate? Share meals with her?

'Well, you should definitely come and help us eat this pineapple cake, once you've helped me make it look pretty. I've made the mix, I just need to put it all in the tin and cook it. It's a surprise – it's Mary and Charles's wedding anniversary and they used to have one here every year when this was a tearoom. I hope it's edible.' She frowned.

'I'm sure it will be fine. Come on then, let's see the pictures you found.'

Jack was pretty sure he had never, ever had an upside-down pineapple cake, or even remotely entertained the thought of making one.

'Tinned pineapple?' He lifted an eyebrow.

'The cake was popular in the 1950s, and so was tinned pineapple!' Kate retorted. He tried hard not to laugh – and failed.

'What?'

'You've done your homework.' He could imagine her researching thoroughly. She'd already mentioned how she used spreadsheets to plan and work out timings – a world away from how he'd cooked. It amused him, but he wasn't making fun of her. He was quite impressed.

'Of course! And glace cherries were on-trend as well.' She held up a container of bright red cherries and laughed at his expression.

'I suppose,' he said slowly, 'it will make a striking retro photo. You'll be obliterating my memories of good food at this rate, let alone pushing them to the back of my mind.'

She laughed, and just hearing the sound made him want to do it again.

'Although if I can't taste the pineapple overload in it, you might as well shoot me now!'

'Or just put you out to pasture,' Kate said, still smiling.

He really did want to kiss her. She was cute, funny. He suddenly felt a pang of jealousy about Eddie. Eddie had shared this kitchen with her, shared his dreams. He'd never had that — apart from with his mum.

He had to stop thinking like this, concentrate on the food one hundred per cent, like he used to. Except concentrating on a pineapple didn't quite have the hook that making a good sauce did.

'Okay, let's try and get a hint of sophistication —' he shook his head and she laughed again '— by cutting the pineapple rings in two, then laying the segments a bit like a tarte tatin. But with a complete ring in the centre?' As he watched her carefully lay out the slices in the tin, then concentrate on cutting the cherries in half, it was a hundred miles away from the food he used to cook, a bit like being a child again. In fact, he'd have to send his mum a photo, it would make her laugh.

'I'm going to do regular Thursday baking sessions with Mary.' Kate straightened up, studying the pineapple slices. 'Because who knows how much longer she'll be able to do it.' She bit her bottom lip, and despite the fact that he hardly knew her he couldn't help but reach out and touch her arm.

'Nothing will be able to top this cake though.' He patted gently, resisting the urge to pull her into the type of hug his mother used to give him.

'Nothing, it's going to be awesome.' She sniffed. 'Hey, you could give me a hand with something else next time you come. I need to come up with some ideas for David to try and tempt his daughter Harry with. She's avoiding food. Mary thinks it's because she feels helpless since her parents split up, and Della thinks it's the only thing she has control over.'

'And you think?' He watched her carefully, the thought of there being a next time scaring and exciting him in equal measures. Well, not quite equal. He wanted to see Kate again. And it would be good for his photography. He was doing them both a favour.

'They're both right, but maybe if we can tempt her with tasty tiny things that she can help David make then she'll be tempted but feel like it's her own decision?'

'I'll have a think.' He could always just message her with some ideas.

'Great, and you've got to come back to show me the photos! Right, this is ready for the oven. Fancy a cup of coffee while it's in there?' He hesitated, wondering if he should go before he somehow got caught up in something he wasn't sure he was ready for. 'You've got to stay. This has to be worth a photo or two if it comes out okay.'

He nodded. If change was about focusing on building a new life, then pineapple upside-down cake was definitely a long way from the old life that was out of his reach. He'd found his new direction. Now he had to embrace it. God help him, he tried not to groan.

'Okay. Smells good already.'

She grinned. 'Wow, so you can smell it! Maybe your senses are starting to come back after all.'

She looked so enthusiastic he didn't want to put a damper on things, he didn't want the haunting sadness that he'd seen the first time he met her to come back. So, he just grinned and shrugged. 'Mebbe!'

'Promise me you'll come back and try a slice with us?

Please, see if it tastes of cardboard? It's their wedding anniversary tomorrow and Della and David are coming as well.'

The cake might not have been exactly fine dining, but when it came out of the oven Jack was sure he could smell more than just cake, he could actually pick out some of the individual elements. He could tell it was piled high with enough sweet pineapple to feed a street. When he smiled at Kate, he almost felt triumphant, and he laughed when he saw the look on her face.

'Wow, it almost looks edible!' She laughed, a throaty laugh that pulled at something deep inside him, locked them together in a strange moment.

He really wanted to take a step closer. Ruffle up her hair, kiss that perfect upturned nose, her generous mouth.

He ducked away and grabbed his camera, to cover his confusion. This was madness – being able to smell bloody pineapple shouldn't make him want to kiss the nearest woman. She was bereaved, she was as muddled up as him.

'Looks good,' he said, knowing his tone was curt. But distance was better than the alternative. Hiding behind his camera, in the same way he used to distance himself behind his chopping board.

His finger stopped pressing the shutter.

He *had* done that. Always. He had separated himself from the rest of life. He'd not exactly been hiding, but nobody and nothing had come between him and his cooking. He lowered the camera and looked at Kate. She was suffering because she'd let somebody in, she'd given time, she'd loved. He'd never let himself do that, had he?

'Okay?' She was frowning.

'Sure. I think I've got enough now.'

'Oh, I almost forgot, can you do one with these freesias in the background, please? Charles brought them round, and they're so pretty.'

'Sure.' He took the final snaps, then put his camera to one side. 'I'll get them over to you tomorrow. Birthday?' He spotted a white envelope on the dresser with her name on, and it seemed a good way to deflect attention.

'No.' She shook her head, colouring up in a way that made him think he'd upset her rather than embarrassed her. 'It was —' She hesitated.

'It's fine, sorry, I didn't mean to be nosy.'

'It was from Eddie.' She looked straight at him then. 'It was in the car when… I'll open it one day, it might sound stupid, but I don't feel ready. It's like … the last thing.' She shrugged, and she did look embarrassed, as well as upset now.

'You don't have to let go of him you know. Even if you open it, it's not goodbye.'

'It's the final words, the ones he never got to say.'

'Maybe you should read them, maybe they were important.' He shrugged. 'We all deserve to be heard. But hey, don't listen to me, I'm the guy that pushed everybody away when they tried to help me, because I didn't want to admit I was a failure.'

'You're not a failure.' She sighed. 'I'll open it soon.'

Jack walked back down the street and wondered who the hell he was to tell Kate what to do. What he'd told her was true. He'd hardly spoken to his own family since his life had gone tits-up, since he'd had to admit he was a failure.

Had he been wrong? Did they deserve to be heard, to be allowed to be a part of the bad as well as the good? Maybe it was a mistake, maybe it was leaving it too late if he waited until his life was properly back on track. Kate felt bad because she'd never had a chance to talk to Eddie, to share his future. Was he heading towards the same kind of future – regrets and guilt?

He pushed his front door open and fished his mobile phone out of his pocket. He could at least message them, tell his mother he'd got a new hobby. The short laugh escaped before he could stop it. Hobby? He'd never had time for anything but a career – his parents would love this.

He'd never live down this flaming cake.

Smiling, he hit send on the message.

Chapter Twenty-Five

KATE

The wedding anniversary

K ate opened the door, a smile already on her face. She was ready, the beautiful (even if she said it herself) cake on the table, the best china out, old-fashioned saucers, bubbly glasses, an assortment of sandwiches cut into delicate fingers. She'd even found a lace tablecloth, and some bunting to brighten up the room and make it look more like the tearoom it used to be. She didn't want to overdo things, but she did want Charles and Mary to be surprised and happy.

Jack had sent over some photographs, which she'd already (with his permission) uploaded to her Instagram, and she'd had a great response. She'd even had a comment from an old schoolfriend, who had said that the pineapple cake had reminded her of her grandparents and had messaged asking if she fancied a natter over a slice of cake and a coffee sometime.

Kate had instantly replied yes. She'd shut herself off, abandoned her friends, and now, alongside the new friends she was making, she knew she was ready to invite her old ones back into her life.

Today was going to be a good day. A celebration of Charles and Mary's life and marriage, and a step forward for herself. She was going to show them all the Instagram account, share things in a way she'd not done since Eddie had died.

'You're early!' But it wasn't Della, with the expected bottle of prosecco in her hand. It was Jack. He didn't smile back.

The feeling of elation she'd felt a second before died.

'Kate, you need to come. Now.' He grabbed her hand, and her instinct was to pull back.

'Hang on, I need…' She shifted her weight back abruptly, and he let go.

'Please. It's Mary.'

The look on his face and urgency in his tone stopped her in her tracks. Jack was grounded, sensible; he wouldn't look like that unless it was serious.

Her heart thudded in her chest. Dragging her apron over her head, she tossed it back into the hallway and pulled the front door shut behind her.

Jack was already striding down the road, glancing briefly over his shoulder. 'I was walking past when the ambulance arrived and went in to check everything was okay. The paramedics are with Mary now, but I thought it was best for somebody to go in with her, and somebody to take Charles in the car.'

Kate really wished she'd got something else on her feet, not useless flipflops, as she did her best to keep up with him. She was out of breath by the time they got to the house, where she could see a pale Charles in the hallway.

'I hope I did the right thing.' His hand trembled as he

reached out for hers. 'I was just so worried, she looked so poorly.'

'You did exactly the right thing.' Kate squeezed his hand. His grip was firm, but his hand was birdlike – so frail, so cold. 'You're cold.' She glanced at Jack, who disappeared into the lounge and came back a moment later with a patterned throw, which he draped around Charles's shoulders.

'The lad was going past.' Charles hardly seemed to notice. 'So I asked him to come and tell you, because you're expecting us and I really don't know if we'll be back in time. We don't want to be late, we're never late.'

'It's fine, Charles, forget about tea.'

'But you've baked and…' He paused for a second, his eyes clouded and confused. 'It's our anniversary, you know.'

'I know,' Kate said softly, then reached forward to hug him. 'We'll celebrate later, okay?'

'She opened her card, but she's not expecting to go out. We always used to, you know. We went to the tearoom…'

'Okay, folks, if we can squeeze past.' A paramedic, her tone positive, broke through Charles's reminisces, and as he glanced at Mary it was as though a switch had been thrown. He was back in the present, not confused at all.

'Do you mind awfully if I go in the ambulance with her? The lad offered to take me, but I think it's better if I'm with her. I've always been there for her, you know. I promised.' He looked Kate straight in the eye, and her throat blocked up. All she could do was nod. Whisper. 'Of course.'

'You've been so kind, both of you. But I can cope from here.'

'Of course, I know you can, Charles. But we're coming anyway, aren't we?' She looked at Jack, who nodded. 'We'll see you at the hospital, Charles. You go with her, and we'll find you.'

'Splendid. Splendid. Have I got my key?' His normal 'splendid' was so muted it brought a pain to her chest. Is this what being brave, being in love, was all about? He patted his pockets, looked round, patted some more then reached in and triumphantly held it up. There was a piece of paper stuck to it, which he looked at blankly for a moment, and then the confusion on his face cleared. 'Ah, bag. Mary told me not to forget her hospital bag, had it packed for a while just in case.'

He pointed, and Kate suddenly noticed the small overnight bag in the corner of the hallway next to his stick. She picked both up and held them out reluctantly.

'Are you sure you'll be okay on your own?'

'I'm not on my own, I'm with Mary,' he said softly. Charles carefully locked the door, then with the help of the paramedic clambered up into the ambulance, sat down and took Mary's hand in his.

'Nonsense, it's no fuss at all, my dear,' Kate heard him say, before the doors were shut.

'They're amazing, aren't they?' Jack said softly, nursing the cup of coffee in his hands.

Kate nodded. 'He knows how ill she is; he was just pretending to be confused when he came to my place the first time. I hope he's told her.' She stared at the poster on the wall, not really seeing it, only a blur. 'I know he does get a bit confused, but only ordinary forgetfulness, and he wasn't confused that day. He came −' she looked at Jack, frowning slightly, still working it out '− I don't think he came because he wanted to go back to their past, I think he came because he wanted to stop her worrying about him. He came for help.'

'I don't get it.'

'He knows she worries about how he'll cope on his own, and…' The words came slowly, but Kate was sure she finally understood. 'He wanted to show her he wasn't alone; he knew Eddie loved cooking and he'd kind of assumed I could as well.' She smiled. 'He didn't know what a challenge he'd have! But he wanted Mary to be able to bake because it made her happy, and she couldn't do it on her own, and he wanted to show her that her love, her food, would still be there for him when she'd gone. That I'd make it.'

'That's some big ask. How could he know you would?'

She shrugged. 'He's a determined man. It must have taken guts to pretend like he did, to persuade me, chat to you, talk to Della. But you get guts when you're doing it for somebody you love that much, don't you?'

'I don't know.' Jack looked her straight in the eye, a slight flush along his cheekbones. 'I don't think I've ever given myself time to love somebody like that.' He shrugged self-consciously, then frowned. 'Not like you did; not like they have. I guess I got what I deserved.'

Kate raised an eyebrow. Waited.

'To be used. Liked – well, I can't even say liked, let alone loved – *dated* for what I was, not who I am. Apparently Clara didn't have time for me either, she just liked to say she was dating a successful chef. And then I wasn't one, so I wasn't worth hanging with.' He looked down at his hands.

'That's a horrible thing to do.'

He sighed. 'But it wasn't particularly nice of me dating her when I didn't have time to really care, was it? I just never thought about it. Isn't that ridiculous?'

'Not really.' She shook her head. Their voices were low, but she seemed to have blocked out everybody else, the comings and goings in the busy waiting area at the hospital. She could hear every word he spoke. And his words suddenly made things crystal clear. She was like him; she'd never given herself time for anything until recently. But here, in this hospital, when all they could do was wait, it seemed easier to understand, easier to think about.

'I get it. Not the Clara bit, but the bit about not having time. I did love Eddie, but I never gave myself time for most things, like appreciating him, talking to him, missing my grandparents. I was always mad busy working, proving I could be somebody. Proving I wasn't −' she paused '− my mother. But I was, in the end, I was too like her and that's why everything went wrong.' She nodded, but it was more for her own benefit than Jack's. 'Mum was like you, like me, she buried herself in her work, she didn't have time for anybody, she didn't even have time to love me, her daughter.'

'Maybe she was just scared of failure? I've never admitted it to anybody before, but I felt a failure when I couldn't cook, and I pushed everybody away and now I feel so bloody guilty about it.'

Kate stared at him, then whispered softly. 'I feel guilty too.'

'About your mum?'

'About Eddie. About all the things I didn't say to him, to explain.' She glanced down, not wanting to meet his gaze. 'I made decisions that weren't mine to make on my own.'

'That's what you do when you're busy. I definitely did that with Clara, I didn't let her in. She wasn't really a part of my life, she was just there on the outside.' He sighed. 'But you and Eddie weren't like that, you were a team.'

'In most things,' she whispered back. 'We talked about

nearly everything, because I did love him and trust him. But there was some stuff that was kind of non-negotiable. I couldn't talk about it with him because it wasn't straight in my own head.'

'But you would have done.'

'I would.' She would. If she'd had time.

'I've been thinking –' he turned the cup slowly in his hands '– that maybe it's time to take a step back and talk to my family, so I messaged Dad. I'm going to ask them over, cos what happens if I run out of time to say sorry?'

Kate blinked. She'd run out of time with Eddie, and that was what really hurt. That was what had ripped her apart. 'That's a great idea.' Her words were strangled, the emotion threatening to block her throat.

'Oh, Kate.' Jack put his coffee down, then put an arm around her shoulders. She leant into the warmth of his body. It was strong, solid. It felt like a body that could absorb her pain, a body that could shield her.

Any other time she would have pulled back, but at this moment it was what she needed – a big protective force.

'You can't get Eddie back, but maybe your mum couldn't help the way she was either. Look, tell me to shut up if talking about her is off-bounds, but the way I see it, Eddie has gone, but she's still out there for you. Maybe she was just scared –' he glanced up, his mouth twisted into a half-smile '– like me.'

Talking about her mum had been off-bounds for a long time, but she had been creeping into Kate's life one way and another recently. Like some ghost that wouldn't be banished. Through the recipe book, through memories that came to Kate as she slept.

Everything went back to her mum. She *was* important, and Kate wasn't sure any longer if it was purely in a bad way or not. But she was the reason for so many decisions Kate had made in her life, she'd influenced her every step of the way. She had played a part in that fateful night – even if she hadn't meant to.

She was still out there, probably, but was she there for Kate? She'd never seemed to be before.

'She had nothing to be scared of,' Kate said.

'We're all scared of something, things that other people don't give a second thought to. Isn't that what drives us, fear? Fear of failure, fear of not being good enough, fear of not winning, fear of the unknown.'

Oh God, she knew about those fears, so many fears that were *because* of her mother. She couldn't imagine that her mum felt like that as well. Mums just didn't, did they? Mums were strong and coped with everything, had all the answers.

Except mums were just humans.

'She was always confident about everything,' Kate whispered. 'She wasn't scared of anything.'

'Everybody is scared of something, Kate, it's what makes us human. It's not always rational. Hey, you probably have nothing to feel guilty about.' His tone was soft, making her look up and meet his gaze. 'But you think you do, and sometimes it feels more complicated than that, doesn't it?'

She stared at him.

'But it doesn't have to be.'

The emotion welled up in Kate as she let Jack's quiet words sink in. Everybody was telling her not to let the feelings of guilt overwhelm her, control her life, but they didn't understand, did they? She didn't know how to explain, she didn't know what to say to him. But it was as though he wasn't expecting her to, he was just saying it the way he saw it. It was more of a statement than a question.

But she could hardly breathe, she couldn't speak as she looked at him.

'She wants to see you!' The uneven croak broke the moment between them, and Kate spun round so quickly she nearly slid off the hard plastic chair. Jack's arm fell from her shoulders. She'd forgotten it was there, until the warmth was replaced with cool air.

'Charles!' She stood up, then wrapped him in a hug. 'Oh, Charles. She's okay?'

'A bit wobbly but aren't we all.' He tried to do his customary cheerful wink, but his eyes were damp, and he was shaky. It just made her want to hug him even harder. 'I told her not to give me any scares! Now come on, come on, both of you.'

Kate's heart gave a little lurch. Mary looked so small and lost against the big bed and stark white sheets. She was pale, and her smile wasn't quite as bright as it was normally, but she held out her hands as Kate and Jack followed Charles into the room.

'Oh Mary, it's so good to see you,' said Kate. 'You gave us all a bit of a scare.'

'Oh, good heavens, I'm sorry. Well, as you can see, I'm fine, I just had a little bit of a wobble.' She smiled and carefully pulled herself up a little higher on the pillows.

Chapter Twenty-Six

MARY

Different ingredients

Mary wasn't sure if this was what death felt like. She'd always thought there would be pain, then nothing, but this was comfortable. She felt like she was surrounded by good things, the feeling inside her was a like a good friend, and something in her head was saying that she couldn't go yet. It wasn't her time. She had things she had to do first.

She wasn't sure what the things were until she felt Charles's hand on her own, then opened her eyes to see his familiar face. And then she remembered.

'Well now, you're looking much chirpier, isn't she, Charles?' said a strange voice.

Charles nodded and smiled at her.

'I'll get you a nice cup of tea, love.' Mary strained to turn her head slightly and look at the nurse. Ah, that's right, she was in hospital. She remembered the nice man and lady telling her they'd take her to hospital. They kept chatting to her, asking her questions, but she'd been so tired. It was hard to concentrate.

'And what about your friends?' The nurse was still talking as she straightened the sheets that didn't need straightening. 'Would you like me to tell them how we're doing?'

Mary raised an eyebrow.

'Little Kate and that Jack fella insisted on coming as well.' Charles shrugged, but she could see that he was relieved. She smiled. This was what she'd wanted more than anything. Somebody who would be there for him.

They'd been there. It was going to be okay.

'You should –' she croaked, then tried to clear her throat and try again '– ask them in if that's okay?'

The nurse nodded. 'Just don't let them stay too long, you need some rest!'

'I'll have plenty of time to rest.' Mary regretted the words, as Charles squeezed her hand, but there was no avoiding it, was there? They'd always faced life's challenges head-on, and now was not the time to do things differently.

'Well, we are feeling better!' The nurse laughed, adjusted the blinds then walked to the door. 'Ring the bell if you need me, love. And you two lovebirds behave yourselves, I've got my eye on you!' She wagged a finger.

Charles chuckled and then followed her out of the door.

Mary closed her eyes, just for a moment. But she didn't feel as exhausted as she had recently; she felt a strange, not exactly energy, more like a *lightness*.

'Oh, Mary!'

Mary smiled as Kate flew in through the door. She was the granddaughter she'd never had, a girl who might have only come into her life briefly, but one she felt she'd shared an important part of her life with.

'You gave us all a bit of a scare.'

'Well as you can see, I'm fine.' Mary sat up a little straighter, determined to reassure the younger woman. 'I'm so sorry we didn't make it for that cup of tea today.'

'Oh, don't be daft!' Kate brushed her eyes with the back of her arm. 'I'm just so pleased to see you're okay. We'll do it next week instead, shall we, when you're back on your feet.'

'That would be lovely, wouldn't it, Charles?'

'And Della will come. I think she's going to be here in a couple of hours. Will they let another visitor in?'

'I'm sure Charles will chat up that nice young nurse, he's got a way with women, haven't you, dear?'

'Not lost my touch!' He smiled, and she was glad that a bit of his colour had come back. He might have a lot of wrinkles, but to her eyes he looked like he'd aged a decade when she'd returned to full consciousness. Not that she'd really been out for the count; she'd just felt a bit under the weather, weak. That was the word. Weak. Too weak to really want to breathe properly, too weak to want to keep her eyes open. But she'd not gone anywhere. She could hear Charles in the background, could hear those medical people. She squeezed his hand and turned to smile at him. He'd know why. They'd always understood each other.

'You do know I'm going to have to stay in, for tests.' Charles nodded. 'I'd really like my own dressing gown. We didn't put that in the bag, did we? Why not?' She frowned. She'd tried to remember everything – why hadn't she thought of that?

'I'll go and get it, dear. The lovely blue one?'

'I'll take you,' Kate said immediately, but Mary had a hold of her hand, and didn't let go.

'I'm sure Jack wouldn't mind taking you, would you, dear?'

'Of course not!'

Mary watched the relief flood his features and tried not to smile. He seemed a nice young man, but just like Charles had been. Unsure of himself when he was in an uncomfortable situation, not knowing what to do if he couldn't take charge. He'd be much happier on chauffeur duties than sitting here next to an old woman.

'Thank you, it will give me time to tell Kate some of my secret recipes!' She waited for the door to close. 'You need to watch my Charlie, he's a real matchmaker. I think he's got plans for you and that young man.' She watched as colour flooded Kate's cheeks. 'And he does seem a nice man. Charles was a lovely young man.' She sighed, trying not to rush her words as they weren't flowing as easily as usual. Her mouth was dry, her head all woolly. 'Thank you for looking after him. He did enjoy your trifle, you know.'

'And your sprinkles on top,' Kate said, a gentle smile lighting her features. 'I'll make another one, but it's not your favourite, is it? Did you say apple crumble was?'

'You've got a good memory. Oh yes, I do love a crumble – apple and blackberry, I used to love foraging for them. But Charles like his trifle, and that's the point, isn't it?'

Kate raised an eyebrow but waited quietly. She liked that about the girl, she listened. She was patient.

'We're all different, aren't we? We have our own memories, our own reasons for doing things, our own favourite recipes, and that's what makes us who we are.'

'You've not given me any of your own favourite recipes, have you?'

'No.' She smiled. 'I've put together the ones Charles loves, so that you'll make them for him. He'll need them.' She tried to squeeze Kate's hand, make sure she understood. But it was hard, so hard to make the effort. 'He'll need you.'

'Nobody has ever needed me, Mary.'

Lots of people needed Kate; she was kinder and more generous than she realised. But she was troubled. It was more than grief; it was a guilt that ran deep. She'd only told Mary half the story after their Sunday lunch, only told her that she didn't want a child, but Eddie did. Not explained why she felt his death was her fault, what the things she'd wanted to tell him were.

Something had told Mary that Kate was ready, that it was the right time for her to talk. Tell her story. And Mary wanted to hear it. She wanted to be there for Kate, to help her. It was the last big thing she could do for somebody she cared for.

'Eddie needed you, he loved you. Love isn't about lust, Kate, it's about trust.' The cough rose up in her throat and she couldn't stop it. But Kate waited, not speaking, until she could carry on. 'And you trusted each other, didn't you?'

Kate nodded. 'But I lied to him.'

'Lied?'

'Well, I didn't tell him things I should have.'

'But he trusted you, Kate. You would have told him when you were ready, and he knew that. He trusted you, so he waited, he gave you room. He let you breathe. Whatever it was, Kate, he loved you enough to wait.'

'I was using contraception.'

The words came out of Kate in a rush. It was as though they'd been waiting, bottled up for ages. Mary felt a huge sense of relief. She'd known there was something, and she'd hoped Kate would tell her — before it was too late. Kate had already had one 'too late' in her life. She shouldn't have another.

'It wasn't that I *couldn't* get pregnant, I made sure I

wouldn't, and I never told him. I should have told him, and he'd gone before I could, and I hated him.' Tears spilled from her eyes, and her shoulders shook with tears she needed to shed. 'And I hated myself.' She laid her forehead down on the bed, on top of their joined hands, and Mary strained across to reach over and touch the top of her head.

'Why, Kate? Why was it so important not to fall pregnant?' It didn't make sense to Mary. Kate would make a good mother. But she was scared, there was something about motherhood that frightened her.

'Mum.'

Mary waited. She didn't have long left, but she had time to wait for this.

'Mum never loved me, I was an inconvenience, I ruined her life.'

'Did she say that to you?'

'She didn't need to. She ran away and I spent all my time with Gran and Grandad. I tried so hard to be good enough for her to notice, but she never came to things at school or wanted to be with me. Jack said maybe she was scared, but she didn't have anything to be scared of.'

'But you are good enough, Kate. You've been like a grand-daughter to us, you're a natural at looking after people. Why are you scared of having a baby?'

Kate looked up, met her gaze. 'Of being a bad mother, of being like my own mum, too busy, too interested in work to bother.'

'Scared of failure?' She closed her eyes. 'Failure and guilt have a lot to answer for, my dear, and so does self-protection. My father ruled by the rod, and when I met Charles, he forbade me from seeing him. He said he was soft.' She couldn't help but smile. She'd always loved the way Charles tried to be strict but kidded neither of them. 'When Charles asked for my hand, he laughed. He wouldn't give us permission to marry. He said it would be the ruin of me, and he'd strip the hide off my bones if I saw Charles again. But I've never been one to be careful and I knew I'd never forgive myself if I didn't try, so we plotted when we were in your tearoom, and we ran away.'

'You ran away?' The incredulity in Kate's tone made her feel proud, happy.

'We went to Gretna Green. I did feel guilty that I'd gone against his wishes, but I learned that was his problem, not mine. I couldn't get pregnant, and I'm sure it was because of all the guilt and stress I'd got locked up inside.' Her hand rested on her heart. Her tired old heart that had once been so passionate. 'I didn't want to admit to Charles's parents that I couldn't do it, I had failed to present them with a grandchild.' That had been her fear of failure, the one she'd even recently been hiding from herself. She'd told Kate she was scared of bearing a child, and she had been once, but she'd also been scared that she had fallen short. That there was some physical imperfection that had stopped her from conceiving. So she'd buried her head in the sand, and convinced herself and the world that she really didn't want to grow a baby in her womb. 'But we did want one, and I couldn't let my father's spite ruin our lives, could I? We had love to give to a child as well as each other, so that's why we decided to adopt. The wise lady who placed Saul with us said I hadn't *failed* to carry a child, I'd triumphed in saving another.'

For a moment, her breath didn't want to come, but it didn't matter. She could still see tiny Saul on the day he was handed over to them. He'd been wrapped in a checked blanket, his tiny rosebud mouth begging to be kissed, and she'd fallen in love with him before he was even in her arms. She wanted to lie here quietly and remember. To remember the sweet smell of him, the velvet softness of his perfect skin. But she'd do that later. When Kate had gone. 'Don't feel guilty, Kate, life is far too short. Believe me.'

'Do you really think Mum just found it easier *not* to be a mother?'

'You'd have to ask her that, Kate.' Oh goodness, this was making her tired, but if Kate was willing to talk then she was more than willing to listen.

'Maybe I need to ask myself as well.' Kate's words were so soft that Mary could hardly hear them. But she did. And a smile inside of her lifted her spirits, even though her face felt too tired to show it on the outside.

'You'll work it out. But Kate, I made my decisions, I decided I wanted to adopt a child and that's the way it was. If you don't want children, then there's nothing wrong with that at all, that's your decision and nobody has the right to say you should. But if you've made the decision because you're frightened of turning out like your mum, then that isn't good enough. You aren't your mother, so you won't be the same parent she was. Just remember that. Can you make an old lady happy and promise me that, dear?'

'I promise.'

'I just don't want you to have any more regrets, dear. But I know you'll work it out.'

'Gran used to say that – I'd work it out.'

'Well, you should remember her words, take them to heart You need to learn how to live, Kate. I read one of these clever sayings a while ago; it said you have to work out how to thrive, not survive, and that's something we often don't work out until we're old, when we've lost so much time. When it's running out.'

'Oh Mary, don't say that.'

'But it's true, my dear. I don't feel sorry for myself, I've relished every second of the last few years, and you're partly responsible for that.' She opened her eyes. Kate was looking at her intently and was smiling at her.

'You're a beautiful soul.' She reached out, wanting to touch her cheek, and Kate leant in closer. 'I've loved baking with you, thank you for letting me.'

'Thank you for helping me. If you hadn't come, I'd have never even tried.'

'Oh, before I forget, my recipe book is in that little overnight bag. Take it now, before we forget.'

'But you can give it me later, Mary. I don't need—'

'I want you to have it now, dear. I need to tidy up. But you do what you like with it, now you can do it your own way without me interfering.'

'You've never interfered! I love baking with you, I like doing it your way.'

Mary tried to ignore the tremor in Kate's voice. There were things she wanted to say. This was her time – maybe her final time – to dole out words of wisdom. Well, she hoped they were. They were the lessons she'd learned, and it was her job to pass them on. To give Kate a shortcut she hadn't had. 'You need to do it your way. Living for yourself isn't selfish, because showing your best self to people is what they really deserve – not some "yes person", trying to be what they think people want. Nobody admires them, do they?'

'I was never a yes person with Eddie.'

'I don't think he let you be, Kate. I think you built a world with him and your job where you felt safe, in control, but having a baby threatened that, didn't it? You're a good girl, Kate, you've got a good heart, and I don't know what your mother was like but for her to have had a girl like you she must have cared and been good deep down. I'm sure she loves you in her own way.' She stopped talking as she ran out of breath again. Oh my, it was so annoying when she had so much that she wanted to say. 'But you're not her, Kate. You're you. Now, have you got that book out of my bag yet?'

She watched as Kate went over and took the book from the bag. That book had been with her for years. It had a lifetime of love and memories in it. But she knew Kate would look after it. Care for it.

'And even if you don't have the inclination to give young Jack the kiss of his lifetime, though I'm sure a passionate soul like him would be rather good at it, you could help him to become part of life down our street, couldn't you?'

Kate laughed. It was a lovely carefree sound. 'I could!'

'Look who we found.' Charles's voice broke into the laughter.

'Happy anniversary!'

The murmur of pain that had been building in Mary's chest melted away as her tired eyes focused on Della, who was standing in the doorway holding out a magnificent cake.

They really were amazing, these people, this new community that she'd only discovered such a short time ago.

'Oh Charles!' He took her hand and looked down into her eyes, and she saw the love there that she always had. She was safe when Charles was with her. 'You organised this? You sneaky man!' It was Charles who had discovered them, not her, it was Charles who had brought them all together. Who had made this happen.

He smiled, and for a moment she could see that debonair chap who had courted her with cups of tea and cake, who had brought her flowers, who had always supported her.

'Well, I think I need to take a drinks order, don't I? Only tea and coffee, mind you!' The nurse's cheerful tone rang around the room. 'And a knife, or have you got one?'

'I've brought one, and some plates.' Della smiled at her. 'David packed them.'

'Well, I think you'd better go and get this David out of the waiting room.' The nurse winked at Mary. 'I think a special cake like this deserves a few visiting rules to be broken, don't you?'

'Oh, this upside-down pineapple cake is magnificent.' Mary hadn't thought she'd be able to eat a thing, but she had a sip of tea and a tiny bit of the sweet fruit and perfectly light sponge. She held Charles's hand and she was right back there. The day he proposed, the many anniversaries, shared time and memories in the beautiful little tearoom. And she enjoyed watching the young people around them.

'Jack took some photos, and it looks even better in them!' Kate laughed, glancing over at him. He smiled back, more relaxed than she'd ever seen him. Although admittedly, when she had seen him, he'd been rushing past with his head down, looking more moody than magnificent. Charles had said he was a nice chap though, and she trusted his judgement. And maybe he was right about Kate and Jack; they certainly seemed comfortable together in a way that came either from years of knowing each other or from hearts that were meant to be together.

She glanced up at her Charles, the other half of her own heart, and he winked back.

'I think maybe we should leave you in peace. I'm sure you'll welcome a bit of shut-eye.' Della was already putting the rest of the cake back in a tin and gathering plates. 'It's been so wonderful to see you though. I'm glad we managed our little party even if it was in the wrong place!'

'There's never a wrong place if you're with the right people,' said David unexpectedly, and they all stared at him. He didn't blush but laughed, and Mary felt a smile find its way to her lips. She'd always liked the man; he was kind and generous, and he'd soldiered on when his family had been pulled apart. Never complaining.

'And the right food.' Jack broke the silence. 'I hear you could do with extending your cooking repertoire a bit, David? Some easy-to-make tasty stuff?'

David nodded, and the two men drifted out of the room.

'He's a good man,' Mary said in Della's ear as she bent down to kiss her.

'I know. My pup Clint loved him from day one and I always think dogs are a good judge, don't you?'

Mary nodded, then motioned her even closer, so that she could talk softly into her ear. There was something she wanted to ask, something she was sure that the sensible Della could help her with.

'That's fine.' Della gave her a last hug. 'Now you take care, and we'll pop in tomorrow. I'll go and find David, and Kate said she'll wait as long as you want, Charles.' She blew a kiss, then seconds later Mary and Charles were alone.

The way she'd always liked it best. Just the two of them.

'Oh Charles, that was lovely. You've always looked after me.'

'You're my everything, Mary.'

'I know.' She relaxed back against the pillows but held on to his hand. 'I know, and you're mine.' She took a sip of water. 'You have always understood about how ill I am, haven't you?'

'Yes, Mary. I might have lost a few marbles, but there are still enough left. And in my cackhanded way I thought going to the tearoom would help us, give us some support, even though I've only ever needed you.'

'She's a good girl, Kate, she'll make sure you're not too lonely, and so will the others. They're good people.'

'I know they are, Mary. That's why I went to the tearoom – I wanted to show you that I'd get by with a little help.'

'I was worried you didn't understand. I've been a fool, haven't I?'

'You've never been a fool, Mary. I'm sorry. Kate told me off, she said I should have talked to you and told you I'm all okay up here.' He tapped his temple, and she smiled.

'But we've always understood each other, haven't we?'

Charles smiled and squeezed her hand gently. 'We have, my love.'

'You're a clever man. You've always been smart.'

'Smart enough to catch you and refuse to let go.'

They sat in silence for a moment.

'You do know you've got odd socks on, don't you?'

He laughed. She liked to hear him laugh – they'd not done enough of it this past week or two. 'I do. I wondered if you'd notice or not, you daft bat!'

'Daft bat yourself!' The chuckle turned into a cough. If he knew he'd got odd socks on he'd be all right.

'I've called Saul. He's coming over but there was some problem with changing his plane ticket.'

'That's good. He'll look after you if you need him. Charles?'

'Yes, darling.'

'I think I've run out of things that I have to do. I'm happy now. It's all perfect and I feel at peace. I'm not as frightened of leaving you. You'll be okay, won't you?'

'I'll never be okay without you, Mary, but I'll get by. I'll manage. I'll manage, my love.'

'I think it's the best time to go then.' She felt the light brush of his lips against her forehead. He'd always kissed her good-night that way. It was nice. Familiar. 'Will you keep hold of my hand, Charles? Tell me about the day we met. I like hearing about that, about how you knew.'

Mary closed her eyes; she could feel the weight of her husband's hand over hers and could hear his familiar voice and she felt lucky.

'You had that butterfly clip in your hair, and that smile that stole my words away, and I knew, my Mary. I knew that we had to be together, that there would never be anybody else...'

Chapter Twenty-Seven

DELLA

Fish, chips and mushy peas

'It's so strange, isn't it?' Kate blew on a chip and stared out to sea. 'Knowing we'll never see her again.'

'I'm glad you made their cake though, and we could take it in to her.' Della passed a flake of fish to Clint who was patiently waiting, as though he knew that now was not the time to try and jump on her knee and steal the fish and chips from the bag.

'The last thing she said to me was that we had to come here, just the two of us. She was brought up near Parkgate and said it was the best place for chips, and she thought it would be a good place to be –' she hesitated over the word '– scattered. She said the smell of vinegar always reminded her of being a kid in short socks and a dress and she thought life was about completing circles.'

'She said to me that her life really started the day Charles proposed and she had that cake, so I suppose it completed the circle, having it in hospital. I wonder where Charles's circle ends?' Kate said thoughtfully. 'They're a bit like two bubbles that collided, but instead of bursting they joined together to make one bigger bubble.'

'I like that.' Della stroked Clint and held out a pea for him to taste. 'We never really did chips at the seaside when we were younger, it was always Cornish pasties. Give me a pastie and I can practically smell the sea and sand. The nearest we got to vinegar on holiday was cockles. It was more about clotted cream and ice-cream.'

'We did chips.' Kate sighed. 'I think Mary was a bit of a mind-reader, it's almost like she *knows* things about me that not even I do.'

'What do you mean?'

'Well, I swear I never told her, but Eddie bought me fish and chips, doused in vinegar, when he proposed.'

'Maybe Eddie told her?' Della said softly. 'She was the type of person people told things to, wasn't she?'

'Maybe.' Kate nodded. 'He did chat to everybody more than I realised. I guess fish, chips and mushy peas is my upside-down pineapple cake!'

She smiled, and although it wasn't a big cheery smile, it didn't seem to be a sad one either. Just thoughtful.

'I think he always dreamed of having a beach hut and bringing all his children to it for chips.' She stared out to sea for another minute, then turned to look at Della. 'You know what, the smell does take me back, and my eyes are smarting, but I think it's more to do with the vinegar now. My heart *does* ache because I'll always miss Eddie, but you know what, this time it's more of an ache that's okay, it's telling me I was lucky to have him. And −' she passed Clint some fish '− it just wasn't the right time for me to have a baby, and maybe there would never have been a right time, or maybe I would have sorted it and we would have had a dozen of them in some alternative reality, but –' she took a deep breath '– it wasn't meant to be in this life. It's today that matters, isn't it? Because yesterday has gone, and we've no way of controlling what will happen tomorrow.'

'That's very philosophical.' Della smiled.

'Our therapists would be proud of me!' Kate grinned. 'Mine and Jack's, they were both a pain in the neck!'

'But now you've got each other?' Della asked the question not needing an answer. She'd watched Jack and Kate dance around each other, sometimes getting closer as though they couldn't help themselves, then moving apart as though the force fields they'd each built around themselves wouldn't let it happen. But she wasn't worried. The times they were together were getting longer; sometimes they seemed to unconsciously slip under the net, to share a brief moment when nothing, and nobody, else mattered. The barriers were getting weaker, more indeterminate. There would be a right time for Kate and Jack, she was sure of it.

'Oh, don't you start! Charles is bad enough. Mary warned me about his matchmaking prowess!'

'But you do like each other, don't you?' she nudged gently. She wanted Kate to be happy.

'He's a very good photographer and he's been a great help with my Instagram account.' Kate said tartly, and made Della laugh again. But this time Kate joined in.

'I'm glad we came here.' Kate said, when they'd sobered up. 'I wanted, needed, fish, chips and vinegar, even if my eyes are smarting.'

'Mine are too.' Della added softly. At the heat, the vinegar. Life.

Mary had given them a purpose. She'd brought them

together, and now Della guessed it was up to them where they went from here.

'I hope Charles is okay.'

'Jack said he'd pop in and check up on him,' Kate said.

'Busy boy – he's going round to see David as well. They're watching the footie, and David said Jack has given him lots of ideas on what he could make with Harry.'

'I wish Jack was here to take a picture of this fish and chips,' Kate said softly, and Della could tell that it was about more than a photograph. Even if Kate hadn't realised it yet, she was starting to rely on Jack. Look to him for support, to share. It was nice. Della knew that feeling. For the first time in her life she'd found a man that she really looked forward to seeing, that she *wanted* to share her time with.

'I suppose we need to decide what food to put on for the wake.'

'It's got to be a celebration of her life, the things that meant a lot to her,' Kate said firmly. 'All the ideas she gave us were for Charles. It's been about his favourites, his memories.'

'Maybe we need to talk to him again?' Della was worried about Charles. He was putting his normal brave, cheery face on things, but losing Mary had obviously left a massive gap in his life. He'd spent the last few months trying to make things easier for her, not in coming to terms with what would happen and how he'd cope.

'Mary gave me her book; I'm hoping that there will be some hints in there. Maybe we should try and get hold of their son, Saul? Charles said he's on his way back so he should be here soon. It's so sad that he didn't get to see her, but she said they talked to him on the Zoom-y thing! I think they talked a lot.' Kate crunched up the empty chip wrapper, smiling. 'She was so lovely, wasn't she? I think she was quite tough underneath. She told me they ran away to get married.'

'Charles and Mary were a force to reckon with and both so funny. I bet she was full of life and quite naughty when she was younger!'

'I'm not sure how we show that with our food, but I think we should try. I'll see if Jack has any ideas.' Kate sighed. 'I will miss Mary; she was so easy to talk to. I guess I felt comfortable with her because it was like talking to Gran.' She smiled. 'At one stage while I was chatting to her, she opened an eye and said, "I am still alive, you know. I'd hate you to think you were confessing to a corpse"!'

'She was easy to talk to but didn't stand any nonsense.' Della stroked her dog. Mary and Kate had seemed to have a bond that she didn't have with the old lady. But she wasn't envious; Kate had needed Mary, and she hadn't. She'd not been scarred by life like Kate. She'd had a hiccup. Marrying Justin had been a mistake, but everybody made mistakes, or else how did they learn? Grow?

Justin had shown her what she didn't want in her life, and now she had a better idea of what she did. She could appreciate the good bits.

She had David. They'd been spending more and more time together, and the more she saw of him the more she realised how much she liked him, and how well suited they were. He challenged her. He suggested they do things she'd never thought she could (last week it was roller skating, and they were definitely planning that cowboy trip in the Canadian Rockies for next year), and she felt – what was the word? – empowered. She felt strong, and more capable than she had ever felt in her life. It didn't matter if their relationship developed into more, or if they parted company, he'd given her a gift that was far bigger than anything anybody else had given her. True, he made her happy, but she was happy because she had gained self-confidence. She didn't dither anymore, or at least not as much.

'I told Mary I'd tricked Eddie,' Kate suddenly said.

'Tricked? Oh, I'm sure you—'

'I made sure I couldn't have a baby. I didn't tell him that I didn't want to be pregnant, I just pretended it wasn't happening.'

'Oh, Kate, that must have been hard. But you can't help the way you feel about babies, and I'm sure Eddie would have got that. Just like Justin can't change the fact he wanted to be with a man, not a woman. It's not like you didn't want a bump, it was something in here.' She put a hand over her heart. 'I realise now that it's not about me forgiving Justin – I've nothing to forgive him for, apart from maybe leaving it so long. He was just being him, being honest, at the end. And Eddie would have known there was something wrong deep down. He probably knew you really didn't want to, but he was giving you space and time because he loved you.'

'Mary said something like that.'

'Well, you should listen to her. Eddie didn't need you to apologise, it was you that needed that,' she said softly. 'He was just waiting until you were ready to tell him, and, knowing him, I bet he would still have been okay with never knowing. He just wanted you to be happy.'

'I know you're right; I know you are. But it's easy for me to say, it's just hard to accept it, to actually believe it. After I chatted to Mary, though, it made me think about whether it was the fact I actually didn't want kids, or if I was just scared of what would happen if I did. And I did need to talk to Eddie about that. He would have helped me work it out. I really wish

I'd had time. That's what still upsets me.' She met Della's gaze. 'To be honest, I don't think it was about just not wanting a baby, and I don't think it was about being scared I'd be a bad mother like mine was, that I'd turn into her. It was about being in control, being able to guide my own life. And you can't do that if you have a baby, can you?'

'But you can't do that if you fall in love either,' Della said softly, letting Clint clamber onto her knee. She buried her face in his fur. 'If you let anybody in close, it can change everything.'

Kate gave a heavy sigh. 'I think it changed my mother.'

Della thought sadly that Kate hardly ever referred to her as 'mum' – she was always 'my mother'. In fact, she could only remember once when Kate had called her 'mum'. Della couldn't imagine what it was like to not have a mother. She'd needed hers so many times as she grew up – even when she said, or thought, that she didn't.

'Don't you ever speak to her?'

'Not for ages. After she went to the States it got harder. She came home for Gran and Grandad's funerals, but she was so bloody distant. It was as though she didn't care.'

'Or cared too much?'

'I honestly don't know. She was never very demonstrative, and my gran was. It seemed so wrong to be air-kissing at her funeral. She'd have wanted hugs and happiness. Anyway, she's not been back since. Shall we look at those recipes when we get back?' Kate stood up, so Della let her end the conversation.

But something deep inside of her was saying that Mary had been right about Kate. She missed her mother, and maybe it wasn't too late for either of them. They just had to find a way to talk to each other. To bury their guilt and be honest. They might never be close, never have a good mother–daughter relationship, but maybe Kate would never move on until she'd spoken to her mother properly. Just once.

Mary had understood. She wasn't one to leave loose ends and unsaid words. She'd given Della a job to do, and she was going to do it to the best of her ability.

She smiled down at Clint as he stared up expectantly at her, waiting to see where they were going next.

She didn't know.

Because being honest was the hardest thing of all, wasn't it? Being honest meant upsetting the apple cart. Having to start again.

She'd never really thought of Justin as being brave when he did what he had. But maybe he was. Maybe it was time she admitted to herself that if *she'd* been braver, she would have acknowledged the warning signs. She would have confronted him first.

But it didn't matter now.

Chapter Twenty-Eight

CHARLES

Sloe Gin and Christmas Cake

Charles looked around the room and his gaze settled on Mary's chair. It was hard to believe that she had been gone nearly a week now. They'd had warning, time to prepare, but when death came it had been unexpected. Sudden. It hadn't felt like a slow ebbing away; it felt like a switch had been thrown.

He'd thought she would come home from hospital and soldier on. That they'd have time, that they would be ready.

This felt like somebody had reached inside him and ripped out a part of his heart or his soul. Without Mary he felt empty inside. How the house felt, how her chair looked, was unimportant because all he could focus on was the gap inside of him.

He didn't care if he'd put odd socks on, it didn't matter if he couldn't remember why he'd gone into the kitchen, or why he'd found the milk in the oven. He'd done what he'd set out to do so many weeks ago: he'd stopped Mary worrying. He'd got her to believe that he'd be okay, he'd cope without her, that he'd have some friends to rally around.

But he wasn't okay.

That had been a rehearsal, and the final showdown had not been what he'd expected at all. He wasn't struggling with daily life; he was struggling with the weight of unforeseen sadness. Nothing could have prepared him for that. She *had* been his whole life; they'd always been meant to be together.

A knock on the door sent him struggling to his feet.

No Mary there to put a hand on his elbow.

'Jack!'

Jack held out a box. 'I thought you might fancy a few of my pork scratchings.'

He didn't ask how he was, which Charles was glad of. 'Come in.' He frowned. 'I asked you to come, didn't I?'

'You did.' Jack pushed the door closed behind him and handed over the pork scratchings.

Charles peered into the box. They looked crispy; the smell reminded him of their first Sunday lunch at Kate's. It reminded him of Mary; he'd been proud as Punch of her. She'd made this happen, and she'd looked beautiful in her Sunday best.

'That's very kind, they look delicious.' He probably wouldn't eat them though; he didn't feel hungry somehow these days. He walked through to the kitchen and spotted the piece of paper on the worktop. Ah, the note he'd written for himself. His reminder. He had to write them for himself now.

'Eton Mess.'

'Sorry?' Jack had followed him through.

'Eton Mess. It was Mary's favourite pudding. She always made stuff she thought I liked. That's what she told little Kate to cook. She wanted to make sure I had somebody to make the things I loved.'

'She was a wonderful lady,' Jack said softly.

Charles sat down heavily on the kitchen chair. He didn't want to go back in the lounge and look at Mary's spot.

'She was, but this wake thing should have her favourite things, not mine, shouldn't it? She always did like a good spread.' Nothing really seemed important now, except putting on a good spread for Mary. She'd have liked that. She deserved a good send-off, to be remembered. For her life to be celebrated. 'It's in her book.' He nodded. 'She gave it to Kate, but promise me you'll find it, make sure you make it.'

'I'll tell Kate.' Jack sat down opposite Charles. 'I'll make sure she makes it for us.'

'I'd like you to make it.' Charles looked him in the eye. He was a nice lad, a bit slow off the mark, but nice. 'You spend too much time with chickens, you should spend it with people. Women,' he added, trying to make the point more clearly.

Jack looked as confused as that flaming hen he'd always been photographed with.

And then he grinned and laughed. 'I never spent too much time with chickens! That was just for the camera, a bit of good old-fashioned home cooking.' He winked at Charles, and Charles couldn't help himself; he laughed back.

'But you haven't got a woman, have you?'

'I chased them all away, I was too busy cooking pork crackling.'

'Well, maybe He took away your sense of smell so that you'd take some time out of the kitchen, eh?'

'Maybe.' Jack smiled back. 'I brought you this.' He put an envelope on the table, then drew out the photograph inside.

It was one he'd taken at the hospital.

Charles and Mary, and their upside-down pineapple cake. Charles put a finger on it. 'She looks happy.'

'She was happy,' Jack said softly. 'She was with you.'

'It would be nice to think we'll be together again, but no matter if that's not the way it works.' He sighed. 'I'm not sure I want to be here without her though, lad. It was never my time, my life, it was ours.' He stared at the picture, at their joined hands. 'She wasn't scared of dying, you know, she was just worried about leaving me on my own. You lot did a grand job of making her feel better. That's why I went to Kate's, you know.'

Jack nodded. 'I know. I'd love to love somebody as much as you loved each other.'

'Baking was never about herself, you know, it was always about other people, making them happy. You understand that, don't you?'

'I do. Except I think she did it much better than I ever did.'

'Not a bad way to live a life, eh?'

'The perfect way.'

'Mary said to me once that there's no single secret ingredient in life, we each have our own one and it's up to us to sprinkle it wherever we can. She sprinkled it on me. I'm a lucky man, aren't I?'

'The luckiest.' Jack's voice had a rough edge to it.

'If you don't mind, I think I need a quiet sit down.'

'Not at all, I'll pop in tomorrow or get Kate to.'

'Can I tell you a secret, lad?' Jack nodded. 'That pork crackling never was my Mary's favourite, you know.'

'Oh?'

'It was mine.' He smiled. 'I just said that because I wanted you two to talk, you and little Kate. She's a good girl, you know.

A good girl, but it would do her good to talk to a man. It did my Mary good.'

Jack smiled. 'Can I tell you a secret? I'm glad you got me talking to Kate. I like her —' he paused '— a lot.'

'Well, that's a good start then. I always liked my Mary a lot.' It was his turn to pause, but to draw his breath. 'And I do like that pork crackling.'

'Good. I hope you enjoy it. It's on the side.'

'Champion. Don't forget that Eton Mess, will you?'

'Promise. I'll make you a cup of tea before I go, shall I? And Charles, thank you.'

'What for, lad?'

'Showing me what love looks like.'

'Splendid. That's what it is, it's splendid. Look after her, she's a gift. Mary would be pleased. She always did like a happy ending.'

'Don't we all,' said Jack softly. 'I'll get the kettle on.'

Charles pushed the front door gently shut behind Jack and went back into the kitchen. He looked at the flowers on the windowsill. The ones he'd given to Mary on their wedding anniversary. She'd always liked flowers. They were beginning to fade. Wilt at the edges. That's how he felt. Fraying at the edges, the feeling gradually spreading inwards. Is that what death did, slowly creep up until it engulfed you?

He looked at the last slice of the cake which Jack had put on a plate for him, then he picked it and the cup of tea up and put them on the tray. He put the photograph that Jack had taken in his pocket, so that it wouldn't get spoiled if he spilled the tea. It was hard not to when your hands trembled the way his did these days. He normally hated the clatter of the cup against the saucer – it reminded him of his age. His frustrations. But today he wasn't bothered as he walked slowly through to the lounge. He put the tray down carefully, then he turned the radio on. Mary's favourite music station. And he pulled the photograph of them out of his pocket and propped it up against the radio.

Saul had given them that a few years ago. The radio. It was a posh one, DAB he called it. He knew how much his mum loved her music.

Charles slowly sat down and stared at the photograph.

Mary looked beautiful. She always did, of course, but Jack had captured a brightness in her. A spark of the old Mary – the pure happiness in her eyes as she lifted a crumb of the cake to her lips, as she looked at him.

The wrinkles, the greying hair, didn't matter because the photograph drew you to her eyes, to her *happiness*. She looked almost radiant, as she had on their wedding day.

If Charles had one regret in life it was that Mary had never had the wedding she deserved. He'd have loved to treat her to a big party, to have seen her in the satin and lace dress that her mother had worn. She'd still got that dress, he thought, in the loft somewhere. He should get it down. There were a lot of things he had to get down. To sort.

He should tell Kate how much Mary had loved a glass of her homemade sloe gin. And making her Christmas cake – because it meant togetherness and forgiveness. Everybody should forgive and forget at Christmas, she used to say. He should tell Kate, but he'll forget. Nothing sticks these days. In one ear out the other, his mother used to say. Although this was his mind. It had turned into a muddled maze, with things getting lost down dead ends, only to reappear when he least expected.

He reached for the pad that Mary used to keep on the little table next to her chair. She used it to write notes for him. Memory joggers.

He used to laughingly call them her 'billet-doux', love letters.

For a moment he stared at her familiar, tiny, neat handwriting on the top sheet – then it hit him that she wasn't here to write it. That she must have written this final note a few days ago.

Loving you was the easiest thing I ever had to do. Leaving you hurts my heart. Call me selfish but I'm glad I was the first to go and never had to live a single day without you.

Don't forget to bring the cat in and put the milk bottles out. Mary x

He chuckled. She'd never let him forget that, the night he'd brought the empty milk bottles, which she'd already put out for the milkman, back in, and thrown the poor cat back out.

'Oh, my Mary, you were never selfish. You wouldn't know how, dear.'

He put the note down, and wrote one of his own, for Kate, which he put on the tray.

Mary's favourites – homemade sloe gin, making Christmas cake.

Then he picked Mary's note up again, still smiling.

He closed his eyes and remembered. Lucidly – he could picture it like it was yesterday. The day he'd first seen her, in a pretty daffodil-yellow frock. That first slice of pineapple cake they'd eaten together. The cake had melted in his mouth, and something in his heart had melted too.

The day he'd taken her ice-skating and she'd been like Bambi – legs in all directions – but she'd never stopped laughing, smiling. Whatever they did, whatever she wore, she had that smile. The smile that always seemed to be just for him.

She smiled at him from her hospital bed when everybody had gone. She was still smiling as she closed her eyes and asked him to talk to her. Tell her how it had been.

Brave. Seeing the best in any situation.

He'd been as nervous as a rabbit in the headlights when they'd gone to Gretna Green, but she'd squeezed his hand and told him it was perfect. She'd never wanted it any other way.

He'd shaken like a leaf the day Saul had been handed over to them. But she'd taken that tiny baby as though it was always meant to be. As though she had been made for motherhood, for that day.

Mary had always embraced life, had always wanted to give, to nurture. She'd looked after him, and she'd looked after their son. She'd cooked the best food, kept the best house, and given the most love.

She'd always knocked on the front door as she opened it. 'Only me!' she'd always shouted. Only me.

He could hear her knocking now.

She'd come in, in a second.

The knocking carried on. The door opened.

'Only me.' The soft voice wasn't Mary's, it was deeper. He opened one eye a tiny bit, as a warm hand covered his. 'Dad? I'm home.'

'That's nice, Saul.' He smiled and closed his eye again. 'That's nice.'

Chapter Twenty-Nine

SAUL

Two halves

Saul looked at the familiar tea tray laid with the best china, the tepid cup of tea still half full, the slice of cake barely touched.

The small smile was recognition, not humour, as he spotted the notes in his mother's neat handwriting, with little additions in his father's spidery scrawl. His father's writing had been precise once, until age had brought tremors, and cataracts had led to crossings-out.

Age could rewrite who you were, couldn't it? Except his parents had never let go of their young selves more than they had to. His childhood parents had still been there deep inside, glimmers showing through as his dad made old jokes and they looked at each other in that way they always had.

His dad's hand rested in his own, the skin more paper-thin than the last time he'd been here, etched with a fine network of lines that reminded him of the skeleton of a leaf.

It was cold to the touch, as though he had already moved

on, even though he'd spoken his final words only a few seconds ago.

He'd call the doctor in a minute, in a few minutes. He just needed a moment with his dad first.

He'd never really thought about how old his parents were, until now. They were just Mum and Dad, and you never expect to lose them, even though you know it's inevitable. Even as they age before your eyes, they're still not *that* old.

He and his dad had expected Mary to have longer. He knew her prognosis, he knew they were going to lose her, but he'd thought they had a few more weeks, which was why he'd booked his plane ticket for the date he had. Today. Time to come and see her, spend some time together. To say goodbye to the best mother he could have ever hoped for.

He half smiled. Mum had always said he was an easy child to love, but she would have said that whatever. It was she who was easy to love. She might have been firm and had her rules, but she was always fair, always supportive, always there to listen. His mother had been more than just a parent; she'd been a friend to him before it was a fashionable thing to be. He couldn't help the small smile.

Mum and Dad had never stuck to the rules, done what people told them they were expected to do. They'd lived life how they wanted, and they didn't care what other people thought because they had each other.

It was typical of his mother to ignore the medical profession and choose her own moment to leave. When she was ready.

When his dad had called to say she'd been rushed into hospital, he'd done his damnedest to move the trip forward. But couldn't.

Saul glanced up at the tablet, at its spot on the dresser.

They'd had regular Zoom calls, three or four times a week, and the last one had been the evening before his mother had gone into hospital.

She'd looked tired, but happy. 'Don't worry about me,' she'd said, 'don't rush home, I'll be fine, dear. I've got your father.'

And his dad had reached out to take her hand and they'd both smiled at him.

'We're two halves of a whole,' Dad always used to say. 'Two peas in a pod. Two bats in a belfry!' It had made Saul laugh, but there'd been a truth in there. They were two halves. Mum had always known that Dad would find it hard without her. He hadn't found it hard – he'd found it impossible. She'd been the meaning in his life.

Saul had never been able to imagine one of them without the other.

His parents had been a team.

He'd had a lot of time to think, while he was waiting for that plane. Mum's message, after her diagnosis, had always been the same. 'You don't need to rush back, dear. As long as I know you're all right then that's fine, and I do because I can talk to you on this zoomies.' When her health had first started to deteriorate seriously, the first time she wasn't in her chair when he'd called them, and he'd wanted to jump on a plane, she'd looked him in the eye and told him what she did and didn't want.

'I don't want you to watch me die, Saul. You're my son. I don't want you to see me too weak to live, I don't want you to see me suffer. No mother would. Bedside vigils are old-fashioned tosh. I want you to remember the living me. I know how much you love me, without having you weep over my body.' She'd given a weak smile then. 'Not that a strong man like you would weep. But it's what I want, Saul. It doesn't matter if other people are telling you that you should be here playing a waiting game, it's what I'm telling you that matters, eh? It's my last request!'

She'd always 'requested' not 'told'. It was their little secret, their in-joke.

For the first time in his life, he'd tried to disobey her, to get home and hold her hand. But she'd foiled him.

'Mothers always know best, eh?' He patted his dad's hand gently. His mother had been wonderful, but so had his father. Charles had been the quiet figure – the backbone of the family – Mary used to call him. And it had suited him. Steady, reliable, but he'd been fun as well. He liked to make them smile. Dad without a twinkle in his eye wouldn't have been Dad, which was why, he supposed, he'd decided it was time. 'Thank you for waiting to say goodbye, Dad. Love you. I love you both. Say hi to Mum for me, eh?' Then, blinking away the heat in his eyes, he kissed the top of his head gently and reached for the phone.

Chapter Thirty

JACK

Eton Mess

'Eton Mess!'

'I hope that's a suggestion, and not a comment on my hair.' Kate grinned at him. Her hair was pinned up on top of her head in a rather sexy rather than messy way and the smudge of what looked like chocolate on her cheek made him want to lean forward, rub it off and kiss her.

None of which he did.

'I popped that photo round to Charles, and he was insistent that I tell you Mary loved Eton Mess so I thought I'd come over on my way home.' It had been an impulse, or an excuse. He wasn't sure which, but he'd wanted to see Kate. These days, he always wanted to see Kate. She'd grown on him, crept into his life until he couldn't imagine it without her. 'It was her favourite, not one of his.'

'Ahh, that's fab. We were talking about it the other day – everything we baked together was for Charles. She wanted to make sure we'd be able to cook him the things he loved; she said it was important when you start to forget things. The familiar.'

Jack nodded. He got that, even without his memory fading. 'It's a comfort, isn't it, having familiar things around you?' He'd pushed everything he'd loved away, tried to have a completely fresh start, but he realised now that he wanted some of those things – like his family, even, in fact, like his cooking – back. 'Do you think the party will help him, or make it worse?'

Kate and Della had told him they were organising a wake after the funeral, but they didn't want to call it that. It was a celebration of Mary's life. All her favourite things.

'I hope it helps.' Kate bit her lip. 'You don't think it's a mistake, do you?'

'No.' He shook his head decisively. 'He'd have done anything for her in life, and I think he's proud that so many people loved her and want to do this. But it must be hard. She was such a force.' He couldn't help the small smile. 'She insisted on having a word with me, before she sent us out of her hospital room. She wanted me to promise that we'd look after him, said that he was a man and wouldn't want a load of women fussing over him, he might need to talk to another guy now and again.'

'She thought of everything.' Kate grinned. 'She had a word with Della, though I've no idea what about, and she talked to me about Eddie, and Mum. It was almost like she had a tick list she had to get through before she could let go.'

'I think she did. She insisted on touching up her lipstick before I took that photograph. I'm sure she knew it would be the last one, she wanted to look her best and not like some doddery old woman.'

'She was never that!'

'Never. I did promise her I'd do my best, but I'm not sure

I'm equipped to help anybody.' Jack hadn't felt he was the right man to look after anybody, even himself, for a long time. But it was strange; he'd felt much more positive recently. He knew he was actually ready for – not just thinking about – the next stage of his life, ready to accept back some of the parts he'd shut off. Mary had said that once you were ready to accept the past, then you were ready to look to the future.

'She wouldn't have asked you if she didn't know you'd do it.' Kate passed him a mug of coffee and sat down opposite him at the kitchen table, pushing the tray of chocolate truffles to one side. 'She was a clever lady. It's funny –' she wrapped her hands round her mug '– Charles knew she'd be more worried about him than herself, so he pretended to be confused so I'd talk to him. It worked – she could forget some of her worries while she was baking, and –' she smiled '– she did think we'd help him when she was gone. But she spent all her time trying to teach me how to cook the things *he* loved! They each did it out of love for the other one, not for themselves.'

'He's already finding it hard though,' Jack sighed. 'Your favourite food isn't any good if you don't want to eat.' He'd gone through a stage of not having any appetite, but that had been self-pity, not heartbreak. 'When I popped in, he looked frail. He's already lost some of his cheeky sparkle.'

'But I wonder how much of that was put on for Mary's benefit. He must have found the last few months, while she's been ill, exhausting.'

'I've had the same thought. So, who's he going to battle on for now?' Jack asked softly. Charles had seemed more than frail, he'd been distant. As though he'd had enough.

'I miss her, so it must be terrible for Charles,' Kate said.

They sat in silence for a moment. Jack knew, of course, that Kate had lost her husband a few years earlier, but he'd never really *thought* about what grieving, the loss of somebody you loved, was really like. Until now. Until he'd seen up close, first hand, what real love between two people was like. What death was like.

'It won't be the same, baking without her.'

'But you mustn't give up,' Jack said.

'You did,' she retorted, but it was said softly. It wasn't confrontational.

'I know.' He gave a wry smile. 'More fool me.'

'I won't know what to cook, how to do it, without Mary, once the wake is over.'

'You've got your own recipes, your gran's book. Your own memories.'

'That's more or less what Mary said. But it was nice having company, having somebody tell me the best way to do things. I'm such a novice.'

Her tone was light, but he could see the sliver of truth in there. Cooking for Kate had been about doing it with somebody, for somebody. Jack had cooked because he'd been driven to, because he wanted to create – nothing and nobody else mattered when he'd been caught up with food. Which had been pretty much twenty-four hours a day.

'Oh Jack, who am I going to bake with now?' Her eyes glistened, and he saw it then. This wasn't about not having the confidence to cook on her own, this was about losing Mary. This was about loss, about pain, about never mourning her own grandparents. Mary had made her feel safe, let her feel she could delve into her memories. Remember.

'You can bake with me,' he said softly. Desperately wanting to make her feel better, take the unshed tears away. And then he realised that he needed to do something. That if he didn't do this now, he might regret it – and he already had too many things in his life that he regretted. 'We'll bake together, I'll make it pretty.' He smiled at her; she really was beautiful. 'And you can put the pics on Instagram and be famous.' She gave him a small smile back. 'We'll do it together, Kate.'

He cupped her face in his hands, and gave her a chance to pull away.

'Really?' Her voice was husky, her gaze searching his face to see if he meant it.

'Really.' There was a small space between them, but it was as though it didn't exist. All he was aware of was her. The scent of her hair, the softness of her skin, the sadness in her eyes. 'Kate?'

Her lips were slightly parted. He loved the shape of her mouth. He loved to watch her talk, her smile, the way she laughed. He could watch Kate all day, he *had* been watching her more and more, because he couldn't help himself. She drew him in, she made his days better.

She moistened her lips, and then he tore his gaze from them, looked up and met her eyes.

'Jack.' It was the sound of his name on her lips, the way she said it with a certainty. No question.

He didn't know who closed the gap. If it was him, her, both of them. But it was slow, deliberate, a moment in time when they were so close they swapped breaths. And then their lips met.

She tasted of chocolate. Rich, lush, sweet chocolate.

She sighed, a heavy sigh, a shudder, that seemed to come from deep inside and was more about need than regret. It sent a shiver down his spine, made him want to draw her into his arms. Hold her tight. Kiss her hard.

A feeling that took him by surprise.

He put the brakes on. Broke the kiss, while he still could. Brushing his hair back with a shaky hand.

'Wow. I'm sorry.'

'Don't be,' she said, slightly breathless, then tilted her head and leaned in closer again. Her lips were soft, full, slightly parted. Waiting for his.

This time it was softer, a kiss that wanted to linger. That he didn't want to end. He wanted to explore, he wanted to share.

This kiss wasn't deep or desperate. It wasn't filled with lust. It was sweet, gentle. He could feel a sensation build up in his body, a want, a softness, that took him by surprise. He'd never shared a kiss like this before. This was like watching waves gently ripple onto a beach and ebb away, this was like watching a flower slowly unfurl, this was being with somebody, being in a moment you wanted to last.

He pulled away a second time because his heart was pounding. This felt so intimate it frightened him, but at the same time made him want more. This time he wasn't afraid of taking too much, that he was being too passionate; this time he was afraid of being too gentle.

He wanted to hold her hands, just look at her. Instead, he swallowed hard and sat back in his seat.

They looked at each other, the silence longer than the kiss had been.

This felt right, but all wrong. He'd always been selfish, always pushed people away, and Kate didn't deserve that. Kate had married a keeper. Kate didn't need hurting all over again.

He knew she wasn't another Clara. But he'd always attracted Claras because he hadn't had time to love, and girls like that understood. They played that game.

He didn't even know if Kate wanted anybody else, if she

was ready. If she'd ever be ready. He could never be another Eddie for her.

She cleared her throat. 'Mary told me that Charles—'

Her words were cut off by the ring of the doorbell.

Jack buried his head in his hands as Kate went to answer the door. What was he playing at? What did he do now? He'd said he'd come back and help her cook and he knew if he did that then the only way he'd be able to keep his hands off her, keep his distance, would be to be abrupt, businesslike. And that wouldn't be fair on her either.

He didn't want to keep his hands off.

Shit.

'Jack, er…' She was hesitating, her cheeks flushed. And then he noticed the guy behind her. Not that he wasn't difficult to notice. He was tall, broad. Built like a lumberjack.

'Hi there, nice to meet you at last.' The middle-aged man was nothing like Mary and Charles, but the soft Canadian accent gave him away.

'Saul?'

The man nodded, as Jack stood up and offered a hand to shake. 'You made it.'

'Planes.' He shook his head. 'Look, guys, I'm sorry to interrupt, I…'

'I'm really sorry about your mother. She was such an amazing lady, we all loved her, and I'm so, so sorry you couldn't make it back in time.'

'She told me how kind you all were.'

'Have you got time for a coffee?' Kate looked far more flustered than Jack had ever seen her, and his arms were itching to grab hold of her. Reassure her, tell her whatever was bothering her would be fine. He kept them pinned to his sides as Saul nodded, then sat down heavily on one of the kitchen chairs.

'To be brutally honest with you guys, she told me not to rush back. She didn't want me to see her at the end, if she suffered. Hell, she could be bossy.' The guy gave a shrewd smile, and Jack smiled back, warming to him. 'I can't bloody believe I got here too late. Bloody planes.'

'It caught us all out. We all thought she'd be back out of hospital and coming round here baking again.'

'It was nice of you to bake that anniversary cake for them, I know it meant a lot.'

'That was Kate.' Jack smiled at her, worried about the look on her face as she bustled about with mugs and coffee. 'Charles will be pleased you're here. I saw him earlier and he's obviously finding it difficult.'

'Jack——' Kate's voice broke, but Saul's deep voice cut in.

'He, he's gone. When I say I got here too late, I meant for both of them.'

Jack stared at him blankly, then looked at Kate.

'He died, Jack,' Kate said softly. Sitting down next to him, putting her hand over his.

'But I saw… A couple of hours ago.'

'I got here just in time to say goodbye, but I was too late to tell him how much Mum meant to me, how much he…' Saul took a sip of the too-hot coffee, to give himself some time. And as Jack stared at him, he finally clocked the paleness of his skin, the red-rimmed eyes. The face of a man who'd had a shock, who had wept. Shit.

'Goodbye…' Jack let the word hang between them. He didn't quite know what to say.

'It was lucky I knew there was a spare key under that pot. He didn't answer the door, but when I went in, he was sitting there with a photograph propped up in front of him.' Saul said softly, then sighed. 'His eyes were shut, but at least he knew I was there, that I'd made it. He took my hand, and then, he just, he … went.' He blinked, as though making an effort to shake the image from his head. 'It was peaceful.'

'Like your mum,' Kate said softly. 'She was happy, she was ready, Saul.'

'She always did like to plan and do things her own way. And Dad did things her way as well.' He gave a wry smile. 'I reckon he just decided it was time to let go. Simple as that. I guess we always knew that he didn't want to live if he hadn't got her with him. He was holding a note from her, and this; does it mean something?' He fished in his pocket and pulled out a small note.

Jack took the note and nodded. 'Sloe gin.' He smiled. 'We were planning a celebration for Mary. Charles said she'd have enjoyed a good spread. He'd been telling us about some of her favourite things.'

'We don't have to do it now,' Kate said softly. 'If you've got other plans.'

'It sounds great.' Saul nodded. 'She would have loved it, they both would. Please, go ahead. I wouldn't know where to start with doing anything. It's years since I lived round here.'

'You are staying a while?'

'I was planning on staying a few weeks, support Dad, plan the funeral. You know.'

'If there's anything you need help with, I'm more than happy, and if you'd like to stay here rather than…'

Saul shook his head, a gentle smile on his lips. 'That's good of you to offer, but I'm fine staying at home. Help would be appreciated though. I've lost touch with this place; it's been a while. The solicitor is still here, but I'm not sure Mum's favourite florist is.'

They all sat silent for a moment. Florists were supposed to be about joy, colour, life.

'I'm sure Della will be able to help, she loves her garden,' Kate said. 'Do you know her? She's lived here quite a while.'

'Oh yes, I know Della. I always thought that Justin was a bit of a one!' He grinned. 'And Mum always kept me up to date with all the comings and goings, the gossip. She said she'd been helping them with the garden.'

Kate nodded. 'I'm sure she'd love to see you. And she's going to Canada with David next year, so they'll be glad of any advice you can give them.'

'I will. You really did help them both, you know. It gave Mum a real boost coming here, she was full of what you'd been baking together. She loved cooking. Look, I won't keep you.' Saul stood up. 'I just wanted to thank you, and, you know, let you know. I've got to get back, I'm expecting the doctor. I'll keep in touch though; let you know what's happening. Oh, I nearly forgot.' He held an envelope out, then drew something from it. 'This was the photograph he'd been looking at. Is this one you took?'

Jack frowned as he glanced down at the photograph of Charles and Mary. 'I did.'

'Do you mind if I keep it?'

'Of course not. It's theirs, yours.' He placed the photograph on the table in front of him. It was hard to believe they'd both gone.

'You've really captured who she was, you know. Both of them.'

'Thanks. It's just a hobby, but I couldn't help it. She just looked so happy, I thought I needed to capture that moment.'

'I'm glad you did.' Saul nodded. 'I'll keep in touch, guys.'

'If there's anything I can do...' Jack shook his hand, then sat back down as Kate walked Saul to the front door. This was unreal.

True, Charles had seemed incredibly frail when he went round to the house, but this was still a shock. He'd never see him again, never have another conversation.

'I can't believe he's gone. I mean, both of them.' Kate came back into the kitchen, visibly upset, and Jack couldn't help himself. He instinctively reached out and took her cold hands in his. No way could he have any idea of how she'd felt when Eddie didn't come home – this wasn't on that scale – but he felt shaken.

'Me neither.' He shook his head. Thought how Charles had been when he saw him. Lost. 'I don't think he wanted to carry on without her, and I guess she'd have been happy to know he didn't have to struggle on his own. Poor Saul, though, that must have floored him.'

'He'll feel it later, after the doctor has gone. I hope he's okay.'

'He will be.' Jack squeezed her hand. 'We'll make sure he is, eh?'

'Mary would expect it,' she said, giving a weak smile.

They both stared at the note that Saul had left.

Mary's favourites – homemade sloe gin, making Christmas cake.

'I have no idea what a sloe even is,' Kate said sadly.

'I have. Maybe we should check she hasn't got some in her airing cupboard?'

'Why do the worst things always happen on the brightest days?' Kate suddenly blurted out. 'Today is lovely. It felt like it could be a *good* day.' Her voice cracked.

Jack waited. This was about more than Charles.

'It was a beautiful day when Eddie died.' Her tone was softer now, more even. 'When he went out to buy some bloody ingredient he'd forgotten. It was just an ordinary day, but a good day. It shouldn't have gone wrong.'

Jack thought about the envelope she still hadn't opened. He didn't say anything, but instead put his arms round her, pulled her onto his lap, let his chin rest on her head.

She sighed. 'Mary wouldn't have wanted us to be sad, would she?'

'She wouldn't. But we're not, we're just taking a moment,' he said, smiling into her hair. 'She'd want us to do that.'

Chapter Thirty-One

KATE

A bit of a spread

K ate took her apron – Eddie's apron – off and folded it up. Then she poured herself a cup of coffee, sat down at the table, picked up her recipe book and started to turn over the pages slowly, one by one.

It had started off with her gran's recipes, and Eddie's, but it had grown into so much more. It wasn't just about her, it was all the people that she'd got to know, grown to love. It was almost like a community, her community, summed up in one little book.

She smiled. She'd even got bacon sandwiches in there, because this book wasn't about complicated techniques and masses of ingredients, it was about people.

It was about *their* secret ingredients. What made each of them who they were, the things that brought them together.

Without bacon butties, she wouldn't have got to know Della. Della's dog Skip had loved them – and now her pup Clint did too. Those bacon butties that Della had made for her had brought them together, made them both realise that sharing a dish full of memories could bring comfort. She grinned – like the paella! Now making that had been quite an experience, especially when Clint had managed to run off with the packet of squid ink and leave black smears on his tongue and down both his front paws. Poor Clint, but it had given them a laugh, and she was pretty sure that Justin's alarm as he'd watched it all unfold on Skype had absolutely made it all worthwhile for Della. Crying with laughter definitely beat crying from pain any day of the week.

She turned another page. Scones, served the Cornish way – the start of it all. Who could have known that a tray of perfect golden scones could have started the healing process that she didn't realise she was looking for?

Then there was the pork crackling, a gift from Jack. Had that recipe really been the start of something tentative, but quite nice, between them? Though nice wasn't quite the word. He'd been a constant since Mary and Charles had passed away, encouraging her to cook, making her laugh. Baking with her. Keeping her company. Like he'd told her he would.

And he'd kissed her again. Several times – it was strange what rubbing a smear of batter off somebody's nose could lead to.

It wasn't until Saul and Jack had gone and she'd been alone, that day of the first kiss, that she'd realised. The kiss hadn't felt wrong. She didn't feel like she'd betrayed Eddie. She'd felt like he'd have given her the thumbs-up, told her it was okay to start making new memories. New memories didn't mean you forgot the old ones.

Sometimes you needed more than a chocolate brownie to mend a broken heart.

Ahh, trifle. Her gran's special dish, and one that Charles

had loved. With sprinkles. So many things in here that Charles had enjoyed. Mary might have been selfless in her suggestions, but Kate just knew it gave her pleasure. Comfort. And that's what this seemed to be about more than anything.

This little recipe book was unique. It was more than a guide to making dishes, it was like a wellness diary, a journey. She could see the steps – the recipes that helped Mary in her final days, the ones that had brought her and Della closer, the ones she'd cooked as she thought about Eddie, the cakes she'd baked as she told Mary about her secret and her guilt. Who needed a therapist when they could cook?

And then there was Jack. She paused. Jack and his pork crackling. Jack and his fabulous photographs that had made her Instagram account special, invited comments from strangers, and brought old friends back into her life.

Jack and the way he'd made sure she never felt she was baking alone.

There was lots of Jack in this book now. In her life.

The instructions from him had become more detailed and more elaborate as the days went on. Her notes in the margin reminded her of when he said he could actually taste the ingredients, and which ones.

Oh yes, she had notes in the margins, just as Eddie and Gran had. Didn't everybody?

She paused on the page that told her how to make the best chips. She'd found that in Eddie's notes. She smiled. The last time she'd had fish and chips was at Parkgate with Della. After Mary had sent them there. As though she knew.

That April day when Eddie proposed had been all her best days rolled into one. He took her to the seaside, bought her the biggest ice-cream she'd ever eaten (despite the fact it was blowing a gale and they were wrapped up as if it was January), then treated her to fish and salty chips that had so much vinegar on her eyes smarted. Well, that was what she'd blamed when he went down on one knee.

Maybe chips and vinegar would always bring tears to her eyes? Maybe the smell would always remind her of the man she'd been sure would never leave her, sure they'd be there for each other. They had their differences, of course they did, but after she had said yes to Eddie, she had felt like the sands had stopped shifting. She had a firm foundation, she knew where her, their, life was heading.

Except she hadn't. But as Jack had said, sometimes you had to rewrite the ending.

She turned another page. Pineapple upside-down cake. She'd always think about Mary and Charles if she as much as smelled pineapple, she knew she would. She chuckled. Who would have thought pineapple would ever make her think of love?

Parkin. It was funny, but it suited David so perfectly. There was something dependable about a good slice of parkin, but it had enough spice in it to never be boring. He'd given Della confidence, and it had rubbed off on Kate. There was no denying it, each of these people and their contribution to this book had made a difference to her. To how *she* saw life. How could she not be brave, be adventurous, when she had the support of people like these?

Mint sauce. That was Jack. She smiled. Charles would be very chuffed with himself if he could see them now. She hadn't a clue what lay ahead of them, but they got on. In a totally different way to her and Eddie, but they did. He'd got them to talk, and it was good.

He might have been a chef, like Eddie had wanted to be,

but there the similarity ended. He wasn't Eddie, he was nothing like him, which made it okay.

Gran's honey-glazed ham. Now there was one for Christmas, along with Mary's sloe gin. The smell of that ham had always been bittersweet, it had been about drawing a line under her life with her mother and accepting she had to make her own way. It was about being strong, about being independent. But as Mary had said, was it always good to be strong, to pretend to be strong even when you weren't? Was that what her mother had done, hidden her fear by marching on with confidence? Maybe sometimes it was better, braver, to admit you were frightened, ask for help. Talk. She'd started to wonder lately if she should call her mother (if she could find her), because how would she feel if she left it too late?

She'd asked Della if she regretted not having a child, and got the answer no. But had she really been asking the question for herself, already doubting she'd made the right decision? Even more so, when wise old Mary had pointed out that worrying about what kind of mother she'd make wasn't a good enough reason to dismiss the idea.

She wished Mary was still here to talk to, but, as Jack had once gently pointed out, her mother was still around, even if Eddie and Mary weren't. She couldn't bring them back.

She turned the next page slowly. Lasagne. She'd still not made it.

What was her mother like back then when she'd still enjoyed Gran's pasta. Was she still the same person, deep down.

Kate had grown up imagining that her mother probably hoped she'd be in the type of job where she would make scientific breakthroughs, or she'd be in some rainforest saving animals from extinction and making the headlines. Somebody notable – not some unmemorable high-school teacher trying to keep rebellious teenagers in check. And now some stay-at-home widow who baked. But was that true or was that Kate's own invention as she desperately looked for some solution, some easy answer to how to feel loved?

Except she *had* been loved.

By her grandparents. By Eddie. By all the people whom she now shared her time with.

She wasn't unlovable, she knew that. And she knew that she couldn't chose who did and didn't love her. That was out of her control.

She wasn't desperate now for love, so maybe now was the right time to look for answers.

Mary's small recipe book caught her eye, and she picked it up with a smile. 'Oh, Mary.' She'd slipped it in her pocket that day in the hospital, meaning to look at it when she got home, but she'd then been too shocked to pick it up for days. When she did a note slipped from the pages.

She wondered how many notes like this Mary had found the energy to write in those final days.

She'd left one for Charles. Saul had shown it to them. She'd never wanted to leave Charles, but she couldn't have imagined life without him either. It had been one final, lovely, love letter. She was glad that it was one of the last things he'd read, and that Saul's voice was the last thing he'd heard.

Family was important.

Which is what Mary had more or less been telling Kate, in *her* own note, she supposed.

Darling Kate,

Sometimes we need to forgive wrongs we don't understand, sometimes forgiveness is the first step and until you do that you won't learn the truth.

The Secret Ingredient

Open your heart, Kate, it's plenty big and generous enough. If you want to do one last thing for me, then open the door to your mother, invite her in, because she might not be brave enough to take the step on her own. We all need people and love in our lives.

Oh, and seize the day, as they say! I did, I took my chance with Charles and ran away, I threw caution to the wind because I never was one to tread carefully, and I just knew he'd be worth it. Eddie will always be in your heart, in your head, but Charles told me seeing you and Jack together made his heart skip, and he didn't think it was arrhythmia. I trust my Charles, I always have, and he's never let me down. Don't live cautiously, Kate, live well. And bake. Bake lots. Mary x

Kate glanced up at the clock. She needed to get cracking and put the finishing touches to everything before everybody started to arrive. She'd got up early to prepare for the celebration party that they'd planned to remember Charles and Mary. It was quite an impressive spread with, of course, a pineapple cake taking centre stage.

Jack had popped in earlier with some pork crackling, apple sauce, and the Eton mess. And, of course, his camera so that they could capture the memories, the food that was so much more important than it looked.

She'd made scones, with lashings of Della's strawberry jam, and David's daughter Harry had insisted on making tiny, delicate sandwiches with every filling imaginable. She must have spent hours preparing the roast beef and horseradish, the coronation chicken, the egg and cress, and the salmon. She said they were the types of things her grandparents always gave them when she was little, and they reminded her of family picnics, and Sunday tea.

Kate was counting plates (the best china – she would never

insult Charles and Mary with paper plates) when the doorbell rang. Whoever it was was early. Very early.

Straightening the corner of the lace tablecloth, she frowned. Could it be David, bringing more wine?

It wasn't; it was the postman asking her to sign for a letter. She took the big white envelope with her name and address typed neatly on it and was just about to open it when the doorbell rang again.

'Hi! All sorted?' Jack grinned, handing over the biggest bouquet she had ever seen in her life, and a bottle of champagne, and then leant forward to kiss her.

'Hey, that's cheating – making sure my hands are full!'

'And would you have objected if your hands hadn't been?' She grinned back. 'Wow, something smells good!' He pushed the door shut behind him, took the presents out of her hands and pulled her into his arms.

'You can smell that?' She raised an eyebrow. There had been positive signs, which she'd secretly been jotting down alongside her recipes, that his senses were slowly recovering – but this was the first time he'd come in sniffing the air like Clint did!

'I can.' He grinned. 'I couldn't tell you exactly what was in there, but it definitely smells like food!' he said teasingly.

'Oh, stop it!'

He kissed the tip of her nose. 'Seriously though, I'm definitely starting to pin down more flavours and smells. I don't want to tempt fate, but it feels good.' He grinned and squeezed her. 'Amazing in fact!'

'Totes amazeballs,' she said, which made him laugh and shake his head.

'I don't know where you get things like that from.'

'David's daughter, she's full of them!'

'I bet,' he said drily. 'But it is amazeballs.' His voice had a rough edge that showed just how much it meant, and it brought a lump to Kate's throat.

'It's fantastic.' She went up on tiptoes, and her lips met his. A long, lingering kiss that left her flushed and wanting more.

'Hey, be careful, you've got guests coming soon!'

'Bugger! This is what happens when you've got friends!' she said mock-crossly, and he laughed.

'We could ditch them.' His fingers played on her waist, and she groaned before pulling away.

'We do need to celebrate it later though!'

'I'm always up for a celebration.' His eyes twinkled, then his voice softened. 'It is brilliant, but it's funny though –' a small frown settled between his eyebrows '– it's amazing, and I am stoked, but food isn't the be all and end all, is it?'

It was Kate's turn to laugh. 'Really? You've just said cooking isn't *everything*.'

'I know, weird, eh?'

'"Be all and end all." You're beginning to sound like Mary!'

'There's nothing wrong with that, we all need to be more like Mary. There's more to life than fancy flavours, you know!'

'But there's not more to life than baking, and now you'll be able to taste the pineapple properly!'

Jack groaned, then said, 'Mm, you smell pretty nice as well.' He nuzzled her neck, and as the goosebumps ran down her back, he kissed her. Properly this time. 'Okay?'

'I am now!' She laughed. 'A bit frazzled, but fine. Now you'd better stop that! Come on, come through.' She led the way through to the kitchen.

'What's this?' He took the envelope out of her hand.

'No idea, it just came. Can you put it on the dresser for now, please? I'll look at it later.'

. . .

It was quite late, and she'd had more than a few drinks, when Della and David – the last of the guests – finally left, and there was just her and Jack.

'Mary would have been proud of you,' Jack said softly, drawing her onto his knee. 'I'm proud of you.' He kissed her lightly.

Kate kicked her shoes off. 'I think we did her proud, don't you? I think both of them would have been pleased. Thank you, by the way.' She kissed him back. 'I couldn't have done it without you.'

'Teamwork,' he said, smiling. 'Aren't you going to open that letter?' He nodded in the direction of the dresser.

'Nosey!'

'I can't believe you're not dying to see who it's from.'

'Signed-for letters are usually official, and official is usually bad news!'

'You might have inherited a stately home. Somebody could have heard about your cooking and be offering you sponsorship.'

'You reckon?' She laughed.

'Or more likely they've seen your Instagram and want to know who has taken the brilliant photographs!'

'Haha. Okay, okay.' She slowly stood up, padded over in her bare feet to pick up the letter, and then grabbed his hand. 'Let's go and sit on the sofa, I need to just splodge.'

'Splodge?'

'I'm too tired to do proper words.'

Two minutes later she didn't feel in a state to do any words.

'It's from my mother.' She held up the sheets of paper, her hand trembling. 'It's like a bloody essay.' She'd been thinking about getting in touch with her mother, but that had still been a thought, something intangible, not yet formed into actions. This was real.

'Do you want me to go, so you can read it in peace?'

'No, I don't.' She swung round, so that she could lean against him. 'Stay, please.'

Dear Kate,

I'm sorry for writing, and not coming round in person, but you still petrify me, and I don't have any expectation that it would be like in the movies and we'd fall into each other's arms. I've got no delusions, this is life, not a movie.

'Why do you petrify her?'

'I don't know, shush, and stop reading over my shoulder.'

I've wanted to get in touch with you before, but I didn't think you'd want me to, and I didn't want to mess up your life. But a friend of yours got in touch, she said Mary asked her to. She told me all about Charles and Mary, I'm sorry I never met them, but I'm glad you did. Your friend told me all about this wonderful woman, my daughter, who brought everybody together with her food. You're like your gran, she was always a nurturer, she liked to make people happy, and that's why I knew you'd be better off with her than me.

'Who got in touch with her? Who would Mary ask?'

'Della,' Kate said softly, as things slotted into place. 'It was Della.' It made sense now, Mary's final chat with Della in hospital. 'She asked Della to find her.'

'You are a wonderful woman, you know.'

'Shhhh.'

When you were born, I wasn't well. They'd call it post-natal depression now, but by the time I realised what was wrong with me it was too late. Or maybe that was just me, maybe I should have tried harder.

I loved you, Kate, from the moment you were born, you were so small, so perfect. So fragile, and I was so sad and tired, I felt like I was hopeless. That I'd break you. I was doing everything wrong. I was so used to being good at everything, I couldn't cope with being so bad. Work was easy, but I felt completely out of control with you. Babies live by their own rules, and it scared me.

Your gran said she'd help me look after you, until I felt better, and she was so brilliant at it. She was so much better than me. It made me see even more just how bad I was. I'd always been able to do things, I'd always been able to be the best if I tried hard. And I couldn't. I was a total failure.

I tried to look after you as you grew up, but it was always hard. You sometimes looked at me as though you wondered how you could have deserved such a terrible mum. I think you much preferred it when I was at work, and you had to go to Gran's.

When you were little, I used to love making things with you, we'd make gingerbread at Christmas, and Easter bonnets, and bake, but then as you got older I never seemed to be able to get it right.

You were so clever and independent, and you scared me. Mum used to seem to know exactly what to say to you, but whatever I said was wrong. We ended up arguing. So I thought you'd be better off with her. I thought if I took the promotions at work, at least I'd be providing for you even if I couldn't do anything else right. I did know how to do my job.

I'm sorry I didn't stay at Gran's funeral long. I wanted to cry, she was my best friend as well as my mother, I was completely wrecked because I'd not realised how little time she had. She was good at hiding stuff, and I was miles away. Yeah, I know that was my fault. I wanted to break down at the funeral, but you were so together. I didn't want to show you up, let you down. You were so beautiful and poised, and it all seemed so fucked up. Except good mothers don't say that, do they?

But I was crap at it. The whole motherhood thing. I thought if I came back then, I'd mess your life up even more.

I never intended to be a young, single mum, it was how it happened, but I always loved you. I loved your dad as well. But I didn't want to mess up his life, so I didn't even tell him about you. Which was wrong. I've written to him now. I'll let you know if he replies.

Anyway, I'm glad you're happy now, I'm glad you're baking. I miss making Christmas cakes with you, even if we did eat more mix than we put in the tin.

My address is on here, my email and my phone number, so if you want to ask me anything, or see me, then I'd really be pleased to hear from you.

I know this is way overdue, but I want to say sorry.

I wish it was true that 'love is never having to say you're sorry', because then you'd understand. Mary told your friend that you were scared you'd make a bad mother. You never will, Kate. You'll make a wonderful mother – but if you ever have a baby and you feel that you can't cope, that you're not good enough, then ask somebody. Be brave. The biggest mistake I made in my life was not to be.

Love, Mum x

Kate put the letter down and closed her eyes.

'Okay?' Jack squeezed her hand.

'I think so. I need time to think about it.' There was nothing she hadn't really expected in the letter. It was like Mary had said, sometimes people are scared. Sometimes it's easier to hide than admit it, like she'd done with Eddie. It hurt; she'd be lying to herself if she said otherwise – because who wants to be told that they were too difficult to look after? She was a baby.

Her mum was an adult. But a young one. Fresh out of uni. Alone.

'You want me to go?'

'I want you to stay. Please.'

'Is it time to open that other card as well, or is that too much for one day?'

Kate stood up slowly, went into the kitchen and picked the white envelope up from the dresser. She went back to Jack and sat down beside him. Staring at it.

'Don't if you don't want to,' he said softly. 'Not if it's going to make you unhappy.'

'I think I do want to,' she said. 'Who knows, it might make me happy. There might not be a secret ingredient to happiness, but it all adds up, doesn't it?' It was one of those days, a day to tie up loose ends, like Mary had done before she'd let go.

Mary had let go of life, but Kate wanted to let go of regrets, of guilt. Of not knowing.

She slowly peeled back the flap of the envelope.

Drew out the card.

Opened it.

Remember, you're all I ever wanted, the rest is just a bonus. Eddie xxx

She smiled. Why had she ever been afraid to open it? This was so Eddie. This wasn't an ending; this wasn't saying goodbye. Eddie was a part of her life that she'd always have with her.

Why had she never thought about it this way herself though? The core of their relationship, them, had been this. Love. Just as it had been for Mary and Charles.

Part of that was about trust, about believing in each other, about being prepared to wait for answers – but it really all came down to this, Eddie and Kate, Kate and Eddie. As long as they'd had each other they could work the rest out. Everything else was negotiable. Everything else was just icing on the cake. Where they lived, what they ate, what they bought, who they saw. Whether they had children.

All Eddie had wanted was for her to be happy. He wanted her to have what *she* needed in life, not what anybody else said she should. And maybe, just maybe, he'd understood her better than she did. Maybe he knew that if they had a baby, she'd be even happier.

But he would have been happy with any decision she'd made.

He didn't think there had to be three of them. All he'd wanted was her.

And she'd known that. She'd always known that, because that's who they were – that's why she'd loved him so much from the start, that's how she'd known that Eddie was the man for her.

Grief had made her blame herself, because it gave her an answer. And she'd needed an answer, a reason for Eddie dying. Because we all need answers, don't we? Guilt had been easier than not knowing.

She went back into the kitchen and propped the card up on the dresser. 'Thank you, Eddie. We had a lot of bonuses, didn't we? We were lucky.'

They had been lucky. He should never have died, but he was in the wrong place at the wrong time and who knew whether fate has everything mapped out for us from the start.

He'd be glad she was happy, he'd be glad she was surrounded by good people, he'd be glad she had started to use his kitchen.

And she was sure he'd be glad she'd got Jack. He'd be glad

that she'd met somebody who loved food with all their heart (although it might be quite good that he wasn't as totally obsessed with it as he'd been once upon a time), who'd offered to take up a sledgehammer and help her start to knock down some of the walls in the house.

Jack had slowly chipped away the barriers she'd built around her own heart, as she'd done for him, and now it seemed strangely right for them to peel away, together, the changes that somebody had made to the tearoom. It was right that the kitchen truly did become the heart of the home again.

She went back into the lounge and stood in front of him. He might be her future, he might not. But he was her present. And she was happy to live in the present. It was a nice place to be these days.

'I think I'll get in touch with Mum.'

'That was a quick decision.' He smiled.

'I might ask her over, make lasagne.'

'That sounds good to me.'

'You know you said you'd give me a hand to knock that wall down?' She pointed behind the sofa.

'Yep.'

'I think it's time we did it. Not now,' she added hastily, laughing at the look of panic on his face. 'Next week maybe.'

'Sounds a good idea.'

'It would be a shame to stop getting everybody together for Sunday lunches and afternoon teas, I think Mary would have liked us to carry on. And doing the house would make it better.'

'I think you could be right. And Della and David have got heaps of vegetables that need eating up!'

'And you've got your taste back, so you've got no excuse!'

He laughed. 'Cheeky.'

They shared a smile. He had a nice smile. Sexy, very sexy, but gentle. 'Will you stay?' She held out a hand, waited.

'That sounds good.' He took it in his, but instead of letting her help him up, he pulled her down, onto his knee. For a moment he stared into her eyes, a stare so deep, so constant, Kate could feel her pulse quicken.

And then he kissed her.

Author's Note

As an author I lead quite a solitary working life, but I think that these days it is increasingly the norm for people to work alone, and often live alone. Friendship, community, a meaning to life, aren't always easy to find, and even for somebody happy with their own company there are times when somebody to talk to, a shoulder to cry on, somebody who will listen, or just willing to share a coffee and cake break with, can make life look brighter.

We go through different stages during our lifetime, and the things and people we rely on may change, but I've often found my community through my hobbies and met incredibly nice and supportive people who share my passions and my interests. But is there something we all have in common, that we all share?

The Secret Ingredient grew from the idea that sharing food can be wonderful – food can be healing; it can bring people together. One person's greatest pleasure may be to see somebody else enjoy the dish they've cooked; another may just enjoy eating it!

We've heard the term 'comfort food', but I really feel that

cooking can help people heal in a way extending beyond that warming dish that is our go-to when we feel down. For the cook, the routine and sense of control can be therapeutic – I enjoy preparing the ingredients as much (or more) than the actual cooking process sometimes. It gives me time to think, to take stock (no pun intended!).

Cooking with and for other people can create a connection between people whose lives are very different in every other way. Cooking dishes that are nostalgic or have links with a special person can provide a link with the past and bring to the surface memories.

We recently moved house, and the central island that links the kitchen prep area and the dining area is one of the reasons I fell in love with our new home. Preparing food is now very much an integral part of our evenings, it can be the best part of the day, and I wanted Kate, in the story, to share that same feeling.

I absolutely love *all* the characters in *The Secret Ingredient*. I have dedicated this book to my great aunt and uncle, who were the inspiration for Charles and Mary. They never had children (they did have a gorgeous cat!), but they had each other and loved and supported each other with a quiet passion that was beautiful.

I love Della with her quiet resilience, and courage as she comes out of her shell and discovers the real her, and the gentle, unassuming, dependable David. Then of course there are Kate, Jack and Eddie – the central characters whose lives are touched with grief and guilt, in a story which I hope you find uplifting and heart-warming.

I really hope you enjoy reading the story, and that you will cook some of the recipes that mean so much to the characters (keep a careful eye on the pork crackling though – I've burned mine to a frazzle and set the smoke alarm off before now!), and of course me. I'd love to hear from you if you do, or if there are other recipes that are significant to you.

There is no single secret ingredient to happiness in life, it's different for everybody. I hope this story can play a small part in helping you find yours, if you haven't already done so.

Acknowledgments

This book draws upon so many important ingredients of my own life. I really believe that we all need passions, loves, and beliefs that can inspire and motivate us, and that can help us through the good times and the bad. Things we have discovered that give us mental support and help our mental health. Things that make us happy. If you have read my previous 'Zara Stoneley' books, or followed me on social media, you will know how important food, cooking, walking with my dogs, being outdoors, travelling, family and love are to me.

To write a story that draws on these things, that is as heartwarming and satisfying as a good bowl of soup, that can lift your spirits like a fluffy pancake, and that can guide you through grief has been a huge emotional journey. One I wouldn't have dared set off on, or be able to finish, without the encouragement from, and amazing support of, my longstanding incredible publisher Charlotte Ledger, and my agent Amanda Preston. I consider myself extraordinarily lucky to be able to work with such talented, inspiring, creative people who are brimming with ideas and inspiration, along with practical help and guidance.

I'd like to also thank all the other people on the team at One More Chapter, and HarperCollins, who have worked on this book, polished it, produced the perfect cover, marketed it, and spread the word. Your support is amazing, I feel privileged to be a small cog in your enormous wheel!

Thanks to my family who (sometimes) allow me the solitude I need to write but make sure I also have the fun times in my life that inspire and motivate me, and just make me flipping happy. Without 'happy' I'd be unable to write. Without going to new places and trying new things my life would be stale. Without their support I'd have less confidence that people will want to read my scribbles.

I can't end this without also mentioning my two dogs – Harry and Tilly - who keep me sane, insist I exercise, and are also relentless in their quest to share my bacon butties and cake so that I don't put too much weight on! As personal trainers go, they're pretty erratic, probably cost more, and don't stick to a timetable so my books take longer to write than they should – but they're loving, make me laugh, have introduced me to lots of new friends, and are always there for a chat, a cuddle, and a sloppy kiss so I forgive them!

And lastly a big thanks to you, for reading this story. Without you, there'd be no point.

ONE MORE CHAPTER

YOUR NUMBER ONE STOP

FOR PAGETURNING BOOKS

The author and One More Chapter would like to thank everyone who contributed to the publication of this story...

Analytics
Emma Harvey
Maria Osa

Audio
Fionnuala Barrett
Ciara Briggs

Contracts
Georgina Hoffman
Florence Shepherd

Design
Lucy Bennett
Fiona Greenway
Holly Macdonald
Liane Payne
Dean Russell

Digital Sales
Laura Daley
Michael Davies
Georgina Ugen

Editorial
Arsalan Isa
Charlotte Ledger
Jennie Rothwell
Tony Russell
Caroline Scott-Bowden
Kimberley Young

International Sales
Bethan Moore

Marketing & Publicity
Chloe Cummings
Emma Petfield

Operations
Melissa Okusanya
Hannah Stamp

Production
Emily Chan
Denis Manson
Francesca Tuzzeo

Rights
Lana Beckwith
Rachel McCarron
Agnes Rigou
Hany Sheikh
Mohamed
Zoe Shine
Aisling Smyth

The HarperCollins Distribution Team

The HarperCollins Finance & Royalties Team

The HarperCollins Legal Team

The HarperCollins Technology Team

Trade Marketing
Ben Hurd

UK Sales
Yazmeen Akhtar
Laura Carpenter
Isabel Coburn
Jay Cochrane
Alice Gomer
Gemma Rayner
Erin White
Harriet Williams
Leah Woods

And every other essential link in the chain from delivery drivers to booksellers to librarians and beyond!

ONE MORE CHAPTER

YOUR NUMBER ONE STOP
FOR PAGETURNING BOOKS

One More Chapter is an
award-winning global
division of HarperCollins.

Sign up to our newsletter to get our
latest eBook deals and stay up to date
with our weekly Book Club!
<u>Subscribe here.</u>

Meet the team at
<u>www.onemorechapter.com</u>

Follow us!

 <u>@OneMoreChapter_</u>
 <u>@OneMoreChapter</u>
 <u>@onemorechapterhc</u>

Do you write unputdownable fiction?
We love to hear from new voices.
Find out how to submit your novel at
<u>www.onemorechapter.com/submissions</u>

06/2/24

PILLGWENLLY